MEMENTO

A.D. Price

Copyright © 2023 A.D. PRICE

All rights reserved

The characters and events portrayed in this book are fictitious. Any similarity to real persons, living or dead, is coincidental and not intended by the author.

No part of this book may be reproduced, or stored in a retrieval system, or transmitted in any form or by any means, electronic, mechanical, photocopying, recording, or otherwise, without express written permission of the publisher.

For Jodie,
Without whom Memento may not have come to be at all.

CONTENTS

Title Page
Copyright
Dedication
Prologue

1.	1
2.	10
3.	19
4.	25
5.	36
6.	43
7.	48
8.	56
9.	62
10.	67
11.	72
12.	75
13.	86
14.	95
15.	101
16.	107

17.	112
18.	115
19.	120
20.	124
21.	129
22.	133
23.	136
24.	149
25.	154
26.	163
27.	167
28.	170
29.	177
30.	191
31.	204
32.	213
33.	218
34.	223
35.	232
36.	238
37.	255
38.	262
39.	268
40.	280
41.	288
42.	303
43.	307
44.	311

45.	321
46.	326
47.	331
48.	338
49.	343
50.	347
51.	366
Acknowledgements	369

PROLOGUE

Bowen stood rooted to the spot, his eyes fixed on the body before him. The Memento pulsed like a giant anxious heart and the vibrations resonated through Bowen's legs. His feet began to move him out of the darkened room leaving the corpse on the floor. Drenched in sweat and blood and with the screwdriver still protruding from his chest he began walking the corridors. Bowen's vision began to shake and blur as distantly he heard shouting and gunfire. At the top of the stairwell Bowen gripped the banister with a weak hand and looked down the shaft. Cool air was blowing up from below that eased his stinging face. Down there was a way off the ship, he could find a spare door that wasn't being watched and he could leave, he could walk to his hotel and sleep until he departed on the Benign Summer back to Saxon. Tears ran down his face as he thought of his mum and dad. What would he say to them? How could he explain? How could they understand? Bowen looked down the stairwell and wished he had never left home. He could have waited for Jules to come back and maybe everything would have been alright, but it didn't matter, not now. Everything was different.

Bowen walked back from the railing and moved through a haze of pain, his thoughts becoming muffled by the second. At another stairwell he began to climb, following the noises of the fighting. The Memento shook violently and the humming increased, it was a power Bowen had never felt before. Every step felt like it would be his last. At the top of the stairs on the main deck his legs gave out, but someone caught him.

"Bowen? Bowen!?" A distant voice was calling him. He recognised it, but he couldn't remember where from. Gunshots and yelling voices echoed around his battered head. Moving was no longer under Bowen's control. Bright lights passed overhead and all noise began to shrink. His world slowly turned as soft hands lay him down on the floor. Thoughts swam in and out of Bowen's head as his senses began to fail before a flash engulfed him. And then only darkness remained.

1.

The skies above the Brittanica valley grew darker. The light from the sun quietly fell behind the horizon as the long summer was coming to a close. Slowly, the stars began to emerge above the planet of Saxon. Up on Beetle hill by a lone, ancient ash tree, Bowen sighed as a ship launched from the market port of Allchester. With his mismatched blue and brown eyes he watched as it left the atmosphere to make its journey to Pennine warp gate that sat in orbit. Bowen lowered his head and ran a hand through his blonde hair. He turned his back on the view to join Simon by the car. As Bowen leant against the bumper of the sleek ground vehicle, Simon sparked a cigarette with his lighter, illuminating his face. Simon was taller than Bowen and wider at the shoulders with red hair and a sharp handsomeness about him. The light from his cigarette reflected in his piercing blue eyes. Bowen tried to think of something to say, but nothing came to mind. He and Simon didn't talk as much as they once had. Bowen just took in the view. Miles away through the heat haze of the evening was the colossal sky station that sat on the lip of the valley. Bowen watched as the towers belched out their steamy contents, maintaining the atmosphere of Saxon. The weather was scheduled to change to rain in the coming days. A warm breeze found them and rustled the leaves of the giant ash tree. Simon retrieved a can of Dizz from the cool box and cracked it open. Bowen watched as the lights of the massive suspended motorway flickered on. He watched a lone cargo lorry become smaller as it drove towards Allchester.

"When did you last hear from anyone?" Bowen asked.

"I heard from James about two weeks ago, why?" Simon replied, scratching his stubbly chin.

"It's been a few months for me. I got a com-disk from James when he got to New Tethys. I sent a message out to Sal and Sol for their birthday, but they didn't reply. I haven't heard from anyone else much since they left."

"Hmm..." Simon took a few swigs before deciding against his can of Dizz and he threw it off the hillside.

"I mean, I get it. They've all got careers and lives now." Bowen continued.

Simon burped.

"I just miss them" Bowen said. "What about Jules...?" he said finally, his head now lowered, "you hear from her much these days?" Simon took a breath as he flicked the butt of his cigarette into the dirt.

"Yeah sometimes." he said without looking at Bowen. Simon pulled his smoking box out of his jacket and busied himself rolling another cigarette. Bowen had noticed he was smoking a lot more than he used to.

"And? How is she?" For the first time in a while, Simon met his eyes.

"She's gone too. She got her off-world papers a few weeks ago. She's performing on a Leisure Fleet ship." The words sank into Bowen like a bad stomach ache. Bowen looked away. "Oh." He ran his fingers through his hair. "When did she leave?"

Simon lit his new cigarette and took a long drag.

"About two months ago." He said through a cloud of smoke. Bowen got off the bonnet of Simon's car. He walked over to the edge of the hill and rubbed his eye, stifling a tear or two.

"Didn't she tell you? She told me." Simon stated.

"I gathered." The sound of a train flying along the hyper tracks behind the hill muffled Bowen's words and Simon didn't hear the way he spat them out. His anger lifted as the image of Jules drifted across his mind. Her untameable mess of ginger hair and freckled face. Her green eyes, her smile and her laugh, and the way she would kiss him, all gone.

Bowen was left with a sadness. Jules had gone and not told him. She had told Simon and maybe others but not him, and after everything. The two had grown very close through college and dated when they found the time after they had graduated. Bowen had probably watched her fly up to the Pennine gate and not known it. Bowen's stomach sank a little further when he thought of all the com-disks he had been sending to her grandparent's house in New Mersey as recently as a few days ago. He tried not to think about the fact that the last time he saw her could have been just that. Bowen turned away from the edge of the hill back to the car.

"Do you have her details, so I can write to her?" Bowen tried.

Simon sat up and with a faraway look on his face.

"I'll have to check and get back to you." The moment hung in the air. "How's the job hunt going?" Simon said to change the subject. Bowen had to think hard for a moment to bring himself away from thinking about Jules. He had been out of work ever since they graduated from Allchester College a few years ago. At the age of twenty five now the two friends were on different paths.

"Yeah. I mean, I'm still looking. I'm waiting on some replies, hopefully this week."

"Oh, like what?"

"A cleaning job over in the archives, a ranger's assistant at Hadley's farm and a phone job over in the industrial zone. I had my interview for that one last week, I actually really hope I get it."

"What's that about?" Simon asked puffing out another cloud of smoke.

"I'd have to contact crew members in ships landing in arrivals from the warp gate and log their information, registration codes, where they've been, what they're hauling, stuff like that."

"That sounds important." Simon sounded almost impressed.

"I'd just be the last person they talk to before they can disembark, they would already have landed. It's not like I'd be in aerospace traffic control, just an office in the tower. And they'd have already passed inspection on both ends of the galactic highways, so it's really not that important." As Bowen was describing it out loud, he realised it sounded like busy-work.

"Oh," was all Simon could say. "Still though, it'd be a job wouldn't it?"

"Yeah I suppose. It'd only be on weekends too that's another thing." Bowen added.

"Huh."

"What about your job on that Free Trader ship that's coming up? You excited?" Bowen asked.

"Excited is the wrong word." Simon replied casually. "I'm happy to be doing it, but it's just a stepping stone to better things. I'm only in the navigation suite." Bowen came and sat on the bonnet of the car again next to Simon.

"Right. You'll only be in the navigation suite of a free trader ship going all kinds of places and seeing the the galaxy. I'd be really excited."

"Yeah I suppose when you put it like that."

"What's it called again?" Bowen asked.

"Its Free Trader name is Memento. We'll be stopping at a planet called Davarak, then Obelisk station and then some moon Vibana." Bowen was watching the glittering lights at the warp gate way up past the night sky,

"Wow. I'm jealous." Bowen hopped down from the car again and paced over to the sloped edge of the hill still looking up at the gate. "I wish I was going with you."

"I know man," Simon replied as he flicked his cigarette stub into the dirt.

"They don't need any farmers on board do they?" Bowen asked with sarcastic hope.

"No, sorry."

"Trust me to spend four years studying the subject that would be next on the list for full automation. I'm going to struggle to even help dad out around the farm after tomorrow." Bowen kicked a stone off the hill and sighed.

"Is it happening tomorrow?" Simon asked. Bowen was sure he had told him more than once already but still he answered.

"Yeah the new combines are being brought over in the morning with the auto balers too. I suppose I'll still be able to look after the cattle." Bowen sighed. "And my mum could always use more help around the house since Niamh left."

"That doesn't sound so bad." Simon said. Bowen felt he sounded a little forced.

Bowen turned away from Simon. He looked at Allchester and back up to the Pennine gate. Some nights Bowen felt as though the warp gate was teasing him. An unreachable ring of lights beyond the sky. He watched as a new ship that glowed with a green exhaust trail descended from space and landed behind the skyline of Allchester. He really wanted that job, just to know where some of the ships had been, maybe get a close look at some of them and perhaps see some of the alien crew members.

"So, when do you leave?" Bowen asked.

"My papers were sorted last week so I'm all set but the packing. I don't expect to be coming back any time soon either." Bowen sighed. Simon opened his smoking box and rolled another cigarette. "You know I think I remember hearing there's kitchen staff wanted onboard." Simon commented. As he said that Bowen turned around and saw that Simon had stopped rolling his cigarette. For an instant it seemed that Simon had not intended to speak out loud. But he had.

"Wait what!?" Bowen reacted.

"I mean, I think I remember hearing that, but I could be mistaken. I could have been hearing about one of the other ships."

"At the aerospace offices?"

"Yes." Simon repeated sounded a little flustered. Bowen suddenly started pacing,

"Maybe I'll go down there and ask about it, wouldn't it be great if I ended up on the ship?" he said. Simon started fidgeting, clearly irritated by Bowen's sudden turn of optimism.

"Listen Bo, even if there was a job going, and even if you got taken on, you don't have any kitchen experience, do you?"

"Well, no."

"And besides it can take up to two months to get papers sorted, it can be a real hassle, I mean Jules ended up waiting nearly three." With that, the conversation was dead. Bowen felt his cheeks flush with a mix of frustration and embarrassment. He returned to the car and leant on the bonnet a little heavier than before.

"I'm sorry." Simon said. Bowen didn't know what to say. Simon was not the apologising type. "Something will come up for you, like that job in the tower, I bet you get that. If you're good you might be taken on full time and then you can climb the ladder like I'm going to do. And besides," he lightly smacked Bowen on the shoulder, in a somewhat patronizing way. "not everyone can leave the planet, if that were the case no one could hold down the fort while the rest of us go gallivanting into space. If you went up there you might hate it, it's not for everyone, and you'd be stuck up there for at least a year until you could come home again." Bowen shifted where he lent against the car.

"I suppose that's true." He said looking down at the floor.

"And hey who knows, maybe in the future we'll all arrange a big homecoming and have a catch up, I'm sure everyone would be happy knowing that you're keeping the place running for us. Maybe by then you could be supervising the flight tower?"

"Yeah, maybe." Bowen tried not to advertise how disheartened he was. Simon had done his best to sway him away from the idea of signing up to the Memento, or going off-world in general.

Perhaps it was just his lot to stay at home.

Simon sighed and finished rolling his cigarette. Bowen watched him. The pack of tobacco, grown on the faraway planet of Gondwana sported its name Ruby Sun in fancy lettering and was framed with artistic illustrations of some of the alien creatures that lived there, Atlas Hawks and Sand Hydras. He imagined what it would be like to see them for real. There was a quiet. A warm wind blew in from the sky station massaging the grass and the crops. The night birds were silhouetted against the lights of Allchester, hunting in the fields. The ships took off and landed. Occasionally cargo lorries would come and go from the town on the motorway. Bowen finished the flat Dizz he had been nursing and put the empty can aside.

"You mind if we just have some music on?" Bowen asked.

"Sure." Bowen ducked his head into the car. He flipped on the switch and started up the radio. The equalizer graphic across the stereo rose and fell with the synthetic notes.

"When might you next be free to hang out..?" Bowen asked as he returned to the bonnet. Simon exhaled a cloud of smoke that seemed to find Bowen's airways perfectly. Bowen coughed and waved his hand.

"I'm not sure, I've got lots to figure out before I leave for off-world, like with my dad and stuff. So, I don't know." Bowen just nodded his head. He knew that was Simon's way of saying he wasn't interested.

"Yeah okay." The electronic synth track that was currently playing was an old one.

"I like this one." Simon said.

"Me too." Music was one of the last things that the two friends still had in common. Simon was a different person than the one Bowen had known in college, and certainly removed from the lanky shy boy he had made friends with in school. They'd been through a lot together, along with the rest of the gang, but they were the only ones left. And Bowen was soon to be the last.

Bowen tried to think of something to talk about but all subjects eluded him. He just wanted to sit there and enjoy the view and the music. He looked up at the warp gate and at the faded galactic highway gently swaying into the depths of space. The stars glittered in their millions. He wondered where all his friends were right at that moment. Were they happy with wherever they had ended up? Did they miss home or even think about it? Did they ever think about him? Could he still call some of them friends? The person who sat beside him was not the Simon he used to goof off with in school. Simon was a changed person, a shadow of the friend he used to know. A ghost. Bowen recognised that he was different also. It seemed to be a normal part of getting older, but he hadn't noticed until recently that he had changed. He still felt like he was the same old Bowen. Perhaps that was the problem. He knew he wasn't as calm and carefree as he used to be. He would get nervous and worry about the slightest thing. And he wasn't as silly as he once was. But maybe that was because he didn't have anyone to be silly with. Especially now that Jules had gone. His memories played out in is mind as he looked around Beetle Hill. Everyone used to go up there when they were in college. They had named it after the small black beetles that would buzz around in the midday sun. Bowen didn't remember who first said it. The group would spend their weekends and free afternoons up there and stay until after sunset. Over the years they had all scratched their names into the giant tree. Where had the time gone?

Beetle Hill was only realistically reachable with a vehicle. If Simon didn't want to hang out again before he left on the Memento, Bowen might never be back there. A melancholy overcame him as he looked at everyone's names on the tree.

"I want to go home." Bowen stated finally.

Simon took the last couple drags of his cigarette and flicked it. Bowen crushed his cans and put them in his rucksack. Simon threw his can off the hill before he entered the car.

Bowen opened the passenger door and stopped to take one last look at the view. He looked around at the tree, and the rocks and the grass, even the dirt.

"You staying?" Simon asked with a smirk.

Bowen took his seat and closed the passenger door. Simon turned the ignition key and the engine came to life. The headlights flickered on and they left.

2.

Bowen exited Simon's car after a blindingly quick drive. Simon raced well over the limits to get Bowen home. Not Bowen knew, for making sure that Bowen got home promptly, but because Simon looked for any excuse to tear around in his car. They took the slip road off the motorway and drifted around the large wind turbine stations.

By the time they reached the entrance to the Rhys family farm, Bowen's stomach had rolled over. He took a deep breath of cool air and composed himself again. He dipped his head back into the car and retrieved his bag from the footwell.

"We should hang out again before you leave." Bowen tried. Simon was busying himself with his rear view mirror and didn't meet Bowen's eyes.

"Yeah, maybe."

"Okay. Well... see you." Bowen closed the door of the car and threw his bag over his shoulder as he watched Simon leave. He was bathed in red from the rear lights of the car as Simon drove off, almost clipping the hedges at the side of the road. Simon cranked the car up a gear and Bowen heard muffled ironwave music begin to blare just as the car disappeared out of sight.

Bowen took a deep breath and walked the gravel path to the house with his head down. Clouds were already beginning to form in the sky. The many sky stations of the northern quadrants of Saxon had begun their transition to the autumn programs. The huge Douglas trees, cloned from earth stock seeds, swayed in the cool wind. As he approached the yard, he heard the cattle mooing to themselves over in the fields.

Sheltered behind a thick wall of conifer trees, sat the stone and wood house. As he approached the porch, the wind chimes sounded. Bowen looked up and saw smoke puffing out of the chimney as the small wind turbine began to spin with the approaching weather. His legs ached and complained as he took the last steps up to the door. He touched the oak door frame as he entered the house.

Bowen was immediately met with the smell of food along with the sound of muffled talking and music from the radio. He hadn't realized how cold he had become on the walk to the house until that moment. Bowen shivered slightly upon entry as the warmth of the house enveloped him. He removed his bag from his tired shoulder, took his boots off in the hallway and left them by potted houseplants and other muddied shoes. Suddenly feeling relaxed, he made his way down the hall, past the dark lounge and into the kitchen.

The music from the radio became clearer as he entered the room and found his parents. His father Mason, was busy gathering up plates and cutlery to the sink as his mother Ida, was sat at the table with a small pile of com-disks and the disk reader computer before her. At the same time they both noticed Bowen.

"Evening." Mason said smiling as he turned back to begin washing the dishes.

"Hello darling." Ida beamed at him as she removed her glasses and rose to hug him. She had to stretch upwards to put her arms around his neck as she gave him a long hug and a kiss on the cheek. As Bowen bent down to hug her back he must have been more tired than he realized. He closed his eyes and felt as if he could fall asleep standing. She let go and returned to the table and pulled out his chair for him as he realized there was a place left with a bowl and a glass of water.

"I'm sorry I missed dinner again." Bowen said as he sat down. Curled up on an armchair by the stove was the black house cat Samhain. The cat stretched himself out before he came and leapt into Bowen's lap to say hello and nuzzled his chest in exchange for scratches behind the ears. Ida went to the oven to fetch his late meal.

"It's alright, you're here now." Mason said.

"This is still warm enough." Ida said as she brought over

a pan and dished out the food into his bowl. She presented him with a classic dish of hers; a hearty pork broth with carrots, celery and onions with some home-made buttered bread on the side. Bowen's stomach yelled at him to start eating as he forked out the first chunk of meat. Ida smiled as she took her seat again at the table opposite him. She put her glasses back on and resumed reading the com-disks. No one spoke to him as he ate as was the way in their house. The kitchen was filled with the sounds of Mason at the sink, Ida inserting com-disks in and out of the reader. Across the table was his older sister Niamh's chair. No longer at home, one of her scarfs was tied around the wooden ear. The soft New Jazz music played on the radio along with the ticking of the clock above the large stove that gently crackled with burning bio turf. Bowen felt relaxed again.

    Ida was a short woman in early middle age with curly blonde hair and kind brown eyes. Her face was wrinkled somewhat from years of laughing and her large reading glasses sat at the bridge of her long, ever so slightly hooked nose. Mason was in the depths of his autumn years. He was taller than Bowen with wiry strength. His grey hair was loosely gathered into a long ponytail. He had a strong jawline that Bowen had not inherited and he was washing the dishes with his strong leathery hands. Mason also wore glasses like Ida although he required them for day to day vision. He had a smart pair of thin square glasses that framed his handsome but ageing face.

    Bowen finished his dinner in no time at all. Mason took his bowl and glass away to the sink.

    "Thanks dad." Bowen said as he suppressed a burp. Ida looked up from the screen of the terminal.

    "Did you have a nice afternoon with Simon?"

    "Yes, Mum, I did." He didn't consciously give the wrong answer, he was too at ease with his surroundings and he had a pleasantly full stomach.

    "Did you enjoy the movie?" Ida asked.

"Hmm? Oh… yes thanks." Bowen had to make himself pay attention all of a sudden and remember the day that had just passed. "What are you doing?" he asked Ida.

"Just replying to your sister."

"She wrote? How is she?"

Ida leant back in her chair.

"She's well. She's busy."

"I can imagine."

"Professor Wilhelm is planning a survey expedition for them which she's excited for. And she says she wants to come home for another visit maybe next year if she can get away."

"That'd be good." Bowen replied. "I wonder what she's doing right now." he imagined as Ida finished typing. Bowen thought about his older sister. Niamh had left home five years earlier. She had studied at the Federation College of Galactic Archaeology on the planet Metro for three years and had joined a well respected team of scientists under Warden Academic Professor Wilhelm Volkov along with numerous other scientists. Their work had taken them to a wild planet called Saurophos. In her com-disks, Niamh had described the wet heat of the dense rainforests and the cacophony of birds, insects and howling creatures at all times of day and night. Niamh was having her own adventure.

"By the way," Ida said to Bowen. "One of these is for you, the post came this morning after you left with Simon." Bowen suddenly perked up. He sat up in his chair at the kitchen table and felt excitement, anticipation and panic simultaneously manifest in his throat and stomach.

"Which one?" He spluttered out. Ida searched through the pile on the table and found the one addressed to him. She handed it to him smiling, seeing his obvious state and stood up from the table. She made for her comfy armchair opposite Mason who was snoozing in his own.

"Go on then I'll get out of your way." she said. Bowen's hands were sweating all of a sudden. He looked at the flat grey cartridge in his hands as he made for the other chair. There was an embossed label across the front;

>Mr. Bowen Rhys
>Rhys Farmstead
>Meath Village
>Habitation Zone 10F
>Allchester District
>Britannica Valley
>Saxon

Bowen's mind raced. Who was it from? A job response? Maybe a message from one of the guys? Perhaps Jules? His heart pounded harder. Bowen took a deep breath and slotted the cartridge into the top of the pastel blue box. The reader whirred and buzzed as it accepted the com-disk. In the centre of the black screen appeared a pixelated logo of the Federation Postal Service, a pink and blue image of a planet with a couple of starships zooming around it. Along the top of the screen was a read out of the current time, the local date and the federation star date. Below in orange text were the words;

>WELCOME!
>YOU HAVE A MESSAGE!
>READ? Y/N

Bowen clacked the Y key on the analogue keyboard. There was a bleep. He heard the internal fan kick in as the computer began to work.

>PLEASE WAIT...

Bowen hated getting com-disks these days. He used to enjoy it much more. When Bowen was younger, the only ones he received were birthday messages from his grandparents and other relatives that would play silly melodies and simple cartoonish images would flash up on screen. Nowadays it had become a stressful event. The anxiety of hearing back from job applications for interviews. The waste of time reading personalised advertisements after making the slightest of purchases in town. It had even become stressful to message and keep track of all the com-disks from his friends. Not that that ever happened any more. Just when he was about to give up, the computer sounded with a beep. On the screen once again flashed up the symbol of The Federation Postal Service this time in the top corner. Then the sender address came up on the opposite side of the screen;

ALLCHESTER
INDUSTRIAL ZONE
TOWER TWO
OFFICE OF RADIO COMMS

He was disappointed that it was not a message from Jules or one of his friends, but that very quickly became anxiety and anticipation. Line by line the orange text typed itself out on screen.

DEAR MR. RHYS,
We hope this com-disk finds you well. Thank you for attending your interview, it was a pleasure to have met you. We regret to inform you that on this occasion you have been unsuccessful. The office of radio comms is always evolving & due to the current rise in automation and the advancements in robotics we're sorry to say that the department of:
IMPORT / EXPORT REGISTRATION
will no longer be taking applicants. As a courtesy we will keep your application details and interview recordings on

file for any future applications you may make to any other department here at the   O F F I C E   O F   R A D I O   C O M M S . We wish you the best of luck for your future.

REGARDS
END OF MESSAGE

At the bottom of the screen in harsh red lettering were the words;

DO NOT REPLY TO THIS MESSAGE

Bowen sat back in the chair, feeling empty despite the food in his stomach. He watched as Ida dropped another block of dark green bio turf into the stove. Bowen sat there trying not think on how he'd just lost the chance of the best job that he could find. And he'd lost it to some robots no less. The fire crackled inside the stove. His mind was soothed as he heard the pipes gently shuddering with warmth through the house. He listened to the ticking of the clock on the wall above the fire, the quiet music coming from the radio and Mason's light snoring.

Bowen clicked a few keys and the cartridge reader beeped and clicked. The coloured texts on the screen all went away as the com-disk loosened itself in the slot. He flipped the power switch off and the computer closed down. Bowen took the com-disk out and held it in his hands. For an instant he considered hurling the message into the bin behind him, but he didn't. He just wanted to close his eyes and teleport upstairs into bed and forget about everything.

"So that was a reply from the tower." he said flatly. Ida looked up from the book she had been reading and Mason snapped out of his light sleep.

"Oh right?" Mason replied.

"And?" Ida prompted him. Bowen said nothing for a moment, trying to find the words.

"Apparently they're going fully automated." His parents both knew exactly what that meant. They looked at each other for a moment and then at Bowen.

"Ah sod them." Mason said. "You don't need it." Bowen wished that were true.

"I really wanted that job." he said glumly.

"Someone's bound to say yes at some point" Ida said with a sympathetic smile.

"Keep your chin up." Mason said.

"Why don't you call Juliette about it?" Ida suggested. "She always makes you smile. We've not had her round for dinner in a while come to think of it." Bowen rubbed his hands through his hair and down the back of his neck with some force as he stood up to exit the situation. He left the com-disk on the table with the others. Ida's motherly intuition kicked in. She stood up and came to give him a big hug. Bowen succumbed to it and rested his head on her shoulder. He heard Mason stand up from his chair and Bowen felt his fathers strong hand squeeze his shoulder. They all stayed that way for a moment. When they all released each other Bowen felt a tear run down from his blue eye and into his stubble. He meant to say thank you though he couldn't manage the words, but they knew. Mason patted him on the shoulder.

"Things will get better." he said. Bowen could only hope that they would.

Bowen left and walked through the cluttered hallway to the staircase. The soft wool carpets massaged his achy feet. As he climbed the steps Bowen passed framed paintings and old photographs of holidays and of family members long gone. He walked past Niamh's door and the last corner with the bathroom before he reached the smaller set of stairs. It was a hard climb, every step was a mile high for his legs. As he reached the tiny landing and found his door, the rain was hard on all sides of the house. His room was the only one on what was the third floor of the house. He found the knob in the dark and entered. Even in the black he stepped around the clutter with finesse. Bowen's bed pulsed with an invisible energy that drew him closer. He managed to remove his clothes and flopped onto the bed. He ran his hands through his unkempt hair and scratched his tired, stubbly face. The soft mattress sank and reshaped itself to his form as he lay on his back on top of the covers. His eyes adjusted to the darkness slowly. Above him on the low, sloped ceiling was the wide sky light window. Right now it was just rain. Behind the rain though was a faint light in the sky. The Pennine warp gate. A tormenting, beautiful sight. Bowen rolled over and looked to the bedside table. The clock radio read twenty four fifty. It wasn't even midnight of the twenty six hour Saxon day, but he felt like he could sleep for weeks. His eyes were drawn to the black and white photograph stood next to the mechanical table lamp. In the warm darkness of his room he could only see the shapes of the picture, but he knew it well. It was an old image. Two people lay on their backs on Bowen's bed, heads touching top to top. One with frizzy hair, freckles, kind eyes and a sweet smile. The second person held the camera above them both. This person had short hair, a clean shaven face and a big, silly smile. Both people were gone. Bowen rolled over and enveloped himself in the bed covers. The sound of Saxon rain had him asleep in seconds.

3.

Morning. Bowen awoke slowly. A pale light filled the room and the rain still hammered. He rolled over in his warm bed and lay there for a few minutes as his eyes refused to open fully. Bowen's shoulder ached and his legs were stiff. With great effort he forced himself to sit up. Bowen sat forwards and ran his hands through his hair before he stood up on tired legs. After dressing himself with a random assortment of clothes he made his way downstairs. It hadn't always been the way, but now he was usually awake before anyone else. Bowen walked around the house switching on lamps and opening the curtains followed closely by Samhain. In the kitchen he brought the stove fire to life after putting out some cat food in Samhain's bowl. He idly prodded at the bricks of bio turf with the iron rod as they hissed and cracked in the heat.

As the house began to warm up, Bowen went to the lounge. Comfy, old armchairs were sat around a long coffee table and almost every wall was lined with shelves that overflowed with books. In a corner of the room sat a small, circular, wooden table. Bowen knelt down in front of it. On the table were candles, an incense burner, a jar of stones and old herbs and framed pictures of family members long gone. Bowen had known some of them, albeit briefly. He took a match from a box and lit a squat candle. The trail of smoke rose upwards. That day was the birthday of his great grandfather Arnold. His picture was amongst the others. Ida sometimes said Bowen looked just like her grandad, but Bowen had trouble seeing it. In his picture, Arnold posed in his flight suit at the landing platform of his Gun Dog star fighter. Inside the frame next to the photograph were three medals. Bowen sat before the table a while and watched the candle burn. The rain patted on the windows and he listened to the wind chimes sound outside. He gently touched the table before he left.

In the entryway, Bowen donned his raincoat and rubber boots as well as his knitted beanie. He unlocked the front door with his key and stepped out onto the porch. He made his way around to the back of the house to a large shed. From inside he pushed out a large wheelbarrow that he took to the greenhouse. Inside, the sound of the rain doubled on the high glass ceilings. Fruit trees that produced all year around stood in their growing plots and deep trenches of soil sprouted all manner of vegetables. At the back of the building the large temperature regulator hummed along with the irrigation machines. Bowen slowly made his way around the greenhouse filling the wheelbarrow, pulling heads of broccoli and cabbage right out of the ground. He plucked sweet potatoes out of the soil, snapped off peppers, picked apples from the branches and grapes from the vines. Working the greenhouse was a small point of pride for Bowen. It was the only task that he had much passion for. Finally when the barrow was full, he heaved it outside.

At the bottom end of the garden, the trees grew larger and had been left to grow wilder than the rest. Within them was a small clearing where Bowen came to a stop. It was much quieter there, thanks to the walls of evergreens and the hedges. The thick canopy above shielded the area from most of the rain. Under the roots of the largest tree was a wide, deep hole. Bowen overturned the wheelbarrow in the middle of the clearing. After a few moments, Bowen cleared his throat.

"Virgil. Breakfast."

From within the cosy hole were sounds of slow and heavy movement. The hefty shuffling grew closer until Bowen was met with the ancient face of Virgil the tortoise. One by one his large feet slowly pulled him out of his home under the tree. Bowen felt a smile crack on his face as Virgil looked up at him. Virgil held his gaze for a moment before lowering his head to carefully chew through a sweet potato. The tortoise had been purchased in a pet shop in Gaul by Bowen's grandfather Gawain, when he was a teenager. At eighty three years old, Virgil was a large creature with a gentle nature and Bowen had always loved him. Virgil was so big that his shell almost reached Bowen's waist. When he was younger Bowen would sometimes come down to Virgil's end of the garden to read a book aloud to him or to just talk. Bowen found his slow and thoughtful personality comforting. Just as Virgil was effortlessly biting into a huge melon, Bowen sighed as he looked at his watch.

"Right, I have to see to the cattle. See you later Virgil." The tortoise raised his head slowly and looked at Bowen as he gently scratched the top of Virgil's head before he turned to leave. With his hands in his pockets, Bowen walked the length of the garden and the house until he reached the yard by the gates into the fields. He unlocked one of the huge sheds and found the old tractor. He clambered into the drivers seat and turned the key that was already in place. The vehicle shuddered as it coughed to life. It was an obsolete model of old world design that ran on out dated plasma fuel, but it was reliable. Bowen could operate it in his sleep he had become so familiar. He carefully drove it outside and around the back where he connected up a trailer that he filled with supplementary cattle feed from a gigantic silo. He activated the gates and trundled the tractor down the well worn track.

From over the fields, the cattle mooed to each other as Bowen drove the tractor towards the troughs. The creatures lumbered their way from over the hill and came to see what was happening. As Bowen came to a stop, the entire herd had arrived and were waiting by the large troughs. They stood silently in the rain, their huge bodies steaming as their mouths dripped with cud. As Bowen began to operate the trailer, the cattle watched him with vacant stares. As the trailer raised itself they started shoving each other suddenly realising what was happening. The tonnage of feed was emptied into the troughs with a cacophonous noise. The cattle began to fight for the prime spot before the trailer despite the feed being evenly displaced around. Bowen reset the trailer and sat back down in the driver's seat of the tractor. Bowen watched the creatures eat as they finally all found a spot. Genetically modified to be many times larger than their old earth ancestors, Saxon cattle were huge. Some species, like the shaggy haired cows of the Northern Reaches were even larger still.

The sounds of the cows eating was all Bowen could hear. They snorted and grunted as they wolfed down mouthfuls of the foul smelling feed. Bowen always thought the smell of the cattle eating smelled like hot porridge with meaty gravy. Occasionally the sound of slopping was heard as the cattle defecated where they stood. Bowen turned his back on them and looked into the misty view. The stretch of the potato field gave way to the neighbouring green spaces between farms, the small clusters of trees and hillocks where he used to play with his friends. In the distance beyond the fields, he could make out the shape of the motorways disappearing into the mist. Even fainter than that was the distant skyline of Allchester. If any ships were landing or departing from the port, they couldn't be seen. The Pennine Gate wasn't visible at all. Bowen thought about Jules, then Simon and the rest of his friends. Glancing behind him, one of the cows was looking at him stupidly chewing and drooling. He sighed and started the tractor up to leave.

Once the trailer was in its place by the silo and the tractor was parked in the shed again, Bowen returned to the house. He hung up his raincoat and left his muddy boots in the entryway. He ate breakfast alone in the kitchen. He was still the only one up. Samhain nuzzled at Bowen's ankles as he played with his muesli and nursed his glass of apple juice. Eventually Bowen found himself in the lounge again. As he flopped into a deep armchair, Samhain jumped into his lap. The cat purred loudly as Bowen scratched behind his black ears. Bowen looked at the clock above the old mantelpiece. His chores for the day were over and it wasn't even close to midday. Bowen idly flicked around on the television but found nothing he wanted to watch. Samhain sighed in his sleep. Bowen's gaze landed again on the small table. The candle that he lit would last all day. For a while, he watched the candle burn. The clock ticked on the mantel and the rain fell against the house. The photographs displayed silent memories.

Eventually the quiet of the house was broken by the sounds of Ida arriving in the kitchen. Bowen could hear her humming and singing quietly to herself as she pottered about. Samhain meowed as he hopped off Bowen's lap and left the room. Bowen heard his mother greet the cat warmly from the kitchen. Without thinking on it much, Bowen stood and made for the hallway. He put his raincoat back on and his walking boots before he entered the kitchen. Ida didn't immediately notice him. She was making breakfast in her yellow pinafore and she still had a messy head of bed hair. Mason was also sat at the table rifling through paperwork dressed in his work clothes. The smell of toast and strong tea filled his head as eggs and bacon crackled in a pan on the stove. Bowen cleared his throat. His parents both noticed him.

"Oh, Morning," Ida said with a smile. It wasn't much of a surprise any more that Bowen was the first up. "You've eaten?"

"I have. So has the cat." he said. He saw that Samhain was curled up on Mason's chair by the fire.

"Have you seen to the cattle?" Mason asked over his glasses.

"I have, and Virgil."

"Is everything alright?" Ida asked him as she brought Mason a plate of eggs and bacon. Bowen couldn't begin to answer that innocent question.

"I'm going out. To town."

"Are you getting the bus? Do you want a lift? The rain?" Ida attempted as she sat down with her modest sized plate of food.

"No thanks. I was going to go on my bike. I could use the exercise." Bowen answered with forced reassurance. Bowen knew his parents were not stupid. He was very aware that being this vague would be sending up red flags for them.

Mason watched him as he took a thoughtful sip of tea.

"Well alright then," he said. "How long do you think you'll be?"

"Just a couple of hours."

"When you get back, the men from town might still be here setting up the new gear."

"Oh is that today?" Bowen asked pretending not to have been thinking about it for weeks. "Well I'm going now."

"Since you're going out..." Ida began. Bowen's mouth tightened into a forced smile.

"Yes Mum?"

"Could you be a star and pick up a few things for me?" She retrieved a list from her pocket and put it in his hand. Bowen gave it a quick glance. Two loaves of bread, milk, eggs, tea and blank com-disks. He smiled as he sighed through his nose.

"No problem." Ida cupped his face in her hands and kissed him on the cheek.

"Ooh, I can tell you've been with the cows." she jested. Bowen couldn't hide his smile.

"Be safe on your bike," Mason said. "Mind those Auto Trucks."

"I will." Bowen left the room and grabbed his backpack off the hook by the door before he ventured out into the rain once again.

4.

Up on the motorway, Bowen rode against the rain. He stuck to the cycle lane but still became soaked by passing trucks more than once. His legs began to ache as he finally reached the turn off for the town. The great stone gateway adorned with flags welcomed him as he entered. The seldom used shield generators hummed from within the walls. Allchester was awake. Compared to the peaceful farmlands of the Britannica Valley, inside the walls the place was bustling. The buildings were constructed of huge stones and dark brickwork to withstand the weather and the great wooden doorways and slate rooftops were adorned with gargoyles of dragons and demons that vomited the rain in torrents. As Bowen biked through, he heard accents from Gaul and Engelreich, Pen Morgan and New Hibernia. The rain did little to deter the Saxon people. Once or twice he heard languages from off world that he couldn't pin point, and not everyone he saw was human. Bowen stopped for a moment to catch his breath in the great square. There he was in the shadow of the 'Old Woman', a colossal beech tree that had survived the journey from earth. In the rich atmosphere of Saxon she had flourished. The base of her trunk was over a hundred feet around and she stood almost three hundred feet high. Ribbons, chimes and bells hung from the lowest branches. The belfries sounded across town and he carried onwards to the industrial zone.

Red faced and near exhaustion, Bowen came to a stop in the wide plaza before the aerospace offices. Statues of important figures from all across federation space watched him disapprovingly as he fitted his bike in a public rack by an ornate fountain. The area was more modern than the rest of town albeit still old. The zone had been built after the Great Induction to the Federation after nearly two centuries of isolation since the landing. The area was fairly quiet despite its size. Beyond the tall buildings of the plaza, Bowen heard a faint roar through the rain, a ship taking off. He squinted up into the iron grey sky but couldn't see it. Emboldened, he ascended the wide stone steps to the building. Statues of great wolves and fierce birds from earth guarded the pillared entrance. Bowen heaved open the wood and glass doorway and was met by warmth.

As the large door closed behind him it silenced the weather. All that could be heard then was the ticking of a huge clock. The interior was like much of Allchester, dark wood and more brick work however there was an air of importance and grandeur. His wet clothes dripped silently on the carpet as he walked. Old tapestries adorned the walls as well as framed paintings of Saxon landscapes. Ornate sculptures and exotic plants were placed here and there on wide marble bases. Dripping wet, Bowen approached an open area where a wide, wooden desk sat opposite a grand staircase. His footsteps echoed as he walked the marble flooring of the atrium. High above on the ceiling were intricate paintings of the history of the world.

"May I help you?" came a woman's voice. Bowen was snapped out of his thoughts. The woman had emerged from a door behind the desk. She was tall and had a striking beauty that Bowen found somewhat unnerving. Her long black hair was perfectly straight and fashioned into an elegant modern style. Her flawless face was younger than her years. Bowen noticed the prestige marks of expensive vanity surgery about her face and neck and down her exposed shoulders and slender arms. She seemed to glide across the floor as she approached her high backed chair. The woman moved with a dreamlike grace even as she adjusted her silver white gown before she sat. Bowen watched as she caressed a portion of the desk. The wood silently unfolded itself and a full administration suite emerged. Bowen cleared his throat and approached. He was acutely aware of how he reeked of the cow fields. As he stepped forward the woman looked him over from head to toe. Bowen felt his face flush.

"I'm enquiring about a job on one of the ships in port, the Memento." he said. Bowen noticed one of the woman's eyes had begun to glow. Federal issued implants. Her fingers drifted across the flat screen keyboard of her terminal and he saw a faint light within her fingers as they traced invisible keys. She gazed into the screen of her computer that to Bowen appeared as a pane of stained glass framed with wood. She did not look at him as she responded.

"Do you have an appointment and paperwork?"

Bowen was stumped. He scratched the back of his damp neck. "No I don't." he replied.

"One moment." The woman's eyes were now both illuminated. She touched another portion of the terminal with her graceful hands and a small wooden box with a slit appeared before Bowen from within the desk. The woman faced Bowen with her glowing stare. "Your identification please." Bowen retrieved his wallet and pulled out his federation citizen card. He inserted the small metal rectangle in the box. "Thank you." she said as she turned back to her terminal. The woman's eyes flickered through various coloured lights and the glass screen swirled and churned with data. She raised her hand up to her neck. A spot on her throat glowed. Bowen heard a chime and the woman smiled.

"Hello. I have mister Bowen Michael Rhys with me interested in Free Trader vessel 22891 Alpha. Yes. Memento. Yes. Is Officer Garber still in the building? I'll send him up. Thank you." The woman's eyes stopped glowing as she looked back at him. "Please ascend to the nineteenth floor and speak to the attendant at the desk there. You have an appointment with Officer Sol Garber of the Memento." She motioned with her hand over to the elevators across the atrium. Bowen thanked her and she bowed her head slightly. He turned away and made for the elevators. As he waited for the doors to open he glanced back to the woman at the desk. She was still human, but was distinctly different from almost anyone Bowen had met before. Being the son of farmers he had never met any federation workers or seen much in the way of the wondrous technology. He wondered if the core worlds of the federation changed everyone as much.

A bell sounded and the doors opened before him. Bowen was surprised to see a polished metal and glass interior with dim lighting in the floor and ceiling. There were no buttons on the walls. Instead, as the doors closed a voice spoke to him.

"Your floor please."

"Nineteen... please." Bowen didn't feel the motion, but a single strip of lighting indicated movement. Within seconds, the bell sounded again and the doors slid open without a sound,

"Floor nineteen." the elevator said. Bowen stepped out onto the floor. He saw another atrium similar to the entrance with doors leading off into other rooms. A huge fountain adorned with statues dominated the space. In the centre was a series of long and expensive looking leather couches. What caught Bowen's attention was a huge window that overlooked part of the landing bays of the port, but the rainfall obscured much of the view. Bowen composed himself and turned to the desk opposite. There was another administration attendant sat operating a computer console. This woman had the dark skin of the faraway planet of Province. Her eyes were obscured completely behind an optic visor and her perfect white hair fell about her shoulders like a cloak. When he checked in with her she passed him a portable computer terminal screen that displayed a digital application form for the Memento. Bowen wasted no time. He filled it in without even thinking before giving back to the woman. He then made to sit down on one of the couches that looked out over the landing bays.

While he waited, he saw the blurry figure of a ship descend from the rainy sky. It was silent from behind the glass, but Bowen noticed the smallest of tremors in the window as it landed out of sight. He sat back in the chair as his mind wandered. He wondered what he was doing there. What did he expect to happened when he met this officer Garber? He had just filled in an application form to join the crew of a Free Trader vessel. Before his thoughts got away from him too much, there was a chime sound behind him from the desk. He turned around in his seat. The woman at the desk looked over to him.

"Officer Garber will see you now Mr. Rhys. Room Three." With a dry mouth, Bowen stood and smiled at the woman in thanks before making for the room. He reached the door, turned the gilded doorknob and entered the room.

Inside was a fairly small office space, but the architecture still retained the aesthetic from the rest of the building. The walls were lined with bookshelves and the furniture was lavish wood. The high windows gave a dim light into the room. At the far end of a long desk, working at a portable computer terminal was a woman. She was an alien. When Bowen entered she looked up at him from her small box screen. She stood and approached him and outstretched her hand to shake his. Bowen breathed a sigh of relief. After interacting with the unnerving administration attendants, it was a nice change to be meeting a normal person, albeit an alien.

"First Officer Sol Garber. Pleasure to meet you Mr Rhys." Garber had cobalt blue skin and a head of long, dark purple hair that appeared to have the texture of silk. She had it tied at the back of her head in a plait that hung over her shoulder. Her eyes were hot pink and had no pupils or iris. She was a few inches taller than Bowen and she had a firm handshake. Garber was dressed in a flight jacket sporting patches under which she wore a white tank top that hugged her physique. Her bright red jumpsuit trousers were tucked into her leather knee high boots. As she had stood from the table Bowen had noticed the gun belt at her waist and the shoulder holster beneath her jacket. Bowen cleared his throat.

"Weird." Bowen said without thinking.

"Excuse me?" Garber said as they were locked in the handshake.

"I'm sorry, I used to know someone called Sol that's all. I mean, I still know her. Him."

"Is that right." Garber said as she released his hand. Bowen felt his face go bright red. Thankfully Garber took a professional approach as she brushed over the moment.

"Please have a seat." she offered as she motioned to the nearest chair to hers at the table. Bowen did as he was bid. Garber sat down and tapped on her keyboard as she read from the screen with her pink eyes. Bowen had the suspicion she was looking at his application.

"So," she began. "you're a local."

"Yes."

"And you state here that you're a farmhand. But you've applied to work in the galley, the cargo bay or be hired as a science officer assistant." Bowen nodded his head with a stiff smile. Officer Garber was speaking fluent Saxon to him, but with the accent of Laurentia. Bowen was still taking in the situation, he found Garber fascinating. Bowen had never seen one of her race before. He did his best to concentrate. Garber began typing on her keyboard. She turned the small screen around so that Bowen could see it and there he was. His federation citizen profile complete with medical records, a clean criminal record, his education history and more. It made Bowen feel naked.

"Good to know you're not a criminal." Garber said. "You studied Agricultural Science and Management here in Allchester? Why don't you work in that field now?" Bowen felt a pang of embarrassment along with a flash of sadness as the reality of the situation came to the front of his mind.

"Everything's becoming automated, my family farm is next up."

Garber observed him and exhaled a deep breath. "That's the federation for you I'm afraid." she said to him quietly. Bowen smiled trying to hide his feelings. For a moment Garber gave him a sympathetic look before resuming the interview. She pulled the screen back around to herself and began typing again.

"Okay. So on your farm what are your responsibilities?"

"I tend to the cattle."

"Is it just a livestock farm?"

"No we have a potato field. I can operate the seeder machine and the pesticide sprayer. We have a greenhouse station too for private use."

"Okay," Garber typed on the keyboard again. Bowen tried not to think about what she could be writing. "We have a garden on the Memento." she said.

"Really?" Bowen felt a jolt of excitement at where this thread could be going.

"But were not currently hiring for it."

"Oh." Bowen's excitement died a death.

"You don't have any hard scientific qualifications beyond agriculture, so I can't really put you down for the science officer assistant. You've never worked a dockyards, used forklifts? No cargo mech license."

"No." Bowen replied. Garber typed again.

"That leaves us with galley hand doesn't it?" Bowen nodded with a stiff, forced smile. "Do you have much of a kitchen background?" Bowen couldn't hide the sigh that came out of him as he replied,

"Not particularly. I can cook for myself but I'm no chef." Garber leant back in her chair and gave his profile one last look.

"If we were to take you on in the galley you would be part of the cleaning crew, you wouldn't be preparing food."

"Right."

"Your hours would vary depending on the shift rotas and your rate of pay would be six hundred kardona per week, which converted to federation credit is around five hundred and sixty with change."

"Wow okay." That was substantially more than Bowen would have guessed.

"Let me ask you this." Garber said. "Are you aware of the basics of free trader law?"

"I don't think so."

"In short, we can trade wherever we please in terms of galactic territory, slipping under all sorts of red tape that applies to other merchant fleets. Now the pay is so high because we don't pay taxes to any government, but that means local authorities are not obligated to protect us or even host us in port. Luckily Saxon is very trusting. I was fortunate to be granted a temporary workspace here for the time being. Do you have any questions?" Bowen tried to wrack his brain.

"Who is the Captain?" was all he could think of. Garber smiled.

"He's a good man." was all she answered. Bowen noticed that Garber glanced up to the corner of the ceiling as she spoke. She cleared her throat and changed the subject. "Now then, you've never left the planet?"

"That's right."

"Not even up to one of your local warp gates?" Bowen shook his head.

"That's no trouble. If we decide to take you on you'll be sent all the details in plenty of time to prepare in terms of medication and the minor procedures required for space travel."

"My older sister had to go through everything when she left for Metro a few years ago. So I sort of know about it." Bowen said.

"Okay good, then it wouldn't come as much of a shock to you." Bowen remembered a flash of seeing Mason take Niamh to the medical centre for her operation. He swallowed as the thought of having to go through it himself became that much more real.

"Just out of interest." Garber said. "I know Saxon is a mostly human population, have you met many off worlders before?" Bowen went red.

"Well, you're the first person I've met properly, more

than just in passing anyway."

"Okay, well just so you know, the crew of the Memento is mostly non human, but it's a good mix. Also I'd advise you refrain from using the word alien. Some don't mind it, but others take offence, so I recommend just avoiding it." Bowen acknowledged. "Again, this is all *if* we take you on."

"Right." Bowen had struggled to grasp whether the interview was going well or not. Garber's professionalism made it difficult to know what she was thinking. There was a moment of quiet where she just looked over his profile on her screen.

"You finished your education with high honours." she said finally.

"Yeah, I miss it." Bowen replied without thinking. Garber typed on the keyboard one last time before she pushed it away from herself. Bowen's heart sank.

"Bowen, why do you want to get away?" Bowen opened his mouth to answer but no words came. He looked down at the table as he summoned a response.

"There's nothing for me here." he said. Garber just looked at him. "I literally decided to come and ask about the job this morning." Bowen added.

"Really?" Garber sounded impressed.

"It feels like everyone else my age has started their lives off world. All my friends have got things figured out." Bowen looked down a little embarrassed that he had divulged his feelings like that.

"Believe me, they haven't." Garber smiled. "Do you have any family here..?" she asked.

"I do."

"I just want a sense of your motivation."

"The career I had planned on starting can't happen now." Bowen sighed. "My last friend from home has actually joined your crew, Simon Van Hoff."

"He's your friend?" Garber asked a little surprised.

"Since school, do you know him?"

"I signed his papers not too long ago, honestly I wouldn't have guessed you were friends."

"Really?" Garber didn't respond to that. She sat up in her seat and changed the subject.

"Now if we were to take you on, we would have you for a short trip out, roughly six to seven standard galactic months at eight day rotations." Bowen nodded even at the idea of being away from home for so long. "We'll be travelling the galactic highways on course for stopping at Davarak at around the half way point until we reach Obelisk station at which point your contract would be terminated. Depending on your performance until then we may offer you an extension or you could get an express trip back home on another ship."

"Great." Bowen replied. He did his best to retain everything Garber had said. At that point, Garber looked at her wristwatch. "Do you have any questions for me?" she asked.

Bowen had a hundred questions. He fumbled to pick one.

"Where are you from if you don't mind me asking?" Bowen felt a flush of embarrassment. The question sounded much less juvenile in his head. Garber seemed surprised at the question but she smiled.

"I was born on Laurentia, hence the accent. But the Merran people are all over the territories."

"Have you ever been to your homeworld?" Bowen asked.

"No, I haven't. I'd like to one day." she replied. Garber had a thoughtful smile on her face for a moment before she composed herself and looked at her wrist watch again.

"Okay Bowen, it seems we've run out of time." She began to type on her console quickly as she spoke. "I'll take into account everything we've talked about and I'll be meeting with the galley supervisor. Between us we will make our decision." Garber stood and Bowen followed suit throwing his backpack over his shoulder. She came around to him and they shook hands. "It was nice to meet you Bowen."

"You too." Bowen smiled.

"Don't dawdle leaving the building." Garber added quietly with a smile. Once again, she glanced up to the corner of the ceiling. Bowen thought not to ask. He turned to leave. As he did, he saw a small wooden orb floating in the upper corner of the room. A glint of a lens caught his eye as he passed.

Bowen stepped out into the large atrium again where the attendant was still at her desk, motionless but for her hands gliding across her sleek console.

"Thank you." Bowen said to her politely without thinking. She did not respond. Bowen heard his footsteps become quicker as he made for the elevator. He felt watched in the elevator as it took him back down to the ground floor. On Garber's advice, he walked briskly out of the elevator and through the quiet atrium. The first attendant in the lobby was no longer there. There was an uncomfortable quiet about the place as he walked to the entrance, hands in his pockets. He was surprised at how happy he was to be out of the building when he found himself descending the steps two at a time. He didn't look back even as he unhooked his bike from the rack before he rode back into town.

5.

Some time later with a backpack full of groceries, Bowen arrived back at the farm. On the way the hyper train speed past him towards New Mersey. He always envied Jules for living close to a platform. His legs had almost given out on the ride home. As he reached the gates of the farm, he dismounted and walked his bike to the house. Through the rain he could hear machinery and voices. On the drive was a huge work van with a massive trailer. As he reached the yard, Bowen found Mason speaking with a shorter man dressed in overalls and a helmet bearing the logo of Federation Agriculture Technologies. They were both standing by the fence that overlooked the potato field. Mason stood under a large umbrella as the other man was shouldering a tech pack that was almost as wide as he was. Bowen sighed, he knew exactly what was happening.

"Bowen look at this." Mason beckoned as he noticed him. Leaving his bike lying on the ground Bowen joined his father under the umbrella by the fence. Mason pointed out into the field. A low cloud had settled over the land but through the rain, Bowen saw the shape of a large vehicle slowly trundling through the potato field. There were also two more workmen busying themselves around it.

"What is it?" Bowen asked.

"It's called..." Mason started trying to remember its proper title when the short man finished off his sentence for him.

"The AFV580 Farm-Hand. All terrain, all weather, all produce, all the work."

Mason nodded along as he finished. The man was shorter than Bowen, older than Mason by some years and very stocky. He had a thick grey moustache that covered his mouth. His sleeves were rolled up showing his immensely thick and hairy forearms that were retaining large raindrops. The rain didn't seem to bother him at all as he lifted his helmet off to scratch his balding head. On his overalls his name tag read Jean Phillipe and he spoke with a gruff voice with the accent of the Gaul region.

"Jean Phillipe and his boys are just monitoring this one for a test run." Mason said.

"So what are we supposed to do with it?" Bowen asked.

"Well, we have to program its scheduling, make sure its routines are all in order, check it's always loaded with whatever it needs. Seeds and pesticides and the like. It's automated to a point, but we have to give it orders and of course we'll have to keep it relatively clean for the job. We're not authorized to go tinkering with it unfortunately and it'll need servicing twice a year, which will be down to Jean Phillipe," he said smiling to him. Jean Phillipe raised his wrist and looked at his watch.

"The feeder will be back in a minute. Claude and Jack will be finished soon." he said.

"Feeder..?" Bowen quietly asked no one in particular. It was then that he noticed that over the work shed, the large silo containing the cattle feed was gone. Bowen's heart skipped a beat and sank at the same time. He was about to say something when the sound of another vehicle came from behind the hedgerow. Splashing through the puddles and already splattered in mud was a massive machine. It came to a stop in a new designated parking zone on a flagged area where the old silo had been. Bowen saw a series of mechanical arms reach out from it and connect to a brand new charging station that had been fitted.

"Wait, hang on..." Bowen tried.

"Fantastic isn't it?" Mason said. Despite the rain and mud it was a brand new machine. Bowen thought it looked like a larger, uglier tractor with no drivers compartment. It had six huge wheels that were caked in mud. Bowen recognized the four barrel fusion engine that sat atop a federation class chassis. The CPU core that sat at the front of the machine instead of a driver was a ghastly orange box with green detailing with the words, Federation Shepherd Technology. On its back were two huge tanks, each one almost as large as the old feed silo. One tank was a bright tropical blue, the other a deep forest green. Bowen didn't need to ask what they contained.

"Come have a look." Mason said, putting his hand on Bowen's shoulder. The three of them came to a stop by the machine. Jean Phillipe pulled a bulky handheld console off his utility belt that was wired to his tech pack and connected it to the vehicle. The console in his hand beeped as Jean Phillipe began pressing buttons.

"Where's the old tractor?" Bowen asked. Whether he had not spoken loudly enough over the rain or not, neither man seemed to hear his question.

"Come see here." Jean Phillipe said to them both. Mason seemed eager to learn about the new toy and moved away from Bowen who was suddenly exposed to the rain. Bowen watched for a moment as Jean Phillipe gave his father a rundown of the vehicles performance and test run diagnostic.

"Dad, I'm going inside." Bowen said. Mason didn't look up from what Jean Phillipe was showing him but he gave a cursory thumbs up. Bowen turned and made for the house. Under the shelter of the porch, the wind chimes sounded. He touched the oak door frame as he entered. Samhain came to say hello as he removed his coat and boots. After giving him a scratch on the head, Bowen entered the kitchen and met Ida. She was sat by the stove in her chair reading a book. Ida thanked him as he emptied the items he had bought for her onto the kitchen table.

"Where did you go again today? I don't remember you saying?" she asked.

"I just went to the library. I just got distracted because I ran into someone."

"Who was that?"

"Just someone I used to know from college." Bowen didn't notice the look Ida gave him over her glasses. He moved and stood by the sink and looked out the window into the rain.

"I didn't realize we were getting a cattle feeder." Bowen said.

"No it was a surprise for us too. Apparently it's included in the program now." Bowen turned from the window.

"We don't need all this though do we?" he said. Ida removed her reading glasses and closed her book.

"Unfortunately sweetheart it's just the way things are changing now. We're one of the last villages in the valley to upgrade. We'll be able to produce a higher quality yield and the cattle will benefit too." Bowen knew she was right. By all accounts the automation was making vast improvements across the planet. He folded his arms and looked down.

"There's nothing for me to do here any more." he said quietly. Ida gave him a sympathetic look.

"Something will come up." she said. He wanted to come clean about going to the plaza of the federation and the meeting with Garber, but the words wouldn't come. It wasn't the right time. Ida stood and began busying herself with the groceries.

Upstairs, as he showered himself his mind mulled over everything. He was embarrassed at how naïve he must have seemed to Officer Garber. He expected that he wouldn't hear back from her, he had sat better interviews for other jobs and not received offers. He lathered his head in soapy water that smelled like tropical fruits from the planet Fujigante. The water ran the stress off him. He thought of the train to New Mersey. It was a line he knew very well. The last time he had travelled that way was to see Jules at her grandparent's house. He tried to forget.

Afterwards he found himself at the dining table in the late afternoon. As was the way for many Saxons, they had invited in Jean Phillipe and his boys to join them. They ate cheese and pickle sandwiches with some apples from the greenhouse. Ida had brewed a pot of tea and brought out some iced pound cake from the cupboard that she had baked that week. Mason was talking with Ida and Jean Phillipe all about the new machinery. The enthusiasm in Mason's voice felt bittersweet. Despite his father previously seeming indifferent, he was now positively giddy. Bowen spoke with Claude and Jack a little. The two were a few years younger than him, having graduated from Bedivere College on the Caledonia coastline the year previous. Earning a degree in the new form of Agricultural Science and Management that Bowen had studied years earlier, Claude and Jack had also learned how to build, program and maintain machines like the ones they had been working on out in the field. The two had been propelled into a promising career immediately after graduating. Not like Bowen. Judging by the quality of boots they wore and also from the exquisitely well done tattoos that Claude was sporting, the two were earning a considerable amount of money. Bowen tried to seem interested in all the conversation, but he just wasn't. Nor was he absorbing any of the information that his father was spouting about how to calibrate the seeding schedules and how to program in the gathering and sorting subroutines of the Farm-Hand. Bowen traced the logo of the Dizz can that he was nursing for a few minutes. After a while, he could take no more and he excused himself.

 Without thinking, Bowen made for the phone table that was by the staircase. He pulled the chord on a shaded lamp that illuminated the space as he sat on the old stool. The hefty phone book with hundreds of place markers dominated the table. Bowen lifted the phone onto his lap and picked up the receiver. He punched in a series of numbers that he knew off by heart. Holding the receiver to his ear he heard the call ring out until it cut off. He reset the phone and tried again.
This time the call was answered.
 "Yes who is it?" said a familiar voice. Bowen cleared his throat and replied,

"Mr. Van Hoff it's me Bowen." Even after over ten years Simon's father Charles didn't recognize Bowen's voice.

"Oh right... he's not in." Mr. Van Hoff grunted.

Bowen sighed through his nose. "When he gets back please can you let him know that I called? I just need to talk to him about something."

"Why don't you ask the ginger one he's usually with her."

"Wait, what..?"

"Look Ben I'm very busy here." Charles said as Bowen heard the crack of a ring pull on a can. "Just leave a message next time." The line went dead as Mr. Van Hoff hung up.

A few hours went by. Bowen sat in his room in his old arm chair. The rain beat down on his windows as the wind picked up from the sky station. The conversation with Mr. Van Hoff had hung around in his mind like a parasite. Simon had already left for the Memento. Did that mean that the ship had also left? Had they gone early for some reason? Had his interview all been for nothing?   Jean Phillipe, Claude and Jack had left in their huge vehicle after they had hosted them. Bowen felt he had unfairly given the boys a cold shoulder after learning what they studied and seeing where they where now. Bowen had heard Mason come back into the house after setting up the Farm-Hand to see to the potato field. It was strange to know that no one was in the fields, but the crops were being seen to by the machines. It made him bitter to think that a machine was looking after his cattle too and doing a more efficient job at that.

Bowen sat in front of his modest sized television. He had closed the curtains on the world as the last of the weak light tried to intrude. His video games did nothing to occupy his mind. Samhain had scratched at the door and meowed until he was allowed inside. The black ball of warm fur was curled up on Bowen's lap as he flicked about on the channels. He watched a few minutes of a game show where a bone headed contestant blundered their way to ten million credits and a brand new top of the line hover car. He found a movie and watched a couple of scenes but nothing caught his attention. On another channel the news bragged about a record low level of unemployment across the territories. A Federation Command ad tried for his attention showcasing the benefits of enlisting. One of them being to see the galaxy and get paid doing it. After bitterly switching off the television, Bowen ushered the sleepy Samhain out of his room before he got into bed himself. It had been an odd day.

6.

The days passed. Clouds blew in from the sky station and the Britannica Valley was awash with rain. The fields and the forests swelled with life in the closing days of summer and time ticked away. From his bedroom windows, Bowen watched the farm-hand in the fields and the cattle feeder trundle backwards and forwards. He busied himself where he could. Bowen fed Virgil every morning and he checked on the greenhouse regularly. He had neglected his appearance somewhat as his hair had grown out and his beard had emerged. Bowen took to walking the length of the fields, the quiet gave his mind a chance to breathe.

There was still a heat in the sun when it wasn't raining, but the days were becoming shorter.

On a clear and breezy morning, Bowen was returning from a walk down the fields. As he entered the house, he could smell lunch from the kitchen. Bowen meant to head straight up to his room but as he turned towards the stairs he found his father by the phone table.

"What's going on?" Bowen asked. Mason looked at him carefully through his glasses.

"What do you make of this?" he asked. Mason pressed a button on the wooden box answering machine and it whirred into life. The sound of a recording began. A robotic voice spoke, "Unknown number called today at nine thirty am. Message…" There was a few seconds of silence and then,

"This is First Officer Sol Garber calling for a Mr. Bowen Rhys following our interview two weeks ago. After consideration I have decided to officially offer you a place as a galley hand onboard our Free Trader ship the Memento. I have compiled a standard welcome package for new crew members to be sent via express courier including signed off world papers and your assignment contract. Bear in mind that our departure date is fixed and we will commence take off whether you are onboard or not. If for any reason you cannot make the voyage, your off world papers will be valid for two standard galactic years and can be used onboard any registered ship. I hope this message finds you well, Garber out."

The answering machine beeped as the message ended. There was a silence but for the sounds of Ida busying herself in the kitchen. Bowen stood blankly with his mouth open. Mason had his arms folded with a concerned look on his face. They hadn't left yet. Which meant Simon hadn't either. Bowen started to speak but Mason beat him to it.

"So the other week, when you went out that morning, is that where you went? To meet this Officer Garber?"

"Yes."

"Right." Mason said.

"I didn't think I'd actually get it. I didn't want you to find out like this." Bowen rubbed the back of his neck. "Are you angry?" He asked.

"No. I'm not." Mason said. Bowen could see the concern on his face however. "You know how your mother's going to take this don't you?" He said with a smile. Bowen smiled back. Mason took a deep breath. "You went and got a job, that's great." Bowen found himself in a warm embrace.

"Thanks dad."

Just then there was a strange noise from outside that caught their attention. A faint, low humming sound was getting louder.

"We have a visitor." Ida called from the kitchen. Bowen and Mason made for the front door and out into the yard. The sound was coming from a hover bike, its repulsion engine kicked up puddles and dirt in its wake. The noise vibrated Bowen's chest as it came to a stop in the yard. It was a sleek machine, orange and white with the word Marathon printed across the faring. The rider was dressed all in matching leathers.

"Good morning," Mason said politely, "Nice day for a

ride." The rider did not acknowledge him. Bowen and Mason exchanged a look. The rider stiffly and precisely dismounted the bike and turned to the rear where they opened a small cargo crate. Bowen looked the rider up and down. It was a robot. The whole planet was slowly being automated with farming machines, but even in town, a bipedal and intelligent robot like this was a rare sight. Was there a metallic head with lights for eyes behind the visor? Or was the helmet its head? The thoughts both intrigued and discomforted Bowen as he watched the machine take out a parcel made of smooth foil. It walked right up to him and outstretched its arm. Bowen took half a step back from the machine as a flat toned voice emanated from the helmet.

"Express delivery for Mr. Bowen Rhys courtesy of Marathon Couriers." Bowen took the silvery parcel from the gloved hands of the machine. It removed its glove and held out its hand as if it wanted to shake hands.

"Your signature is required." it said. Bowen looked down at the smooth metal hand with a sensor covered palm that was dotted with holes. Bowen carefully put his hand out. The robot took it in its own and there was a glow from between their palms. Bowen felt a slight warmth as it scanned his print. There was a beep from somewhere as it released Bowen's hand.

"Thank you and goodbye from Marathon Couriers." Bowen and Mason watched the robot put its glove back on as it mounted the bike again. The engine hummed to life and they watched it speed off towards the main road. Bowen clutched the parcel in his hands.

"Well, that was impressive," Mason said finally. "Never seen a postman like that before." Bowen secretly agreed, but he didn't say so. He had applied for a job with Marathon the year before and received a blunt response about how they were branching into the ever efficient world of automated drivers on state of the art vehicles.

"What was that?" Ida called from the porch.

"A robo-postman would you believe?" Mason said with a

smile.

"What's that?" Ida asked Bowen as he approached the house holding the parcel.

"I'll show you."

Bowen took a deep breath as they entered the kitchen and sat around the dining table. Bowen knew Ida would be starting to worry already. Bowen took the parcel in his hands. He saw the stamp of the aerospace offices in the corner where he tore it open and spilled the contents.

The neatly organised paperwork spilled out as well as a com-disk with the title 'Orientation.' There was also a small green wallet that unfolded to show his off world papers. A small laminated card with his face on it that mirrored his federation id picture. Below in a dotted square box was Officer Garber's signature. A free pass to leave the planet. Bowen smiled as he looked at it. He took a moment to observe the items himself before he looked up at his parents.

"I've got a job." he said with a stiff smile.

"Oh …excellent!" Ida said with genuine delight. Bowen could tell there was a slight hesitation with her words. Ida would know there was a lot more to say, but she was allowing herself to be happy in the moment.

"It's on a ship called the Memento. This is the welcome pack for new crew members." Bowen said plainly. He saw Ida's face change back to concern. Bowen continued, "I'm going to be working in the galley. The pay is really good." Bowen cleared his throat and continued, "I've been offered a short-term contract that will last until I get to Obelisk station and then I'll come home. The woman who interviewed me, she was an alien. Officer Sol Garber. She secured my papers." He showed them the small green wallet. "Simon told me about this, he's going too. I know this has come out of nowhere but it's what I want. I'm sorry I didn't tell you before now." He took a breath and looked down at the table. "I missed the boat finding a job in farming, with all the automation now. I have no prospects here." His parents both looked at him with a mixture of concern and pride the way only parents can. Ida leant forwards and picked up the com-disk.

"What is the ship called again?"

"Memento."

"What kind of ship is it?" she asked.

"Well, it's a.," Bowen tried.

"Federation Merchant Fleet." Mason interrupted. Bowen felt a pang of relief laced with guilt as he realised what his father was doing. Bowen looked at the floor and chose to affirm his father's lie.

"Yeah that's right." He forced himself to look into his mother's face. She was making herself smile.

"Well it's nothing that new to us really," Ida said, "Niamh had to travel to Metro and now she's on that science vessel."

"When will you be going?" Mason asked.

"In a few weeks time." Bowen said.

"Right," Ida said, "we'll have to get you an appointment at the clinic to get you started on your meds and get you fitted for your implants like your sister. It'll probably detail it all in what they've given you. You should read through this com-disk this afternoon and then read through it again a couple of times before you go." Bowen reached out and held his mother's hand, she was shaking slightly.

"Mum," Bowen said. She looked up at him with watery eyes, "It'll be okay." She smiled at him and nodded.

Mason cleared his throat and said, "I'll make a call to the clinic and I'll take you to your appointment."

Bowen swallowed his rising sense of guilt before he said, "Thanks dad.."

7.

The next morning came with a clear sky and the fields bore a heavy layer of mist. Bowen stood in the yard waiting with an anxious mind. He gazed upward. In the distance was the skyline of Allchester poking through the mist. High above beyond the sky, the Pennine warp gate glinted. Bowen watched a tiny dot rise upward. It sparkled as the sun's rays hit it from over the horizon. Beneath his anxiety was excitement. The gate seemed a lot closer now than it ever had.

From out of the work shed came Mason driving his truck. It was a bulky utility vehicle that sat on eight wheels. Mason wound the window down and called to Bowen over the noise of the engine.

"Ready?"

"Ready." Bowen ran around the front of the truck and climbed the short step ladders on the passenger side. When he was buckled in, the vehicle shuddered as they set off down the trail to the main road. With one hand Mason found a selection of cassette tapes and slotted one into the radio. The new jazz music filled the quiet.

Bowen tried to enjoy the view from up on the motorway but his thoughts were distracting him. Mason broke the quiet.

"So do you understand what's going to happen with these implants? Did that orientation com-disk detail it much?"

"Briefly," Bowen replied.

"Well Niamh said it wasn't awful, just that the adjustment period after was a little weird." Mason said. "I'd be excited to be eligible for something like this."

"I'm not nervous." It was a half truth. Another quiet fell until Bowen couldn't contain it any more.

"Dad why did we lie to Mum?" Mason didn't immediately respond. He shuffled in his seat and checked his rear view display screens.

He took a deep breath before he answered Bowen. "You know what your mother's like. She's going to worry about you, a lot. She was the same with Niamh. And she's heard one too many stories about Free Traders over the years."

"What do you mean?"

"Apparently they can be a dodgy lot. Some turn pirate. I'm not proud of it myself, but if your mum thinks you're with the Merchant Fleet she'll sleep a little easier." There was a moment of quiet between them before Mason spoke again. "This Officer Garber, what was she like?"

"She seemed like a decent woman. Respectable."

"She sounded very authoritative. Not someone to cross."

"Yeah, probably. She had two guns on her in my interview."

"You said Simon's on the crew didn't you?"

"I did."

"Well at least you'll have a friend from the get go." Bowen didn't respond. As they turned off the motorway at Allchester, he realised his fist was clenched.

***

Bowen and Mason sat on leather couches in the large waiting room of the surgery. It was quiet. They had found their way up to the second floor of the medical clinic to the auditory and neurology department. Bowen tapped his fingers on the arm of the leather chair he sat in. Next to him, Mason was reading a pamphlet on zero gravity aerobics. The huge building was one of the oldest in the town. The tiled floors were pristine and the sun beamed through coloured glass windows. From speakers in the ceiling came a robotic voice.

"Bowen Rhys to room four. Bowen Rhys to room four."

"Do you want me to come in with you?" Mason asked.

"If you like." Bowen replied. The two walked through a large doorway and followed the signs up a set of stairs and found room four. Bowen took a deep breath and knocked.

"Yes?" A voice from within came. Mason gave Bowen a reassuring look as he opened the door. Inside was a dimly lit, windowless room. Bowen saw an elderly man with wispy grey hair sat behind a desk at a computer terminal. He was illuminated by a large standing lamp that loomed over his cluttered desk. "Mr. Rhys?" the doctor said. The short man stood as they entered.

"That's right. This is my dad." Bowen replied as they shook hands.

"Hello dad." he said as he shook Mason's hand. "I'm Doctor Dietrich."

"Hello doctor," Mason replied.

"Please sit down." the doctor invited them. Dietrich spoke with the accent of Engelreich. As Bowen took his seat, something caught his eye. Behind Doctor Dietrich in a small alcove was a robot. It was not unlike the Marathon courier. This one had a more slender body shape with red and white colouring on its body with a series of large amber lenses in its head. It also sported two sets of arms.

"That's Missy," Dietrich said. "my assistant nurse bot. She'll be helping me with the procedure today. Much better than my human assistant." Bowen was uneasy at the presence of Missy. However Bowen was reassured when he noticed the numerous awards and placards dotted around the room. Doctor Dietrich turned to his terminal and began typing.

"So, you need the standard issue spacer's auditory implants." he asked.

"Yes that's right." Bowen replied.

"Do you have your paperwork for me?"

"I do." From inside his jacket Bowen retrieved the paperwork that had come with the welcome package and handed it to the doctor. Dietrich began skim reading them, muttering the odd word under his breath. Bowen looked at Mason who was twiddling with his pony tail. He looked at Bowen and smirked with raised eyebrows. Bowen's tension lifted somewhat.

"Journeying across space are we Bowen?"

"That's right."

"I'll also be installing the vital sign micro chip. Simple procedure, I numb skin on back of your neck and install the chip. It connects to the spinal cord and brain stem over a few days." Bowen swallowed hard.

"Right, okay."

"Painless. Very easy especially with Missy's help." The doctor said noticing Bowen's anxiety.

"Great."

"We'll do the chip first, then the implants. They'll work better together if the chip is inserted first." Bowen smiled with tightened lips, he did not like the word inserted in this situation. "Shall we get started?" the doctor asked. "If you would take off your jacket and make your way to the chair in the theatre." Dietrich pointed over into a darkened area through an open doorway. Bowen removed his jacket and handed it to his father.

"You'll be fine," Mason said.

"Come watch if you like?" the doctor offered. Mason considered and stood up to follow them.

"Lights." the doctor commanded. As he did so the theatre lit up showing off what was inside. Bowen's throat dried up. Through the door was a wide room. The walls were obscured by darkness as well as the ceilings. A series of bright lights illuminated a seat in the centre of the room. It was the most intimidating chair Bowen had ever seen. It was all white and chrome with various arms and apparatus connected. He saw a series of mirrors and magnifying lenses and a small computer terminal. Bowen stopped at the entrance but had no time to take in the sight. Doctor Dietrich was behind him urging him inside. Stood up, the doctor was quite short compared to Bowen, he had a small stool that he mounted next to the operating chair. He began outfitting himself with a pair of robotic goggles and a wrist mounted computer. Bowen sat down on the seat. He turned to face Mason who was standing out of the way just within the light. The doctor powered up his wrist mounted computer and said,

"Wake up Missy. Come meet Bowen." Bowen swallowed hard again. From within the office came Missy. A cheerful and polite female voice came from the robot.

"Hello Bowen, it is lovely to meet you." She said with an expressionless face.

"Hello…" Bowen said with an awkward smile.

"I am detecting anxiety." said Missy.

"You're telling me."

"Correct."

"What?"

"Music." Dietrich said. He brought the goggles down over his eyes and activated the terminal. Suddenly from somewhere came an operatic singer bellowing along with pipe organs. Bowen's brain was scrambled. The doctor pressed more buttons and the chair fully reclined. Bowen gripped the arm rests as the chair was then raised upwards a few feet. Doctor Dietrich lowered his stool so that he was now underneath Bowen who was then acutely aware that the back of his neck was exposed through a gap under the headrest. The opera singer began his next verse as the music swelled. Missy was now stood by Bowen's head. Bowen took a deep breath and swallowed. Missy gently but firmly placed her red rubber hands either side of Bowen's face.

"Please do not move" she instructed. His muffled response received no reaction. Bowen could hear the doctor tinkering with metallic instruments and his heart rate increased. "Try to think of something positive," Missy advised. "A rainbow, or puppies perhaps."

Suddenly Bowen felt a cold spray on the back of his neck that accompanied a floral bleach smell. After a moment, the doctor asked,

"Can you feel this?"

"No." Bowen managed despite Missy's soft rubber vice on his face.

"How about this?" the doctor asked again. Bowen gave the same response. "Good, we will begin now." The opera music swelled as another verse climbed to crescendo as Dietrich got to work. Bowen sensed movement but he didn't feel anything. During a lull in the music however, he heard a wet, sharp sound. Suddenly the opera didn't seem so bad. Bowen periodically heard the doctor changing out his instruments. A few minutes passed as Bowen's neck began to feel warmer along with what sounded like a small laser.

"Just sealing the wound now." Dietrich commented. "Now for the implant." Missy released Bowen's head as the chair raised up a few degrees into a reclined position. Her second set of rubber hands were holding him firmly but safely by the shoulders. He heard a hissing sound from above him as Missy reached to a large contraption that had been hiding just beyond the light. She pulled it down on its hydraulic arm and set it just above Bowen's head.

"Please don't move Bowen." she said as she held him. He couldn't of if he tried. To his side, Dietrich was flipping switches on the apparatus above Bowen's head. The doctor stopped for a moment and said,

"This will feel strange, but there should be no pain."

"Great." Bowen replied. Dietrich resumed his work. The machine whirred and beeped as internal gears shifted. Bowen felt a soft, fuzzy fabric surround both of his ears. He could still hear the music but now it was as though he were underwater. A strange new noise came from within the machine like the scurrying of tiny metal insects. In both ears he felt small cold touches and a gentle pinching sensation as the machine was reaching deeper.

Bowen tried to distract himself. He thought about trying to call Simon again. Why had he not been around lately? He thought about the Memento and that he was going to be leaving home behind. It was only temporary but still, almost a year in space on a ship was a long time.

"Done." Dietrich said. Bowen hadn't realized how tightly

he was gripping the arm rests and he was suddenly aware of how much he had been sweating.

"Well done Bowen." Missy said.

"Thank you." Bowen sighed. Missy's hands supported his back as he sat up. He touched his neck and rubbed his hands over his ears expecting pain, but felt nothing.

"Did it go alright?" Mason asked.

"Indeed it did." Dietrich answered as he was clearing up his work station. He removed his goggles and his wrist computer "If you would both like to return to my office I will join you in a moment." Bowen swung his legs off the seat and felt blood rush down his legs. Mason helped Bowen stand.

"Are you alright?" he asked.

"I think so." Bowen replied. Mason smiled at him and squeezed his shoulder. Dietrich joined them and began typing at his desktop terminal. Missy stayed behind disinfecting the theatre.

"Now then." Dietrich started. "You have just received a Personal Bio Vital chip or a "PBV". It is familiarising itself with your body as we speak. It is an all in one health monitoring piece of technology, it'll help your ship's doctor diagnose you should you fall ill to plague, parasite, virus, anything." Bowen nodded and rubbed his ear.

"You will feel some slight discomfort for a few hours as the implant settles. You also now have the federation standard spacer auditory implant in both your ears. If you encounter anyone who speaks a registered federation language you will hear your native Saxon and the implant will trick your eyes to make them appear to be speaking the words exactly. After a few days it will take effect. Now, I'm prescribing you some medication so that your body will adjust to the shock of outer space." He clacked away at his keyboard and a small printed square of paper emerged from the side of the computer. "Bring this to the front desk and follow the instructions on the box. Do you have any questions?"

Bowen had a hundred questions. Will the implant last

forever? What if my body rejects the PBV chip? What does shock of outer space mean exactly? Bowen finally managed to say, "Are there many plagues out in space?"

"Yes." Dietrich replied, "but nothing a federation doctor worth his salt can't handle." Bowen felt the colour leave his face. He was not boarding a federation vessel. "It says here that you are going to Obelisk station." Bowen nodded. "Well there have never been any recorded outbreaks between here and there so don't concern yourself. I'd be more conscious of sexually transmitted diseases among crew mates." Bowen smiled awkwardly and went red. "I'll include a pamphlet with your prescription." Dietrich said. "Any last questions?" he asked. Bowen's head was a little fuzzy and the smell of the disinfectant from Missy's handiwork was now drifting into the office.

"No, I don't think so." Bowen said.

"Thank you very much doctor." Mason said. All three of them stood. They both shook hands with doctor Dietrich.

"Good luck on your voyage Mr. Rhys."

"Thanks a lot." Bowen said. Missy, who had completed her work was stood by the open door. "Goodbye Bowen." She said cheerfully. He stammered a thank you and left with Mason.

8.

Time began to blur for Bowen. He did his best to fill the days with preparation. He had started the course of pills straight away, one with every meal as was prescribed. The little white capsules went down easily enough and he felt nothing despite the instructions carrying a hefty list of mild to serious recorded side effects. Bowen got permission to haul the com-disk reader up to his room so that he could have privacy to study the orientation disk. It detailed his new responsibilities, shift patterns, the pay and the name of his supervisor; a person named "Wotll". He signed all the papers and packed them neatly back into the folder. As he read through the orientation, it was hard to tell if it was anxiety, impatience or if it was just dull but Bowen found it hard to read for any length of time. Phrases like, "hull integrity failure", "sudden gravitational reversal" and "emergency ditch procedure" had all jumped out at him as he skim read the section entitled, "In the Event Of..."

Amongst the paperwork was a folded print-out cross section map of the Memento. More than anything yet this grabbed his attention. When fully unfolded it was too ungainly to hold forcing Bowen to clear floorspace to lay it out. It wasn't a true representation and much of it was too technical to make sense of, but it was his first real look at the ship. If he had been anxious, his mind now turned to excitement. He couldn't wait to see it. The closest Bowen had ever felt to flying was taking the suspended hyper trains up and down the country. The idea of not only flying through the air but then leaving the planet entirely made his imagination soar.

Bowen continued with his daily routines such as they were. He fed Virgil and checked on the greenhouse, pruning and picking what was ready. He watched the machines trundle around the farm with disdain. Mason had finished programming their routines and seemed to be happy with them. Bowen was pleased for him but he couldn't help but feel a tug of resentment and a flair of jealousy which made him feel privately ashamed. Bowen had been looking forward to herding the cattle into their huge shed down where they would live for the cold months, but no, the machines were taking care of that too.

In the days following his procedure at the clinic, after dinner everyone sat around the television for a little while. For a few minutes every night they tuned it to fuzzy alien channels to see if they took effect. It was an odd sensation for Bowen, but gradually they worked. On the night it was confirmed to have been successful, Bowen translated a whole ten minutes of programmes spoken from a multitude of races, much to everyone's delight.

Mason and Ida were of course, nothing but supportive during his preparation to leave and he loved them for it. Ida had remained strong despite her worries. She would ask the occasional round about question, but never anything too specific. Bowen thought not to speak about some of the emergency procedures he had read about in the orientation.

Some days later, Bowen took a break from worrying about the dangers of space travel and set to tidying his bedroom. He would be leaving in less than a week and he thought that the last thing he'd want to come home to was a pigsty of a room. He dismantled piles of books and put them back on their shelves. He salvaged spare plates and glassware that had been sat around for weeks. He stripped his bed and began making a huge pile of dirty clothes for the wash room.

As he rummaged under his bed for stray socks and forgotten t shirts, his hand felt a distinctly foreign material. As confused as he was for an instant, Bowen knew what it was before he retrieved it from the dark. A black lace thong. He removed a clump of stray hairs that had collected from under the bed and he sat on the bare mattress, holding it in his hands. He felt a clench in his chest. The last time that Jules was in his room was months ago in the early summer. Bowen sat there, listening to the light rain on the windows and the quiet ticking of his beside clock and he gave in to reminiscence.

The balmy morning that day was but a taste of the heat that would dominate the rest of the day. By the time Bowen had cycled all the way to Allchester station he had sweated through his shirt and he very much regretted wearing jeans instead of shorts. He had just enough time to catch his breath before the train flew in on the hyper track. The usual trickle of passengers disembarked and with them Juliette walking her blue bicycle. Juliette was of course dressed for the heat. A loose, bright yellow tank top and a floral short skirt that billowed as she stepped onto the platform. As passengers moved around them, Jules greeted him with a kiss and she whispered something in his ear that he couldn't recall. They wandered town a while before they rode their bikes away, down the dirt roads that ran parallel to the motorways. The warm wind came across the endless fields to chase them away. As they weaved in and out of the gigantic concrete pillars of the motorway, Jules began to stand up while she pedalled. Bowen remembered how she glanced back at him smiling, giving him a glimpse of the dark lace.

His memories blurred much of the afternoon beyond that. All that remained was the rising heat and the feeling of his shirt sticking to his back. He could still hear Jules panting as she rode her bike, if he listened for it. They ordered take out and watched some television in his room. After the sun went down, it was still oppressively hot. Bowen opened all his bedroom windows and left the curtains wide open to let in what little air there was.

He remembered her waiting for him on his bed wearing the thong with the matching bra. Her ginger hair fell about her sunburnt, freckly shoulders that were glistened with sweat. She knew exactly how to look at him with her green eyes when she wanted to fuck him. Jules knew full well that she had been a tease and led him on all day. She stretched herself out like a cat, showing him everything she had to offer. Jules would never make the first move when she wanted sex, in fact she rarely even spoke of it. But she knew just what to do to get what she wanted.

His mind toyed with him, making him remember it all. Bowen remembered Jules' fruity lip balm combined with the taste of the sauce from the burgers as they kissed. He didn't specifically remember removing the thong, but he remembered her fingers running through his hair as he ate her out. He couldn't remember taking off her bra, but he remembered her perky breasts filling his hands. She straddled Bowen and rode him, taking herself to a shuddering orgasm, having to bite into his neck to stop herself crying out. The smell of her body butter mixed with an undercurrent of latex and lubricant drifted through Bowen's mind as the memory quietly faded into the back of his head.

That next morning, after she had discreetly showered herself, Jules declined breakfast as she often did and she left for the train home. Whether she intentionally left without her underwear or not, he couldn't know. Bowen had almost told Jules that he loved her before she left. In a way he was glad that he had not. He thought he would feel even worse discovering that she had left Saxon. He sat holding the forgotten thong in his hands. He wasn't sure what to do with it. After a moment, he reached across to his bedside table and opened the bottom drawer. Inside were a couple of boudoir burlesque magazines along with his box of condoms. His mother never exactly came into his room to clean any more, but he still had a secret drawer of material. He couldn't quite bring himself to throw the thong away, so he left it in there.

Bowen lay back on his bed and his mind trailed away. She must have known that day that she was going to be leaving the planet. She must have known when they were riding their bikes and when they were eating dinner, and when she was fucking him and when she kissed him goodbye. Wherever she was, she hadn't written to him. Was she angry with him for some reason? He was quite sure he hadn't done anything to upset her. Would she ever come back? How would he know? Would she reach out to him is she did? If she did, what would he say to her? What would she say? Would she apologize? He felt like he deserved an explanation at least.

Why did he have to hear from Simon that Jules had left Saxon? Simon had apparently had more contact than Bowen had with some of their other friends after they had left. Was Simon still in touch with Jules? Simon knew enough to say that she was on a ship by the treasure nebula, which to Bowen's knowledge was the far side of the territory. How could she leave without saying anything? Were they even still an item? Should he consider her his ex now? His insides sank. Maybe their relationship just meant more to him than it did to her. He sat up and wiped the tears that had begun to pool at the corners of his eyes and he continued with tidying his bedroom.

That evening Bowen found himself sat by the phone in the hallway. He had called the Van Hoff household again, this time conceding to leave a message to Charles asking for Simon to get back to him when he could. Bowen knew that the Memento hadn't left yet, so why had Simon gone quiet? The next day after no response, Bowen left another message this time directly to Simon.

"Si, it's me Bowen. I was hoping we could at least talk before you left, I've got a few things I want to tell you. And I've got a couple things I want to ask you." Bowen thought for a moment whether to leave it at that, but his mind made him say more, "I went and asked about that job you told me about and I got it. So, I suppose if you're too busy to talk I'll see you on the Memento."

He put the phone down with more force than he meant to. Bowen realized that his heart was beating something fierce in his chest. He felt angry. How hard was it to pick up the phone and talk? Was Simon avoiding him? Come to think of it he had been particularly off with him for a long while. If Simon was simply bored of Bowen's friendship, he would rather he would just come out with it. What was going on? It was then Bowen's mind recalled something that Mr. Van Hoff had said when he spoke to him a few weeks back.

"Why don't you ask the ginger one, he's usually with her."

9.

The rain spattered the windows. The neon green glow from the clock showed 5:46am. Bowen's eyes had already adjusted to the darkness. He had been drifting in and out of sleep all night. Sunrise wouldn't be for another hour or so, but it wouldn't be much of a sunny day in the Britannica Valley, the scheduled weather was more clouds and rain. He sat up in bed with his hair splayed across his face. It was just too early to get ready, but just too late to go back to sleep. His large dark leather case and accompanying satchel were sat waiting at the foot of the bed, both bulging with clothing, toiletries and books along with his binoculars and camera. He brushed his hair behind his ears and made a last-minute decision.

Bowen quietly made his way to the bathroom. His skinny physique greeted him in the mirror. He ignored his less than presentable reflection and began rummaging in the cupboard under the sink. He retrieved a small metal box and set it on the counter top. Inside was a set of electric razors. He set up the razor to charge and looked himself in the mirror. He grabbed a pair of long scissors and trimmed his hair down. The lengths mostly fell into the sink. Once the razor was charged, he set to work. The buzzing gently rattled his skull as he carefully scoured every inch of his head. When he was done his locks were everywhere. He plucked the biggest clumps of hair from the sink and filled the bowl with warm water. He set about shaving off his now scruffy looking brown-blonde beard with a small hand razor. His new reflection soon stared back at him. The last time Bowen had seen himself like this was when Jules decided to buzz his head to make him "look tough". Bowen couldn't keep eye contact with himself, but he did quite like the shape of his skull.

After cleaning up he stripped nude and jumped in the shower. As the steamy hot water cascaded from above him, he wondered what the showering situation would be like on the Memento. He was apparently getting his own bathroom in his quarters, but nothing specified whether he would get his own shower. Perhaps there was a communal block that he would have to use with all manner of off worlders. Hopefully that wasn't the case. He made the most of the last shower he would have at home for a long while.

Back in his room, he dressed and he set about lugging his case and satchel down the flights of stairs. He flopped onto the couch in the lounge and caught his breath. He regretted not getting into shape before leaving.

Samhain found his way into Bowen's lap. The cat nuzzled at his face and purred as he licked Bowen's neck. The rain pattered on the windows and the wind whistled down the fireplace. He looked at the photographs on the table a while.

The day earlier he had brought the com-disc reader from his room and set it up on the coffee table. Bowen looked at his new clean-shaven reflection and for a moment he didn't recognise himself. The clocks chimed. His parents would soon emerge. Bowen went to the kitchen and brewed a pot of tea. He made for himself some lightly buttered toast which took him almost twice as long as normal to eat. The nerves had started, he realized as he stirred his strong tea.

Mason and Ida soon joined him in the kitchen and had their own breakfast. Mason asked sensible, fatherly questions as Ida fussed over Bowen, suggesting he have more toast or some cereal that he politely but firmly refused. Bowen took his pills and downed a glass of water to tide over his stomach.

Before long Bowen didn't really register what they were talking about as he answered last minute questions. He had triple checked his belongings the night before and he was more than prepared for the day ahead, on paper at least. Despite his anxieties forcing his brain to not fully absorb the conversations, before long the kitchen was echoing with jokes and laughter. For a little while, Bowen was calm.

From the hallway came a noise. The post had arrived.

Mason rose from the table and went to the hall. When he returned he passed around the com-discs. The majority were for Mason and Ida, but one was for Bowen, to his amazement.

Bowen's mind raced. Had there been some problem with his work placement? Had the Memento been forced to cut costs and let him go before he'd even been taken on? Bowen picked up the cassette and made for the lounge. In the dim light of the room he fumbled to turn on the machine. The old thing made its usual hissing and clunking as it came to life. He initially tried to insert the cartridge backwards with his now sweating hands but eventually succeeded. The screen greeted him finally. The Federation Postal Service logo appeared and gave way to the message.

WELCOME!
YOU HAVE A MESSAGE!
PLEASE WAIT!

"Come on." Bowen said impatiently. He was right on the edge of the couch, hunched over the table, tapping his finger on the wood. After what seemed like an age, the screen shifted. The Federation Postal Service logo appeared in the top corner opposite the sender address.

COMMS SUITE
CREW DECK ALPHA
LEISURE FLEET PRIME
FEDERATION VESSEL:
EMPRESS DOWAGER

Hey Bo,
We haven't spoken in a while have we? I'm letting you know I'll be home in a few months. I asked Simon to let you know I had left. Honestly I'm having the best time! I can't wait to tell you all about it. You can buy me a burger in town!
Love Jules x

Bowen felt sick. He retreated from the screen and sat back into the couch. His stomach was on the floor and his brain was static. Bowen rubbed his chin and sat back up to re-read the message. There was no apology, no explanation. No, "how have you been?" Not even a, "Sorry I just ran away like that, didn't mean to forget about your feelings…" She had entrusted Simon to tell him that she had left, which was not how things had gone. Even so that would not have made things any better.

Bowen didn't know what to think. He felt happy that she had written, relieved that she hadn't forgotten him, but he was angry at the vagueness of the message along with her apparent disinterest in his life since they last saw each other. She said she would be home in a few months. Not exactly specific.

There was a part of him that wanted nothing more than to wait for Jules to come back. When he was with her his worries disappeared, at least for a while. The clock sounded on the hour and shook Bowen out of his thoughts. Not long now. Mason would be taking him soon. Bowen looked back at the screen of the com-disc reader. He hesitated for moment on whether to reply and return. He decided against it. He pressed the appropriate buttons and the message disappeared. The machine relaxed its hold on the cartridge. Like the thong the other night, he wasn't sure what to do with it. Bowen made the decision to not make the decision and he placed the cartridge in his jacket pocket.

There was little else to do to prepare. Mason stood in the hallway in his raincoat and woolly hat, the keys to the truck in hand. Bowen checked his bags and his papers. His identification card was in its new home in his wallet. When he stood up from lacing up his boots Ida approached him sniffling but smiling, handkerchief in hand. She clutched him and kissed him on the cheek and he received a hug that only a mother can give.

"It's not forever." He remembered saying. There was a

meowing from the ground. He looked down and saw Samhain padding at the cuff of his jeans. A single little claw trying to hold him back. "Hey now mister." he said as he leant down and picked him up. Bowen nuzzled Samhain's thick black fur and he stroked him behind his ears. "See you soon okay?" He handed the cat over to Ida.

"Time to go." Mason said, looking at his watch, "I'll be back soon." He said. The cold air rushed in as they opened the door to the rainy yard. Mason had already parked the truck out front. Bowen wrestled his case and satchel into the storage compartment before he remembered.

"Oh shit! I'll just be a minute." He said before running around towards the rear of the house. He ran right past the sheds and the greenhouse. He splashed his way down the garden path to Virgil's clearing. The huge tortoise was out of his hide, drinking from his pond. As Bowen reached Virgil the creature looked at him slowly. "I'm sorry, I can't believe I forgot to feed you." He knelt down and met Virgil at his eye level and scratched him gently on his large head. Virgil looked into his eyes and blinked. "I'm going away for a while," Bowen said. "But I'll be back." Virgil simply looked back at him. "I'll miss you." Bowen said without thinking. He felt his eyes welling up, so he stood and left. When he returned to the truck, Mason was stood there in the rain,

"You forgot to feed him, didn't you?" he said with a stiff smile.

"I'm sorry." Bowen said.

"Don't worry about it, I'll see to him when I get back. I'll be feeding from now on anyway." Mason said before he climbed into the truck. Bowen turned back to the house where Ida were stood under the porch. Ida was dabbing her face with Samhain in her arms but she was beaming at him. He called out a goodbye through the rain and she waved before he climbed into the truck to leave. Bowen watched the house in the wet wing mirror until it was out of sight.

10.

    The drive to Allchester felt different. Bowen felt as though he had never truly paid attention to the route before. Before long they had reached the gates to the port. Through his rain-soaked window Bowen saw the foggy silhouette of the high perimeter wall. They came to a stop in a marked-out spot among hazard stripes where a large red light stared them down from the gate. Armoured guards were stationed around. One approached Mason's side door. Mason rolled the window down to greet the man.

    "Morning." he said. Bowen could see that the guards were federation patrol men, he recognized the grey and white urban pattern body armour, and he saw their tool belts and bandoleers. They carried plasma rifles close to their chests that hissed in the rain.

    "Business?" the guard asked Mason. As he spoke the voice sounded as though it was being played through a small speaker.

    "I'm taking my son through to departures." Mason said. Bowen noticed that the other guards had quietly surrounded the truck. The guard climbed the step ladders of the driver's side to see inside the cabin. Mason sat back with his hands on the wheel. The guard's faceless, rain-soaked helmet observed Bowen for a moment. A small camera on the side of the helmet focused in and out at him before the guard spoke again.

    "Identification." The guard requested. Bowen carefully pulled out his wallet. He retrieved his card and handed it over. The guard took it with his gauntlet, angling it down and towards the light. Bowen noticed that even though the guard had stopped looking him in the face, his helmet mounted camera was still watching him. Bowen and Mason exchanged a look. The guard returned Bowen's identification to him and said, "Cleared for entry. Wait for the signal." Bowen and Mason both politely thanked the guard as he left them.

"Did you see his gun?" Mason said as he rolled his window back up.

"I did."

"It's a far cry from my old ballistic."

Bowen looked through his wet window at the huge metal and stone gate. A series of security cameras were all pointed at their car along with automated gun emplacements at the ready. The red light became amber as the gate began to lift upwards. After a moment it flashed green as a small alarm rang. Mason crawled the truck forward as they were waved through.

Before long they had parked up and unpacked. Once Mason had paid for the parking they followed a covered walkway that directed them to a place called the village. They came down some wide steps and into a sprawling courtyard bustling with people, and not just humans. They saw a huge awning four stories above, sheltering the area from the rain. Every edge of the place was a store or a bar of some kind with people coming and going. The upper levels of the village looked to be hotels and rest stops. On the courtyard itself were numerous stalls and vendors and in the centre was a command post with more guards. Across the village centre were huge entrances to landing pads and docking bays, each with their own check point. Bowen's eyes were drawn upwards to a large control tower that loomed over everything from beyond the rooftops. From a series of huge speakers came a robotic voice that occasionally spouted rules and regulations.

Mason pointed to a huge digital twenty-six-hour clock on a departure screen. Bowen read the words Memento Docking Bay Three. He swallowed.

"Come on let's get you gone." Mason said with a smile and patted Bowen on the shoulder. The pair moved through the crowd towards the checkpoint for docking bay three where they fell into line behind others. Further down, guards were inspecting identification. Bowen noticed people breaking off and leaving up a set of stairs to the side, while behind the checkpoint was a wide set of concrete stairs that led downwards. Eventually they reached the front. Bowen was asked to show his card again by a guard while another scanned him and his belongings. Bowen's heart rate increased. The guard returned Bowen's identification and turned to Mason.

"Sir if you aren't boarding, I can't let you past. You may go to the observation deck if you wish." the guard said. Mason turned to Bowen.

"Okay spacer, I'll be watching." Bowen found himself in a warm, firm hug. Bowen's nose filled with his father's earthy, farm scent with the edge of his aftershave. Bowen tried to say bye but his voice caught in his throat. Mason patted Bowen on the back and released him as the guard showed Bowen the stairway. He was beckoned through and he began to lug his case down the steps. He chanced a look back, but Mason was already gone.

As he reached the bottom a cold wind rushed towards him. He followed a series of passages that were lined with travel boards before falling into line again with some passengers as they waited to be let out through the guarded metal doorways of a wide lift. There were no windows, but Bowen could hear the wind whistling through the passages beyond. Bowen took a deep breath and patted his pockets to make sure he still had everything. As he did so, he felt the com-disc from Jules.

From further down the line, a small face was looking at him. A young girl with blonde hair and big blue eyes was being carried by her mother. She was wrapped up in a yellow coat and she was wearing a soft knitted hat with floppy bunny ears. Bowen was taken a back for a second and he wasn't sure how to react. Without thinking he went cross eyed and pulled a silly face. The girl giggled to herself and Bowen felt his face go red as he smiled back.

There was a buzzing sound as the metal doors opened and everyone was ushered through into the lift. It was large, but still Bowen found himself wedging in between a lanky insectoid person and a heavy set alien with skin like an old couch. The doors closed as the lift was illuminated in dim green light. As they ascended, the little blonde girl was being fussed over by her parents. Her father was gathering her hair up with a bobble and zipping up her yellow coat tight. Bowen took another deep breath as he checked his satchel strap and patted his case that he had sat between his legs. The lift shuddered to a stop. The opposite side of the lift opened and a rush of cold, wet air came through. The passengers were beckoned out by another guard. They were on a long, wide bridge with a cage roof that ran all the way to an enormous building. Large dark holes in the sides were belching a thick mist. An immense fog horn sounded periodically. The rain was coming down in sheets. As Bowen walked out into the rain, he looked out and saw that the walkway was at least a couple hundred feet in the air. He noticed a few people stopping for a moment and waving to their right. He looked out into the rain and saw another caged area not too far away from them. It was the observation platform.

There weren't that many people there, but through the mist and the rain he saw his father. He waved at Bowen as they noticed each other. Mason began to call out something to him, but as he did so, the foghorn blared again.

"What!?" Bowen shouted, but Mason was just waving to him and laughing.

"Last call!" someone shouted. Bowen realized now that he was the last person on the bridge. He hurried towards the far doorway to the huge building lugging his leather case. Bowen was now soaked. He looked up through the cage at the immense shape of the structure. The foghorn sounded again and blew away a wisp of cloud to reveal the word Memento.

Bowen's mouth fell open. The ship was huge, far bigger than he had imagined. He finally reached the end of the walkway and was met by a crew member. The man was a head taller than Bowen. He looked human but had no nose and bright orange skin with black eyes, a Duuboss male. He was dressed in a green armoured flight suit and wore a gun belt similar to Garber's. A tag on his chest read Kytos.

"Crew or passenger!?" he shouted to Bowen.

"I'm a new crew member!"

"Turn around!" Kytos requested as he brandished some kind of scanner. Bowen did as he was bid. He felt the alien tug down on his jacket and expose his neck. He heard a buzzing noise and felt a warm patch where his Personal Bio Vital chip was. The sensation passed and there was an electronic ping from the scanner. "Welcome to the crew Mr. Rhys!" he said after looking at the device. Bowen couldn't suppress his smile. "Find a seat in commercial for now!" Bowen nodded as Kytos stood aside to allow him to enter. Bowen looked over his shoulder. He couldn't make out Mason any more. The moment passed and Bowen took a step onto the Memento.

11.

Kytos the security guard followed Bowen inside. The sounds of the rain and wind outside were immediately silenced as the door was shut and locked. Bowen followed the directions through a series of automatic doors to commercial seating. His wet case now felt double the weight it had earlier. Commercial seating was a long cabin with rows of three seats with an aisle through the middle. There was a line of windows that ran down the right-hand side that let in the grey light. Bowen shuffled along with his case and found an empty aisle seat on the right. He heaved his case up into the overhead storage. Keeping his satchel on him he sat down. Next to him was a large, sleeping alien with a rubbery gut hanging out of his shirt. Sat by the window was a slim alien with the aspect of a cat who was reading a book. Bowen took off his wet jacket and laid it over his lap. He looked around and saw a smattering of humans among the passengers, but they were mostly aliens as Officer Garber had said. Bowen caught himself looking for Simon's face. He made eye contact with the little blonde girl instead. She was sat in the seat opposite him across the aisle. She swung her legs as she smiled at him. He smiled back.

A note chimed through a speaker in the low ceiling above his seat and a familiar voice came through.

"Ladies and Gentlemen this is Officer Sol Garber speaking. The Captain would ask that you now take your seats and buckle in as we prepare for launch. We are prepared and on schedule for our departure to Pennine warp gate. Expect some minor turbulence as we take off but it will ease as we ascend to orbit. For your own safety remain seated during take off. The Captain and crew are happy to have you and we hope you have a pleasant journey. Officer Sol Garber signing out."

There was a small racket as the passengers all buckled themselves in. Bowen adjusted the shoulder straps and fastened the central buckle. He looked across the aisle. The mother of the blonde girl was helping her strap in. From down the front of the aisle came a guard through the doorway. The alien was dressed in a blue armoured flight suit similar to the crew member who scanned Bowen at the door. This guard however was almost crocodilian in appearance and he wielded a large rifle with a drum barrel. He surveyed the passengers with beady eyes and stood to the side of the door. Bowen craned his neck around to see the door he had entered through. There was another guard with the same gun as the other, however this one looked avian in appearance with a sharp black beak and garish pink and green colouring about his head. They did not take a seat despite the passengers having been instructed to do so.

Bowen took a deep breath and looked past the fat alien man who had gone back to sleep after buckling himself in. He looked out the window that the cat-like person was thankfully not obstructing. The rain still hammered down from the grey skies of Saxon. Bowen noticed a pulsing yellow light was catching the glass from somewhere outside as he felt a rumbling from within the ship. It was happening. He sat back in his seat and took another deep breath. The rumbling grew and grew and grew. A sound like rolling thunder came as Bowen gripped the arm rests of his chair. There was a shudder through the floor and then, nothing.

All of a sudden, the ship roared and the entire cabin began to quake. He had never experienced such a force. His heart pounded in his chest. Bowen strained his neck to see out the window. The clouds rushed downwards. The engines thundered as the ship crashed its way into the sky. There was a stomach clenching sensation as he felt the ship angle itself upwards. Bowen stifled a panic as the ship began to rock against the wind. Just as it seemed that the storm might win the fight, sunlight flooded into the cabin. The Memento stopped thrashing as it broke through the clouds. Bowen leaned forward and looked out the window. His mind took a second to adjust to what he could see. His anxiety gave way to exhilaration as he saw the vertical horizon of Saxon. They were leaving the clouds way behind as they flew through the clear blue sky. Bowen had never seen anything so incredible. He saw the distant peaks of Pen Morgan jutting through the clouds way off in the distance but even they seemed small and they were getting smaller by the second.

The sky soon grew a darker shade of blue. It became darker and darker until the upper atmosphere of Saxon was left behind entirely.

12.

The chaos of the launch eased as the ship left the upper atmosphere of the planet. The last of the wind rocked the ship before there was nothing but the rumbling of the engines. Bowen took a few deep breaths as he looked out the window at the slowly curving horizon. Nothing could have prepared him for the sight and he felt the last of his nerves fade away.

The fat alien next to him snored. He wished he could see out the front of the ship from the bridge. He would have loved to get a good look at the Pennine warp gate as they approached. Bowen's attention turned to the guard at the front door. The launch had not phased him in the slightest. Bowen strained to read the name patch on his broad chest. It read Vargoth. Vargoth's sharp green eyes scanned the cabin. As they made eye contact, Bowen gave an awkwardly stiff smile before sheepishly looking away. He busied himself checking his pockets once again as the passenger next to him rumbled sleepily. Bowen wondered how something such as a space launch could ever be so mundane.

Before long the ship was approaching the warp gate. The overhead speakers chimed, "Ladies and Gentlemen this is Officer Sol Garber speaking. We are approaching the Pennine warp gate now. We have clearance to dock however we will be circling the station due to some light traffic. We ask that you remain seated until we have docked and the ship comes to a complete stop." Bowen checked his seatbelts and watched out the window. There was a low rumble from deep within the ship as the Memento gradually altered its pitch forwards until Saxon was below them. Bowen's stomach tensed for a moment. He was glad he didn't give up on the medication, or else he'd be making his way to a bathroom. The planet looked incredible. A vast expanse of swirling grey clouds above swathes of deep green and wide stretches of cold, dark blue. He was leaving his whole life behind, albeit just for a while.

The view now began to move past them as the ship began to circle the station. Bowen wondered if his dad had watched until the Memento was completely out of sight. He thought about just how far away that was already, how far down below him Allchester was. His feet curled in his shoes as his stomach clenched a little again. He swallowed hard and tried to think of something else. The ship juddered as the engines altered their movement. Bowen sat back in his seat. From the speakers came beeps and buzzing. Bowen imagined what it must be like to pilot something roughly the size of a stadium and then to accurately dock with another colossal object. He wondered if maybe one day he would get a look at the bridge. Just then the engines whined and strained as they brought the ship into its docking position. The internal systems fluctuated and pulsed as the ship came to a stop and the engines powered down.

"Ladies and Gentlemen this is Officer Sol Garber speaking, we have arrived at Pennine warp gate station. Passengers travelling with us can now find their cabins following the signs. All new crew members are required to deposit their luggage in their cabins and immediately report to their supervisors for their orientation. Please have your identification ready to present to the guards at the doors. Passengers seeking connecting flights, make your way to the arrival tunnel following the signs. Myself, the Captain and all the crew wish you well and thank you for flying with us this morning. Officer Sol Garber signing off."

The cabin was filled with noise as all the passengers began to stand and gather their luggage. Bowen soon had his case from the overhead compartment and found himself being moved with the flow of passengers with his satchel tight across his body. As he stood in the aisle to leave, Bowen caught himself looking for the back of Simon's head, but before long he was face to face with the guard at the rear door. His yellow and black beak twitched as Bowen approached him.

His vibrant head cocked to one side slightly as his beady eyes surveyed him. Bowen read his name patch as Zaziik. Bowen was about to speak when Zaziik beat him to it with a quick, sharp voice.

"Identification." Bowen showed his open wallet to him as Zaziick clicked his beak and examined his details. "Up the stairs."

"Thanks." Bowen said as he stuffed his wallet back into his jacket pocket. Zaziik gave no further response as Bowen was ushered into the entryway where he had boarded. The orange skinned alien Kytos was still there guiding passengers off the ship into a disembarking tunnel that had been connected from the docking bay. Bowen took a deep breath as he climbed a grated metal stairway. His arms ached as he lugged the case upwards. The walls were mostly exposed piping and metallic panelling. Large technical read-outs were printed in painted stencil work here and there. He passed other crew members who shuffled past him. Officer Garber wasn't kidding when she said the crew was mostly non-human. He passed access corridors for engineering, passageways to cargo lifts and maintenance hatches, many of which bore large red lettering and restricted symbols. Bowen was really starting to feel the weight of his luggage as he finally reached the crew decks.

The corridors there was wide enough for roughly half a dozen people to stand shoulder to shoulder. The floor was a worn grey carpet and the walls were much more substantial than the stairwell. In the gaps between cabin doors were huge screens that seemed to periodically change. As Bowen walked the hallway he passed images of locations from around the galaxy and vistas of space as well as advertisements for items that could apparently be purchased from an onboard store called Gricky's. In the ceiling were neon panel lights that shone with fake daylight. The deck appeared to run the whole length of the ship as it curved out of sight further down. There was a distinct ambience as he searched for his cabin. There was a low chatter from the few crew members that were stood around idly as well as a constant low hum from the engines as they rested.

He finally found his cabin and massaged his shoulder as he dropped his case. He withdrew his identification card from his wallet and inserted it into the slot in the door. A small green light blinked and there was a mechanical shunting sound as his cabin unlocked. His shoulder complained as he heaved his case inside.

Through a short corridor the cabin opened up. It was small but not cramped. A sizeable bed slab sat across from a fixed desk under a wall lamp. The more he looked around he noticed a plethora of cleverly hidden storage compartments. Thin light panels around the coving of the ceiling illuminated the room. He dropped his case by the foot of the bed and he placed his satchel by the side table. Across from him was an open door where he discovered a small bathroom with a shower to his relief. He removed his jacket and shirt and took the opportunity to freshen up.

After washing and changing his shirt his curiosity took over. A small series of buttons by the window controlled the metal blinds. After working it out, the shades retracted and the view of Pennine station was presented to him with Saxon spread out beneath like an enormous carpet. An incredible view of the colossal ring structure with hundreds of other ships docked up. He watched passengers from other ships disembark from tunnel hatches that snaked into the body of the station.

Bowen found his camera and snapped a few pictures, zooming in and out to some of the other ships. He could have stayed there and watched the view for hours, but he was there to work. He decided to lose his jacket for the day and brought with him only his wallet. He stood in the centre of the cabin, took a few deep breaths and ran his hands over his shaved head before he made to leave.

In the crew deck corridors again he followed a sign that

clung to the ceiling that said Rec Deck, Galley and Cafeteria. He found his way to some stairs passing more crew members on the way. There was more buzz of activity as he explored. Walking through more corridors where he was more often than not the only human, to his relief he eventually found a huge atrium across which was a large set of double doors that opened up onto the cafeteria.

It was a massive room with a high ceiling. Taking up a whole side of the room was a set of windows that ran from the floor to the ceiling. All that could be seen through the glass was the enormous station. The space was large enough to seat everyone on the ship at once on a series of stools, long benches and tables all fixed to the floors. Towards the far end, a line of people queued up at a long service counter getting lunch. Bowen's stomach rumbled. The toast he had forced down seemed like forever ago and his insides were telling him it hadn't been enough. To the side of the serving line, he saw a swinging doorway with staff in matching black and white aprons and hats coming and going. Bowen swallowed and made for the door. On his way over he felt watched. He tried to look casual but he was conscious of the fact that he was a stranger and knew no one. There were sure to be other new starters but there was no way of knowing who they were. His mind again made him look for Simon, but to no avail. He walked through the swinging double doors a little more brazenly than he intended to and a few faces turned and looked at him.

"Bowen Rhys I presume?" came a gruff woman's voice. Bowen scanned the room to see which person the voice had come from. His gaze landed on the only body who wasn't moving. A squat, overweight alien was stood in the centre of the busy kitchen looking directly at him. She had the appearance of an amphibian. Her skin was glossy and a deep yellow with mottled brown patches. Her large red eyes were startling with their vertical slit pupil but the woman was smiling at him. Her bulbous throat wobbled as she spoke.

"Wotll?" Bowen asked.

"That's me sunshine." she said as she hefted herself over to him. She wiped her long dexterous hands on her grubby apron before holding out a hand. As they shook hands Bowen smiled and did his best not to focus on how cold and oddly rough her skin felt despite its appearance. He also did his best to not think about how he could quite easily fit his whole head in her mouth it was so big and wide. "You don't look like a farmer." she chuckled causing her throat to inflate.

"No?" Bowen replied with a bemused smile.

"But then I don't look like a chef now do I?"

"I wouldn't say that." he said even though he secretly agreed.

"Garber said you were a good kid." Wotll said as their handshake ended. Bowen felt his face go pink. "Well, this is it." Wotll said. She turned around and outstretched her chubby arms motioning to the kitchen as a whole. "The most important part of any spaceship. Doesn't matter what kind of ship it is or where its going, a crew that's well fed is a happy crew." Bowen's eyes ran across the kitchens after Wotll's introduction. It was a wide single room with many work stations with staff working like frantic clockwork at their tasks. There were no windows but the whole room was well lit with hanging bulbs and lots of bright strip lighting. Like with the rest of the ship he had seen so far, as a human Bowen was definitely a minority.

"First things first Rhys," Wotll said as she turned back to Bowen. "Let's get you suited up so you look the part." Bowen followed Wotll through the kitchen. As they passed the workstations, some staff raised their gazes to look at him. He nodded greetings as he passed. Occasionally Wotll would give orders as she kept a watchful eye on everything that was going on.

"Watch the heat there... Good stuff... Two of each remember?" Bowen kept up with her as they reached what Bowen thought was a locked cupboard door. Wotll reached into her supportive under-shirt and withdrew her own key card. She unlocked it and beckoned Bowen to follow her inside saying, "Step into my office."

Inside Bowen was surprised to see that it was indeed a tiny, dimly lit office. The windowless walls were lined with filing cabinets and storage units. At the back sat a small desk with a couple of chairs. Bowen recognised the com-disk reader on the desk as the same make and model as the one from home. The most striking thing in the room was a hanging heat lamp that glowed a warm orange.

"Cosy isn't it?" Wotll said breathlessly as she shuffled her way to a large metal cabinet. "Used to be a pantry once upon a time." Wotll crouched down on her fat legs and began rummaging until she stood and tossed Bowen a plastic wrapped parcel. Bowen fumbled the catch and had to pick it up off the floor as Wotll said, "Go on try those on," before she sat herself down on her chair wheezing. Bowen unwrapped the plastic and found a black and white chequered hat and an apron with similar patterning. As Bowen began to tie the apron around himself Wotll continued, "Doesn't really matter what you wear on shift, as long as you wear all that. But it's dirty work, so don't wear anything too precious."

"Right no problem," Bowen said as he completed the look with his hat.

"You don't seem particularly hairy but if you grow it out you'll have to keep it short and neat." Bowen nodded. "Seems like I sized you up fine, now lets show you round a bit." Bowen was ushered out by Wotll's massive frame. After she locked her office behind her again, she began to walk Bowen about the place. "Garber told me you don't really have too much kitchen experience."

"Yeah that's right." Bowen said.

"Well don't worry I won't have you cooking anything. You'll be washing, cleaning and tidying up after the rest of them. You won't be alone either. The rest of them have all gone to stretch their legs on the station. They'll be back after lunch.

I'll introduce them to you when they come back."

"Sounds good to me." Bowen said dutifully. Wotll showed Bowen the clean storage with its array of mops, buckets and chemicals. As Bowen looked inside his nose burned with the smell. Wotll then showed him the tableware cart. "When you're on shift you'll go out there with this thing and clean up after the crew, bring their trays and cutlery back here and start a wash." Bowen acknowledged with a nod. "Let me show you the stores. The cooks may ask you to fetch something if they're busy."

Bowen was escorted to another corner of the kitchen where there was a large metal door. Wotll heaved it open and they both entered. This room was a lot bigger than Bowen thought it would be. There were huge crates of fruit and vegetables, a lot of which Bowen didn't recognise. Glass jars full to the brim with various species of nuts and seeds, some of which were the size of his fist. On metal shelving were huge tins of oils and other liquids of all colours as well as boxes containing bright foil bars. There were three huge, squat refrigerators that were each about the size of Bowen's cabin. Inside them were hanging sides of meat and a multitude of eggs of all sizes and colours. Bowen spotted large glass containers with little scuttling insects and next to it a tall tank of red liquid with long worms or snakes swimming around. He saw a vat of bubbling warm water full of what looked like smooth stones until he noticed one of them was looking at him with tiny eyes.

"So as you've gathered already a good deal of the crew aren't human," Wotll said, "There's enough food here that anyone can find something good to eat and with enough variety. Pretty much everything in here is safe for human consumption so don't you worry."

"So the others I'll be working with? Are they an alright bunch?" he asked.

"Oh they're some characters, I'm sure you'll get on." Wotll reassured him. At that moment, Bowen's stomach had finally had enough. He felt a ripple within himself as his innards growled.

"Hungry?" Wotll said.

"Just a bit. I ate light this morning. You know, nerves and all."

Wotll's huge mouth widened with a smile pushing her eyes further away from each other.

"Well that won't do. Since there's not much to do around here for you just yet, you go and get some lunch. Service has got just over half an hour then the others will be back and we can get you started proper. Here take one of these." she said. She thrust a pink foil bar into his hands and said, "I recommend the Venox meat pie with Saxon spinach and treat yourself to one of these too. Don't worry the price will be deducted from your first pay slip. The Zordo bar is on the house though." Bowen looked down at the bar and saw the words 'Zordo, Backflip flavour' in bright blue lettering. "After service has ended just come back and there'll be enough work to be getting on with."

Bowen pocketed the confectionery and did his best to remember Venox pie and spinach. As he made his way back through the kitchen he caught a glimpse of some of the other staff members. A lanky red skinned alien with a face like an angler fish was delicately peeling the skin off slimy cuts of meat with a dangerous looking knife. A small insectoid was clambering up a set of stepladders and gathering small tins from off of shelving in his multiple arms.

A curious character caught Bowen's eye who was stood at a lowered counter top. A short, slender alien was expertly slicing black cheese with a knife. As Bowen passed they looked up at him and stopped cutting the food. This person was wearing a full face mask. Bowen was a little unnerved as he looked into the dark lenses that observed him. The hand that held the knife was pale green and small with a thin membrane of webbing between three fingers. He noticed a name tag on his apron read Kabé. Bowen felt his face go red as he realised he was staring. He casually nodded with a stiff smile and hastily made for the swinging double doors.

As he turned his back on the kitchen his chest jolted in a flash of pain for an instant as he collided with someone and a tremendous metallic crashing rattled Bowen's brain. As the accident formed before him, Bowen heard a combination of sighing and laughter from the kitchen staff as well as a sudden raucous cheering from within the cafeteria itself. Bowen immediately fell to the floor gathering up the empty basins that had caught him in the chest.

"My bad." Bowen said as he fumbled. "I should have looked where I was going." He gathered up the dirty metal basins and attempted to put smaller ones into larger ones. "Are you alright?" Bowen asked. It was only at this point that he registered who he had collided with. Another human, but not a Saxon. She had olive skin and pale green eyes. Her prominent but pretty nose was decorated with a jewelled septum piercing and Bowen saw flicks of black hair trying to escape from underneath a brightly coloured headscarf. She was clearly flustered by the incident but the girl composed herself.

"Yes. Thank you," she flicked the trails of her scarf behind her head and tucked a stray strand of hair behind her ear that was pierced with gold rings. Bowen smiled unintelligently.

"I'm Bowen." he said as she took the basins out of his hands. Just as he thought the incident couldn't become any more cringe inducing he felt more words erupting from within him. "I'm from Saxon and I'm new." As the words left his mouth he suddenly felt the urge to throw himself through the nearest window and end his own life from sheer embarrassment. He was sure he heard some snickering coming from behind him. His face bloomed red.

"I'm Safiya. I'm from Phoenicia. And I'm busy." With that Safiya briskly walked away. The tail of her headscarf whipped at Bowen as she left him with a hint of floral perfume in his nose. Bowen raised his hands and pulled at his face. He slowly turned towards the kitchen. There were a few cooks clearly stifling laughter as they worked at their stations. Bowen's gaze fell on Kabé. They looked at each other for a moment, before he looked down and resumed slicing the black cheese in silence as Bowen left.

13.

Bowen stood in line with his head down, his apron and hat stuffed into his pockets. He wondered if this had been such a great idea after all. Before long he had shuffled his way to the front of the line. Through the glass was a dazzling rainbow of food. Bowen had a hard time making sense of some of it.

"What'll it be?" came a gruff male voice from behind the glass. Bowen looked up at the grossly overweight alien brandishing a metal ladle in one large hand and a pair of tongs in the other. He was black and hairy and on his name tag read Jungga. Jungga's face was wrinkled and intricately layered with nasal flaps that went up to his forehead between his large pointed ears.

Bowen rubbed his head thoughtfully. "Venox pie? And Saxon spinach?"

"Pie's out." Jungga replied. With that Bowen was lost. His eyes scanned across the alien landscape of food for anything that looked vaguely familiar.

"What would you recommend?"

"Human?"

"I'm sorry?"

"Are you human?" Jungga clarified.

"Oh, yes I am." Jungga gave a guttural laugh and began scooping and grabbing at various items. Before he knew it Bowen was looking down at a tray full of food. His stomach demanded it at once. He flashed his id card at the pay station, grabbed some cutlery and turned to find a seat. The cafeteria was bustling with all manner of folk. There was no trace of Simon. Bowen found a seat at a mostly empty table facing the huge windows onto Pennine station. He placed himself on a stool at the far end. One or two of the alien crew glanced up at him but quickly returned to their conversation. Bowen busied himself with eating.

He had a portion of tangy purple beans and some herby breaded meat on a wooden stick of some creature he was sure he'd never heard of before. He also had thin red crackers with some of the black cheese Kabé was slicing. For desert he ate a bowl of yellow and orange berries that exploded with thick juice in his mouth. For his first meal off world Bowen thought it was pretty great. He had gone with the safe option of a can of iced water to wash it all down.

It was hard not to look around at the mass of aliens but Bowen's attention was well and truly on the view of the station. He was curious as to what exactly constituted as "Backflip" flavour as he tore open the foil. The pinkish Zordo bar was chewy and felt like nougat but was distinctly different. Bowen tried to place the taste, but it would not come to him. All that he knew in that moment was that Backflip flavour was a new favourite.

As he looked out the window, Bowen saw the true scale of the station. From this viewpoint there was a plethora of advertisement boards and glowing signs showcasing everything from fashion and movies to food and cigarettes. Dotted here and there were windows with people stood looking out past the Memento. They looked miniscule from this distance. He was content to sit and stare a while.

Bowen watched the cafeteria slowly empty as the remainder of the lunch rush passed. Through one of the doorways across the room came a gaggle of crew who were dressing themselves in aprons and hats. Bowen watched them walk into the kitchen. His nerves kicked in. Bowen stood and returned his tray to one of the trash stations. Taking his hat and apron out of his back pockets he adorned himself with his new uniform with a small amount of pride and made for the kitchens.

Bowen was careful to open the doors again lest he repeat the incident from earlier. As he entered, he heard people talking and kitchenware being clattered about. He saw that most of the kitchen staff had left and they had left quite a mess. Stood around by the door to the equipment room were the rest of the cleaners along with Wotll, who noticed Bowen come in.

"Here he is. So how was your first meal courtesy of the Memento galley?" The conversation the staff were having stopped as they all turned around to look at him. The motley crew of people looked Bowen up and down. He felt naked. Bowen cleared his throat and approached.

"Really good thanks." he replied. Wotll smiled widely forcing her red eyes to look away to the sides.

"Ladies and gents this is Bowen Rhys the newest member of the team. Which reminds me..." She plunged her hand into her apron pouch. "...I forgot to give you this." she tossed Bowen a small plastic card which luckily he caught. It was a tag with his name printed onto it. Bowen was surprised that he felt a smile spread across his face as if this was what made it all official. As he looked up from pinning it through one of the straps of his apron he noticed that the group had surrounded him.

"It completes the look wouldn't you say?" Wotll said. "Introductions I suppose before you all get started then." Wotll waved her hands around the group "Jist, Duggy, Ramphry, Steg, Ellbo, Qirus, and Roo." Bowen did his very best to keep up and was thankful when Wotll added, "Don't try to remember all that. It's why you all have name tags." Bowen smiled and set about greeting the aliens that surrounded him. Ramphry was the first to speak up. He looked like a large red humanoid boar with a snout, short tusks and dark bristly hair all over his lump of a body.

"So you're a he? Right? Is he a he or a her?" Bowen looked up into Ramphry's small black eyes with a bemused smile.

"You're such a bottom feeder." Qirus responded in a sharp, raspy voice. Qirus was a slender woman with dark brown skin covered in fine hairs like a spider. Her startling white eyes darted over Bowen. "He's a guy obviously, you've seen humans before." Bowen couldn't help but notice her insanely sharp teeth behind her lips as she smiled at him. Ramphry shuffled on the spot.

"It's useful to check." he said. Bowen chuckled.

"Yes I'm a male human."

"You've got odd eyes." said Ellbo. "One's green and one's blue. Is that normal?"

"It's uncommon for humans but it's normal for me." Bowen replied. Ellbo was stout, rounded and with little to no neck to speak of. His skin was like metallic rock except for his smooth, featureless face. Ellbo's own eyes sparkled like gems. Bowen smiled at Ellbo's concern.

"Wotll tells us this is your first trip out?" Jist spoke with a silky, dream like voice. She was taller than Bowen with her thin neck and bald head. She had grey, hairless skin that had been tattooed with silvery ink. "How did you find the launch?" she asked.

"It was, exciting." Bowen replied. Jist smiled as Roo interjected.

"Exciting?" Roo said with his arms folded. "Wow."

"Yeah, I've never left Saxon before today." Roo looked the most human of them all except for the fact that he had deep purple skin and bright orange eyes. Roo's wild, dark hair was much thicker than a humans and seemed almost rigid.

"Ah! Bowen, from Saxon, you're new!" exclaimed Duggy. Bowen's face went as red as Duggy's eyes. Of course the word had spread already about the clumsy new guy. Bowen sighed and gave a stiff smile to the black scaled lizard Duggy.

"Yeah that's right. Not my best first impression." Duggy laughed, showing off his multiple rows of teeth. He slapped Bowen on the shoulder.

"Relax Saxon I'm just taking a shit."

"What?" Duggy turned to Steg, a humanoid canid with sharp ears and a fanged snout.

"Isn't that what humans say?" Duggy asked shrugging.

"No Duggy, it's not." Steg scratched under his long jaws. "Who do you want showing him the ropes Wotll?" Wotll scratched her throat sack as it inflated.

"It's up to you Steg, my dear. Show him how to work the blitzer and then it's all hands on deck for the clean up. Bowen quickly realized that Steg was Wotll's second in command as he began to instruct who was doing what.

"Okay Roo and Ellbo you two fire up the blitzer and run a hot cycle. Qirus and Jist, you start gathering up the crap from in here with me. Ramphry and Duggy take Bowen into the cafeteria." There was a collective affirmation from the group as they broke off into their teams. Bowen was trying to imagine what the blitzer was when Ramphry's large red hand grasped Bowen's shoulder.

"Come on Human let's get to it." Bowen helped Ramphry and Duggy get out the huge collection trolley from the clean storage room and the three of them wheeled it out through to the cafeteria. It was unwieldy but between the three of them it was manageable. When they had hauled it through, Bowen saw the true size of the cafeteria now that there was no one around. He hadn't noticed the line of brightly coloured vending machines along one wall. One of them was hot pink with a flare of blue that only contained Zordo bars.

Next to him, Duggy retrieved a metal electric lighter from his pocket and sparked up a short red cigarette. He took a puff and sat it at the corner of his scaly mouth.

"Don't just stand there, start grabbing stuff. Remember to scrape into the slop bucket. Qirus will eat you if she finds bits of food clogging the blitzer."

The three of them began making their way down the tables gathering trays. The sounds of them working echoed around the room. The smoke from Duggy's cigarette was slightly purple in colour, and a small cloud followed him around as he worked. Bowen reached one of the large trash stations where some empty trays had been stacked neatly by crew members.

"How come some people do this and others just leave their stuff all over the table?" Bowen asked. Duggy responded through a purple haze.

"Because some people are inconsiderate slugs. If everyone left their crap by the bins and scraped their shit for us our job would take half the time." Duggy was dumping handfuls of dirty cutlery into the collection trolley when he continued, "You'll quickly learn that us galley cleaners are way down the food chain on this ship." Bowen brought over a stack of trays and inserted them into the trolley when Duggy was lighting up another cigarette.

"How long have you two been working here?" Bowen asked.

"I've been on here just over two years. Ramphry just less." Duggy said as he adjusted his apron. "I jumped on at Gargant station. I can't remember where Ramphry joined. Where were you when you joined the crew Ramphry?" he asked. Ramphry had been shuffling about at one of the tables with his back to Bowen and Duggy. He heaved himself around after hearing Duggy's question. Ramphry's bristly face was smeared with food from eating the scraps off the trays. Bowen's face creased up slightly.

"Don't do that Ram, that's disgusting." Duggy said thoroughly unimpressed.

"Sorry." Ramphry said as he gathered his apron up and wiped his face.

"See what I mean?" Duggy said to Bowen as a purple trail left his nostrils, "if folks did the decent thing and cleared up after themselves we wouldn't have to deal with that."

Ramphry made a dim, confused noise as he placed an armful of plates onto the trolley.

"So where were you before you worked here Ramphry?" Bowen asked. He heard himself ask in the same manner as he would a child. Ramphry shuffled over clearing tables.

"I was on a back-to-work scheme on New Appalachia." he said in wheezes.

"What were you doing there?" Ramphry made another confused noise.

"What were you doing on New Appalachia Ram?" Duggy asked him loudly.

"Oh …the gold mine ran dry."

"Oh wow." Bowen replied. He looked at Duggy who made a gesture referencing Ramphry's intelligence.

"What were you doing on Gargant station Duggy?" Bowen asked as he started another table.

"Pest exterminator in maintenance."

"Oh, sweet." Bowen replied.

"Yeah, moved up in the galaxy haven't I?" They both laughed. After a while, they were almost done. Duggy finished his current cigarette and sparked up another as he leant against the collection trolley.

"What about you Bowen from Saxon? What were you doing down there?" Bowen thought for a moment. What had he been doing? A whole lot of nothing in comparison to working in a New Appalachian gold mine or being an exterminator on a space station. Bowen felt his face go red, not from how Duggy referred to him as "Bowen from Saxon" again, but at the thought of his dull answer.

"Well," he started as he lugged the last of the trays to the cart. "Not a lot, just helping out around my family's farm… you might say this is my first proper job." Duggy took a long drag of his cigarette.

"What was that like?" Bowen could tell from how Duggy spoke that he wasn't truly interested. But he answered all the same.

"It was okay. A bit boring. I've got a friend who works on the ship who told me about the vacancy and I thought I might try for it." Duggy seemed to perk up slightly.

"Oh yeah? Whose your buddy?"

"Simon Van Hoff, he works in Navigation." Duggy blew a purple smoke ring and squinted his red eyes.

"Don't know any of them stargazers do we Ram?" he said. Ramphry was sitting on an empty stool breathing heavily with his hairy red hand resting on his large belly.

"Nope," he said after a deep cough, "not nice."

"Really?" Bowen asked.

"They're all full of themselves, and we're just lower forms of life who clean up after them at meal times."

"Simon's not like that." Bowen said quietly taking offence on Simon's behalf.

"Did he start today same as you?" Duggy asked "Did you launch together?"

"I think he started today, he wasn't with me when we launched. We haven't actually spoken for a little while." Duggy squinted again as he exhaled purple smoke from his mouth.

"Why?" Ramphry asked bluntly. Bowen wasn't sure of how to answer. His mind flashed.

"I asked Simon to tell you I'd left..."

"He's usually with her..."

"I've been busy preparing to leave that's all." Bowen said as he folded his arms and looked down at the floor. There was a moment of silence but for Ramphry wheezing. Muffled clattering could be heard in the galley. Duggy finished his cigarette and stubbed it out on top of a trash station.

"Best get back in there before Steg loses his ass." Duggy said.

"I think you mean loses his shit." Bowen said as they began to move the now incredibly heavy collection trolley.

"What'd I say?" Duggy asked.

The remainder of the shift went by in a hazy, tiring blur. Bowen, Duggy and Ramphry heaved the trolley into the galley and joined the rest of the team in the clean up. Steg showed Bowen how to use the blitzer, which was an industrial sized dish washer. It was baby blue in colour and was large enough that a person could climb inside. After everyone joined in loading it up, Steg instructed Bowen how to programme in the appropriate cycle with the correct temperature. Bowen was assailed by yet more questions about life on Saxon from mainly Duggy and Qirus, with Ramphry often getting confused. The smell of bleach was clearing Bowen's airways as he worked with Ellbo to wipe down the meat stations. Ellbo asked simple questions about humans like whether most humans had no hair on their heads and whether humans laid eggs or not. Bowen smiled as he answered the innocent questions. As a team they all mopped the floors with Steg orchestrating the whole operation. Jist pleasantly spoke to Bowen about music in her pensive voice while Roo came across as uncaring and rude as they worked. By the time they were done the kitchen was gleaming. Bowen was exhausted as they stood in the cavernous cafeteria talking. Steg was the first to leave.

"See you all in a few hours." he said. As he left, he patted Bowen on the shoulder with his clawed hand. Jist and Ellbo left together and Roo exited without a word to anyone. As Bowen removed his hat and apron he asked Qirus a question.

"So what does everyone do during downtime around here?"

"The rec deck's about the only place to kill time." Bowen was invited to tag along, but as they reached the stairwell he decided against it and politely excused himself. His legs and back were utterly shot. Bowen groggily made his way back to his cabin. Once locked inside he forced himself to unpack his case. After shoving his clothes into one of the storage compartments under his bed he removed his shoes and sat down on the mattress. There was a digital clock fixed into the side table in which he programmed an alarm into so he did not miss dinner. Bowen didn't bother to close the blinds on the cabin window. He flopped back onto the bed that was softer than it appeared. Not a moment went by and he was unconscious.

14.

Bowen felt as though he had been asleep for minutes as the alarm woke him. He freshened up in his bathroom and he changed his shirt again. Dinner service would be on soon. He took a moment and looked out of his window at the station. He thought about Simon. His frustration was slowly mounting. Bowen left his cabin. The lights in the crew deck corridor were now dim and golden simulating evening light.

Bowen reached the cafeteria just as service started and he fell into line. Every time the doors opened he craned his neck around to see who had entered, but none of the faces he saw belonged to Simon. Finally he reached the front of the queue, grabbed a tray and came face to face with Safiya.

"Oh, hi." Bowen said as casually as he could.

"Hey." she replied not meeting his eye. "What are you having?" Bowen composed himself and looked down through the glass. He was glad to see more Venox Pie had been made so he went with it. As he shuffled down the line with Safiya serving him food he stopped himself from making embarrassing small talk. As she handed him a can of ice water he heard himself speak.

"It was Safiya wasn't it?" she looked at him just as he noticed her name tag.

"Yeah." she confirmed. Bowen motioned to her chest.

"Awesome." Safiya looked down at herself and back at him with raised eyebrows.

"Name tag." he clarified.

Safiya rolled her eyes. "Next please." she spoke past him. Bowen moved down the line looking at the floor. Bowen flashed his identification at the pay station and he turned to find a seat, kicking himself. He found an empty table towards the back end of the room and sat down facing the main doors. Outside the windows the light had changed as they orbited

Saxon in what was now early evening. He wondered what his mother would be making for dinner.

Bowen hardly noticed the taste of the Venox pie. Nor did he give much attention to the delicate cake with a two-toned fruit topping. He watched the doors until the canteen was very full. He had a good view of the service counter, but still Simon didn't show.

On a couple of tables away from him were a group of human passengers. He spotted the family who had boarded the ship with him. The mother was tying up her daughter's blonde hair into a braid as she ate her child size meal. The father was reading pamphlets and occasionally showing the other two pictures. The mother made eye contact with Bowen for a moment and smiled at him with kind eyes. Bowen smiled back stiffly.

He thought about Jules and the com-disk that was sitting in his cabin. He had seen the signs for a comms suite as he walked the corridors. Even if he found a moment to go and use it, he still had no idea what he would say to her. He wondered what she would think of him going into space. It wasn't a glamorous ship, and it wasn't a glamorous job, but perhaps she would still be impressed. There were still a lot of questions that he wanted answering however. Why did Jules leave Saxon without telling him herself? Why had Simon avoided him for weeks? Had there been something going on between them? All of a sudden his view was blocked as someone sat across from him.

"Hi Ramphry." Bowen said as he swirled the last mouthful of water in his can.

"You changed clothes." Ramphry said bluntly.

"Yeah, thought I'd dress up for dinner." Ramphry didn't pick up on Bowen's sarcasm as he set about stuffing his face. His tray was piled high with what looked like one of everything going. The table shifted next to him as Duggy hopped onto a stool next to Bowen.

"Evening." Duggy said.

"Alright." Bowen replied. All that Duggy had on his tray was a bowl of green fluid with shelled insects swimming around in it. He also had a Kickass flavour Zordo bar. Duggy began picking out the small creatures from his bowl and crunching on them casually when he said,

"So how's it going for a first day?"

"Not bad." Was all he could say. Bowen excused himself while he emptied his tray into the trash station just to get another proper look around the cafeteria. He surveyed the service line, the doors and the row of vending machines. No Simon. When he returned to the table with Ramphry and Duggy he asked a question to no one in particular,

"Are crew members allowed to leave the ship onto the station?"

"You need a shore leave pass but yes. I'm not sure they'd give you one on your first day though." Duggy replied.

"I was just wondering." Bowen replied. He was starting to suspect that Simon had been on the ship a while.

The dinner service ended and the crew members slowly began to leave. Bowen watched as some people cleared up after themselves and as others did not. He felt himself judging them already as the workload revealed itself. Ramphry cleared his tray and let out numerous belches as he began picking at his tusked mouth with a podgy red finger. Duggy had eaten all of his insects as well as slurped all the liquid from the bowl. He pushed his tray away from himself as he retrieved a cigarette and his lighter.

"You smoke, Saxon?" Duggy asked as he held out his small silver pack.

"No, thanks." Bowen replied. Duggy began playing with his lighter in his hands.

"Dinner clean up's always the worst." he said.

"Yeah?"

"Yep. Always." Duggy said blowing purple smoke to the side.

"They make the most food for dinner." Ramphry

commented. The three of them sat a while as the cafeteria cleared out around them revealing where the other team members had been sitting. As one they all adorned their hats and aprons and they got to work.

For the evening, Qirus, Ellbo and Jist cleared the canteen while Ramphry, Duggy, Roo, Steg and Bowen got a start on the kitchen. Duggy hadn't been exaggerating when he said that the kitchen produced the most food for dinner service. The place was a state. Wotll had stayed behind after the service and helped to get the job done. However after she helped set up the blitzer she sat on a chair by her office door with what looked like a bottle of green wine offering words of encouragement. Bowen was glad that he had freshened up before he came back to dinner, as he began sweating right through his new shirt. The blitzer needed three cycles to get everything cleaned and huge extractor fans in the ceiling were activated as it put out an incredible amount of steam. Bowen had to partner up with Roo to clear down the vegetable stations that were positively dripping with fluids. Bowen had to hold his tongue as Roo became irritable and began snapping, but Steg barked for quiet as they all finished up.

The shift went on for a long while, Bowen was glad when it was over. Steg assured Bowen that he would get used to the workload after a few days. He hoped that was true. Again, Roo left without saying anything. Jist, Qirus and Ellbo bid their goodbyes and left while Steg stayed behind and had business to talk with Wotll. Bowen was left with Duggy and Ramphry.

"Coming for a drink?" Duggy asked.

"Yeah why not."

"I need a snack." Ramphry said.

"Course you do." replied Duggy. The three of them made their way through the ship until they found the recreation deck. Due to the hour, it was quiet inside. The long, large room was comfortably furnished with couches, arm chairs and coffee tables along with numerous televisions. There were vending machines dotted about and a large music player and a few arcade machines. Huge potted plants, most of which looked alien to Bowen were decorating the bar area that made up the back end of the room.

As was advertised on the screens around the ship, Bowen saw the entrance to the onboard store Gricky's currently closed with electric shutters down. His attention was drawn to the wide window. The rec deck looked out onto the other side of the ship. Spread out beneath them was the vast expanse of Saxon at night. Bowen leaned his head against the glass and tried to look straight down, to see if he could spot Allchester, but of course he could not. It looked beautiful. He looked upwards through the window into the void of space at thousands of stars. The thrill of space travel came back to him as he began to imagine the sights of other planets and places.

"Quite a view." Duggy said from behind Bowen.

"I know."

"Great legs." Duggy continued. Bowen, now confused turned around and saw that Duggy was sat in an arm chair watching an advertisement on the nearest television. There was a leggy alien woman in a swimming costume lying across a black hover car.

"Oh." Bowen said. Bowen took the seat next to Duggy who had put his feet up onto the wooden coffee table. As Duggy was lighting up a cigarette, he gave his identification to Ramphry.

"Hey Ram I'm buying the drinks. Get us two Sun Fossils and whatever you want. Don't get talking to Techno."

"Thanks Duggy." Bowen said. Duggy just waved his hand. Bowen watched as Ramphry trundled off. Bowen saw a robot behind the bar, Techno he presumed. A minute later, Ramphry returned placing the drinks on the table. It turned out a Sun Fossil was a tall orange coloured drink with a thin layer of bone white foam. For himself Ramphry had a glass mug full of a dark and flat beer. The label on the glass read Burn Back. The three sat there in content silence with the television on. Bowen enjoyed the taste of his Sun Fossil as he sipped it.

The television transitioned to a news article. The flashy animations crossed the screen with intense music as an anchor narrated footage.

"Breaking news. There has been a devastating explosion on the federation science base Noble Pursuit on the human controlled planet Atlanticana." The screen showed stock footage of a massive station jutting out of a dark sea. "Details are scant at this time, but early reports state that most of the base has sank beneath the waves of the ocean world. It is thought that as many as four hundred lives have been lost. Conflicting information from survivors blames everything from mechanical failure, to the explosion being intentional. One report points towards the work of the pirate faction Sapphire Wind lead by one Zoltan Hayashi, however this cannot be confirmed at this time." Bowen saw as an image of Zoltan Hayashi came up on the screen. A stern man with short white hair, his eyes were hidden behind small glasses.

Ramphry snored. There was a purple cloud forming above them as Duggy finished up his cigarette. He sat up and stubbed it out into an ash tray on the table.

"It's all a load of shit isn't it?" he said. Bowen had no response. Duggy reached for the remote control and began to flick around the stations. He finally settled on a music channel. Bowen finished his Sun Fossil as half naked women from a variety of species danced with each other on screen. Duggy walked to one of the vending machines and bought himself another pack of cigarettes as Ramphry rumbled quietly.

Bowen turned to the window. As he looked to the northern reaches of Saxon, he saw a borealis form silently before his eyes. He had never seen it in real life before, he felt lucky to catch it then from above the world. He wondered what his family were doing at that moment. He thought of Samhain curled up somewhere comfortable. He imagined Mason feeding Virgil in the rain and Ida tying a ribbon around his chair at the dinner table. It wasn't forever.

15.

The next morning after showering, Bowen ate breakfast alone. A bowl of fibrous flakes with rich rhinoceros milk from Province. During service, the speakers chimed echoing around the cafeteria.

"Ladies and gentlemen this is Officer Sol Garber speaking. All crew members will be required to attend the Captain's briefing this evening immediately following dinner service. This message will repeat throughout the day. Officer Sol Garber signing off."

The ambience of the canteen resumed. Another human entered the cafeteria. He wore a grey uniform covered in official patches and he carried a large messenger bag. The man was tall, dark skinned and middle aged. When he spoke his voice filled the whole room over the noise of breakfast.

"Last day to send messages! Last day to send messages until Davarak! Cut off point tonight's night cycle!" the man commanded. He spoke with the accent of Laurentia. As he spoke, some crew members approached him and handed to him small packages containing com-disks.

"Messages to me now or deposit them at my office! Any time before tonight's night cycle!" he repeated. The comms officer stood there a while repeating his instructions for a few minutes until he repeated himself once more with his booming voice and turned to leave.

After his work shift, Bowen returned to his cabin and retrieved his satchel before he set off to find the comms suite. As he explored the upper decks, he passed crew members dressed in armoured flight suits carrying holstered weapons and he began to feel more out of place. Finally he found it.

The Comms suite was a large windowless room. The low ceiling was mostly exposed wiring and there was dim strip lighting illuminating the booths that contained private com-disk readers. There were small rotating fans here and there battling against the muggy heat that came from the computers. On the back wall there was a door labelled,

SERVER ROOM – AUTHORISED PERSONNEL ONLY

A few crew members were sat around, each at a com-disk reader, clacking away, their faces illuminated by dim green light. Some looked up to see Bowen as he passed. Bowen chose to sit at a terminal in the corner. The machine was a more advanced model than he had seen before. It was black and the keyboard was illuminated. Bowen entered his identification card into the slot in the black tower and waited. The inner workings buzzed and whirred with quiet efficiency. In no time at all he was greeted with an operations screen. Bowen tapped the appropriate keys and selected the option for communications. The computer beeped and waited to accept a com-disk with a small yellow light. He retrieved a couple of blank com-disks from his bag. He inserted one and the computer accepted it with a silky smooth function. The screen changed and he began to type.

MASON NATHANIEL RHYS
FEDERATION IDENTIFICATION:
140358DP

Hi everyone,
The launch went fine.
The ship has been docked at Pennine but we're leaving on the highways tomorrow.
I'm settling in okay, I got put to work immediately.
The work is tiring, but the people I work with are an alright bunch.
The view from up here is amazing.
I hope you are all doing well.
I will write when I get the chance.

Love, Bowen

Bowen finished up the process and exchanged out the disk for another.

NIAMH MARGOT RHYS
FEDERATION IDENTIFICATION:
030389EP

Hello Niamh.
I hope you're doing okay.
Sorry it's been a while since my last message.
I finally got a job. I'm in a galley on a ship
headed for Obelisk station.
When I get back home the money I'll have
earned will go towards moving out.
I want to start my own farm in the Northern Reaches.
Hope you are careful in those jungles.
Keep safe.
Love, Bowen.

Again, he finished up the procedure and put it safely in his bag. He retrieved the message from Jules and played with it in his hands. He wanted to speak to Simon first. He logged out of the machine and left. He was glad to be out in the cooler corridor. As he turned to leave down the stairwell, Bowen noticed a sign to Navigation. He adjusted his satchel strap and took a deep breath. He didn't want to wait for Simon to show up any longer. He confidently strode off down the corridor. He passed a few more crew members in their armoured flight suits, but no one stopped him. He walked past long thin windows that looked out onto Pennine station but he didn't stop to look. At a junction he saw a sign for an officer's suite and an armoury. Finally he reached the closed doors of the navigation suite. It had a more advanced key card lock with a digital readout screen. In red lettering it read;

AUTHORISED PERSONNEL ONLY

Bowen sighed. He was just about to leave when he was struck by a moment of irresponsible daring. He took out his identification and spun the metal card in his fingers

"Fuck it." he said quietly to himself swiping it into the key card lock. The words on the small screen vanished and nothing happened. Bowen was about to turn to go when there was a beeping sound. He heard the release of electronic pistons as the door unlocked itself for him. Bowen frowned in confusion. He leaned in closer to double check what had appeared on screen. In green lettering were the words;

WELCOME, LIEUTENANT RHYS

Bowen swallowed hard, was this some sort of malfunction? Sheer curiosity drove his now sweaty hand as he reached out and pressed the activation button. The doors opened for him and he tentatively entered. In front of him was a thin, dark corridor with access panels that blinked with coloured lights. He could hear fragments of transmission signals coming from deeper in the suite. The corridor opened up to a wide room. Inside was a series of galactic map screens around a central bowl shaped table that showed a complicated star map. He tightened his grip around his satchel strap as he approached the table. Towards the centre of the bowl was a symbol labelled Obelisk. There was a very definite trajectory marker that ended at the station that Bowen assumed was the Memento's flight path. There was also multiple other directive signatures that came from other directions including from a nearby planetoid. As Bowen looked down into the concave map table, he jumped as a voice came from a doorway in the corner of the room.

"Who are you?" Bowen said nothing, as no words would come. He stood there with his mouth open like an imbecile. The man who had entered the room was a human in a smart suit jacket uniform with navigation officer patches. His name patch read Officer Denton. Bowen's heart missed a beat. His long blonde hair was gathered into a tight bun at the back of his head and his eyes were dark. Denton had a stern, clean shaven face and he spoke with the twang of New Appalachia.

"You aren't supposed to be in here." Denton said matter of factly. Before Bowen could attempt to speak properly Denton glanced down to the corridor to the entrance and then called behind himself. "Who left the main doors unlocked?" he said with an annoyed sigh. There came no response. Denton came over and was roughly the same height as Bowen. His strong hand landed on Bowen's shoulder as he began to frog march him out the corridor. Bowen attempted to speak but he was cut off. "Can't you read? Authorised personnel only."

"Sorry, I'm just looking for.." Bowen stammered.

"The main stairwell is down that corridor and to the right," Denton interrupted. "I suggest you use it before I report you. Now get lost and don't come back here. Tourist." Bowen was lost for words as Denton pressed a button and closed the doors and locked them. The red lettering appeared on the key card lock again. Bowen was somewhat relieved that Officer Denton had mistaken him for a passenger. Perhaps, in part due to his comparatively shabby clothes and his messenger bag.

Bowen thought not to linger and made for the stairwell, frustrated. Another dead end looking for Simon. Sooner or later he was going to give up trying. The thought swirled around his head as he found the postal centre.

The postal centre was a large kiosk set back against a wall across from a doorway to an observation deck. Bowen approached a service hatch where he came face to face with the postal officer from breakfast. Bowen saw at his chest was a patch that read Officer Horner. Inside, Horner was sitting at a cluttered terminal desk. Officer Horner looked up at Bowen.

"Can I help you?" he asked. Bowen reached into his satchel and pulled out his com-disks.

"I'd like to send these please."

"In the slot." Horner instructed as he opened up a secure deposit box. Bowen followed the instructions and Horner collected them.

"Any replies can be collected here the next time we dock." Horner said flatly.

"Do you know when that will be?" Bowen asked. Horner sighed and looked up at his terminal and began clicking at the keys.

"We're making a stop at Oasis City on Davarak. That's a four month trip."

"Four months?" Bowen repeated. His family at home would likely get a copy of his message that next day, but he wouldn't get their reply for four months.

"That's right." Horner confirmed. Bowen swallowed. "Problem?"

"No, no. Thanks." Bowen said as he turned to leave.

16.

The remainder of the day flew by. For lunch, Bowen ate a pork sandwich courtesy of the farms of Engelreich with a tangy blue fruit that was a mutated species of banana. Most of the clean up crew bar Roo and Steg happened together on the same table for lunch and Bowen was pleased to realise that he was fitting in. The announcement from Officer Garber played out again whilst they ate.

The lunch clean up went by quickly. Bowen set the blitzer to work without assistance and it seemed as though the kitchen staff hadn't left the area quite as much of a bomb site. He spent the afternoon in the rec deck with Duggy and Ramphry. Duggy introduced Bowen to a curious game involving cards and polyhedral dice called Usurper. Bowen made sure to bring his bulky camera and he spent a while taking photographs of the view. He already couldn't wait to get the pictures developed when he got back home.

At dinner that evening, the cafeteria became the most full Bowen had seen it so far. The kitchen staff had remained in the cafeteria at one table, some of them still in their messy white jackets. Bowen noticed a collection of burly aliens in utility jump suits who came up from the cargo bays. Technicians, janitorial and laundry staff as well as engineers and security were all present.   Bowen noticed Officer Horner stood at the vending machines. He tried, but couldn't get a good enough look at the room to spot anyone from Navigation, however Bowen wasn't sure he wanted to come across Denton again. Roo, Duggy and Qirus began the collection as more crew members were filtering in through the main doors and through the side entrances, whilst Bowen and the others fired up the blitzer and began organising the kitchen. Bowen had his head underneath a cabinet fetching a dropped ladle when Wotll came through wheezing,

"Come on out, the Captain's on his way down to brief the crew." Bowen got to his feet and followed the rest of them through. The rest of the team were now stood behind the service line and Bowen fell into place between Ellbo and Steg. From behind the double doors came an odd sight. A tall alien clad in a strange and complicated body suit made of equal parts metal and rubber entered the cafeteria. Their steps thudded and clanked as they walked. On the suit was a series of tanks and cylinders with connecting pipes and wires that weaved in and out around the body and up towards the head that was hidden behind a series of glass viewports.

"Doctor Jinn-Quo and the nurses." Ellbo whispered to Bowen. The doctor was followed by a number of assistant nurses who all wore matching pale coloured ensembles of sterile rubber and vinyl bodysuits. A few of them wore intricate face masks with just their eyes showing, while some sported full head gear with similar breathing apparatus to the doctor. Despite this being a briefing the whole team of them including Jinn-Quo seemed equipped to deal with any situation there and then. Each was equipped with tool belts and surgical gear at their wrists, waists and down their gloved arms.

A familiar face then appeared from the main doors as Officer Garber strode in dressed in a leather trench coat that flowed behind her. She was accompanied by a human. His stern, haggard face told of years of action. His black crew cut was sharp he had broad shoulders. Dressed in a short combat jacket and the bottom half of a dull blue flight suit, he strode in confidently.

"Whose that?" Bowen whispered.

"First Officer Lennox," Ellbo replied, "he's serious." Lennox and Garber made their way towards the huge windows where they stopped. Garber stood with her long legs apart, hands on her hips. Lennox reached into his jacket pocket and retrieved a black wrapped cigar that he sat between his teeth.

"Captain on deck!" he commanded. When he spoke

Bowen heard the accent of the federation planet of Ocker. The whole canteen fell silent as the double doors opened.

He appeared a similar age to Mason, but he was wide and muscular. His thick, dark beard had a hint of grey, much like his short, sharp hair. He wore a scuffed leather jacket and grey flight suit bottoms that were tucked into black buckled boots. There was a hint of labour to his confident walk as he passed through the tables towards the windows. Like Lennox, the Captain's face had clearly seen conflict. A portion of his left ear was missing and a scar ran from his temple down to his cheek. As he turned to face the crowd, Bowen saw the right side of the Captain's head. It was dominated by a mechanical augmentation that covered the spot where his ear should have been and reached around to his eye socket where a cybernetic yellow eye sat.

The Captain surveyed the quiet crowd with his intimidating stare before he spoke. When he did, he spoke with the strong accent of Kovoztoy on the borders of Federation space.

"We pass through the Pennine warp gate in ten hours. It is a four month voyage to Davarak. For the benefit of new crew members, I am your Captain Ezekiel Quinn. Know this, trouble making will be dealt with swiftly and the punishment will fit the crime. Take pride in your work. Show each other respect and dignity and there will be no problems. If at any point you require assistance that your supervisor cannot help with, you are free to approach Officer Sol Garber or First Officer Harper Lennox." Captain Quinn motioned to each of them accordingly. "If at any point you require medical aid, Doctor Jinn-Quo and his medical team are sworn to aid you." he said stretching his arm out towards the group. When he did, Bowen noticed his right hand was mechanical. Quinn turned towards the kitchen serving line and announced, "Our departure time means that breakfast will be served one hour later than normal isn't that correct?"

"Indeed that's right." Wotll replied. There was a

murmur of displeasure from the crew. Just as Bowen turned to look back at Captain Quinn, he saw that the Captain was looking right at him.

From across the cafeteria Bowen felt unnerved as Captain Quinn's robotic eye seemed to study him from a distance. The Captain seemed confused for an instant. Bowen felt his face go red as his immediate thought was that he had been reported for trespassing in Navigation. Of course the Captain would know when someone went somewhere they shouldn't.

The crew who had suddenly began to protest at the delay of breakfast meant that no one else seemed to notice. Bowen shuffled in his place uncomfortably as he began to sweat at the thought of his upcoming punishment.

"That's enough of that!" Garber ordered. The crew were silenced and Quinn's attention was ripped away from Bowen.

"Anything you would like to add?" Quinn asked Garber and Lennox who both declined. He turned back to the cafeteria. "Are there any questions?" he asked the room to which there was a murmur of declination. "That'll be all." Quinn finished.

He left the room with Lennox and Garber following behind. As he did, Bowen watched and expected Quinn to look back at him. Bowen's heart was in his throat as the Captain strode out. He let out a sigh when the Captain left without a second glance. As they left, the crew rose and began to shuffle out through the doors as one.

"Right you lot," Wotll called, "get to it." As Steg began to call out instructions, Bowen's head happened to snap up to exactly the right place. Simon shuffling through the crowd to leave. Without thinking, Bowen broke away from the others and attempted to get a better position. It was indeed Simon. He was wearing his navigation uniform and his red hair had been cut short. He could see him chatting and laughing with some other crew members as they tried to leave with the crowd.

"Simon!" Bowen called out over the din. No response.

Simon was getting closer and closer to the doors. "Si!" he tried again.

"Oi!" came a voice from behind him. It was Steg. "What are you doing?"

"Sorry." Bowen sighed. He rubbed his head and returned to the group.

The clean up shift was difficult. They were at a constant stop and start all night. They were interrupted frequently by members of the cargo crew who were arriving through a back door from access corridors. The burly cargo crew members were wheeling in huge crates of food and large drums of liquids for the kitchen. At one point it fell to Bowen to move a set of barrels containing cleaning fluid into storage. Afterwards he had to muck in with the others to rearrange the kitchen's store room for the sheer amount of deliveries that were being left with them. Roo made it clear that it should have been the job of the kitchen staff, not them. The rest of the group were slowly becoming irritable as the night went on. Steg was losing his patience with Ramphry who constantly needed to sit down. Duggy and Roo were not working well together no matter what they did. Qirus was snapping at Ellbo who was working just slow enough to annoy her. Bowen became exhausted cracking open a crate full of jars of blue sauce with Jist and placing them on the shelves. Bowen did his best to keep his mouth shut as Jist began to waffle on about the beauty of the intergalactic highway. When Bowen tried to think of other things to relieve the tedium he merely managed to worry about how much trouble be might expect to be in for trespassing into Navigation, or how infuriatingly close he was to Simon in the cafeteria.

The Captain's stare was fixed in his mind.

17.
The cabin was dark. A constant low hum came from deep within the ship as the engines awoke in preparation to leave. Bowen had stirred before his alarm. He was excited to be passing through the warp gate but his mind was all over the place. He rolled over trying to forget it all.

Just then a faint scratching sound came from above him. Bowen slowly rolled onto his back and looked up at the ceiling. The pipes and panelling were still, but there it was. Every few seconds, a scratching and a shuffling. He lay still in bed tracing his eyes across to estimate the movement. In the corner of the ceiling was a small grated vent. It seemed to be moving towards there. Bowen sat up slowly and quietly moved to the end of his bed. His bare feet met the cool floor as he stood, dressed only in his briefs.

Now completely awake, he wasn't exactly sure what he was doing, but he waited to react to something. The shuffling came closer. Bowen held his breath. He crept over to the corner without making a sound. Standing under the vent, he heard the sound one last time and it came to a stop just before the grate. His vision had adjusted to the dim cabin, but his eyes strained into the blackness of the vent. Bowen blinked hard and focused his eyes. Three small eyes were peering back at him. Bowen gasped in surprise. As he did so, a small fanged mouth flung open and the creature shrieked. Bowen leapt back onto his bed as the animal screeched again before it scrambled off into the ship rattling the ventilation passages as it went.

Bowen sat on his bed with the hairs on the back of his neck standing up. He composed himself after a minute, assuming that whatever it was wasn't coming back. After a wash and brushing his teeth he opened his blinds and watched the view of the station. He retrieved his camera and snapped a few pictures, realising that it would be his last opportunity. In the minutes before his alarm was due to go off he took some time to look over his schedule, he was pleased to be having a day off soon. As he dressed in fresh clothes he hoped that it would at least coincide with someone else's.

He left the cabin and locked the door, watching the vent above the doorway with a suspicious eye. Bowen made for the cafeteria, despite the delay on breakfast. As he entered he saw that he was alone but for one janitor. He was a short, hunchback alien with a blotchy face and skin like crispy bacon. He was grumbling to himself and emptying the trash bins into a large wheeled trolley that was marked with a label that said 'Incineration.' His grubby uniform had seen much better days. Bowen minded his own business as he found a seat by the windows. As he took in the view of Pennine station a series of noises came through the speakers. Quick successive beeps and electric chimes came through along with fragments of signals as the Memento's computer brain fired up. Bowen sat forward on his stool. It was happening now.

"Attention all crew members. Departure commencing." Garber's voice echoed around the cafeteria. The Memento began to stir. The low hum from the ship's bowels increased and caused a vibration through the floor. Garber's voice came through again.

"Boarding tunnel detached. Cargo bay doors sealed. Exterior hatches locked. Go for departure." The view from the windows began to change as the Memento reversed away from its docking bay. The signs and screens of the station began to get smaller as the ship pulled back. The Memento turned, manoeuvring and yawing into position. The view of morning on Saxon suddenly came into view as the ship turned around to face the entryway of the warp gate.   Bowen stood from his seat as the planet passed slowly in front of the window. He walked towards the glass and put out his hand. The view of Saxon passed as other ships came into view, waiting to pass through the gate. The warp gate itself was colossal. The interior of the ringed station was the entry point. A great swirling mass of blue warp energy filled the entirety of the view from the window. The gateway into space. The docking bays, now far out to the side looked small as the Memento fell into line and straightened out. The ship vibrated again as the engines flared up. Bowen felt it through the glass. The Memento moved closer to the warp gate and the station ring moved past slowly.

The alien janitor finished up his work and wheeled out the trash trolley through the double doors, coughing as he went. Bowen didn't notice. The speakers crackled.

"Entering the warp gate. Thirty seconds." The engines revved in anticipation and the entire cafeteria shuddered. Bowen stood alone at the window with his heart in his throat. The view of the station ring was gradually becoming distorted, disfigured and stretched.

"Twenty seconds." The great blue void was swirling with glittering white and streaked with cuts of darkness. Closer the Memento approached.

"Ten." Pennine station now looked murky and began to flicker like fire as the ship reached the threshold. Bowen braced himself.

"Five, four, three, two."

A harsh, crushing white light flooded through the windows. It was warm and cold all at once as Bowen's entire body was consumed by it. The Memento shook with tremendous force as Bowen felt the power of the warp gate propel the ship through space. As quickly as it came, the light vanished and was replaced with blue roiling energy. Flashes of white and dark lightning arced outward from the Memento as it flew through the galactic highway. The shuddering eased and the vibrations settled back to a gentle state as the ship adjusted to a cruising speed. Garber's voice came through the speakers as Bowen sat back down.

"Warp successful, e.t.a. four months to Davarak."

18.

Bowen watched out the window as the ship flew on the galactic highway. The Memento felt alive. If he concentrated on it, Bowen felt gentle rocking and vibrations. He remembered how far away he felt Allchester was when they were docked at the warp gate. At that moment as the Memento flew through space it seemed like now he truly was leaving home.

The gargantuan blue tunnel the ship flew through gave the sense of movement, but there was no way to know just how fast they were going. Bowen sat there a while as crew and passengers began filtering in to the cafeteria. The kitchen staff began pottering around in the kitchen and quickly finished up preparing as people began to queue up for breakfast. It was clear that a good deal of crew had spent their time on Pennine station for meals as the cafeteria was becoming very crowded. Bowen fell into line and chose a bowl of Saxon bran with cow milk, a portion of toasted salt cake loaf with a soft, red fruit topping and a can of iced orange juice from Laurentia. Duggy and Ramphry called him over having saved him a seat after spotting him in line. Over breakfast they chatted idly about the warp jump. Apparently he had experienced an easy start by working some shifts while they were docked at Pennine. According to Duggy, the mess that the kitchen staff would leave for them would be worse from now on with many more crew and passengers to feed. Bowen tried to remain positive about his situation, but he could already feel that the novelty of his new job was wearing off.

Bowen finished his breakfast and took his tray to the trash station. As he reached it, he sighed as he noticed that virtually no one who had finished eating had done the same. As he sorted his bowl and plate into the racks at the trash station, his attention was drawn to a table not too far from him. A familiar voice was speaking. Bowen's ears traced the room until his eyes found Simon. He was sitting with some others smoking, having finished eating. Simon wore a smart navy blue shirt the same as the others on his table. Thankfully Officer Denton was not present. Bowen was on auto pilot as he approached. It felt like a long walk.

"Simon." Bowen said, "Hey man." Simon looked up at him with a mixture of surprise and confusion. The whole group fell silent as they each turned to look at Bowen. All of a sudden Bowen felt naked. Simon exhaled a puff of smoke with a slight cough.

"Bowen. You're... here." he stated. It almost sounded like a question.

"Yeah I... I went and asked after you told me about the galley job."

"Right, right. I remember." Simon replied. Simon cleared his throat. "Bowen, this is Murrow, Liio and Qizic." Bowen made eye contact with the crew sat around the table and politely greeted them. Murrow and Liio vaguely acknowledged Bowen's presence. Murrow's pearlescent feathers shimmered as he looked at Bowen through his beady eyes. Liio's grey skin looked wet and his ashen hair was styled in long braids. The insectoid Qizic looked at Bowen without even turning his head, his mantis eyes observed him from all angles. He merely clicked his mandibles.

Bowen found himself in an awkward silence. The moment passed for Simon to introduce Bowen to them. He could feel a wave of embarrassment incoming. All of the questions Bowen had for Simon were falling out of his head. Bowen cleared his throat.

"I'm Bowen. Me and Simon grew up together on Saxon." There was a mixture of responses. Liio seemed to at least fain interest with his facial expressions. Murrow and Qizic ignored him. Bowen's heart sank as Simon looked down with a flush of red on his pale and freckled cheeks. Bowen took a deep breath.

"So, you got a day off soon..? I'm off work in a couple of days." he said. Simon sniffed and took another drag from his cigarette.

"Yeah man, I'll let you know." he looked up at Bowen and gave him a very weak, stiff lipped smile. From behind Bowen came a loud voice.

"Saxon! Oi Bowen!" It was Duggy. Bowen turned to see that he and Ramphry were making their way across the canteen towards the kitchen, hastily donning their aprons and hats.

"You're with us," Duggy shouted through a purple haze. "We've gotta get a move on because of the late breakfast!" Duggy hadn't seen where he was walking as he finished the last of his cigarette and barged right into Ramphry's back as he fumbled with his apron.

"Ram you dumpster, keep moving!" Duggy shouted, turning some nearby heads. Bowen turned back to Simon and his companions to see that they were all looking over at Duggy and Ramphry with smirks on their faces. Simon just looked down, stubbing his cigarette into an ash tray.

"Come on, you want Wotll to burst her throat?" Duggy called to Bowen, clearly flustered. Simon's friends barely tried to hide their amusement. Bowen looked between each of them and then to Simon, his teeth beginning to clench.

"Right well, see you." Bowen said. He turned to leave and took his apron and hat out of his back pockets. He swallowed hard as he heard hushed talking from behind him with some snickering. He wanted to turn around, but he walked away with boiling blood.

Bowen entered the kitchen through the swinging double doors to see the full kitchen staff in the last throes of preparing food. The sounds of metal on metal and scraping shoes on the tiled floor rattled his aggravated head.

"Hey Bowen." came a quiet voice that cut through the chaos. It was Safiya. She was piling up pots and pans into a neat stack as she watched him.

"Morning." he replied rather flatly.

"Are you alright?"

"Fine. Thanks." Bowen replied with a forced smiled.

As he turned, Kabé was watching him from over the pastry counters, his head cocked to the side slightly.

"Morn ...ning?" Kabé's voice sounded distinctly foreign, as if Bowen's implants had not registered his voice. Bowen blinked and frowned as he strode over to the cleaning cupboard to meet the others.

"When you're quite finished socialising..." Roo started with a venomous undercurrent.

"Waiting for me were you?" Bowen replied with a flush of anger. He looked into Roo's flat orange eyes as he aggressively leered back at him. Steg shuffled his athletic frame between them.

"Cool it both of you. Roo I asked you to fire up the blitzer. Bowen you start the collection with Duggy and Ellbo." Steg seemed just as touchy as everyone else. Bowen took a deep breath as he joined Duggy and Ellbo in hauling out the collection trolley.

Many had left the cafeteria already but it was still extremely busy as they began working. They separated the cafeteria into sections that they each tackled simultaneously. Bowen sighed as his section just happened to be where Simon was. Bowen did his best to circle around the edges first so as to give them time to leave, but it seemed they were leisurely riding out the clock to return to work. None of them had cleared their table. Eventually there was no more avoiding it as Bowen approached them.

Bowen stopped himself from speaking as he began to collect their trays and tableware. Their conversation died away as he worked. Bowen found himself actively not looking at Simon, but in his peripheral vision it appeared that Simon had once again lowered his head. As he leaned over to collect Qizic's tray, Bowen was more than aware that he was being observed.

Embarrassment turned to quiet anger as he brought their trays to the trolley. He met Duggy who was eyeing the table. Duggy took out his lighter and sparked up a cigarette as

Bowen returned to take their last items.

"That you're friend?" Duggy asked quietly as Bowen came back to scrape food into the slop bucket. Bowen nodded without looking at Duggy. Duggy sniffed as he retrieved a spray bottle and a rag from the trolley and strode over. He brazenly leaned between the group and squirted the spray bottle onto the table saying,

"Don't mind me fellas." Duggy exhaled a huge breath of purple smoke without a care, that crashed against the table and grasped at them all. Bowen watched as all their faces creased up in disgust as Duggy began to recklessly swipe his cloth over the table. They all rose from their stools and began to leave. Qizic stood to face Duggy, clicking his mandibles. Duggy stopped wiping the table and looked up at the insectoid. Qizic was a whole head and shoulders taller than him. The rest of the crew including Simon had stopped and turned back to watch. There was a moment of tense silence as Bowen swallowed. He turned and saw that Steg had emerged from the kitchen and was watching from behind the serving line, his sharp ears pointing forwards at attention. Duggy leered at Qizic with his red eyes.

"See you at lunch." he said as purple smoke rose from his nostrils. Qizic clacked his mandibles once more and turned to leave with the others. As the group left, Bowen noticed Simon turn back briefly. They made eye contact for a moment and then he was gone. Duggy returned to the trolley.

"I think I made a friend." Duggy said.

Bowen chuckled.

"Is that a smile?" Duggy nudged Bowen in the side. "Come on then lets get this bull chips back before Steg loses it."

"I think you mean bullshit?" Bowen said with a laugh.

"What did I say?"

19.

Most people had left by the time they finished work. Steg gave Duggy a warning for almost causing a ruckus on day one of the voyage. The rest of the day went by slowly for Bowen. The lunch rush was suddenly upon them after breakfast had been late. At both lunch and dinner he spotted Simon from a distance but he refrained from approaching him. At the start of the dinner clean up, Bowen asked Wotll about the creature that he had seen in the vents in his cabin that morning but she had no idea what he was talking about. Neither did Steg or Qirus when he asked them.

Later that evening Bowen was in his cabin. The ever moving blue light from the galactic highway had been mesmerizing but he found it distracting after a while, so he had closed his blinds. The cabin was illuminated only by the dim strip lights and his lamp. Bowen lay on his bed reading a book he had brought from home called "War for Everest", a dramatised story allegedly based on true events from the history of Earth. As he flicked the yellowed pages he got the smell of the sitting room from home. For a moment he thought he heard the quiet ticking of the clock in the lounge, but it was just a heating pipe adjusting itself. He idly held the leather bookmark in his mouth as he read.

There was a knock at the door. It had not been aggressive, but Bowen had jumped at the sound of it. He placed his bookmark inside and set it down on the bedside table. His mind rifled through all possibilities as to who could be knocking as he got up. Wotll? Duggy? Steg? Safiya perhaps? No. Denton? Garber? The Captain? Perhaps he was about to be punished for his instance of trespassing. He began to sweat as he unlocked his cabin door. He slowly opened the thick metal slab to find Simon stood in the corridor.

"Oh." Bowen said surprised. Simon stood with his hands

in his pockets.

"Hey." he said plainly. The crew deck corridor was quiet and the lighting had gone into evening mode. Bowen shut his cabin door behind him. He felt the worn grey carpet beneath his bare feet. The two were both illuminated by the advertisement screens.

"How did you find my cabin?" Bowen asked.

"It's all in the logs." Simon shrugged.

"Oh, right." Bowen couldn't help but notice that Simon was looking up and down the corridor every few seconds.

"I didn't recognise you with the skin head earlier." Simon said.

"No?"

"Looks okay, you've got the skull for it."

"Thanks." A silence fell. It seemed like a long time ago since they last spoke. "So. What's going on with you?" Bowen asked tentatively. It was all he could think of to say. Simon didn't answer the question.

"Look I'm sorry about, today..." he blurted. Bowen was taken aback. Simon had never been one for apologising, at least not without coercion. "...the guys can be a bit funny with other departments." Bowen folded his arms across his shirt and looked down for a moment.

"It's okay," he lied. Simon sighed with apparent relief.

"So... It's pretty weird us both being here isn't it?"

"Yeah. I suppose it is." Bowen took a breath. "So when did you board the ship?" he asked.

"Oh a few weeks ago." Simon replied flippantly. He didn't let Bowen respond. "Yeah, they wanted me onboard as soon as, so I could get the crash course for the navigation suite."

"Hmm. Right."

"Pretty advanced stuff they've got me doing already." Simon bragged. "What have they got you doing?" Bowen again looked down and shuffled his feet.

"Well, what you saw today really. That and doing the big

clean up in the kitchen with the others."

"Oh right ...awesome." Simon replied with a feigned interest. "So they've not got you cooking anything?"

"No."

"Oh that's a relief then." Simon jested. Bowen forced a smile. "So you said you had a free day coming up soon?"

"Yeah I have in a couple of days."

Simon reached into his jacket pocket and pulled out a small notebook with a silver pen. He flicked through the pages.

"Do you always have the same days off every rotation?"

"Yes."

"Well that works for me next rotation, so we can have a catch up, how's that?"

"Okay yeah. Sounds good."

"How about I meet you on the observation deck? Do you know where that is?"

"I've passed it."

"Great. So day six next rotation." Simon said quickly as he scribbled in his notebook and returned it to his pocket. Bowen could feel his heartbeat in his throat. Simon looked up and down the corridors again and was about to say something when Bowen managed to speak up.

"You know, Jules wrote to me." It wasn't quite a question. Simon's attention was instantly commanded.

"Oh right?" Simon looked at Bowen properly for the first time since he had arrived.

"I got a com-disk from her before I left home." Bowen teased. The current advertisement screen was glowing red against Simon's face and Bowen couldn't be sure if Simon's face had gone flushed or not.

"How is she?" Simon asked. Bowen's heart was now battering at his rib cage. He took a deep breath.

"Oh you know Jules." he replied as casually as he could. Simon glanced down at the floor and stammered a laugh. Bowen rubbed his stubbly scalp as he changed the subject. "So next week then after lunch on the observation deck?"

"Right." Simon answered. He seemed distracted.

"I feel like we've got a lot to catch up on. It's been a while you know?" Bowen said.

"Yeah it has." Simon's body language suggested he was more than ready to leave. "Well, I'm gonna go it's late."

"No problem man, see you."

"See you around." Simon said as he turned to leave.

Bowen fumbled to open his door. He turned his head to see Simon walking down the corridor briskly. Bowen's heart was still pounding. As he entered back into his cabin, he was kicking himself. He had too many thoughts all at once. He was angry at himself for not speaking his mind to Simon. But he was equally mad at Simon's very weak apology that Bowen knew in Simon's mind would mean the end of it. He was angry that he hadn't voiced his feelings on how Simon had made him feel earlier that day. Bowen locked his door and made for the bathroom. He removed his shirt and ran the water in the sink. After a minute he threw the icy cold water on his face and he took a few long breaths.

He came back out into the cabin and sat on the end of his bed. Perhaps he wasn't that angry with Simon. It had been a long day after all. He yawned and took off his trousers. As he got into bed, he was about to turn off his light when he heard it. A scuttling sound in the ceiling by the vent. Bowen watched the metal grill as he turned off his light. He waited a moment.

"Fuck off!" he shouted up at the vent. A small, sharp shriek followed by chittering came from the grate as the creature scampered off into the airways.

20.

The view from the windows did not change as the days began to bleed into one another. The Memento hurtled across space through the galactic highway. To Bowen, the highway started to look like the ocean but for the dark streaks of lightning that sparked off the ship keeping it stable mid flight. Shifts came and went, each one more or less like the last.

On Bowen's first day off he found himself needing to do laundry. Ever since they set off from Pennine he had seen crew members coming and going from the dry cleaning station carrying white sacks full of clothes. He found his own stretchy net bag in his storage and filled it with all his laundry including his work clothes and bedding. Situated on the same level as the rec deck, it was simple enough to find what Duggy had charmingly called the wet house.

Through the deck's large atrium, he passed an onboard gym. Inside Bowen saw crew of all shapes and sizes hard at work on the machines and free weights. As he passed the doorway he heard the ambience of panting and grunting framed by high octane power synth music. Further down was the wet house.

There was a steamy air and it was warm as he entered. Ceiling fans attempting to cool the room and each wall was lined with stacks of washing machines. A handful of crew sat on sets of coloured metal benches that ran the length of the long room, waiting for their cycles to finish.

Bowen dumped his sack onto a bench and attempted to catch his breath.

Sat at the other end of the bench was an alien woman. Wearing a large pair of headphones attached to a small tape deck, she rested her elbows onto the back of the bench in a relaxed manner. She had white skin, but not like how humans knew most Saxons as "white". Her skin was white as frost.

Everything else about her though was ink black. The sides of her head were shaved exposing her small, sharp ears and her dramatically styled, black hair fell well behind her shoulders. Her black eyes were larger than a humans and ever so slightly further apart. As she stared into space watching her laundry, her black tongue played with a pink lip ring that pierced her thin black lips. She raised her thin, sharp eyebrow that was also pierced as she noticed him looking at her. As they looked at each other, from her mouth she inflated some bubblegum that was a mesmerizing silvery purple. Bowen gave an awkward, stiff smile and set about doing his laundry. Despite the ambience of the washing machines, he could hear the muffled sound of the music she listened to. It sounded like incredibly fast breakbeats and heavy bass synthesizers. He could tell that he had gone bright red.

Bowen chose one of the upper machines. Each one was a huge hot pink cube with a slot for a crew id card next to a small key pad. Instantly he was flummoxed. There was what appeared to be a series of instructions printed on a panel, except that his implants were not translating the words. It was the same for the key pad, what might have looked like numbers and letters were just alien symbols that Bowen had no chance of deciphering. He was aware that he was being watched. Taking a deep breath, he began grabbing all his dirty clothes and carelessly shoving them into the large open door. He closed it and heard a click as he entered his identification. Bowen began blindly pressing buttons and turning knobs. An aggressive beep sounded which Bowen took to mean the machine did not like him. From behind, he heard the muffled music become clearer all of a sudden along with a jingling of bracelets and buckles. He rubbed the back of his head and looked blankly at the alien writing.

"Hey." came a voice from his side. Bowen turned and looked into the large black eyes of the alien girl as she leaned against the next machine, headphones around her neck. She inflated her bubblegum until it popped.

"...Hey."

"It's Karukash."

"What?"

"The instructions. They're in Karukash. From the Gol Katharr empire."

"Oh. My implants aren't..."

"No they won't. The Federation hasn't fully translated it." As she spoke Bowen heard the same Laurentian twang as Garber. "You washing everything at once?"

"I was going to."

"What about these?" she said as she dangled a pair of his briefs in front of his face that had dropped to the floor. Bowen felt his face go almost purple with embarrassment.

"Thanks." he stammered. He quickly opened and closed the door again fumbling to stop more clothes from falling out. Bowen didn't notice the smile play at the edge of the alien girls black mouth.

"Back up a second and watch me." she instructed. Bowen did as he was bid. She altered her exposed bra strap and began turning the dials into different positions. She pointed to each of them in turn.

"Gentle, medium heat, wash and dry. Yeah?" Bowen nodded. "See these?" She motioned to a row of multicoloured square buttons with various coloured patterns. "These are your detergents and softeners. Which one do you want?" She inflated her bubblegum as Bowen considered.

"I suppose I'll have the first one?" The button for the one he had chosen was sky blue with white and pink streaks.

"Lillummii Dawn-Flower. That's a good one." She pressed the button in and it illuminated. "It's what I use. Now do you know your crew id number by heart?"

"...No."

"Okay come here." Bowen stepped up next to her. Because of her thick, stompy boots she was the same height as him, but her exaggerated hair gave the illusion she was taller. "Check it out." she said as she pulled his card out of the slot. "Cute." she said as she looked at the picture on the card. "So," she said as she traced her black nail across the plastic. "See under the bar code?" Bowen peered closer and there was indeed a series of twelve numbers.

"Yeah."

"You have to input them manually on the key pad before you insert it."

"Right. Okay."

"It's stupid I know." She tapped her finger on the key pad jangling her rainbow of bracelets. "These first three aren't numbers but from this one to this one is a zero to a nine. So go on." She handed back Bowen's crew card and he cautiously began typing onto the key pad. The girl watched him as he carefully entered his numbers.

"Now press that last button, the blue one… Put your card in the slot…" As he did so he heard a locking mechanism fire. "…Take your card back… And there you go."

The machine began to shudder slightly as it started up the wash cycle. "You see that little screen?" She pointed to above the door of the washer to a digital readout in red, alien lettering. "Doesn't look like it, but it's a timer counting down from three hours." Bowen rubbed the back of his head. As he was about to speak, the machine next to his and down one beeped twice. The girl opened it and she retrieved her own laundry sack from the back pocket of her dark, skinny trousers. She bent down at the waist and began taking out her dry washing and stuffing it into her stretchy sack. Bowen cleared his throat.

"Hey. Thanks for that…" he paused. She stood and tied her laundry sack together firmly as she faced him.

"Vetura."

"Vetura." he repeated. "My name's Bowen."

"I know." Vetura replied as Bowen looked at her confused. "Your card…" she said raising her thin black eyebrows.

"Yeah, obviously." Bowen said as he blushed. She

chuckled. "But yeah thanks for giving me a hand."

"It's no problem." she said as she slung her laundry sack onto her shoulder. "But you've done it now… you owe me one."

"Oh okay," Bowen said with a sheepish smile. She inflated her bubblegum until it popped.

"See you around Bowen." Vetura said as she lifted her bulky headphones onto her head, flattening a portion of her extreme black hair.

"Yeah… see you." Bowen said as she left him. He watched her until she was out of sight.

21.

The next week one evening after a hard shift, Bowen sat on the rec deck with Duggy and Ramphry. The blue warp was no longer there through the windows. Instead a series of shutters had been lowered and there was a digital expansive view of a city on a rainy day complete with rain hitting the window and running down the false glass. The televisions showed slowly changing screensavers, as channels could not be viewed while on the highway.

Having earned some money, Bowen explored Gricky's. He picked up a magazine on video games and one on combat sports as well as a can of Dizz and three Zordo bars. He took his items to the counter where an alien sat reading a book and smoking a blue cigarette. The skinny, green alien reminded Bowen of a stick insect complete with twitchy feelers. On his vest, he wore a name tag that read "Gricky". Gricky looked up from his book at Bowen and observed him with four eyes behind a set of large goggles.

"Yep?" he asked in a dry and cracked voice.

"Hey." Bowen replied as he set his items down before him. Gricky exhaled a puff of dark smoke as he placed his cigarette between small and flat teeth and began scanning Bowen's items with a handheld device.

"Ten point six kardona bud." Bowen swiped his card.

"You need a bag my dude?" Gricky asked.

"No, thanks."

"See you next time." Gricky said as he returned to reading.

Bowen returned to the rec deck. His heart dropped when he saw that Duggy and Ramphry were gone.

"Bowen!" came Duggy's voice from behind him. Bowen span around and saw Duggy sitting at the bar at the far end of the rec deck. Ramphry was off to the side filling his arms with snacks from the vending machines. Bowen sighed in quiet relief as he made to join them.

"I thought you'd left." Bowen said as he took a stool at the bar.

"You think we'd just bail on you like that?" Duggy asked with a slap on the shoulder. "Nah it's getting a bit slow we needed a drink."

"Good call."

The robot bartender everyone knew as "Techno" spoke with half intelligence. It observed them with a head like a computer screen.

"Drinks? Snacks? Problem?"

"No problem, can we just get three pints of Burn Back? I'm paying." Bowen said raising his crew id card. Techno's lanky metal skeleton clanked over and raised a small card reader.

"Fifteen point nine five kardona." After Bowen paid, Techno turned around and began grabbing glasses off the shelves. By the time there were three pint glasses full of the dark drink, Ramphry had heaved himself onto a stool with them at the bar.

Bowen saw himself in the large mirror behind the bar outlined with neon lights and signs. There was a smattering of people about the deck and there was an ambience of low chatter as well as soft music from the nearby machine. The three sat in content quiet for a while. Bowen flicked through his thick combat sports magazine entitled Ultimate Chaos Biannual. Bowen shared out two of the three Zordo bars to Duggy and Ramphry. The Point Blank flavour he had gotten for himself crackled in his mouth as he ate it. Next to them, Ramphry was openly looking at a pin up magazine and crunching on his own bar.

"So how's things with you?" Duggy asked Bowen.

"Yeah, they're okay. How about you?"

"Ah I'm not bad. You settled in alright then?"

"I think so." Bowen replied thinking. He had fallen into

the routine completely and he was waking up in the morning like clockwork. The strict meal times helped him wake easier and it was the easiest he had fallen asleep in years. Despite this, during the short time he had been on the Memento, he felt he had now seen and done most things that were on offer to him.

"You wanna do something tomorrow night?" Duggy asked.

"Like this you mean?" Duggy shook his scaly head as he inhaled purple smoke back into his mouth and out his nostrils again.

"After hours in the cafeteria about once a month some of the guys get together, have a drink, play some Usurper, talk about shit you know?"

"How come you don't do that in here?"

"It's private, quieter."

"I don't know, maybe." Bowen said looking into his drink.

"It'd do you some good to meet some more folks, considering your friend from Saxon hasn't given you the time of day."

"You're right... But it's funny you should say that, I'm seeing him tomorrow on my day off."

"Oh yeah?"

"We're meeting up on the observation deck after lunch."

"Bit out of the way that isn't it? Not much going on up there."

"We're just gonna catch up and talk about stuff."

"Sounds a little formal."

Bowen felt a little uncomfortable remembering what exactly it was he wanted to talk to Simon about. Duggy stubbed out the end of his cigarette.

"Still, that's great. I'm inviting you to guys night all the same."

"Okay sure. I'll come."

"That's right." Duggy said as he slapped Bowen on the back. "You'll have a great time, won't he Ram?" he said, turning around to Ramphry. Bowen looked over Duggy's shoulder and saw that Ramphry was sat upright, but fast asleep.

22.

Bowen's day off was tarnished by agonising over meeting up with Simon. His mind constantly planned and reimagined what he was going to say. He wasn't sure if this meeting was going to become a regular occurrence or if it was just a one off and Bowen was unsure of what approach to take with Simon. They had seldom argued over the years they had known each other, but Bowen knew Simon had a real attitude when he thought someone was having a go at him.   Bowen was glad he didn't have to work. He couldn't concentrate on reading his video game magazine before lunch, he would have had no hope of keeping his thoughts on the mundanity of work. He found himself staring out his cabin window for a good while. He thought about Jules and where she might be, but it only served to agitate him.

During lunch Bowen kept his eyes open for Simon about the cafeteria in the hope that he might catch him leaving and they could go to the observation deck together. Perhaps the walk there would make the conversation flow a little easier. Bowen finished his meal and hadn't seen Simon. He waited until a good deal of people had left the cafeteria just to make sure he wasn't there. When he finally gave up, he made for the doors.

As he left, Safiya caught his eye as she was gathering up empty basins from the serving line and taking them through to the galley. When she looked at him she smiled. It caught Bowen off guard, but he managed to smile back before Safiya broke eye contact. For a moment his tension was lifted.

Out in the atrium beyond the cafeteria main doors, Bowen made straight for observation. Climbing the huge stairwells, he kept his eye out for Simon as he passed crew members, but to no avail. He reached the atrium in front of the postal kiosk and saw that Simon was not waiting outside the doors to observation. In the centre of the space was a group of technicians who had opened up a floor panel and were tinkering with something. They were making a lot of noise.

Bowen took a deep breath and pushed open the doors and found himself in a dark corridor. He felt as though he had just entered a theatre as the door closed behind him and cut out all noise from the technicians. There was a series of small lights at the edge of the floors as Bowen walked inside. The floor began to slope downwards and went on for longer than he anticipated until there was a sudden left turn that opened up onto the huge deck.

Bowen was suddenly drenched in the blue light from the highway. The deck was like a combination of a cinema screen and an auditorium with a similar seating arrangement. There was something like a conservatory about the deck also, with a huge window that curved upwards and became part of the ceiling. He was awestruck by the view. The windows were more forward facing than anywhere else he had been on the ship so far. Bowen saw the scope of the highway now mostly out in front. It was mesmerizing, he couldn't believe there weren't more people there.

It was like they were travelling through a colossal tunnel with a darkness at the far end that never came any closer. Bowen ripped his eyes away from the windows and looked around the deck for Simon. Above the walkway tunnel he had just entered from, there was a digital clock. He was on time.

There were exactly one hundred seats evenly spaced around. He had the time to count them. There was no one, and no Simon. Bowen walked up the steps and chose a seat in the centre of the room. No big deal he thought, he had rushed there after all. He made himself comfortable and enjoyed the view while he waited.

As he waited and watched the spectacle of the highway, recent events played out in his mind. He thought about what his parents were doing at that moment. Had they sent a reply to his com-disk by now? Would he receive it by the time they reached this planet Davarak? He wondered if Niamh had received his message yet. Saurophos was much, much further away than Saxon was. Perhaps not. He wondered where Jules was. He would have loved her to be with him now. If not for Duggy and Ramphry and the random kindness of Vetura he would have felt very alone. He stretched out and rubbed his head with his hands. Where the hell was Simon?

As he sat there, he thought that this was the perfect place to talk with someone, especially since no one could be heard outside and probably from within. After a while, Bowen began to pace. He walked down to the front of the room to the window across the wide carpeted flooring. There was a metal barrier stopping him from reaching the glass. Bowen started to tap his fingers on the cold steel. He walked the length of the window, counting each step out of boredom. The barrier again stopped him from reaching the very end, but he discovered that the room was just short of two hundred feet long.

Bowen sighed. He sat down on the carpet in the open. Looking at the digital clock he saw that there were minutes left before dinner would start. In fact the time it would take to get to the cafeteria meant that if he was to get there on time, he would have to leave there and then.

Bowen took a deep breath and stood up. Despite having spent a good portion of his day in a pleasant environment such as the observation deck, he had spent the whole time alone with nothing to do. If he had known he would have been on his own the time he would have brought something to read at least. His stomach growled at him for food. He deliberately walked slowly back over to the tunnel with some shred of hope that Simon would appear in the last few seconds of his time there. But he didn't. With a tensed jaw and clenched fists wedged into his pockets, Bowen left.

23.

The nervous knot in Bowen's stomach was laced with excitement. The cafeteria was off limits to all but janitorial and security personnel after hours and the consumption of alcohol was prohibited outside of the rec deck. Bowen wondered how the guys would even have any. As Bowen dressed himself, he considered that this was the first social event he would have been to in a very long time. Part of him was excited to break some rules and he hoped the evening would take his mind off things. Bowen threw his leather jacket on for the first time since the day he joined the crew and he left.

The ship was quiet but for the sound of the engines humming. If he didn't know any better, he might have thought the ship was less than half populated. Bowen passed no one through the corridors and down the stairwells. In the passage to the lower atrium he saw two tired looking crew members carrying laundry sacks as well as a janitor buffering the floors with a ride on machine. As he reached the doors to the cafeteria he heard muffled voices. Bowen took a deep breath before entering.

The cafeteria was dark. Sitting around a circular table at the far end of the room was a group of men. The huge windows had been shuttered and the group was illuminated by one of the hanging lights. A dim rainbow glowed behind them from the vending machines.

"There he is." Duggy called over. He stood and jogged the length of the room to meet Bowen by the doors. "I thought you'd reconsidered."

"Almost." Bowen said with a smile.

"That's everyone then!" Duggy announced back to the room.

"Get the doors!" came a voice from the table. Duggy retrieved a set of keys from his pockets and locked them in.

"Come on then." he said as he clapped Bowen on the shoulders. The two of them walked the length of the huge and empty room to the table where they stepped into the light. The table was dominated by a game of Usurper. Cards and dice were scattered around as well as bottles, cans and food packets. Unlike the last time he approached a table of strangers, he was introduced. Duggy whistled between his sharp teeth.

"Oi this is Bowen." A diverse range of faces observed him from under the light. A wave of reactions all came at once.

"Hey." Bowen replied with a nervous wave. The table, Bowen saw, was not full of strangers. Ramphry was present as well as Gricky.

"Now then," Duggy started. "Bowen's a human obviously, despite him being the total opposite of Bao Bao over there." The remark was met with friendly laughter and Bowen laughed too as he saw who Duggy was talking about. Across the table was Bao Bao. Bowen had never seen a larger human in his life. Bao Bao was a hugely fat man and bald but for a long black plaited braid that came from the back of his head. Almost every inch of his flabby skin that could be seen was covered in tattoos. Bao Bao wore a necklace that showed an ancient symbol for Fujigante. When he spoke with his incredibly deep voice, his accent confirmed the heritage.

"Just coz all Skalosi look like you lizard boy." he said with a belly rolling laugh.

"Black scaled Skalosi are less than one percent of the population actually…" Duggy reacted causing more laughter. "…very desirable to the ladies."

"I've gotta say Bowen, you could eat off these tables they're so clean." the new voice came from a green skinned alien with striking blue eyes and hair like tendrils that fell about his broad shoulders.

"He wasn't working today Shillok that was all me." Duggy replied sounding offended.

"Oh my bad."

"Thanks anyway." Bowen said.

"Bowen did you bring more snacks?" Ramphry asked whilst scratching his belly.

"No, sorry Ram."

"You're gonna explode, my dude." Gricky commented, puffing on a blue cigarette. Gricky was shuffling a deck of cards in his thin insectoid hands as he spoke. "We've still got bags of Jinkos if you want some, courtesy of the store." Gricky said to Bowen.

"Yeah go on then." Bowen said as he sat down on a free stool. Gricky flipped the card deck over in one hand as he reached under the table and tossed a bag of Jinkos to Bowen with his other. Duggy sat himself down and motioned to Bowen's sides.

"Bowen, Zaren and Moryys." Duggy stated as the three exchanged greetings. To Bowen's left, Zaren was a cat-like humanoid covered in a light orange and white fur. In his clawed hands he held the polyhedral dice for Usurper. "He hasn't got a drink." Duggy stated. "Grab him a Roddenberry, Zazz." Zaren passed Bowen a can from the crate on the table.

"There you go bud, let it breath for a second."

"Thanks." Bowen replied as he cracked it open. To his right, Moryys was the largest at the table. Moryys had thick skin like a shark with similar colouring that Bowen could tell was equal parts fat and muscle. He was incredibly wide and a head and shoulders above everyone else. He had small, pachyderm ears and dark eyes sat in his whale-like head.

"Sweet shirt." Moryys commented. Bowen hadn't remembered that he was wearing his Battle of Ages t-shirt.

"You watch Battle of Ages?"

"Seems you've found yourself another nerd, Moryys." said Shillok.

"Have I seen you somewhere before?" Bowen asked Moryys.

"Probably." Shillok teased.

"You were in a magazine I was reading." Bowen realised. "You're a house fighter in Blue Dragon Arena?"

"Yeah I was." Moryys answered with a sigh.

"Mister Mega-Fist himself!" laughed Bao Bao.

"You watch Bludgeon Brawl Assault then?" asked Zaren.

"No, no. So are you retired?" he asked Moryys.

"Sort of."

"Ever since he went to MX-12" Duggy said through a cloud of purple smoke.

"What's MX-12?" Bowen asked.

"Ooh that's a sore spot." Duggy teased. Moryys laughed and gave a rude gesture to Duggy. Zaren nudged Bowen and winked one of his cat eyes.

"Don't ask." he advised. Before Bowen could feel too awkward, one of the doors to the bathrooms clattered open from across the cafeteria. An odd silhouette appeared in the doorway for a moment before it disappeared in the dark.

"You good Jo?" Gricky called out. A loud grunt came in response as Bowen heard a mechanical whirring sound coming towards the table. From out of the darkness that surrounded the table came an alien in a large wheelchair.

"Bowen this is Jothazar." Moryys said as he parked up at the table. Jothazar was a frail rodent man. The chair looked like a mobile work station as much as it was a mobility aid. He squinted his small eyes towards Bowen.

"Pleasure..." Jothazar said in a very dry tone. "...are we playing or what?"

"You know how to play Usurper, my dude?" Gricky asked Bowen.

"Duggy introduced me to it, but I'm not great."

"Don't sweat it you're probably better than Moryys."

"Hey." Moryys reacted causing a round of laughter. Gricky began dealing out cards and distributing coloured chits to gamble with.

"So where you from?" Jothazar asked Bowen.

"Saxon." he replied. Jothazar sniffed as he pieced together what looked like a smoking pipe made out of spare parts from around his chair.

"Never been to Saxon." He commented.

"We were docked there for weeks." Zaren said. Jothazar didn't seem to register the comment and was busy filling his pipe with crushed black spices he had obtained from a pouch in his jacket.

"He barely leaves engineering never mind takes shore leave." Moryys told Bowen.

"It's hard enough to convince him to come up here for game night." Shillok said as he observed the cards he had been dealt with a frown. "I've got fuck all." he said bitterly.

"Same." Bao Bao added. Bowen looked down at his hand to see that he had two Jade Hearts, a Tattered Map, the Dead Prince and three Poisoned Feasts. Bowen did his best to remember everything Duggy had taught him.

"Fifteen chits to start us off." Gricky said as he slid his hand out to the middle of the table. He rolled an eight sided dice into the centre. "King card is up. Round one."

"I bet Seven." Bao Bao said as he added his chits to the pile. He rolled his ten sided dice and played a card. "The White Whore." They each placed bets, rolled dice and played a card as the round played out. Bowen just about had a grasp of the rules as they went.

"King still rules." Gricky said as the round concluded. The pile of chits on the table had swelled. Moryys had lost out already as well as Shillok and Ramphry. Bowen chose to place his Tattered Map card which seemed to illicit a laugh from Gricky and a sigh from Zaren who then had no choice but to place his "Sun Spider" card. As they played the chatter continued.

"So what do you do Bowen?" Jothazar asked as he lazily smoked his pipe and held his cards in his small hairy hand. Bowen took a swig of his Roddenberry before he answered.

"I'm on the clean up crew with Duggy and Ram." he replied. Jothazar made a noise that seemed to be recognition as Bowen asked, "What about you Jo?"

Jothazar coughed and didn't answer.

"He's the head of engineering." Moryys answered for him. "Keeps the ship ticking over don't you Jo?" Jothazar's small black eyes were busy squinting at his cards which he held in front of his face. "Don't take it personal, my man," Moryys said to Bowen, "He's half deaf as well as being a grumpy old shit."

"What's that?" Jothazar asked looking up from his cards.

"We're just talking about you Jo." Moryys teased. At that moment, Bowen jumped out of his skin as a small creature landed on his shoulder from above.

"Toki, where have you been hiding!?" Jothazar shouted from across the table. Bowen tensed his shoulders as he felt two small and delicate hands inquisitively touching his ear. There was quick and interested sniffing in his ear as the creature padded its small feet onto his shoulders. On his neck Bowen felt a fuzzy tail as it swiped to and fro. The whole table had stopped what they were doing and were now watching Bowen.

"Don't panic Bowen he's not dangerous." Shillok stated. Bowen forced a smile as he felt his stubbly head being rubbed and inspected by Toki.

"He likes you." Bao Bao said.

"Come here." Jothazar demanded. At the appearance of Toki, Jothazar had definitely perked up. The creature hopped from Bowen's shoulder to the table and turned to face Bowen. Toki looked like a blend of simian and marsupial. His body and long bushy tail were covered in stripey purple and black fur. Toki's face had two dominant eyes that were large and reflective with smaller eyes flanking them towards the sides of his head. His small puckering mouth constantly widened into a smile, showing off a series of fangs. Bowen watched as the animal began picking up cards to taste them. He picked up a chit from the pile and held it right up to his eyes and turned it over in his hands curiously.

"I saw him in the vents in my cabin a while ago." Bowen

stated.

"He hides in the vents when we launch from anywhere and he ends up exploring." Moryys said.

"Put that down." Jothazar ordered firmly. Toki did as he was told and walked over the table to Jothazar with his little hands in the air. He clambered up onto Jothazar's outstretched arms and sat behind his head. Toki was content to sit in a nook behind Jothazar's head as he passed up small brown pellets for Toki to eat.

The game continued. Bowen drank Roddenberrys, ate the strong and moreish Jinkos and felt content as the banter ebbed and flowed between the hands and rounds of Usurper. He lost out as Duggy displayed a ruthless edge and Ramphry surprised everyone by dominating another round. Bowen had fun despite losing hand after hand. On one round Bowen found himself playing directly against Moryys after everyone else had lost out.

"King's in his winter years." Gricky announced as everyone watched intently. He tossed a few more chits into the pile and passed Bowen a ten sided dice. Bowen rolled against Moryys and felt the whole table's eyes on him.

"Seven." Bowen announced. Moryys, who at that point in the game only had a four sided dice took a deep breath and rolled against him. His huge hand rattled the tiny orange plastic die and threw it out.

"One." Moryys called.

"What you got big man?" Gricky asked. Moryys weighed up his three cards. Bowen saw a look of intense thought play out on his bulky face as he played. "The Accursed Onslaught." Gricky announced. The table leaned in with a murmur of anticipation. Bowen saw the artwork on the card depicted a flaming castle under siege from an army of demons.

"Ooh he's becoming mighty!" Duggy japed at Moryys.

"Shut up." Moryys grumbled clearly flustered under the stress of the game.

"Go on my dude, what you got for him?" Gricky asked.

Bowen considered his cards privately and decided. He made his choice and placed a card down face up in front of himself. The whole table gasped with surprise and elation.

"The Crystal Dragon." Gricky announced. "The King is dead." Moryys groaned as Gricky flipped the King card face down. Bowen beamed. He couldn't believe it as there was a small round of applause and congratulations from everyone. Even Jothazar who had seemingly fallen asleep gave an approving nod to Bowen. Gricky pushed the pile of chits over to Bowen with his long arms as Moryys patted Bowen on the back with his large hand. Gricky retrieved a small notepad and a pen and began scribbling. "And he's officially on the table." he said. Bowen felt a small swell of pride in his chest. He also felt the need to piss. He excused himself and made his way to the bathrooms. As he did so, Bowen felt the effects of the Roddenberrys he had been drinking, more than once, he had to steady himself against the tables. The automated lights in the bathroom were blindingly bright in contrast to the cafeteria. As he stood in the stall relieving himself, he was happy to feel like he might have finally fallen in with some proper friends. As he thought that, Simon's face emerged in his mind's eye. Bowen burped as he felt a touch of bitterness. He spat into the bowl.

When he had found his way back to the table, cans of Roddenberry were being passed around again, to which Bowen accepted. Duggy, Gricky, Shillok and Bao Bao were all smoking variously coloured cigarettes and Jothazar had fallen asleep with Toki picking through his grey hair. Bowen stretched out his legs under the table and felt relaxed.

"You got a girlfriend, Bowen?" Shillok asked. The sudden question threw him. Shillok looked him dead in the face across the table with his bright blue eyes as he waited for a response.

"Uh, no. No I haven't." Bowen replied as he cracked open his drink. As the words left his mouth, Bowen wondered if he had merely gone with a simple answer or if that was his heart speaking for him. He took a thoughtful swig of Roddenberry.

"Well there's plenty of action to be had on this ship let me tell you." Shillok said knowingly. Bowen wasn't sure how to answer such a statement. Part of him knew it was inevitable that spending time with a group of males would result in such a conversation.

"I've spotted you eyeing up that one in the kitchen." Duggy said raising his scaly brow.

"Safiya?" Bowen asked.

"Oh aye?" Duggy said as a murmur went around the table. Bowen felt his face go red.

"I mean she's nice but I'm not, I mean… I don't know. I'm not sure I'm her type." Laughter circulated the table. Zaren patted Bowen on the shoulder with his paw.

"There's about fifteen hundred people on this ship, chances are there's someone who wants a go."

"Besides, from what I've seen there's virtually no other human women on the ship." Bowen said. The comment garnered an odd reaction from the table. Bao Bao laughed loudly.

"You'll be missing out on a lot of fun…" he said. Bowen was stuck for words as he laughed. Sex with an alien was not something that had ever entered his mind. "…Go see the good doctor Jinn-Quo. He'll get you a com-disk pamphlet on spacer's sexual health."

"I mean, yeah, sounds like a plan." Bowen replied with a hint of sarcasm.

"Tell you what I'd love to have a few rounds with Officer Garber." Shillok said as he flicked his green tendrils over his shoulder. Jothhazar, who had seemingly been sleeping grunted in agreement and nodded slowly.

"Garber would eat you alive." Moryys laughed.

"Oh I bet." Shillok replied causing laugher to bounce around the room. "She's way out of my league anyway." he added. "Wouldn't wanna follow on from the Captain anyhow."

"You believe that?" Gricky asked.

"You've seen how she looks at the Captain." Duggy said.

"Ah I think that's just rumours." Gricky replied sparking up another cigarette.

"You still sleeping with that pink dolly, fuzz ball?" Bao Bao asked Zaren as he opened another pack of Jinkos.

"That's right." he replied with a fanged smirk. Moryys shuffled in his seat.

"Their outfits give me the creeps." he said.

"Yeah?" Zaren said. "She leaves most of it on for me usually." Jothazar grunted in approval again as everyone laughed. Bowen had gone bright red.

"Like I said Bowen," Shillok said as he crushed his empty can. "...you find someone whose willing and as long as you're compatible you can go at it like there's no going home." The laughter of the group echoed around the cafeteria.

"I'll remember that, thanks." Bowen replied as Zaren and Moryys each patted and slapped him on the shoulders. His head was swimming from the conversation, or perhaps the drink. Safiya floated through his head, and for a moment, so did Vetura, inflating her bubblegum and looking him dead in the eyes. Duggy stubbed out his red cigarette in an ash tray and stood up.

"When we get to Obelisk station," he started. "...we'll go and have a real guys night. I'm talking drinks at the Old House with all you can eat, put some money on a fight at the Hot Box and round it off with a strip show at Madame Valentha's." There was a resounding approval from the table. Duggy winked a red eye at Bowen.

"Don't worry mate, we'll get you seen to in the end." Bowen smiled right through his embarrassment. He was powerless against the tidal wave of machismo.

Just then, Toki's head snapped up. He chirped and hopped off Jothazar and scampered into the darkness. Everyone at the table paused as they heard the sound of someone unlocking the main doors.

"Busted, my dudes." Gricky said grimly. The dim light

from the atrium spilled into the cafeteria as someone entered through the doors. No one spoke as footsteps came towards them. After an uncomfortable amount of time, out from the dark stepped First Officer Lennox.

"Evening fellas." he said as he came under the light. "What's on?" Lennox observed the cards and dice on the table with some disdain.

"Just having a get together sir." Shillok said after clearing his throat.

"Yeah?" Lennox replied putting his foot on an empty stool. "Something wrong with the Rec Deck?"

"Quieter here, sir." Duggy replied bravely. Bowen's heart rate increased.

"That right?" Lennox replied. He picked up an empty bottle of Roddenberry and looked it over. "You boys remember the rules on alcohol right?" There was a murmur of affirmation from the group. "I've gotta say I'm disappointed, especially in you two." Lennox pointed to Jothazar and Gricky.

"Aye sir." Gricky said. Jothazar smoked his pipe and said nothing. Lennox surveyed the table. Bowen's heart skipped a beat as Lennox's gaze fell on him.

"What's your name?" he asked directly. Bowen cleared his throat. The Roddenberry's had well and truly gone to his head. He had to really think about his answer before he spoke.

"Rhys, Bowen Rhys, my name's Bowen ...sir." he fumbled. Lennox seemed to take his time to process the information as he looked at Bowen thoughtfully. There was an uncomfortable quiet that hung in the air as everyone waited for Lennox to speak again. Ramphry broke the silence by snorting, which brought Lennox out of his thoughts, frowning.

"Well gents, I'll let you off this once. Next time I'll dock your pay. Understood?" His voice dropped the false friendliness as he spoke. There was a collective shuffle and a muttering of confirmation from everyone. Lennox took his foot off the stool and stepped back, waiting for everyone to leave.

"Come on man," Moryys said quietly to Bowen and they both stood up with the others. Lennox watched as Gricky quickly gathered up the game of Usurper into a carry box and the others collected their trash and deposited it in the bins. He watched them all as they passed him on the way to the doors. Bowen walked behind the hulking mass of Moryys as they exited into the dim atrium. Lennox followed them out jingling keys until he locked the doors behind himself.

"Good night fellas," he said as he turned back to them. "Crew decks that way." he motioned across the atrium to the stairwells. He stood and watched them leave.

"Fucking jobsworth." Duggy growled under his breath.

"We knew there was a risk of being caught." Shillok said. "We should count ourselves lucky he only gave us a warning." Bowen turned back around and saw Lennox swinging his keys, watching them. They reached the stairwell when Jothazar drove away from them towards doors to an access corridor.

"Next time we'll just suck it up and go to the rec deck eh, Jo?" Zaren said. Jothazar grunted.

"Til next time old man." called Gricky. Jothazar grunted again loudly in response. As the group ascended the stairs, Bowen realised he was steadying himself by holding Moryys' large arm. All of a sudden there was laughter as Bowen's world spun around. It took his brain a moment to realise that Moryys had slung him over his huge shoulder and was carrying him up the stairs. Bowen chuckled to himself as he saw the steps moving away from him. The cool air in the stairwell rushed past his head.

"Crew Deck A or B?" Moryys asked as they reached a landing. Bowen's brain struggled to comprehend for a moment before he replied.

"B... like bees."

"What's bees?" he heard Duggy ask. The goodbyes from the others sounded distant as they reached the crew decks. He felt the ground beneath his feet as Moryys put him down.

"Are you good? You know where you're going?" Moryys asked him.

"Yeah I'm okay."

"Alright then." Moryys held out his large hand to which Bowen gave him a clumsy high five.

"Hey Moryys." said Bowen.

"Yeah?"

"We should chill out some time you know?" Moryys smiled with his wide mouth.

"Sounds good, I'll take you up on that."

"Okay. I'm going to bed now. I'm gonna be late for work tomorrow I can tell."

"Make sure you drink some water first." Moryys said pointing his large finger at Bowen's chest.

"Water's good." Bowen said.

"See you man." Moryys replied as he turned to leave.

24.

Bowen balanced himself on the walls as he made his way to his cabin. The advertisement screens slowly morphed as he passed them, making him squint in the dark. As the corridor slowly curved around, he was in sight of his cabin door. Down the dimly lit corridor he saw someone walking away from his doorway, hands in their pockets.

"Simon?" Bowen called louder than he meant to. The person wheeled around startled. It was indeed Simon. Bowen reached his cabin doors as Simon walked back to meet him. The corridor was coming in and out of focus for Bowen but he could tell that Simon was standing in front of him.

"What happened man? How come you weren't at the observation deck today?" Bowen asked without a thought. Simon had a surprised look on his face. He took a moment to answer as Bowen was slightly swaying on the spot.

"...I had to work. Overtime you know."

"Well you could have let me know. I was waiting in there for like three hours."

"It's not my fault. I've got responsibilities." Simon stated, importantly.

"Oh yeah, navigating with Denton and the fly boys."

"What? ...Look I came here to rearrange for when I'm next free."

Bowen cut him off.

"That was a really shitty thing to do man," Bowen felt his heart drop.

"Ugh your breath stinks what have you been drinking?" Simon asked.

"I've been making friends actually." Bowen replied with a layer of anger.

"Right." Simon said firmly as he looked up and down the corridor.

"You know you've been acting different with me since I got on this ship. And honestly for a long time before that." Bowen said. He could feel his throat closing up with his heart beat rising upwards.

"What do you mean?" Simon asked frowning.

"I think you know what I mean..." Bowen had tears in his eyes.

"You're just drunk Bowen. Where's your key card?"

Bowen reached into his pocket and retrieved his wallet.

"It's here." he said waving it.

"Right, get inside before you make a fool of yourself." Simon ordered. Bowen felt Simon snatch his wallet out of his hand and before he could make sense of things, Simon was marching Bowen into his cabin.

"I'm quite capable thank you." Bowen tried as he felt the bed under his bottom as Simon sat him down. "I've still got stuff to talk about you know."

"Leave it for another time when you're not drunk." Simon left, slammed the cabin door shut without so much as a good bye. Bowen felt tears falling down his face. Bowen struggled to take his boots off before he found the bathroom and carefully poured himself a glass of water. He took a few swigs before he undressed. Bowen wiped his wet face with his arm as he lay down. Sniffling, he went to sleep with one foot on the floor.

***

The rotations passed and the weeks blurred.

Bowen remembered his encounter with Simon that night, but as the days started to blur together, all he was left with was a feeling of embarrassment and frustration.

Bowen made no attempt to speak to Simon despite spotting him more than once in the cafeteria. Despite this, Bowen began to walk about the ship with his head up. He frequently crossed paths with Moryys as he made deliveries from the cargo bay. He also often ran into Zaren and Shillok in their armoured security suits. When Bowen found himself in the onboard store, Gricky would often shave off a few dona from the price of items for him. Bao Bao became a more noticable presence among the galley staff ever since Bowen had met him. Bao Bao would occasionally shout to him during service above the din asking him whether he had researched interspecies compatibility. Bowen was grateful to Duggy for including him in the fun that night, more than he could have said.

One evening in his cabin, Bowen caught himself remembering that in a few months he would be going home, and these aliens who had become his friends would suddenly be as distant to him as his school friends were to him now. Unless he didn't go home. Bowen couldn't concentrate on his book after the thought entered his mind. There was nothing to say that he had to go back to Saxon. When they reach Obelisk, he would have the opportunity to get a flight home or carry on with the Memento on a longer voyage.

Bowen stared out of the window into the blue. When the trip to Obelisk was done, he was sure that he would have had enough of cleaning up the cafeteria. Garber never made it clear as to what a longer voyage would look like, it could be another year or more. And there was nothing stopping Captain Quinn taking the Memento away from Federation space. They could end up on the other side of the galaxy, perhaps further. The thought was frightening and enticing. To travel further than Niamh on Saurophos. To perhaps travel to unknown and unmapped worlds. His imagination began to fire. But then he thought about his parents at home. Samhain and Virgil too. And Jules. Bowen caught her mass of ginger hair and freckly smile in the corner of his mind. The thought of Jules made him think of Simon. As time had passed, Bowen didn't miss her as much as he once had.

Time began to wash over him like a slow moving river. He took to sleeping with his blinds open which threw the deep blue light of the highway across the walls of his cabin. The ambience of the ship relaxed him. The ever present hum of the engines through the walls wasn't as intrusive as it had been previously. A couple of times, Bowen was again visited by Toki in the vents. Instead of scaring him off, Bowen had discovered how to remove the metal grate on the vent and he allowed Toki to jump down onto his shoulder. Toki seemed initially hesitant but soon he was exploring Bowen's cabin, inspecting and tasting things curiously. The little creature took to hanging from the pipes on the ceiling just watching Bowen or looking wide eyed out the window.

    When he was working, the shifts often blurred past with the same activities. Once everything had become routine it became more a case of how to pass the time. The monotony was broken when during the clean up after a busy breakfast, Wotll approached Bowen as he was setting a cycle on the blitzer. She tapped her long fingers on his shoulder.

    "I need a favour when lunch comes around." she said.

    "Yeah sure, what is it?"

    "We're down a few people today, breakfast service was a nightmare. I need you to work the pay station for me. It'll be instead of doing the clean up." For a moment Bowen felt a surge of excitement at the notion of doing something different despite it being a rather mundane job otherwise. Wotll cleared her throat and continued. "Come out to the line I'll show you what to do." Bowen finished setting up the blitzer and followed Wotll. Roo, overhearing the interaction shot him daggers from over the meat counter as he was preparing to wipe down, but Bowen gave him a rather smug smile. He followed Wotll out to the empty service line and to the pay station at the end. The last of the crew and passengers he saw, were sat around the cafeteria smoking and chatting. Bowen had encountered the pay station every time he had eaten a meal but from the other side it was completely different. The bulky machine was covered in a multitude of buttons and the small digital screen blinked waiting to be used.

"All you've got to do is set the machine to the shift time, like so," she pressed a couple of buttons and the machine beeped. "Then insert your id card in the slot so it knows whose using it. Then when someone comes to the end of the line you ask them for their id which will be crew or passenger. If they're crew press this button," she pointed out a square blue button. "If they're a passenger, press this one." Wotll showed him a corresponding orange one. Bowen nodded along. "Then you get this thing." She picked up the wired scanner device and wielded it like a pistol. "Press the button and pull the trigger when you point it at their card and the meal will go through. It'll come up on the screen. Crew don't pay directly, but passengers do so it's important you get it right."

"Okay no problem." Bowen said in confidence.

"Any questions?" At that moment, he heard a voice that caught his attention. His eyes drifted from the machine up to over the cafeteria where he saw Safiya leaving with a couple of other women from the galley staff. They were all laughing about something together. He had not seen Safiya smile before.

"Bowen?" Wotll snapped him out of his distraction.

"No I think I got it." he said.

"Sure?"

"Yes."

"Good."

25.

Bowen arrived at the cafeteria early to mentally prepare for lunch service. The rest of the galley staff began to emerge and a steady stream of crew and passengers soon followed. Bowen took his position behind the pay station. He set the machine to the shift time and inserted his id card. The service line was stretched, but still manned. The first of the crew were slowly making their way down the service line towards them. Next to Bowen on desserts was Kabé. Bowen watched as he twirled a pair of tongs in his hand like it was a knife. Further along the line was Safiya by the hot veg. She was adjusting her blue floral head scarf when her eyes met his.

"Hey." he said casually.

"Hi." Safiya replied. She then busied herself with last minute preparations to her station. Kabé was now balancing the tongs on one of his long, green fingertips. Bowen cleared his throat and attempted conversation.

"Those Plutonium cakes look good." Kabé turned his head and looked at Bowen through the large dark lenses of his mask. Bowen motioned to the cakes he referred to. Small green cupcakes with sugar salt chunks topped with radiation hazard labels made of sugar paper.

"Cake." Kabé replied plainly. Bowen smiled awkwardly as he felt the slowly mounting pressure of the shift with the line growing closer.

"So... Ka-be. Am I saying that right?" Kabé did not respond and had resumed spinning the tongs in his three delicate fingers. "...I'm Bowen."

"Bo ...wen.." Kabé repeated carefully.

"Where are you from then?" Bowen asked as casually as he could. Kabé clutched the tongs and looked back at him.

"From..."

"Yeah you know, Saxon's my home planet, what about

you?"

Kabé looked into the serving line at the Plutonium cakes.

"Home…" Before Bowen could think on the odd interaction with Kabé he was face to face with an alien with a tray full of lunch.

"Hi. Crew or passenger?" The man was already holding out his id card. "Oh." Bowen said with a nervous laugh. He obtained the scanner and pressed the activator whilst pulling the trigger. The card was scanned and the meal wet through. The machine beeped as Bowen saw a small readout on the screen flare up. "Enjoy your lunch." Bowen said. But the alien was already finding a table.

From that point on the shift began to blur forwards unrelentingly. He served crew member after crew member with the occasional passenger. Part of Bowen wished he could have greeted everyone he served but it just wasn't possible. It was also not possible to chat or make small talk with anyone on the serving line.

There was a brief moment of respite when a particularly slow moving and choosy alien was considering his lunch further down the line. Bowen had a minute to stand back. The heat from the hanging lights above the line was beginning to be bothersome. Kabé seemed utterly unaffected by the unforgiving pace of the shift. Safiya took a moment to step back herself and wipe the sweat from her neck. Bowen saw that she had put aside a can of water and he wished he had done the same as he watched her take cool, long mouthfuls. It was only for a brief moment as the line caught up with the service again.

Before long the family of human passengers from Saxon came to the front of the queue with three trays of lunch. The blonde girl was sat on the hip of her mother. The father adjusted his glasses as he began to fumble finding his id card.

"I should have had it ready I'm sorry." the man said to Bowen.

"Don't worry there's no rush." he replied. When the

man spoke, Bowen heard the regional accent of the Hibernian Steppes.

"Are you from the Dales?" the mother asked Bowen.

"Yes I am." he said with a smile.

"I recognised your accent." she said. "You boarded the ship from Allchester with us didn't you?" She shifted her daughter on her hip as she flicked her own long ginger fringe out of her eyes. "Daddy's a faff isn't he?" she teased to her daughter. "Come on Colum." she added quietly to her husband.

"Where are you going if you don't mind the question?" Bowen asked. Colum answered.

"We're eventually headed for Bolgotha. Have you got your card, Orla, I must have left mine in the cabin." Orla tutted and reached into her pocket.

"Oh wow, that's a long trip." Bowen said as Orla handed him her card. Bowen had never seen a diamond grade federation citizen card before.

"Mammy he's got one blue eye and one green eye." the girl said pointing at Bowen with a small finger.

"He has Erin," Orla commented. "...but it's rude to point." Erin was looking at Bowen with her big blue eyes.

"I wish I had two nice blue ones like yours." Bowen replied with a smile. Erin hid her face in Orla's hair. Bowen scanned Orla's card.

"With plenty of sightseeing on the way and a few rest stops it should take us a couple of years." Colum commented as he wiped his glasses.

"Well good luck to you." Bowen said secretly jealous. He reached over into the dessert section and retrieved a Plutonium cake. "This okay for her?" he asked Orla. She nodded and Bowen placed the cake on Erin's tray.

"Well Erin that sounds like a great adventure you're having." Bowen said. Erin peeked out from behind her mother and her eyes fixated onto the green cupcake.

"Oh wow, that's nice isn't it Erin? Say thank you to Bowen." Orla said looking at Bowen's name tag.

"Thank you." Erin said quietly.

"Any time today..." came a voice from further down the queue.

"Sorry sorry." Colum said as he hurriedly picked up two of the three trays. As Orla picked up the last one with Erin's lunch she thanked Bowen as Erin waved goodbye to him. Bowen didn't notice Safiya watching him.

The shift blurred on with a tiring pace. As Bowen served people, his arms and particularly his fingers were becoming tired. They complained at him with every pull of the trigger and clack on the pay station. Unintentionally, Bowen discovered that if he kept the activator pressed down, he could have the trigger constantly pulled, which relieved some of the cramping that had begun to build up in his hand. He cautiously experimented with a couple of crew members and it appeared to work. He felt content that he had streamlined his workload as he continued scanning id cards.

Inevitably, he came face to face with crew from the Navigation suite. Qizic came first presenting a meal of squishy red maggot creatures that fidgeted in their bowl of thick fluid. He brandished his id to Bowen and clicked his mandibles without a word. Bowen's heart rate had increased as he noticed Simon further down the line who hadn't noticed him yet. Bowen lifted the scanner device up to Qizic's card, and nothing happened. No beeping came from the machine. Bowen released the trigger and attempted it again using the original method. Nothing. He began to panic as Qizic began to display impatience. The smell of Qizic's meal was turning Bowen's stomach with every passing moment.

"Sorry can I just see your card?" Bowen said as he delicately took the card from Qizic's clawed hand. Qizic began to click his mandibles faster as his large unblinking eyes observed Bowen. Bowen attempted the process a few times but to no avail. The screen displayed an unhelpful hint that there had been a failure and that something had to be reset. His heart sank when he noticed that the end of the scanner device was ever so slightly fizzing with electricity. He had broken it.

"Come on what's going on?" came a voice from further down the line. Bowen's mind went into overdrive as the consequences began to rifle through his mind. They were about half way through lunch, meaning roughly half of all crew and passengers were yet to be served and now he had disrupted the whole thing. His breath began to become short and fast.

"Dead." Kabé said next to him looking at the pay station.

"Yeah." Bowen replied, his sweaty hand rubbing down his face.

"What's happened?" came another voice. It was Safiya. Bowen jumped as she emerged between him and Kabé. The smell of her perfume laced with sweat filled his head.

"It's fucked. Look." Bowen said as he showed her the scanner. Safiya took a deep breath.

"I'm sorry about this." She said to Qizic. He clicked his mandibles at her.

"I'm hungry." he said. His voice was deep and unnerving.

"Somebody get Wotll!" Safiya called down the serving line. Bowen buried his face in his hands. A ripple of questions and realisations went down through the crew resulting in complaints flying and loud sighing. Some hungry crew members began to eat their food in the line with grumpy expressions on their faces. Bowen couldn't look at them. Qizic simply stood looking at Bowen. The rest of the navigation crew were all quietly finding it hilarious that Bowen was drowning before them.

"Simon your friend's a little out of his depth here isn't he?" said one of them. Part of Bowen wanted to leap over the service line and start swinging his fists whilst another part of him wanted nothing more than for the Memento to spontaneously explode there and then. After what seemed like forever, Wotll wheezed her way from the kitchen and shuffled down to them.

"Right what's the problem?" she asked. Bowen tried to speak but he struggled to find the words.

"The scanners broken." Safiya answered for him. Wotll thought for a moment and took a deep breath.

"Right Saf, go to my office an fetch a pen and notebook and be quick about it." she commanded. Safiya disappeared with a whip of her head scarf. Bowen was trying to take deep breaths. "How did that happened then?" Wotll asked him. The way she asked the question made Bowen suspect that she knew exactly how it had happened and she wanted him to say so.

"I was scanning but, I think..." Before he could finish his pathetic explanation Safiya reappeared which sprung Wotll back into action.

"Right Rhys, this is what your gonna have to do, the scanners dead so you'll have to take the id cards." she said as she took Qizic's card in her hand. "And you're gonna have to jot down names and card numbers to be entered in manually at a later time." Bowen took a deep breath and nodded. "Okay well go on then folks are waiting."

Bowen was painfully aware of the fact that everyone was being held up. He could barely contain his embarrassment that his shortcut had caused a huge backlash. Wotll waddled away.   "Somebody get a technician down here as soon as possible!" she cried out. Bowen began to take crew id cards and note down names and the twelve digit numbers that went with them attempting to find the sweet spot between writing quickly whilst also legibly. Bowen didn't even register when he took Simon's card out of his hand and wrote his name and crew id on the paper. He also didn't take any notice when Safiya placed an icy can of water on the counter next to him.

The flow of service eventually began to pick up again but there had been a clear delay. Bowen took a moment to crack open the water can and downed half of it before resuming the laborious task. After an agonizing amount of time the technician had arrived.

"The techy's here!" Someone shouted. Bowen breathed a sigh of relief and stood back from the counter. As he stood up straight his back ached and cracked. There was still a steady stream of passengers and crew but at least now the machine could be looked at. From out of the blurry haze and the stress came a familiar voice.

"Not great with technology are you?" It was Vetura. She was dressed in a blue grey jumpsuit. At her waist was a tool belt and she carried a sturdy looking case. Her hair was neatly tied up and she wore work appropriate shoes. Bowen saw her at her true height. She was almost a head shorter than he was. Bowen smiled weakly and laughed.

"No I'm not." It was all he could manage to say. He had no choice but to continue working as more customers were passing through. As he began writing a crew member's details, Vetura plonked her tool case onto the counter next to him.

"What's happened then?" she asked looking at the pay station.

"I broke the scanner." He admitted. He spoke quietly enough that only Vetura could hear him.

"You know what'll happen now don't you?" she whispered in response.

"What..?"

"The Captain's gonna throw you out the air lock."

"I can't wait." Bowen laughed. So did Vetura. Bowen felt his stress being defeated. He didn't notice Safiya watching them from next to Kabé.

"Straight into the blue as they say." Vetura said. "You'll be burned away layer by layer on the highway."

"That sounds great right about now." Bowen joked.

"Tell me about it." she answered. When Vetura smiled she revealed her naturally black gums and gleaming white teeth. She put her hand on his sweaty lower back as she squeezed past him to get to the pay station. She composed herself and got to work. "Let's see." she said to herself.

After looking the machine over carefully she retrieved

a small key from her tool belt and opened a side panel. Bowen heard her flicking switches and unplugging internal connectors. Bowen realised his heart rate had returned to normal as he caught himself smiling at crew and passengers again. Next to him, Vetura took the scanner in her hands and inspected it. After a moment, she set it down again.

"Right." she said. "I'm gonna have to nip down to the machine shop and get another one of these. Don't touch the machine or the scanner I'll be back in a few minutes."

"Okay." Bowen replied as he watched her leave. She weaved her way down the serving line and jogged through the main cafeteria doors. Bowen's eyes met Safiya's who smiled at him before she broke eye contact.

A short while later Vetura returned carrying a sealed plastic bag containing a new scanner. She hurried back down the line and placed it on the counter next to the pay station before unlocking her tool case with a key. Bowen continued to take note of id numbers as she worked. Vetura worked quickly, obtaining a series of clippers and keys with a small tightening wrench. Vetura carefully disconnected the broken scanner and ripped open the bag with the new one. He noticed her take in the smell of the new part as she opened the bag. Without so much as a hesitation, Vetura was installing the new scanner as if she had done so a hundred times before. The queue for lunch was coming to an end, but Vetura had managed to salvage a portion of his shift for him. She completed the installation of the scanner with a swift few button presses.

"All done." She said at last. Bowen took a deep breath as she handed him the new scanner, smooth and unused. Before he could say thank you to her, Wotll emerged after squashing herself down to them.

"Sorted then?" she asked Vetura.

"Yep, we're all good here. No big deal." she said looking at Bowen directly. He smiled.

"Thank you darlin'." Wotll said as Vetura began to pack up her tools. Wotll patted Bowen on the shoulder. "Don't go anywhere Bowen I'll be back in a minute." Wotll said as she proceeded to walk away out of breath back to the kitchen.

"Thanks a lot, seriously." Bowen said to Vetura as he took a payment from one of the last customers. Vetura locked up her tool case and began to tighten her hair.

"That's another one you owe me." she said.

"It is." Bowen smiled with a nod. Vetura checked her tool belt and took her case in hand.

"See you around Bowen." Vetura turned to leave. Bowen watched her leave down the line. Wotll returned from the kitchens and joined him.

"How was that then?" Wotll asked. Bowen leant against the counter and rubbed his hand over his face. "About right." she commented. Speaking quietly she continued, "You kept the trigger held down on the scanner didn't you?" Bowen felt his face go red.

"I thought I could speed things up. I'm sorry Wotll." She put her long, frog like hand on his shoulder.

"It's done now, no sense fretting." Bowen felt a weight lift off of him. Wotll wheezed as she spoke. "Listen I'll need you to come back for the dinner service, but you swap places with Safiya okay?" she asked so that Safiya could also hear her. They both agreed that was best. "Make sure you leave that list of id numbers in the drawer under the station. There's not enough time now, so you'll have to stay behind after dinner to enter them into the system." Wotll began to make for the kitchen as she finished, "Now then, you get some lunch with the rest of the galley lot and I'll see you later." As she moved away, Kabé was stood watching him.

"You alright?" Bowen asked.

"...Lunch."

26.

Red faced, Bowen sat eating lunch. He could feel judgmental and frustrated eyes on him from time to time. He had opted for a Crocodon meat burger sourced from Ocker with New Appalachia style fries and salad, but he barely noticed any of it. He found a seat with Bao Bao, but due to his embarrassment fuelled exhaustion, Bowen couldn't engage in much conversation. From across the cafeteria, he spotted some of the navigation crew looking over their shoulders at him. Bowen did his best to ignore it.

Before he knew it, Bowen was standing on the serving line at dinner. Having switched places with Safiya, Bowen had his head down. He had not been looking forward to facing every single crew mate and passenger who he had held up at lunch again. Luckily, the bright light from the heat lamps mostly covered his red face. He was working next to Jungga, who had little to say to Bowen during the shift, which suited Bowen fine as he didn't want to draw more attention to himself. Inevitably he came face to face with Simon and his colleagues. Bowen did his best not to meet Simon's eye as he came down the queue. Simon thankfully took a similar approach as he passed on the veg station entirely. Bowen occasionally glanced over at Safiya at the pay station who was performing the task much more efficiently than he had at lunch.

Dinner service seemed to end as quickly as it had started. Bowen was glad that he didn't have to join in with the clean up, but on the other hand, he did have to perform the tedious task of manually inputting the data that he had recorded into the pay station. After he had eaten his own dinner as the cafeteria was becoming quieter, he pulled up a stool to the station. As the clean up crew began to work in the emptying cafeteria, Wotll arrived to show him what to do. She entrusted him with a spare key to lock up the main doors as he finished. She expected him to be working rather late. As she left him typing away carefully into the machine, Safiya emerged from the double doors of the kitchen. He sat up straight and cracked his aching neck. As he did so, he idly watched Safiya approach the vending machines. After a moment, he busied himself entering numbers.

"Hey." Safiya greeted him. Bowen looked up to see her standing across the counter. Bowen rubbed his eyes, he was beginning to lose concentration.

"Hello." he replied.

"You look like you need this." she said smiling. She put down on the counter a tall can of a drink called tusk, she had for herself a can of water. She also withdrew from her pocket a couple of Zordo bars. "I've seen you eat these a few times, I assumed you like them." Caught off by this display of charity, Bowen took a moment to reply.

"Yeah… thanks Safiya."

"You look exhausted." she said as she lifted herself up onto the counter in front of him. She crossed her legs at the knees and exposed her thighs as she motioned for him to give her the notepad. "Let me help, you'll be out of here a lot quicker." Bowen didn't protest as he handed over the pad. He cracked open the sweet smelling can of TUSK and took a swig. "Where are you up to?" she asked.

"I just entered Fibbok Pontuss." he replied. She traced her finger down the page as she flicked her loose hair over her shoulder.

"Okay next one." she began. "Kiiva Shii." She spelled it out for him as she spoke. "identification 923… 647… 111… F Yeah?"

"Got it." Bowen confirmed. To Bowen's relief, he was working quicker than he would have done otherwise. Whether it was the TUSK perking him up or Safiya's presence, he didn't know. Bowen was growing more and more tired as they went along, so he was grateful for having someone else read the names and numbers for him.

After a while, they were finished. Bowen stretched out on his stool. Looking around he saw that they were the only ones left in the cafeteria. The clean up crew had left a while ago and he hadn't noticed. Bowen yawned. "I appreciate you staying behind and helping. I'd have been here struggling if you hadn't, so thanks."

"Don't worry about it, I'm not working tomorrow." Safiya replied.

"I was so embarrassed earlier. I thought I'd be in so much trouble."

"I noticed. I saw you go bright red when you realised something had gone wrong." As she spoke she caressed her thigh idly. "So you already knew the technician girl?" Safiya asked as Bowen was unwrapping the Avalanche flavour Zordo bar that he had forgotten about.

"Vetura? Yeah sort of. I met her once before doing my laundry. She seems cool." Safiya made a noise which indicated that she heard but didn't really care for the answer.

"So how long are you on the Memento for then?" she asked. Bowen was barely noticing the strong chunky flavours of the Zordo bar as he thought over the answer.

"I'm contracted until Obelisk station and then I think I'm going back home."

"To Saxon..? Where you're from..?" she teased. Bowen exhaled and his cheeks went pink as he cringed at the memory.

"Wow, I'd almost forgotten about that." he said with a laugh.

"I'm sorry that was mean." Safiya smiled. As she spoke Bowen felt her graze his forearm with a fingertip. Bowen swallowed hard.

"So... how long are you on the ship for..?" he asked.

"I'm going back to Phoenicia at some point."

"Whereabouts on Phoenicia are you from..?" Bowen asked as she idly tucked in an exposed label on his shirt.

"The upper Crystal Canal Districts in Neo Cairo." she

replied casually.

"Wow." Bowen said impressed. "Your family could probably buy my families little farm and all the surrounding ones and not flinch." Safiya found that amusing.

"We do okay." She answered flicking her loose hair over her shoulder again. "So you're a farm boy..?" she asked. Bowen felt his face go pink again.

"Yeah we have cows, and... potatoes and stuff."

"I can tell from your hands." she said as she traced the wrinkles on his knuckles. Her amber eyes met his. "Your eyes are odd, they're nice." she stated. Bowen struggled to respond. It had taken him a moment but he was now aware that he was being flirted with. Bowen cleared his throat.

"I... like your nose ring. It's cool."

"Oh, I forget it's there." she laughed. Safiya lifted her hand and wafted her loose fitting top and said, "I forget about most of my piercings usually," Bowen couldn't help but notice that she looked down at her chest as she spoke. Bowen cleared his throat again.

"I've never had anything pierced." he said.

"It hurts for a second but then it kinda feels good." Bowen made an odd sound and attempted to pass it off as a cough. Safiya smiled. "Well it's been good talking but it's late and I want a shower." She hopped off the counter, her floral perfume wafting over him.

"Okay." Bowen said as he watched her walk to the doors.

"See you Bowen. Don't forget to lock up." She looked back at him, throwing her loose, black hair over her shoulder.

"Okay." Bowen said again rather stupidly. Safiya bit her lip as she smiled at him before leaving him alone in the cafeteria.

27.

In the following days, Bowen returned to his usual duties. After his late shift in the cafeteria, Safiya was well and truly wedged into his thoughts. She caught his eye in the galley much more than she had done previously. When their shifts happened to overlap, Bowen began to notice her watching him as they both worked. He enjoyed her attention. It shed light on how distant Jules often was in that regard. Safiya couldn't come to sit with him at meal times as their work patterns wouldn't allow it, but she would flash her eyes at him over the service line. When she worked, she wore work appropriate clothing like everyone else, but Bowen began to notice the curves beneath.

One morning Bowen was sat with Duggy in the cafeteria.

"You getting busy with her then?" Duggy jested.

"No, I don't know what you're talking about." Bowen said instantly red faced.

"Oh come on, you've started sitting where you can see the line. Right now, she's pretending to not look at you. Watch." Bowen looked over the tables of crew members at the service line where Safiya was placing more sides of freshly cooked bacon under the heat lamps.

"I don't know man I think she's just working." Bowen said.

"Nah she can't wait to look at you again." Duggy was proved right when Safiya did indeed look up from the line right at them. Bowen felt his insides jolt as their eyes met. Duggy raised his scaly black hand and waved at Safiya enthusiastically smiling at her with his rows of sharp teeth. Bowen saw Safiya look between him and Duggy with a surprised look on her face. Bowen half cringing, half laughing grabbed Duggy by the wrist and wrenched it down.

"Dude!"

"She's into you man. Check it out." Bowen saw that Safiya had returned her attention to working but with a poorly hidden smile on her face.

"Yeah well..." Bowen tried. His smile betrayed him as Duggy slapped him on the shoulder.

"You asked her on a date yet? That's what humans call it?"

"Yeah it is. But no I haven't, there hasn't been a good moment for it. And I don't think I've ever seen her in the rec deck."

"What do you mean there hasn't been a good moment she right there."

Before Bowen could respond, Duggy tried to rise from his stool. "I'm gonna go set you up now." Bowen grabbed Duggy by his sleeve.

"Don't!" Bowen cried out louder than he meant to turning some nearby heads. Duggy sat back down with a mischievous smirk and rubbed his hand over Bowen's now thickening layer of fuzzy hair.

"Nah I'm happy for you Saxon. Just be careful know what I'm saying?"

"What..?" Bowen asked as he took a mouthful of cereal.

"When you get to fucking her don't be spawning no offspring."

Bowen spluttered as he almost choked on his breakfast.

"Steady on." Bowen said wiping milk from his chin.

"When on the highways as they say."

"What does that mean?" Bowen asked. Duggy put his hand on Bowen's shoulder and motioned to the service line and the rest of the room.

"Bowen my friend, space travel gets boring. When men and women get stuffed into a big metal box like the Memento for months on end it's inevitable. It's hard to get out alive. Doesn't matter if it's a station, a science base, military outpost, free trader vessel. Sex palaces, every one of them." Bowen knew he had gone bright red but he couldn't contain his smile. "Just don't keep her waiting."

28.

Duggy's words bounced around Bowen's mind over the next few days. Safiya seemed to keep to herself when not working, much to Bowen's frustration. He was eager to spend more time with her, if he could only catch her somewhere besides over the service line or in the hectic galley. When he did approach her about such a thing, he would very much like to have not smelled of the cleaning products that he worked with.

After a busy lunch rush, Bowen entered the cafeteria with Ellbo and Roo to start the collection. The room was emptying as normal and there were still people around like always. The staff were finishing up their work in the kitchen and were clattering about as normal and the sound permeated into the cafeteria. Bowen winced and wiggled his finger into his ear as he felt a small, niggling pain. He put it out of his mind and got to work. As he began, Bowen noticed a table with the navigation crew sat around waiting out the end of lunch. Simon wasn't with them. Across the room by the windows he noticed Vetura sitting alone at a table with a can of TUSK, listening to music on her headphones. As Bowen cleared away a table close to her she noticed him and smiled. He smiled back and nodded.

Roo was being particularly uncooperative on the collection and his behaviour was drawing Bowen's attention. Unlike the others, Roo often didn't scrape the plates into the slop bucket. Bowen returned with an armful of trays as Roo had reached the trolley with handfuls of cutlery. Ellbo was currently wiping down tables as they went.

"You know it's not difficult to clean the plate before you stack it." Bowen stated as he began to scrape food out of a bowl.

"The quicker we get done the quicker I can get out of here." Roo responded, his purple skin flaring more red.

"Okay, but it only causes more problems for the ones working the blitzer. Not scraping gives them more work."

Roo began tossing cutlery into their assortment slots without a care as to which ones went where. Bowen could feel his anger mounting. He also could tell that they were being watched.

"Honestly, I don't care." Roo said.

"No? Well maybe if you just…"

"What..?" Roo seemed to want Bowen to start something. He was standing in front of Bowen with his hands on his hips, looking up at him defiantly. But Bowen had something else to worry about. The niggling pain in his ear had increased suddenly. It expanded and it seemed to travel behind his eyes and through to his other ear. Bowen closed his eyes and raised his hand to his head. "What..?" Roo repeated. "What's up with you?" The pain in Bowen's head was causing his eyes to burn. Roo's mouth didn't match with what he had said. When Bowen tried to speak he let out a yell of pain as a piercing frequency shot through his brain. It caused him to lean on the collection trolley to steady himself. Managing to open his strained eyes he tried to look for Vetura, but her back was turned and she was still wearing her headphones. Ellbo was down the other end of the cafeteria. Desperately, he attempted to communicate his sensation to Roo.

"My ears… My head." he tried. He looked at Roo for some form of help. The pain was becoming excruciating.

"Tibab…? Mo-ab tibab?" Roo said. Bowen blinked.

"…What…!?"

"Tibab..!? Yonib to-mam ibab!?" Bowen began to panic. His heart was racing and his head felt as though it was about to explode. Bowen managed to steady himself from the collection trolley with his now sweaty hands. His breathing began to quicken as he fumbled his way over to Ellbo who had his back to him cleaning the tables. Bowen reached him and put his hand on his shoulder.

"Ellbo… help." Bowen managed. Ellbo turned around.

"Zishush? Vuss vazoosh?" Bowen stumbled back from Ellbo and knocked over a stool. He could no longer understand anyone. The pain was impairing his ability to think. A human, he needed to find another human. Safiya. Maybe she was still in the galley. Bowen's heart was pounding in his chest as he stumbled over to the double doors. Roo shouted for Bowen in his alien language, but he didn't stop. Bowen barged through into the noisy and steamy kitchen and called out in desperation.

"Safiya!?" The pain in his head was pounding as it bounced from ear to ear. Every few seconds he heard what sounded like screeching transmissions inside his head. They were beginning to wrench his brain. The pain was so severe that he fell against one of the counter tops and knocked over a stack of dirty pans. He felt a hand grab his arm as someone tried to steady him. Through his painful, squinting eyes he saw that he was surrounded by people. Duggy had him by the shoulders in his strong scaly hands. Duggy tried to speak to Bowen as he helped him stand, but when he did, all Bowen heard was a terrifying hissing mixed with a very animalistic guttural nattering. Bowen recoiled in fear. Duggy turned his head and screeched into the kitchen, his black jaws vibrating as he did so. Bowen closed his eyes again from the pain as Roo and Ellbo came into the kitchen. Bowen could not make sense of anything that was being said to him.

Suddenly, Safiya's face came through the noisy crowd and Bowen fell towards her with arms outstretched.

"Safiya... help me... my ears... my head." Safiya looked at him carefully. She, like most others had a concerned look on her face. She turned and spoke to Wotll who had squashed herself into the throng of staff. When Safiya spoke, Bowen was dismayed to hear what he assumed was the language of Phoenicia. Safiya then turned to Bowen and held him by the shoulders. Through the pain and confusion Bowen was surprised at how strong her grip was on him. To his relief, she spoke slowly to him in Saxon.

"Bowen… what is problem please..?" The crowd all seemed to go quiet to listen to what he had to say.

"My ears, it hurts. And, my eyes. I can't understand anyone." The pain and the heat of the kitchen made Bowen feel as though he were going to vomit. Safiya turned to Wotll and again spoke in her native Phoenician.

"Loorkithruuk. Ruthimoork ithikii." Wotll said, her throat wobbling and inflating. Safiya then turned to Bowen again and spoke as clearly as she could.

"Bowen… I help… hospital… doctor." The next thing Bowen knew he was being supported by Safiya and Bao Bao and he had very little control over where he was going. He felt his feet touch the floor but between them, Safiya and Bao Bao walked him to one of the delivery doors at the back of the kitchen. Through the haze of pain, Bowen squinted his burning eyes and saw that they were in the access corridor that led to the cargo lifts. Bao Bao helped Safiya with Bowen to the lift where he left them to it. Just before Bowen saw the heavy metal doors slowly shut together, he saw Bao Bao wave at him with his tattooed hand and he spoke something in Gantanese that culminated in a belly jiggling laugh and a big friendly smile. Bowen smiled back very weakly as the doors closed leaving him alone with Safiya.

Safiya supported him with her shoulder as his head felt as though it were ten times the weight it normally should be. In the miasma of pain Bowen's head also filled with the smell of Safiya's perfume. He heard Safiya say something quietly in Phoenician. Bowen tried to speak but he was worried if he opened his mouth he would throw up all over her. He simply closed his eyes and accepted that he was totally out of control of the situation. Bowen felt the lift start moving upwards for a minute and then sideways for a short time. Bowen felt his stomach lurch when the motions shifted. His shattered ears heard the outer metal pullies and gears whirring and grinding. After a short time, the doors opened again and Safiya moved him along. He heard the muffled footsteps of crew members as well as an array of alien voices that made no sense.

"No worry ...negative," Safiya said in poor Saxon. "Doctor make you good yes."

"Okay." Bowen said simply. His brain felt as though it were trying to escape his head. Bowen's legs were becoming weak from the pain as Safiya walked him through the corridors. Before long, he could smell a sterile environment and he heard the sound of compressing air and shrill beeping that pierced his head. Again Bowen heard odd voices from his alien crew mates. When he tried to open his eyes, the light from above was far too bright. He heard Safiya speak her native tongue with a flare of urgency. She was answered by unusual alien voices before he felt Safiya's reassuring grip leave him.

"You Bowen safe. Help hospital." she said as she let go of him. The pain that radiated from ear to ear had reached a horrific climax as he felt multiple rubber hands carefully yet firmly take him and escort him away. Bowen found himself being lay on a bed under a bright lamp. He could not open his eyes for the pain. Chattering alien voices spoke to one another as they fussed around him. He felt a rubber finger gently pull one of his eye lids up. He almost heard the light as it scorched his mind and he instinctively tried to look away. Bowen's breathing had become rapid as he heard the nurses get to work around him. He hoped Safiya was still in the room but he couldn't know. He felt the latex hands wipe his arm with a cold gel and then he felt an instant of sharp pain as they injected him with a needle.

From somewhere else in the room came different sounds. Heavy metal footfalls entered the room and were accompanied by what sounded like small jets of air and pistons firing. Bowen's painful ears followed the noise until it stopped by his head. A nurse was touching his arm that had begun to feel cool and tingly. A hot sensation struck his neck as something began to scan his bio chip. He heard a series of static frequencies adjusting and muffled switches being flicked. Then a man's voice came. A clear and well spoken voice that sounded like it was playing through a small speaker system. The voice spoke to him in perfect Saxon.

"Hello Bowen. Can you understand me? Just nod if so." Bowen nodded weakly with his eyes still shut. He heard a muffled rush of fluids and a small jet of air as the voice continued. "Excellent. Now then Bowen, I'm Doctor Jinn-Quo, it's a pleasure to meet you." Bowen smiled weakly as the cool sensation from his arm began to climb up to his chest. "You're in the surgery and you're in good hands." As Doctor Jinn-Quo spoke he felt the nurse caress his arm reassuringly. "We've given you a general painkiller solution whilst we look into what's happened. It appears you've suffered an unfortunate malfunction with your translation implants." Bowen took a deep breath. "Is your pain easing?" Bowen nodded again. "Good, good." Jinn-Quo continued. "The painkiller will do its work. If you feel yourself drifting off just let it happen." Bowen breathed a sigh of relief as his head began to feel cool and his pain eased away.

He heard the doctor speaking in another language to the nurses who began to fuss around him again taking his blood pressure and temperature. As Jinn-Quo worked, he heard clacking away at computer terminal keys and more beeping. Again he heard the doctor speak in Saxon. "It's a good thing miss Haddad brought you here so quickly or there may have been risk of serious damage." He heard the doctor shift around to the side. Bowen then felt a pair of rubber hands grip the sides of his head gently as the nurse held him in place. Bowen's head still throbbed, but it was much less than it had been. The doctor spoke again as Bowen's head began to swim. "Don't worry Bowen we're going to fix you."

He heard a mechanical jet of air again as a large contraption was brought down from the ceiling. Bowen suddenly remembered being in Doctor Dietrich's office with his dad. He heard vaguely familiar sounds as Jinn-Quo prepared his large operating machines. Bowen felt two soft cushions against his ears that muffled all sounds. His breathing had slowed to a relaxed pace as he saw faces swim through his mind. His parents, Jules and Simon, then Safiya, Moryys, Captain Quinn and finally Vetura.

Not a minute had gone by when Bowen had fallen into an induced sleep.

29.

Sometime later, Bowen opened his eyes in a quiet, dimly lit room. He felt comfortable and warm. His head felt delicate but it no longer hurt and his eyes stung a little. The low hum of the ships engines was accompanied by a constant beeping sound from a series of machines next to his bed. His right arm was encased in a fabric sleeve. Movement from the corner of the room caught his eye.

"Don't remove that." a woman's voice said. She emerged from the low lit corner of the room where she had been sitting at a small terminal. Dressed in her full medical uniform the nurse was head to toe in clunky metal and sleek, sterile rubber. Around her shoulders she wore a mechanical harness that sported a third robotic arm. Her voice came through in a slightly computerized tone from the chunky head gear that she wore. The breathing apparatus on her back inflated and depressed as she spoke. "How do you feel Mr. Rhys?" she asked him. Bowen cleared his throat as the nurse began to fuss over him. On her long overcoat next to her clip on timepiece her name tag read "Ulla".

"I think I'm okay." Bowen replied.

"Good. I'm just going to take some readings of your vitals and some blood." Ulla said. As she worked Bowen saw she was very tall. Despite him not being able to see her full face due to her sterilized clothing and medical gear, she had a soothing presence. In the small gaps in her uniform, he saw that her skin was a deep pink. "Sharp scratch." Ulla said as she inserted a needle to take some of his blood. Bowen hardly registered the pain. He looked away as the blood filled the vial and saw that there were three other beds in the room, but they were all empty.

"How long have I been here?" Bowen asked groggily.

"A few hours." she replied as she withdrew the needle

from his arm. "Doctor Jinn-Quo fixed you up in just under three hours and we brought you in here. I've just been monitoring you while you came back around."

"Oh." Bowen said sleepily. Ulla glided over to the terminal.

"You can understand me which is a good sign," she said. "You wouldn't be able to if the procedure hadn't been successful."

"What did you do?" Bowen asked. He watched as Ulla placed the blood vial into a machine and began clicking away on her terminal.

"Doctor Jinn-Quo replaced your implants. You've now got the E Series as opposed to the basic B Series you had previously."

"Right."

"It's no different really." Ulla said. "But it runs better. Everything looks good here, your body has accepted the implants with no issue. Now I just need to do a small test." She withdrew a small file from one of the large wall cabinets and she came back to his bed. She helped him sit up as she propped him up with his pillows. She perched on the end of his bed and Bowen saw that she was at least seven foot tall. He watched as she took out some small cards from the file. "Now then could you please read these aloud to me if you can." Bowen cleared his throat and read the card that she held in front of him.

"Hello." Bowen read.

"Good." Ulla said as she switched to the next one.

"Could you please direct me to the departure lounge?" he said.

"Excellent, and this one?" Bowen read more and more cards with increasingly complex sentences until they were done. Ulla put them away in the file.

"Right then well done, you just read words and passages from over forty registered federation languages." Just then there was a beep from the door. "Come in" Ulla called. The door opened and in walked Doctor Jinn-Quo. This was the first time Bowen had gotten a proper look at him since he glimpsed him at the Captain's briefing. The Doctor clanked his way over to the other side of the bed where he came to a stop. Bowen was fascinated to see that the Doctor's suit was full of a light blue fluid. He observed Bowen through a clear, wide view port in his head piece. Jinn-Quo's face looked as though he was a humanoid jellyfish. From his suit, his well spoken voice came through again from a speaker.

"Good evening Bowen, how are we feeling?"

"Okay thank you." Bowen replied. "Do you know what caused my implants to malfunction?"

"Unfortunately no." Jinn-Quo replied puzzled. "Some specific types of energy frequencies can interfere with the implants but yours began to shut down suddenly. This sort of occurrence never usually happens without intent... However it shouldn't happen again we gave you an upgrade didn't we Ulla?" Jinn-Quo said smiling. As he did so, Bowen thought he could see through his skin almost past his delicate eyes to his brain. As the doctor spoke, small fronds from his chin constantly reached out and pressed buttons and pulled small switches right in front of his face within the head piece of his uniform. Ulla got up from Bowen's bed and moved back over to her terminal as the doctor continued. "So just in case, I'm going to send you away with a series of painkillers and I'm giving you some eye protection while your eyes adjust to normality." Bowen watched as Ulla returned from her terminal and handed him a sleeve of blue pills and what to Bowen looked like reflective sunglasses with one singular lens. They were in a sealed and sterile plastic bag.

"Perhaps put them on now before we discharge you." Ulla recommended. Bowen ripped open the bag and felt a little silly, but he put them on, plunging the already dim room into near total darkness.

"Now then." said Jinn-Quo, "I have contacted your supervisor, Wotll Ungamuzh and I've explained the situation and you are to have a few days paid leave to recover.

"Thanks doctor that's really helpful." Bowen said as Ulla began to peel off his fabric sleeve to disconnect him from the machines. The doctor began configuring his suit with a few presses of buttons on his wrist mounted computer and began to leave.

"Not at all Mister Rhys I am sworn to ensure the health of all onboard. Miss Haddad is waiting for you I believe."

"Safiya waited for me?" Bowen asked Ulla.

"She did indeed." Ulla replied as she helped him swing his legs off the bed. "Here let me." Ulla said as she began to put Bowen's shoes on for him. He felt her rubber hands on his ankles in the dark. He thanked her and she helped him stand out of the bed. Ulla walked Bowen to his door into the bright main room of the surgery. "So how long have you and Miss Haddad been together?" Bowen felt his face flush with red as he fumbled his reply.

"Oh, we..."

"Bowen!" Through his shades he saw Safiya stand from a leather waiting room chair. "Are you alright? Is he alright?" she asked them both. Bowen attempted to hide his smile.

"He'll be okay, we've given him painkillers and the glasses to help his eyes recover easier." Ulla replied.

"Yeah I'm alright." he confirmed.

"I was starting to worry," Safiya said. Bowen's insides clenched in a good way.

"Best not to go anywhere too loud or too bright for this evening." Ulla instructed.

"Thank you, I'll look after him." Safiya said. She took his hand and began escorting him away. Bowen looked down at his hand in hers. Even though he could barely see with his shades on in the evening lights of the corridors, Bowen saw Safiya for the first time in clothes other than for work. She wore a loose fitting top with exposed shoulders and snug, form fitting leggings. She wore yet another headscarf, this time a sunset yellow, with her black hair loosely contained. She had with her a colourful knitted messenger bag. Bowen smiled.

"I bet you're starving, you've missed dinner." she said.

"I am." Bowen said just as his stomach grumbled.

"Well don't worry I'll sort you out."

Once again, Bowen was being escorted around the ship without the ability to see very well by Safiya. The thought made him smile. "Somewhere quiet and not too bright…" Safiya said to herself. Bowen just let her walk him around the ship, hand in hand. Her hand felt soft and smooth in his. He couldn't tell if it was deliberate or not, but occasionally she would caress his hand with her thumb as they walked around. Her perfume wafted into his nose at every slight turn of her head or when she flicked loose hair over her shoulder. Underneath his hunger was another sensation he hadn't felt since the last time he was with Jules.

His head still felt delicate with occasional pangs of pain, but it was minor. Wearing the shaded sunglasses helped, but he found himself still closing his eyes as they were quite strained. Before long, Bowen heard their footsteps echoing in the atrium by the observation deck. He knew where she was taking him.

"Here we are." Safiya said as she pushed open the sound proofed door and led him inside. Now Bowen could see absolutely nothing in the tunnel. Safiya gripped his hand tighter as she slowly led him inside. Bowen's heart had begun to flutter a little. His stomach was now audibly complaining too. As they rounded the last corner and entered the observation room the dim blue glow from the highway danced like water on the walls. Bowen could now see more or less even with the glasses. "Have you been in here before?" Safiya asked him.

"Yeah once." Bowen said remembering the failed meet up with Simon.

"I haven't been in here since I first joined the ship." she replied. He felt her guide him to one of the lowest chairs in the room. He gripped Safiya's hand tight as she helped him sit down. Bowen took a deep breath as he relaxed into the comfy seat. "I'm going to get you some food, don't go anywhere." Bowen's heart stammered for a moment.

"You will come back won't you..?" he asked without thinking. Safiya turned back to him and seemed a little shocked by the question.

"Of course I will." she replied. She was but a curvy, dark shape to Bowen against the huge windows but he saw her approach him slowly. He felt her hand on his forearm and he smelled her perfume as she leant down to him and kissed him on the head. "I won't be long." She said quietly. Bowen didn't know how to react. He heard Safiya's running shoes against the carpeted floor as she exited the room. He saw her disappear into the gloom as he was once again alone on the observation deck. He closed his eyes and rested his head back into the chair. He felt almost overwhelmed. It was more than obvious to him that Safiya liked him. Why else would she have stayed behind with him that night to help him correct his embarrassing mistake at the pay station? All at once his mind began to replay every time she had shot him a glance and he hadn't picked up on it. He felt foolish.

A short time passed and Bowen had nodded off. The Observation deck was by far the quietest part of the Memento he had yet seen. The sound of the engines couldn't be heard through the walls unlike many other places. He was awoken by Safiya's touch as she returned. She had taken care to quietly enter the room again and she gently shook his arm.

"Hey." she said. Bowen sat up after having slumped in his chair and he rubbed the back of his neck and head.

"You're back." Bowen said sleepily.

"I told you I would be."

Bowen could see a rough outline of her messenger bag that was slightly bulging. His stomach knew what was inside before his brain did. Safiya began to remove a few of the comfy seat cushions from the chairs and she lay them out on the floor. Bowen felt her soft hand grasp him by the wrist as she pulled him to his feet slowly. She carefully sat him down before she took a seat for herself opposite him.

"How's your head?" she asked him as she began to withdraw items from her bag.

"Better. But it feels fragile."

Safiya made a sympathetic noise.

"Here I found this for you." she said handing him something. Bowen felt a warm and long foil package in his hands with some weight to it.

"What is it?"

"Metro style pizza foot long"

"Oh damn." Bowen said as he unwrapped it.

"Is that okay..?"

Bowen replied with an affirmative noise as his mouth was already full. Safiya chuckled. "Good. I put it aside for you in case you missed dinner."

"I appreciate it." Bowen said as his finished his mouthful.

"It's okay."

Bowen thought he could hear her smile as she spoke. Safiya retrieved two cans of water and opened one for herself. She pushed the other over towards him. She also passed him a Zordo bar. For a little while, the two sat in a comfortable silence as Safiya watched Bowen eat his sandwich. He might have merely been starving or perhaps it was the company, but the foot long sandwich was the best thing he had eaten in days. He took a deep breath as he finished it.

"Thanks Safie." he said.

"You're welcome." she said with a smile.

"What?" Bowen asked as he carefully cracked open the can of water. He saw her outline as Safiya looked down.

"Nothing, my daddy calls me Safie."

"Oh, my bad. I won't say it." Bowen said awkwardly.

"Please do." she reached over to him with her hand. He flinched a little as she touched his face. "You've got cheese on your chin." she said with a laugh as she caressed his stubble.

"Well I did almost go blind today." Bowen jested.

"I'm glad you didn't"

"Me too." He patted on the floor in front of himself as he felt for the Zordo bar. "What have you got me this time?"

"I think it's Point Blank flavour."

"Nice that's a good one."

"I'm glad I didn't mess this up." Safiya said. Bowen could see the vague shape of her playing with her head scarf in her fingers. "How are your eyes?" she asked him.

"I think they're alright. They feel like, you know when you haven't slept at all?"

"Yeah, that sucks." Again she made a sympathetic noise "Well when you've eaten that take a couple of those painkillers." Bowen was not about to argue. He smiled as he finished his Zordo bar.

"What?" Safiya asked him.

"Nothing." Bowen replied. "Just, thanks for looking after me."

Safiya didn't reply, but he thought he saw a smile on her face through the gloom. She began to play with a strand of hair again. He carefully opened the sleeve of the small blue pills. After downing them with a few swigs of his can of water he took a deep breath. He could see Safiya's outline. She appeared to be quietly fussing with her top. Bowen turned his head and looked out of the window. The highway was still beautiful to him even through the shaded glasses he wore. Safiya sighed.

"You know, it's nice to spend some time with another human, even though technically you are an alien to me and vice versa."

"I know what you mean." Bowen replied looking out the window. He thought of Simon. "There are a handful of other humans on board though." he said.

"There are, but I don't know any of them."

"What about Bao Bao? You work with him." Bowen said. Safiya made a dismissive noise.

"Barely, he's not really the sort of person I'd like to get to know better." Bowen swallowed.

"So, tell me about you..." Bowen immediately cringed. "I'm sorry that was such a line." Safiya laughed. "You're cute." she said.

Bowen felt his face go pink and hoped the light of the observation deck would hide it. "There's not much to tell really. I'm from Neo Cairo on Phoenicia." she said. "I have an older brother Jerick. My family owns the restaurant chain Golden Crescent."

"That's impressive."

"Really?"

"Definitely. I'm not sure there is one on all Saxon, it's a bit too expensive for anyone back home. Didn't they film the assassination scene from Midnight Silver in a Golden Crescent on Metro..?"

"That's right. My daddy was there for that."

"Well I'm impressed. Meaning no offence or anything, but what are you doing on a free trader ship of all places?" He saw Safiya look out the window as she considered her answer.

"I'm supposed to take over the business in a couple of years and I don't feel ready for it. I'm not even sure that's what I want to do. The Memento was docked at the Emerald Ports and I think I just wanted to get away for a while. I managed to twist the truth to my parents that I would be assistant head chef onboard, as well as the Memento being a Leisure Fleet ship." Bowen felt a pang of guilt as he remembered how he and his father had lied to his mother about the nature of the Memento.

"That must have been difficult."

"And on top of that, I think my parents are setting me up for a marriage in the near future."

"Oh?"

"The same thing happened to Jerick. They arranged for him to be wed to the daughter of a winery empire. He's perfectly happy though. They started having children immediately and they are making a lot of money together."

"What does your brother do?"

"Do you know of the Hyper Sonic 9000 event on Metro?"

Safiya asked.

"Yeah I've watched it a few times, it's pretty intense." Bowen replied.

"Well he owns the Gilded Raceway Company, so he owns the event along with a few others."

"That's serious money." Bowen said in awe. He remembered seeing the races on tv with his dad a few years ago. Whole zones of the city planet were closed off for the race and millions of spectators from all over the galaxy flocked to see the state of the art hover cars blast their way through the streets.

"It is."Safiya said.

Bowen took a long swig of water.

"So..." he began. "Whose this guy who your parents are gonna set you up with?" he asked cautiously.

Safiya sighed.

"I don't know him. He's called Kadir, or Kaled, I don't remember. He's the eldest son of a family who owns some casinos."

Bowen felt rather insignificant. He couldn't help but compare what he was imagining of Safiya's life to his own. He rubbed the back of his neck.

"So, you don't want all that?"

"No... Not yet anyway. It's all been planned out for me and I don't like it. I haven't had a chance to get out on my own, so I felt like I had to get away before my chances disappear."

"I know how you feel." Bowen said. "All of my friends left Saxon one after another."

"That must have been hard."

"It was. For a while it was just me, Simon and Jules. But then Jules left too..." He paused for a moment.

"What happened to your friend Simon?" Safiya asked.

Bowen scoffed a laugh before he answered.

"He's somewhere on the Memento right now."

"Oh right... Is he that guy I saw you talking to in the cafeteria a while ago? From Navigation?"

"Yeah that's him." Bowen sighed.

"Did you board the ship together?"

"No we didn't."

"So... do you see much of him?"

"No. No I don't."

"Is it your shift patterns?"

"No." Bowen replied with a sigh.

Safiya seemed to shuffle in her seat.

"Why's that..?" she asked.

Bowen took a swig of water before he considered his answer.

"It's sort of complicated. I wouldn't want to unload it onto you."

"Feel free to. If you need to talk I'm listening." she offered. Bowen smiled.

"To tell you the truth, I'm not sure what I'm even doing here any more. On the Memento I mean." Through the gloom he saw Safiya cross her legs and sit up to attention for him. He took a deep breath and continued. "So, my friend Jules... Juliette. She ups and leaves Saxon without telling me for a job on a Leisure Fleet ship. And I end up discovering this from a throw away comment from Simon when were hanging out. He told me about the job in the galley, well it slipped out from him really... and I kinda just went for it because like you were saying, there might not be many chances to get away. And after all, I ended up studying a dying subject that didn't lead to the career I wanted."

"What was that?"

"I studied Agricultural Sciences. But by the time I finished college, the federation was beginning its mechanisation of farming and everything was becoming more automated."

"That must have been frustrating."

"It was. So I spent the last few years helping out around the farm while endlessly applying for jobs that I have no experience or education in."

Safiya played with her hair as she listened.

"I can imagine that was difficult. I feel bad now complaining about my problems."

"No don't feel bad." Bowen said.

"If someone had asked you ten years ago what would you be doing now?" Safiya asked.

"Oh yeah don't." Bowen replied. They both laughed.

"Okay if you could be doing anything with your life right now, what would it be?" Bowen asked.

"Ooh I don't know." Safiya said. "I've always wanted to attend fashion shows. Maybe as a journalist."

"Yeah?" Bowen smiled.

"Yeah, what about you?" Safiya asked.

"I don't even know. When I was little I, no that's embarrassing…"

"No go on."

"No it's stupid."

"Please." Safiya said. As she did so her hand found his knee.

"Okay well, I used to imagine I could be a spaceship Captain and fly around the galaxy fighting pirates and monsters."

"That's the sweetest thing." Safiya squeed.

Bowen smiled.

"I'm probably just gonna stay on Saxon though. I'd like to have my own farm in the Northern Reaches growing vegetables. Perhaps put my education to some use. I'd be happy with a small cottage."

"That sounds nice."

"It gets cold up there but it's a nice country. The hills and the coastlines and all that."

"I'd like to see it one day." Safiya said stroking his leg.

"I'd love to see Neo Cairo I bet it's amazing."

"It's alright." she said. "It gets hot." There was a moment of quiet as they sat together. Through his dark shades he caught himself admiring the details of her he could make out.

"So this friend, Juliette." Safiya said finally.

"Yeah?"

"Was she your girlfriend..?"

"Sort of." Bowen admitted.

"You have a history though?" Safiya assumed.

"We do. And I feel like Simon has more of a part in it than I thought."

"That sounds like a lot of drama."

"Yeah." Bowen said looking down at the floor.

"Do you think they were spending time with each other behind your back?" she asked. Bowen didn't look up from the floor as he felt his eyes begin to water. Perhaps it was after all his eyes had been through that day, or it could have been the fact that it had finally been said out loud. He nodded. Safiya shuffled closer to him and she placed her hand on his arm.

"I can understand you wanting to get away from all of that." Bowen sniffed and wiped his face.

"I feel like Simon resents me for following him and he's done a good job of avoiding me since I joined the crew. You know how I said I'd been in here once before?"

"Yeah?"

"He arranged to meet me here a couple of months ago and he never showed up. I was in here for three hours on my own."

"That's awful. I'm sorry that happened. He sounds like a bad friend."

"I don't know what changed over the years." Bowen wondered out loud.

"People change." Safiya said simply. Her words hit Bowen. He stretched his leg out and winced as his it had fallen asleep. "Come on lets stretch your legs." Safiya said. She gripped his hands and stood up gracefully. He pulled himself up and he found himself stood right in front of her. With his shades still on he looked down into her face. She took his hand and walked him down the long window of the observation deck.

"Hows your pain?" she asked.

"It's better now thanks. My painkillers have kicked in."

"Good."

Bowen held her hand and with his other he held the metal rail before the window.

"You know Doctor Jinn-Quo said that if you hadn't got me to the surgery so quickly I might have suffered more serious damage to my eyes and ears."

"Really?"

Bowen stopped walking and turned to face her.

"Yeah, so thank you. Seriously."

"How are your eyes..?"

"I think they're okay now." he said. She turned him to the side so that the light from the highway illuminated him. She gently raised her hands and removed his shades. The blue light from the highway spilled into his vision and illuminated the whole room and Safiya herself. He took the glasses out of her hands and put them in his pocket. The light from the highway glinted off of her nose ring and pierced ears. She was looking into him with with her big, amber eyes.

"How's that?" she asked as she gently squeezed his hand.

"It's fine. It doesn't hurt any more."

"Good." It was only then that he realised that she had cupped the side of his face with her other hand. He leant into her touch for a moment. "I love your eyes." she said quietly.

"You do?"

Their faces became closer.

"Yeah."

The smell of her perfume filled his head and it soothed his mind. His free hand found its way to the small of her back and he pulled her closer. The light from the highway illuminated them both as they shared a long kiss.

30.

A few rotations passed. One morning, Bowen was sitting at breakfast with Moryys who was eating his way through a plate of meat and eggs. Safiya smiled at Bowen from over the service line to which Moryys gave him a playful nudge with his huge elbow. Inevitably, the guys had caught on about him and Safiya. Bowen enjoyed her company a couple of times a week when their work allowed time for it. They would find quiet spots around the ship, in observation or the rec deck. Bowen enjoyed having someone to talk to on a more personal level. Safiya seemed like a good listener and she would tell him her problems also. Often their conversations would morph into kissing.

Occasionally they were seen walking to the observation deck together which garnered gentle teasing when he spent time with any of the guys in the cafeteria or the rec deck. Bowen and Moryys had gravitated towards each other also. Bowen could talk to him about things that the others couldn't, movies and video games and the like. Bowen had even felt comfortable enough with Moryys once or twice to talk about more personal things. Bowen's thoughts were shook when Simon approached him and Moryys at breakfast.

"Hey Bowen how are you doing?" he asked casually. Bowen swallowed his mouthful of food hard.

"Hey. I'm doing fine. You?"

"I'm alright." Simon replied. Simon looked around the cafeteria as well as awkwardly towards Moryys.

"Oh hey, Si this is my friend Moryys. Moryys this is my friend Simon I told you about from home." Moryys stood up from his stool and towered over Simon to greet him.

"Hey hows it going?" Moryys said with an outstretched hand. Bowen smiled as Simon looked incredibly awkward when they shook hands. Simon's hand was tiny in comparison to Moryys'.

"Hi." Simon replied as Moryys sat back down. "So, I heard about what happened a while back, are you alright?"

"I am. How did you hear about that?" Bowen asked. It was unusual for Simon to express concern.

"Word got around that one of the galley staff had ended up in the surgery. And when I found out it was you I got worried."

"Oh." Bowen replied.

"So... what happened?" Simon asked as he shuffled on the spot.

"My implants messed up. I could have gone blind and deaf if I hadn't got to the doctor in time." Simon again was looking around the cafeteria rather than looking at Bowen.

"Well I'm glad you didn't, cybernetics are super expensive."

"Really."

"Anyway I've gotta go man, got a lot of work to do before we land at Davarak."

"Sounds important." Bowen said. Simon seemed not to hear the layer of sarcasm in his voice. Simon clapped Bowen on the shoulder and gripped him hard for an instant.

"Okay man see you round." he said. Bowen didn't respond as Simon walked away briskly.

"See you around yeah?" Moryys called after Simon who didn't turn back. "Yeah he seems great." Moryys said.

"You ever been to Davarak?" Bowen asked Moryys as he lazily played with his toast.

"No. Not much there apparently. A lot of red sand and rocks."

"I can't wait to see it." Bowen said. He was excited to see his first alien world. "What about this Oasis City we're stopping at?" Bowen asked. Moryys suppressed a burp.

"It's probably like most other rest stops out there. Somewhere to drink, sample some local flavours and such."

"Well I hope we can at least stretch our legs a bit. I might like to go and take some photographs."

"All I know is that me and the cargo boys will be pretty busy when we land. We're exporting almost half the containers and taking on some more stuff. The refuelling will take a few days too." The ambience of the cafeteria was disrupted by the announcement signal from the overhead speakers from Officer Garber.

"Attention. All crew members will be required to attend the Captain's briefing this evening immediately following dinner service. This message will repeat throughout the day. Officer Sol Garber signing off." The sounds of the cafeteria resumed.

"What are you doing tonight? You wanna hang out?" Moryys asked. "I got some drink in a cooler and I picked up a few video tapes from Gricky's. We need a rematch on Quad Shot Trigger X too after last time."

"Yeah sure sounds good."

***

That evening after dinner, the cafeteria was full of crew awaiting the briefing. Duggy's purple cigarette smoke clung to the air above them as Gricky idly shuffled a fresh deck of Usurper cards in his hands. Moryys and Ramphry were engaged in a rather intense game of Sun, Ship, Station, their opposed fists changing with each round counted down.

The cafeteria was bustling as the bridge crew came through the double doors. As Lennox and Garber entered, their presence forced a hush that fell over the echoing room. Garber's sweeping trench coat billowed behind her as she walked and Lennox was playing with a cigar between his fingers.

"Captain on deck!" Garber announced silencing the last of the chatter. Bowen watched Captain Quinn enter and take his place in front of the crew. He shuffled on his stool. He was closer to the Captain there than he had been during the briefing at Pennine station. The Captain's jacket bore old federation naval fleet symbols as well as a few patches he didn't recognise. Behind the white vest top the Captain wore beneath his jacket, Bowen caught a glimpse of yet more cybernetics that seemed to reach up to his neck from his chest. The Captain's robotic yellow eye seemed to scan the room. Bowen swallowed as he was sure he saw it move independently over towards their table. Lennox lit his cigar and set it between his teeth as Captain Quinn began.

"In approximately twelve hours we will pass through Ganderonn's Gate in the Yandehark system. From there it is a four hour flight to land at Oasis City on the planet Davarak. Whilst in port we will be trading with two other Free Trader vessels, the Storm Raven and Bastard Titan. It will take a few days to refuel and to finalise cargo deals, we may be planetside for a week maybe more. It is encouraged that crew members stretch their legs and make use of real gravity, however do not leave the city lest you be severed from the crew. Is that clear?" There was a murmur of acknowledgment from the room.

Garber stepped forwards.

"Anyone who has not done so already may apply for a shore leave pass from myself. But there will be no trouble making with the locals or other spacers, understood?" There was another ripple of recognition.

Quinn looked around the room towards Wotll and the kitchen staff.

"Lunch may be delayed as we land," he said. "But crew members are free to explore the city as soon as we make port." This comment caused another murmur of chatter around the crew. "Questions?" Quinn asked the room. There was no affirmative response.

Lennox moved his cigar around in his mouth as he spoke up.

"As you were then!" he shouted. Bowen watched as the Captain and Lennox left together as the room began to shuffle. Bowen stood to don his apron and hat to begin the clean up but then realised Garber was approaching their table.

"Ma'am." Moryys acknowledged her.

"Gentlemen." she addressed them. Bowen had forgotten how tall she was as he looked up at her. Her pink eyes fell on him.

"Mr. Rhys." she greeted him

"Officer Garber." Bowen replied nervously.

"Are you scheduled to work tomorrow?" she asked.

Duggy answered for him as he floundered to answer.

"No he isn't." he said.

"Yeah, no I'm not." Bowen confirmed.

"After breakfast the Captain wants to see you." Garber said. Bowen was stunned.

"Oh, okay." he replied.

"Make your way up to the main deck. Follow the signs to the Captain's quarters and don't keep him waiting. Understood?" she asked. Bowen swallowed hard.

"Yes ma'am."

"Good. As you were. Gentlemen." she said to the table. Her trench coat billowed as she turned to leave. Bowen turned to his friends with his mouth open.

"Weird." Gricky said.

"You said it." Moryys replied.

"Asking if you're free tomorrow, I thought she was about to ask you up to her cabin never mind the Captain's." Duggy teased.

"What does the Captain want to see me for?" Bowen asked no one in particular.

"Don't freak out, maybe it's nothing." Moryys reassured him.

"Does the Captain often invite crew up for a chat?" Bowen asked. They all looked around at each other.

"No." Ramphry answered bluntly.

***

Bowen couldn't concentrate on the clean up shift. The evening went by in a blur and soon he found himself knocking at Moryys' cabin door. His huge frame filled the doorway as he opened up. Bowen smiled as he looked up at Moryys' big head. He was wearing loose grey sweats and a baggy, blue vest top over his muscular torso. Moryys grinned at him with his large teeth.

"Sorry I'm a bit late, work dragged on a bit."

"No worries come on in." Moryys replied. He shifted his massive bulk and let Bowen in past him. Moryys' dimly lit cabin was a little larger than Bowen's but a similar layout. Bassy and entrancing music was quietly coming from a small player on the tv stand. Where Bowen had a desk, Moryys had a large television cabinet with a low and wide couch facing it. "Make yourself comfortable." Moryys said. Bowen removed his jacket and sat down on the couch. It seemed to immediately swallow him up it was that soft. Moryys' video game console was hooked up to the tv and a mess of cables on the floor ran to power outlets.

Moryys came to sit next to Bowen. As he did so the whole couch shifted a little with his huge weight. Moryys pulled a cool box across the floor from his side. "I've got Blue Eye, Sun Fossil, Roddenberry, what d'ya fancy?" he asked.

"I'll have a Roddenberry, thanks."

"Make sure you pace yourself." Moryys advised.

"Thanks Dad."

For the next couple of hours Bowen and Moryys hung out comfortably eating snacks and drinking. Moryys had acquired some episodes of Battle of Ages on video from Gricky's and they were slowly making their way through them. Afterwards they engaged in some competitive video games. They fought together and against each other, raced hyper cars and shot each other in foggy polygonal environments in the various games they played. Bowen smiled the whole time and forgot his worries for a while. It had been a long time since he had last enjoyed time with a friend as much.

Their last deathmatch ended with Moryys just scraping the win from Bowen.

"Nice." Bowen congratulated as they finished up, with digital stats flashing up on screen. Bowen stretched out and leant back in the couch.

"So, how's thing's with you?" Moryys asked. "You and Safiya doing okay?"

"Yeah, it's good."

"You guys just fooling around or is it more serious than that?" Moryys asked.

"We hang out and talk about stuff mostly, sometimes we make out." Bowen said with a slight blush.

"Nice." Moryys held out his drink and they clinked their bottles together. "So you haven't like, you know..?"

"No we haven't."

"All in good time, these things shouldn't be rushed." Moryys said.

Bowen took a thoughtful swig of his drink.

"I don't know what to expect tomorrow." he said.

"You have no idea what it could be about?"

"It could be a couple of things." Bowen said.

"Like what?"

"Maybe it's because I broke the pay station a couple months ago?" Bowen wondered.

Moryys chuckled.

"Yeah I remember that." Bowen gave a stiff lipped smile as he cringed at the memory of the shift. "Sorry go on."

"Perhaps it caused a more serious problem with stock records or something and I've messed up the finances?" Bowen said.

Moryys scratched the back of his leathery head and one of his little ears flapped.

"Hmm, I don't know. I don't see how it would have fucked things up that bad."

"It could be something else." Bowen said.

"What's that?" Moryys asked.

Bowen sighed.

"Before we had even left Pennine station, I went to look for Simon up in Navigation and I ended up sort of stumbling into the suite even though it says authorised personnel only."

"How did you manage that?" Moryys asked.

Bowen reached into his pocket and retrieved his id card. He played with it in his hands for a moment.

"I don't know what came over me. I just tried my card in the slot and it worked."

"So the door just let you in there?" Moryys asked.

"Yeah."

"So, you went in? Did you do anything whilst you were in there? You didn't mess with any terminals?"

"No no, course not. But before I found Simon, Officer Denton found me and mistook me for a lost passenger and threw me out."

"Denton's famously a shit head. It's probably lucky he thought you weren't crew."

"What's he like, is he a big deal?" Bowen asked nervously.

"He's the lead navigator." Moryys said as casually as he could.

Bowen swallowed.

"Maybe he's recognised me after seeing me in the cafeteria and he's reported it to the Captain?"

"I'm not sure it would take this long for something like that to be handled."

They sat there a moment with the video game on pause.

Moryys had a thoughtful look on his face. "Can I see your card?" he asked. Bowen handed it over. Moryys held it up to his small dark eyes and he studied it carefully.

"You think my card's bugged?" Bowen asked.

"Maybe." Moryys replied. "It looks okay. Maybe there's a problem with the chip?"

"How would we find out?" Bowen asked.

"A good techie could find out. Somone who doesn't mind keeping a secret."

"What do you mean by that?" Bowen asked. Moryys didn't answer. Bowen's mind turned over and he began to worry again. "Maybe the Captain's gonna kick me off the ship on Davarak..." Bowen thought out loud. His stomach dropped at the thought. To be left on his own in a strange place on another planet. He couldn't think of much worse. How would he get home? What about Safiya..?

Moryys placed his huge hand on Bowen's shoulder.

"Don't worry about it man. You're not a troublemaker. The bridge crew are pretty good at sniffing out things like that."

"Lennox would remember me from when we had guys night in the cafeteria. It wasn't a great first impression." Bowen said.

"Nah, Lennox is cool. He let us off pretty easy that night. If it had been Garber who found us she would have docked our pay. I mean, Garber's cool too, but she's way more by the book about things like that. And as far as the Captain goes, I'm sure it's not what you think."

Bowen felt himself sink into the couch. The thought that this could be the last night he spent on the Memento had well and truly defeated his good mood. Moryys suddenly stood up, rocking the couch as he did so. Bowen watched him as he hunched over the shelves by the television. Moryys shut off the video game console, took out the cartridge and set it back in its box.

"What you doing?" Bowen asked. Moryys turned around and leant on the television stand. He held a video tape in his hand.

"I'm gonna take your mind off things for a minute."

"Okay..."

"You remember how I used to compete on Bludgeon Brawl Assault?" Bowen sat up a little wondering where this was going.

"Yeah?"

"Yeah well watch this." He pulled the tape out of the case and inserted it into the player that sat on top of the television. Moryys sat back down next to Bowen who was now both interested and confused. Moryys held out the remote control and pressed a button to play the tape.

Bowen watched as the screen flickered as the playback calibrated. Upbeat music began to play against a flamboyant and multi coloured title screen. An array of different crazy looking fonts appeared and formed the words

MISTER MEGA FIST'S MEGA WORK OUT VIDEO

"Oh, wow." Bowen said as he sat up a little more. Moryys sighed and folded his arms with a poorly hidden smirk on his face. Bowen watched as the title screen swiped away to reveal a younger Moryys in a brightly coloured studio set surrounded by five attractive alien women of various races. Moryys was slightly slimmer, and if anything he appeared even more muscular. He was wearing white sport boots and a brightly coloured animal print leotard with a very low neckline that showed off much of his chest. The women were dressed in matching attire along with sweat bands on their wrists and foreheads that held back their big hair styles. They were all beautiful as they smiled into the camera. The shot panned across the room and zoomed in on Moryys who pointed directly at the viewer.

"Hey you! Yeah I'm talking to you! You wanna shed that weight and look great doing it? You've come to the right place! I'm Mister Mega Fist of Bludgeon Brawl Assault. Let's get started!" Bowen had a huge smile on his face as he looked over at Moryys who had his hand over his eyes in embarrassment. Bowen watched as the troupe began to move around to the music performing stretches. The music began to swell as Moryys concluded the stretching session and declared, "Let's work your upper body with some push ups! Come on girls!" The camera panned around as they all moved as one to begin the exercise with Moryys in the centre. "One handed if you can!" Moryys called out to the camera. The busty women all giggled around him as he began to do push ups one handed and he winked into the camera. Bowen heard Moryys sigh next to him. They both watched as Moryys and the girls would change their move sets and change up the exercises. The electronic music was so upbeat that Bowen found himself nodding along to it. Moryys would occasionally shout out motivational slogans such as, "Focus your energy! Torture those muscles! Crunch that stomach! ...That's it! You're becoming mighty!" Moryys yelled to the camera. Bowen wiped away a tear from laughing as he watched them performing punches to the music. Moryys himself was laughing too as the video came to its end. The crazy music came to a climax as the group finished their workout. A towel was thrown to Moryys from off camera and he dabbed at his chest and neck.

"That was some work out huh? Keep at it and who knows, maybe I'll see you on the BBA course next season on Blue Dragon Station?" The camera began to slowly pan away from the group as the girls all began to clap and surround Moryys jumping up and down around him as the music began again.

"Tune in to Battle Brawler Network or Federation Channel 78B to catch all the highlights and best moments from the BBA as well as the best of the best combat sports events in the galaxy! See you next time champions!" The music began to take over the sounds of the girls clapping and cheering as Moryys began to wave. The screen faded to black as credits rolled on the video.

Bowen sat back in his seat and looked at Moryys who looked a little defeated but he was smiling too.

"Well," Bowen said. "That was something."

Moryys sighed.

"It was in my contract. I didn't really want to do it."

The tape flickered as the video changed to recorded

channel footage. Bowen watched as a huge arena appeared lit by flood lights.

"What's this?" Bowen asked.

Moryys sighed despite the slight smile on his face.

"I'd forgot this was on this tape… it's the Solar Super Charger Games from my third season…"

Thousands of audience members cheered from stands waving signs and banners. The camera panned around to an extreme looking assault course full of pitfalls and over the top hazards. Extreme iron wave music played out as the footage swept across the arena until it landed on a ramped stage. An announcer spoke over the cacophony of the crowd introducing the house fighters. Bowen saw a diverse and dangerous group of fighters emerge one by one, each dressed in over the top outfits, some barely dressed at all. Their names played out on screen as they appeared. Thunder Spider, Gigaton, Zig-Zag Ultra, The Dark One, Mistress Vex, Metal Giant Alpha and finally Mister Mega Fist. Their presence was awe inspiring and intimidating. They were some of the most extreme individuals Bowen had ever seen in every sense. An array of muscles, chest hair, fangs, cleavage, sweat and oil. They took positions around the assault course. The crowd loved and hated them.

One by one, brave and crazed contestants attempted the course, occasionally having to square off with one of the house fighters. Before long, blood was flying and the crowd was in a frenzy.

"Do you miss it?" Bowen asked.

"Yes and no." Moryys replied. Bowen looked at Moryys on the couch. Bowen saw a hint of sadness on his face. "I originally signed up just to compete." Moryys said.

"What happened?"

"The prize money used to roll over every season. That year, the winner would have taken home forty million credits. I really needed the money. But when I interviewed they liked me so much they wanted me to be a house fighter. So I didn't get the prize money, but I got a hefty salary instead."

Bowen listened. He watched as a one on one fight commenced between the beautiful Mistress Vex and a crazed contestant on a raised platform. The contestant was wide eyed and looked ravenous for blood himself wielding a spiked club. Bowen watched as he lost to the graceful and lightning quick Mistress Vex as she stabbed him in the chest with a stiletto knife. The crowd booed and jeered as the contestant fell to the ground where a medical team swarmed him.

"Did people die playing the game?"

"Sometimes..." Moryys said.

"Did you ever..?"

"A few times. It came with the job." Moryys sighed. Bowen swallowed. The contestants that attempted the game seemed to be as extreme as the house fighters, but they each knew what they were signing up for.

"Is that why you quit?"

"I didn't exactly quit." Moryys said. "There was a lot happening behind the scenes in my last season. It bled out into the show one night in a bad way."

Bowen remembered Duggy mentioning a place called MX-12 where Moryys had spent some time. Was it a prison? Bowen thought not to ask.

"You look badass though..." Bowen said finally as the video showed Moryys dressed in a spiked outfit posing for the crowd even as they booed him and threw things. Bowen saw a sadness in Moryys' eyes as he watched the tv.

"Thanks Bowen."

31.

After an uneasy sleep, Bowen awoke early. He showered and dressed and made his way down through the ship to the cafeteria. When he entered, the galley staff were already behind the scenes cluttering and shouting to each other as they prepared for breakfast. As Bowen bought a can of water from the vending machines, his mind began to stray. He felt an odd mixture of anxiety and excitement. In just a short while the ship would leave the galactic highway into the Yandehark system.

Bowen took a seat at the closest table to the windows. He couldn't wait to finally see a new part of the galaxy. In the past he had seen the Yandehark system on star maps, but it had always just been a formless name. He couldn't wait to see it, even just a small part of it. His excitement was marred by anxiety of what would happen before they even landed. Bowen took a hard gulp of icy cold water. He had tried to not think on what the Captain wanted with him but it had caused him to toss and turn all night. Before long, the smell of meat and eggs came wafting over, but his stomach was not interested. He knew Safiya was in there. There wouldn't be time to speak to her before he made the journey to see the Captain. Despite everything, he wanted to still be prompt.

Bowen sat a while watching the roiling blue outside the window. He closed his eyes and listened to the low humming of the ship and he felt the gentle rocking of the highway when he focused on it. It calmed his nerves somewhat. The breakfast spread was slowly set up on the serving line, people began filtering in to the cafeteria and soon the din of the breakfast rush filled the room. He considered joining the throng for some food more than once, but decided against it. He kept an eye on the serving line. Safiya wasn't there. His attention was commanded when over the tannoy came the sound of Officer

Garber.

"Attention all crew and passengers, Officer Sol Garber speaking, expect some light turbulence as we pass through Ganderonn's Gate. Two minutes to arrival."

Bowen's heart thumped in his chest at the announcement. He glanced around at the room. No one else seemed to have even registered what was about to happen. Bowen stood up from the now crowded table and stood by the windows. The outer portions of the Memento he could see out before him looked like frosted rooftops. Flashes of lightning arced outward from the ship as they got closer to their destination. Months of travel were about to come to an end. In no time at all the two minutes were up.

A shuddering went through the ship. Bowen felt it in his shoes and up into his legs. A series of beeping sounds came through the speakers and fragments of transmission signals from the Yandehark system and beyond. The swirling blue tunnel of the highway seemed to be spinning faster and slower simultaneously. The shuddering became increasingly more and more aggressive. Bowen put his hand on the glass to steady himself which made the hairs on his arms stand. From around the cafeteria, plates and cutlery rattled on the tables as the ship vibrated. Still, barely anyone seemed to notice or care. The serving line was rattling and the dangling ceiling lights swayed. The blue of the highway appeared to move and crackle like fire as a vertical structure came into view from nowhere. The shaking increased as the view of Ganderonn's gate came into view. A thousand sparkling stars ebbed and flowed into existence as the view of static space emerged. There was a jolt and a last great shudder as the Memento began to whine and strain. Bowen held his breath until all at once, it stopped. The speakers beeped overhead.

"Traversal successful. Four hours to Daverak. Garber out."

Bowen exhaled. The atmosphere in the cafeteria was unaffected. Bowen realised he was sweating and he became a little self conscious. He turned to the window where the view had completely changed. Ganderonn's Gate was now far behind them and out of view. From what he had briefly seen of it, the warp gate appeared to be a simplified iteration of the Pennine gate. What really captivated Bowen was the view of space. The Yandehark system was red black with spots of golden yellow. Beyond, the stars punctured the colours in their thousands. He was a long way from home.

After a minute of staring open mouthed, Bowen's thoughts were wrenched back to the matters at hand. He turned and saw that a good deal of the crew had left the cafeteria. His heart began to thump again in anxious anticipation as he left the room.

***

Breathless, Bowen made it to the upper decks where he followed the wide corridors to the central hub. From the main junction Bowen saw the ramped corridor that led to the bridge. At the top of the ramp he saw a set of heavy duty reinforced doors. Bowen would have loved to get a look inside the bridge, but it wasn't his lot. He was merely a pot wash, there would be no reason for him to be up there. He sighed and carried onwards.

After a few minutes, he was stood at the entrance to Captain Quinn's quarters. Much like the entrance to the bridge, this set of heavy metal doors looked like it was reinforced and could take more than a few knocks before giving way. Bowen looked at the small keypad by the side and swallowed. He raised his gaze up and saw that there was a small camera pointing down at him. Feeling a little exposed, he cleared his throat and knocked on the door. Nothing happened initially, but Bowen was sure he heard the lenses of the camera shift and get a closer look. He considered whether to knock again, but the doors opened for him. He stepped inside.

He entered a large, dimly lit entryway as if someone had

taken his own cabin and enlarged it many times. He carefully followed the orange strip lighting that led him to where the quarters opened up. There was metallic clattering coming from ahead as well as what sounded like a dental drill firing in short bursts. Bowen turned the corner into the main room and discovered the source of the noises.

Below harsh white lamp light, sitting on a small stool was Captain Quinn. Surrounding him was a small workbench cluttered with tools and there were wires trailing across the floor to power outlets. A small computer terminal on a wheeled stand threw out a green glow. The Captain wore a loose vest that exposed much of his cybernetic parts. The arm caught Bowen's attention. It looked strong and reinforced, but there were numerous scratches and scuffs. It encompassed his entire arm and his shoulder joint. More metallic parts disappeared under his clothes. Quinn's non robotic parts seemed like they had seen as much action. He was scarred with an array of old injuries from clean cuts to bullet entry points and even a small burn mark on his neck. On his human shoulder, Bowen noticed an aged tattoo of a crest of Kovostoyan military, a shield with a clock face crossed with a rifle and a shovel. In his hand, the Captain held a small drill that he was using on his mechanical shoulder joint. Bowen made sure he wasn't gawping. He cleared his throat cautiously. As he did so, Quinn looked up at him from over his workbench. His yellow robotic eye shone at him from under the shadow of his strong brow.

"Rhys. Come in." the Captain said. Bowen came forward slightly and tried his best not to seem nervous. It was very warm in the room. He watched as Quinn finished up tightening his mechanical parts. The Captain seemed to wince in a few places. He disconnected the drill and set it down before retrieving a small metallic box from his tool belt. He opened it and took out two bright green pills. With his skeletal metal hand he threw them to the back of his mouth and dry swallowed them. Bowen shuffled. He had a hundred questions.

The Captain stood from his stool and fixed his vest top before donning a leather jacket that he had been sat on. The Captain approached Bowen who swallowed anxiously. Despite being a similar height to him, Bowen felt rather small in comparison. Even wearing his battered leather jacket, the Captain's strong physique outclassed Bowen's thin frame in almost every way.

Quinn surveyed him. The yellow of the robotic eye glinted.

"Let me see your hands." The Captain said. Bowen did as he was bid without question and exposed his palms upwards. Quinn took them in his own. The Captain turned over Bowen's hands like he was inspecting cuts of meat. Quinn's human hand was ageing but was just as strong as its cybernetic counterpart. His knuckles were tattooed with glyphs and runes from old earth and the back of his hand was dominated by a navigation pattern from star maps of the federation. Bowen thought the interaction was odd but he was not about to say so. The Captain released his hands back to him.

"You've been working with soil all your life." Bowen was taken aback by the statement and replied,

"Mostly, yes Sir."

"You're a Saxon."

"Yes, Sir."

"You can drop the formalities." Bowen swallowed.

"...Alright."

"Ever work engines?" Quinn asked

Bowen cleared his throat before answering.

"Agricultural engineering."

Quinn made a noise that indicated surprise. He began to potter around his workbench disassembling his equipment. He raised the bright spot light into the ceiling, causing more of the room to be exposed. Quinn took another stool from under a desk and slid it over to Bowen.

"Have a seat Rhys." Bowen followed the order. His heart was beginning to thump harder. Quinn sat opposite him on his stool and rested his human arm on his thigh. The Captain was watching Bowen like he had never seen another person before.

"What made you join my crew?" Quinn asked. Bowen took a quivery deep breath.

"I... just needed a job." Bowen replied. He knew there was much more to it than that, but it was all he could say.

"Your family." Quinn changed the subject. "Tell me about them." Bowen had not expected such a question. He proceeded to tell the Captain of his parents and his sister. Quinn was hanging on to every word.

"No one in your family has ever been in the military..?"

"My great grandfather Arnold Rhys was. He was Fleet Major for the 21st Brigade Star Hawks." Quinn didn't respond, he only watched Bowen intently, his yellow eye seemed not to blink. Bowen cleared his throat. "He was killed at Mausoleum." Quinn leant forwards slightly and said nothing. He merely blinked and took a deep breath.

"Your elder sibling. The scientist." Quinn said.

"Niamh?"

"She is on Saurophos?" Quinn confirmed.

"Yes."

"And the name of her vessel..?"

"The Glass Library under Professor Wilhelm Volkov..." Bowen answered carefully. He was aware that he was divulging personal information to the Captain, but curiously his responses were coming naturally. Quinn rubbed his stubbly chin and the back of his neck with his human hand. That moment lingered for an instant. Quinn reached up to the cybernetics on his head as he looked down. Quinn took a deep breath before he spoke again.

"Have you your crew card?" the Captain asked. Bowen's heart rate doubled.

"I do..."

Quinn stretched out his metallic arm and opened its palm.

"May I..?" he requested. Bowen took his wallet out of his jacket pocket and fetched his identification for the Captain.

Bowen braced himself for what was to come. He had not prepared a defence for himself. But he didn't need one. Quinn took a look over his card and handed it back to him. Bowen placed it back in his wallet. He had entered the room with a hundred questions but now he had even more. This meeting had not gone how he expected it to.

"You're a farmer, yes..?" Quinn asked. Again Bowen was thrown by the change of subject.

"You could say that." he replied. Quinn stood up from his stool and put his hands on his hips. Bowen noticed the large sidearm at his hip.

"Walk with me." The Captain commanded. Bowen fumbled a response but before he could speak properly he found himself following the Captain out of his quarters. Quinn opened the door for Bowen and showed him out before locking the doorway behind them.

Bowen walked down the corridors by Quinn's side. As they passed all manner of crew members, they addressed the Captain appropriately. Some looked from the Captain to Bowen and frowned in confusion. They even happened across Simon with Denton and Liio. Bowen attempted to stop his face from going red. He wasn't exactly sure where the Captain was taking him, but his anxiety was bubbling again. They made their way through access corridors and passed maintenance atriums, and they even used one of the restricted elevators. Bowen was totally at the mercy of the Captain, he had no idea where they were. The wide elevator seemed to descend further and further into the bowels of the ship. For a moment, Bowen was afraid they would break through the bottom into space. But they just kept descending. Finally they came to a stop. The wide doorway opened up and a gust of air rushed inside the elevator. As they stepped out into the cavernous hallway Bowen heard the humming of the ship much louder than it was anywhere else.

Bowen felt a slight vibration through his shoes. The engines were close. Their steps echoed around the gaping hallways as Quinn led the way. The lower decks were dimly lit and were far more utility than anything else. The floor was bare metal instead of carpet and the walls and ceiling were covered in exposed piping and wiring. They passed maintenance terminals and access hatches as well as parked forklift trucks with missing parts and loose tools left about. After walking for some time, they reached a corner where they found a doorway. Bowen saw the dusty sign above the door frame that read,

BOTANICAL TECHNOLOGIES

Quinn brushed a layer of grime off the key card lock. He used his own id card and unlocked the doors. He opened them onto another dark room. When the doors opened Bowen's nose was filled with a mix of old dirt and acrid natural smells and the sound of echoing drips bounced off the walls. Bowen took a step into the room as Quinn flipped an old switch on the wall. The sound of a generator charging up came from somewhere as one by one a series of hanging lights flickered on. More than one lamp exploded as they attempted to come back to life. Out in front of them, Bowen could see what the room contained. A whole warehouse sized room with trenches and patches of soil. Set against the walls were huge glass cylinders filled with long dead plants and here and there were more glass structures the size of small houses, each dripping with old growth. High above the stretches of dirt was a series of pipes with sprinkler system taps, the source of the dripping sounds. A damp mist clung to the ceiling.

"Garber mentioned to you that we had a garden." Quinn said finally.

"She did. I didn't imagine something this big." Bowen replied.

"Could you get it up and running again?"

"Well... I mean, it looks like it needs a lot of work."

"It does. Is that a problem?" Quinn asked.

"No not at all." Bowen recovered. He began to walk among the patches and Quinn followed him. "The sprinklers will probably need flushing. The dirt will need to be replaced." Bowen said. "Some of the electrics are completely dead," Quinn stated. "The terminals by the growing tubes, and some of the heat lamps. Would you like the responsibility?" Quinn offered.

"I would love it." Bowen replied. His head was spinning. A real chance to put his skills to use. "I'd need a lot of equipment just to clean the place never mind get it up to scratch to grow things. Humidifiers, dehumidifiers, the chemical agents for the pipes, the amount of fresh soil. And then there's the seeds, the fertiliser, and..." Quinn raised his hand.

"As it happens, Oasis City is a perfect place to acquire everything you'll need. We'll be docked there for a while. If you can get this place cleaned up in a few days, we can sort out everything you need."

"I might need some help with the cleaning." Bowen admitted.

"We can see to that. If you need assistance with anything, go and ask for it. You can tell them your under my instructions. If they give you any problems let me know." Suddenly a thought struck Bowen.

"What about my job in the kitchens..?"

"Wouldn't you rather do this?" Quinn asked plainly.

"More than anything."

"Good. I'll make some adjustments to your paperwork." Bowen was just smiling. "I'll increase your pay too, lets call it thirty percent." Bowen picked up a handful of old, hard dirt. It stunk of rotten plant life. He smiled as it fell apart in his hands.

"Why me..?" he asked. Quinn took a look around the room and his gaze fell back on Bowen.

"It's not often farmers go to space."

"Thank you Captain."

32.

Eagerly, Bowen set to work right away. He was pleased to have this chance to prove himself, his education might not have been for nothing after all. Captain Quinn sent word for some janitorial staff to help Bowen with the clean up and promptly they arrived. Fillius, Virkman, Calciok, Justipher and little Wyella all appeared in heavy duty uniforms of orange and black rubber. Virkman, a shaggy haired brute handed Bowen his own set including some thick rubber boots. Bowen removed his jacket and hung it on a hook in an old changing room. Little Wyella brazenly watched Bowen as he dressed himself. She reminded him of a scruffy rabbit as he awkwardly smiled at her. The group had brought with them mops, buckets, water tanks, chemical dousers, rags and brushes.

When they were all set, Bowen realised that they were all waiting for him to give them directions. Fillius stared at Bowen with a gaping, toothless mouth and huge fish like eyes, while Justifer and Calciok, who looked like blotchy skinned goblin men stood at attention. Bowen cleared his throat and began instructing them.

"Okay thanks for helping me out with this." he started. "The best thing to do first is to remove all this old dirt and chuck it in the incinerator to make room for the new soil. We'll just bag it all up and move them down there with these flatbed tugs." He pointed to a series of pump trucks with built in crates as well as a pallet of large bags that he had found in a storage room. "Then we'll split into teams and tackle the room in three sections bleaching and scrubbing. That okay with everyone..?" They all agreed. "Any questions?" he asked. There were none. "Right masks on." Bowen instructed.

Everyone donned a clear plastic face mask with rubber hoods and then split into three pairs, Calciok and Justipher, Fillius and Wyella, Bowen and Virkman. As they all started shovelling the mossy, rotten dirt, small flying mites erupted from within, disturbed from eating the last of the nutrients. Despite this, Bowen smiled to himself. Being in charge was odd. It was easier than he might have expected. It helped that the cleaners were not very talkative and extremely compliant, but still he admitted to himself that it felt good to have some small modicum of authority over a situation.

Bowen was pleased that it took no time at all to bag up the majority of the old soil into the bags. They all helped each other load the bags into the open top crates and with Justipher and Calciok leading the way, they wheeled the dirt back into the corridors with Fillius and Wyella bringing up the rear. Bowen was glad to be paired with Virkman as the crate was extremely heavy, even with most of the weight off the floor with the pump truck. They made their way through the bowels of the ship, through the echoing hallways and wide passages. The low hum of the ship grew louder as they moved. It was like the lair of some giant beast Bowen thought. The small mites followed the crates in desperate swarms. Bowen was glad of the hooded masks as the insects began to land on them and crawl over their uniforms. They were slowly dying after being forcibly removed from their environment. All for the better, Bowen thought as he imagined the prospect of having to purchase more germination insects. Captain Quinn had assured him that Oasis City had everything he would need.

Before long, the caravan of dirt reached a huge red metal door that looked to Bowen like a vault. It was at least twice the height of Bowen and just as wide. The incinerator. The door was plastered in warning signs and discouraging images, Bowen felt a pang of anxiety. Calciok reached his black gloved hand into his utility belt pouch and retrieved a key chain. His crew id card dangled from it along with his keys and an array of odd knick knacks. Calciok moved to the keypad lock and gained access. There was a surge of power from a hidden generator and two revolving lights began flashing yellow and red. One by one a series of huge internal locks shifted, each one gave the sound of a hammer blow on metal. A loud klaxon sounded as gears began to grind and the doorway opened out towards them. Even through his heavy rubber suit, Bowen felt the rush of hot air hit him and it scattered the last of the mites that hadn't yet died.

Calciok and Justipher began to heave their truck into the room. The inside was rounded. The walls were lined with pressure gauges and computer terminals monitoring temperature and intensity. The room was positively dripping with heat. There were yet more warning labels and instructional readouts plastered on every surface. In the centre of the room was a large metal bowl at the bottom of which was a dark hole covered by a metal mesh. Periodically the incinerator would spew out a gulp of steam. From even further downward there was a hellish orange glow. For a moment, Bowen's attention was on a large image of a cross section of the incinerator. Whatever was thrown into the pit appeared to feed directly into the thrusters. The group all parked up their trucks around the bowl. Bowen was sweating profusely and his rubber suit was beginning to get heavier. They didn't have much time before the task became a lot harder.

Bowen found himself taking the initiative. He heaved a bag out of the crate and emptied it into the bowl. The clods of dirt and rotten moss slid down into the incinerator. The rest of the group copied him. Each time a bagful of dirt fell into the hole there was a muffled roaring sound that came from far below followed by a gulp of steam. Bowen felt as though they were feeding a monster that could never be satisfied. By the time they were finished the whole chamber was steamy and everyone had to wipe at their masks to see. They returned their empty bags into their crates and hauled them away. When the incinerator door finally closed behind them with a thunderous clunking, they all took off their face masks. The cool air of the empty corridors felt good on Bowen's sweaty skin. He hoped to not have to make too many trips to the incinerator in the future.

On the way back to the garden, an announcement chimed. Down in the lower decks Garber's voice sounded far away as it echoed around the cavernous halls.

"Attention all crew and passengers, Officer Garber speaking. We have been given clearance to land at Oasis City and are making our descent to Davarak. Scans show clear skies with some moderate winds. There will be turbulence in the upper atmosphere but nothing serious. Approximate time to landing, ten minutes. Officer Garber out."

As usual, no one batted an eye at the announcement. Bowen felt a mixture of disappointment and excitement. He had completely lost track of time working with the others. He wanted more than anything to drop what he was doing and get the elevator back to the upper decks and watch the descent to Daverak. But there was work to be done. It would be lunch soon and the view from the cafeteria would have to do.

As they returned to the garden, Bowen directed the group to begin spraying the floor with cleaning agents. They each armed themselves with back mounted tanks of chemicals and water and it was back on with the masks. Bowen split them into pairs again and they each tackled a portion of the room power spraying everything as they went.

They had just about started when the ship began to rumble. The Memento had entered the upper atmosphere of Davarak. Bowen felt a surge of power from below the floor as the whole room began to shudder. The pipes above them rattled as the ship fought with the winds of the planet. More than once Bowen had to steady himself as the Memento rocked from side to side. A tremendous mechanical whine came from all sides and the shaking increased as the rumbling grew and grew, until it ended with one final, gigantic thud as the landing struts made contact with the planet. The ship hissed as it began to catch its breath. Through the floors, the engines could be heard powering down. After a moment the ship fell quiet, and all that could be heard was the spraying of chemicals and the lights swinging in the garden.

It was all Bowen could do to control himself and concentrate on working and not leave to get a look at the planet. He did his best to put it out of his head.

It took almost two hours but they succeeded in cleaning every inch of the surfaces. They all removed their suits and left them to dry out on a series of hooks by a wash station. Bowen donned his leather jacket again and thanked them for their help so far.

"I appreciate you all doing this." he said. "After lunch we can start on the glass growth tanks." They all acknowledged him in various ways and they left for lunch.

33.

As Bowen stepped out of the access elevator his cleaning troupe clashed with cargo crew.

"Hey Bowen!" called Moryys from over the crowd. He was dressed in his brown cargo operator jumpsuit and his utility belt was jingling at his waist.

"How's it going man?" Bowen asked.

"Forget me, how did your meeting with the Captain go? And what are you doing coming up from the lower decks with the janitors?" They both hung back from the crowd and they began to walk through the maintenance corridors towards the cafeteria.

"The Captain's put me in charge of the garden." Bowen said.

"No way." Moryys replied. "That's awesome." He patted Bowen on the back with his big hand.

"Thanks."

"So you didn't get in trouble for snooping or for anything?"

"No, nothing." Bowen felt a little silly thinking how he had worried so much.

"So the Captain just wanted to speak to you and boom new job?"

"I suppose so. We talked briefly beforehand in his quarters. He asked me about my family and my experience. It felt like an interview now I think about it. And when I asked him why me he didn't really have an answer."

"Huh. See I said didn't I there wasn't anything to freak out over."

"Yeah you were right." Bowen said. "It still needs a lot of work. The Captain had the janitorial staff help me clean up the place. I think he was on about taking me out into Oasis City to buy supplies for the garden."

"Look at you getting in with the Captain." Moryys said smiling with all his big teeth. "You'll be rocking an armoured flight suit next with a gun on your hip." Bowen laughed. "So we'll be working on the same level then which is cool." Moryys said as they passed through some double doors.

"I suppose it is." Bowen said with a smile.

"We'll be eating home grown fruit and veg in no time."

"Dude I'm starving."

"Same, I'm gonna have to eat and run back to the cargo bay. We've got the loader mechs fully charged and ready to go and impatient truckers waiting outside."

When they entered the cafeteria from the access corridor, Bowen caught a glimpse of the view from beyond the huge windows. A vast, pastel pink open sky. Gigantic rock spires jutted up as high as sky scrapers from out of the red, stony sand that seemed to go on forever. As they joined the queue for lunch, the ceiling began to rattle as the ships air conditioning kicked in. High above them the metal fans shook off a layer of dust as they began to spin.

The cafeteria was considerably less populated than it normally was. A good portion of the crew had opted to leave the ship as soon as they were able. Bowen was torn between wanting to go out to see Davarak and Oasis City or to rush back to the garden and get on with the work. Bowen's plate was piled with Zuko-bird meat courtesy of Jungga. Bowen quite liked the taste especially with the accompanying sauce and starchy blue potatoes but it was the third time that week it had been on for lunch as they were coming to the end of the supplies. He turned his head to Moryys and spoke quietly so as not to offend the galley staff.

"We aren't by any chance taking on more food from the city?"

"I hope so. It's no wonder folks have already made a break for it." Moryys commented. Jungga squinted his beady bat eyes at Moryys. "Looks great though." Moryys fumbled. As they shuffled down the line leaving Jungga grumbling under his breath, Bowen heard Wotll's wheezing coming from behind the service line. She emerged and took over at the pay station just as Bowen reached it.

"I heard a rumour that you don't work in here any more." she said with a smile. Bowen felt his face turn pink as he smiled.

"No I suppose I don't."

"Captain must like you to promote you to our new gardener." She said as she scanned his id card. "I'm pleased for you."

"Thanks." he replied with a smile.

"I'll expect a steady supply train coming up from down there you know." Wotll said as she handed him his cutlery.

"I'll do my best for you." Bowen replied. "Is Safiya working today..?" he asked.

"She's in the back now." Wotll answered. "I'll let her off early shall I?"

"Thanks Wotll."

Bowen and Moryys took a seat at a table close to the windows. As Bowen tucked into his Zuko-bird fillets, he could see just how hot the planet outside was. The heat was blistering off the outer portions of the ship and caused the view of the horizon to shimmer. Bowen cracked open his first of two cans of water as Safiya arrived. Her perfume gave her away before he saw her. As she walked around him, her hand brushed across the back of his neck. His insides seemed to shift as she came into view.

"Hey." he managed.

"Hey yourself." she replied as she sat down opposite Bowen. Safiya had for herself a bowl of tinned fruit and a brightly coloured prism of sugared Gypsy Jelly. Bowen sat up straight.

"By the way Safie, this is my friend Moryys I've told you about. Moryys, Safiya." Bowen said. Moryys picked out a strand of gristle from his huge teeth as he greeted her.

"Hey there."

"Hello." she said rather awkwardly. She brushed some loose hair behind her ear.

"So you have a new job?" Safiya asked Bowen.

"I do. The Captain's put me in charge of the garden." He did his best to contain his pride as he spoke.

"Is that was that smell is then?" Safiya wrinkled her nose.

"Oh, sorry. Yeah it must be. I was clearing all the old growth out of the patches. And then I went to the incinerator." Bowen said now very self conscious. There was a moment of silence that ended when Moryys made to move.

"Well that's me, lots of work to do." he said.

"Yeah no problem." Bowen replied.

"Nice to meet you." Moryys said to Safiya.

"Mhm." she replied with a mouthful of food. With that Moryys left them alone at the table.

"How's things with you?" Bowen asked.

"Yeah okay." She replied simply. "Just a bit bored with work." They sat there for a little while for the remainder of the lunch period until Safiya broke the quiet. "Are you going to be working in the garden permanently then?"

"I think so. The Captain said he would alter my paperwork. When it's up and running in a couple of weeks you should come down and see it." Bowen said.

"I don't really like it down there it gives me the creeps."

"Oh..."

"But yes I'll come and have a look when you've set it up."

"I'll be quite busy for the next few days but then would you like to spend some time together?" Bowen asked. "Perhaps we could leave the ship, see what's what..?"

"I'm not sure about that. This place isn't like a gateway rest stop."

"What do you mean?"

"It's just a mining city with a few rough bars and trading depots. Not much to see really."

"Looks amazing doesn't it?" Bowen commented looking

out the window.

"In a way I suppose it does."

"Everything okay with you..? You seem a bit off." Bowen asked. Safiya seemed to think for a moment before answering. She looked over to him and smiled.

"I think I'll just miss the chance of bumping into you around here."

"I'm only gonna be in lower decks. And my hours will be more my own now. As long as I get the work done, I can work whenever suits me. I won't really have a supervisor." Safiya smiled.

"How about I come see you after dinner tonight?"

"Yeah that sounds good."

"Just make sure you've showered."

34.

The elevator to the cargo bay was hot. Bowen was already sweating through his vest top and his rucksack stuck to his back. Cool jets of air streamed into the lift but they were fighting a losing battle as the heat of the planet was gently roasting the ship. Finally the metal doors slid open and a rush of warm air came billowing inside and made the hair on Bowen's legs ripple. The shorts were a good call it seemed. The cargo bay was buzzing with activity. The high walls were lined with containers and crates, some made of metal, others of treated wood. Bowen stuck to the designated walkway as he entered the room. From below him, sounds of machinery operating dominated the space, pierced every now and then by the men shouting out to one another. As he moved along the suspended catwalk, he saw some crew members checking the locks and mechanisms of the containers illuminated by the daylight that was streaming inside. A huge crane suspended from the ceiling was loading crates and containers into the metal hands of the loader mechs who were then taking them down the wide ramp to the outside. Bowen reached the far end of the catwalk and descended the metal staircase to the cargo bay floor where the Captain was waiting for him at the top of the ramp.

"Morning Captain." Bowen said.

"Rhys." Quinn replied. "Good, you dressed for the heat." Bowen adjusted his bush hat that he had bought from Gricky's. Initially he had felt a little silly with it, but faced with leaving the ship, even in the morning sun it seemed to have been a wise purchase. The Captain wore a duster jacket and an old military scarf.

"Ready when you are." Bowen said. Quinn donned a pair of black out welding goggles and pulled the scarf up over his nose.

"Are your legs planetside yet?" he asked.

"They're a little shaky but they're okay." Bowen replied. In the days since they had landed, the artificial gravity had been turned off onboard the Memento making Bowen's knees and legs shudder intermittently but it was easing. It had somewhat hampered cleaning the last of the garden, but he had still left the place gleaming in part thanks to the others. Bowen reached into his rucksack and took out a lightweight poncho that he threw over himself in hopes of protecting his shoulders and arms from the sun.

From outside in the blazing light came the thumping metal footfalls of one of the loader mechs. When the machine reached the top of the ramp it stood over twice the height of Bowen.

"Hot out there." came the voice of Moryys. His whole head and shoulders were visible in the open cockpit in the chest of the machine. He wore a leather pilot hat with wires attached that ran back behind his head into a small port. The hat had flattened his ears, and his shark like skin was sweating profusely.

"Just a little." Bowen said.

"Gonna need a cold shower later."

"Hows it coming?" the Captain asked Moryys.

"About half way done with the first quadrant, so we're on schedule Captain." he replied. As he spoke, the mech pointed with one of its huge mechanical hands.

"As you were." Quinn said.

"Aye Captain. See you Bowen." Moryys said. Quinn turned to Bowen.

"Let's go." As Quinn lead the way down the ramp, Bowen noticed that the Captain had a gun slung over his shoulder. Bowen almost instinctively asked what he was bringing it for, but he decided he would rather not know.

They descended the wide metal ramp and stepped onto the ground. Bowen smiled for a moment as it sunk it. He had taken a step onto another planet. He followed Quinn across a huge stretch of black tarmac painted with white and yellow markings that was hundreds of feet across. Out in front in the pink heat haze, Bowen saw the smoggy shape of an atmospheric sky station, similar to the ones from home. This one rose defiantly from the desert and presided over Oasis City. Jutting up into the sky like metal trees were the shapes of old mining cranes. The air was filled with chemical smells and odd fumes as well as distant sounds of engines, digging machines and drilling. And there was a great mechanical pulsing noise that Bowen couldn't pin point.

Bowen glanced back towards the Memento. The thick glass windows glistened in the sun as vents were jetting excess exhaust here and there over the hull and the heat was shimmering off it all. To the side, Bowen saw a colossal crane had been attached to the side of the Memento and was connected via a series of massive pipes and tubes to an even bigger tank that read DeBassa Crystalak Fuel. Men were calling to each other over the noise from gangways and platforms all over the machine that sat on wheels the size of Bowen's house. The pulsing noise was the ship was being refueled. Looking past the ship, Bowen saw the shimmering shapes of other ships way out on the tarmac hooked up to their own fuel rigs. Despite working in the large and cavernous lower decks of late, he had forgotten how big the Memento was to behold. He turned and saw that Quinn was watching him look at the ship. He jogged to return to Quinn and they continued to walk.

"Sorry Captain, it's the first time I've really looked at it since the morning I joined the crew. And even then it was shrouded in the fog and rain." They walked together off the large landing pad into a shaded walkway that led into the city.

"What do you think of her?" Quinn asked.

"I think she's amazing." Bowen replied.

"I think so too."

Under the shaded walkway they passed a number of landing pad workers dressed in full body rig uniforms resting on chairs drinking and fanning themselves. The walkway led them to a bustling square that sat under a huge canopy that billowed in the slight wind. The square was something like a marketplace with people selling wares and each competing for attention of passers-by. Bowen was reminded of passing through the village in Allchester with Mason. The area was flanked with a large bar with harsh neon signs buzzing as well as a general store and a brothel. Here and there were huge alien succulent trees in massive squat planters. Some of the trees sported beautiful flowers and others were dangerously covered in vines that sported spines the length of Bowen's arm. In the centre of the square was a great fountain carved of a dark stone. Bowen saw clusters of miners in their clunky gear, helmets off, smoking, drinking and passing the time with cards. There were no humans among them that he could see. More than one had a scantily clad woman on their knee, stroking their heads and laughing at their bad jokes. None of the working girls seemed to be human either Bowen saw. Quinn's presence kept Bowen's anxiety in check.

As the two walked side by side through the area numerous aliens approached Bowen.

"You look like a man who needs to slow down a little. I got these pills..?"

"That's two for one right here, two for one today only sir!"

"Hey gorgeous, twenty dona and I'm all yours for an hour..."

"My friend do you have a moment to talk about the wonder of the Crystal Ziggurat?" Bowen did his best to politely decline each of the market's vendors that approached him, but Quinn put his cybernetic hand on his shoulder and guided him away.

"Just ignore them." he instructed. They followed the walkways passed numerous storehouses and maintenance sheds until they reached a massive trader storehouse. Parked outside were a few off road vehicles with raised suspension and oversized tires. They were parked next to a disused digger machine that was partially stripped down as well at the head of a monumentally big excavator saw that looked more than capable of tearing right through the Memento with ease.

They both entered the storehouse causing an electric klaxon to sound off. When they did, Quinn removed his goggles and pulled down the scarf from his face. It was only then when they were inside that Bowen realised that his face was coated in a fine layer of red sand. The storehouse was massive on the inside and it was much cooler. High above in the ceiling, large vents dispensed cold air and big fans wafted it around. Bowen could see all kinds of things for sale. Nuts and bolts of all sizes. Power tools for every job with appropriate clothing and gear to match. Standing tanks and silos for all purposes. Spare tires for ground vehicles. All in one survival kits for expeditions in all sorts of environments. Quinn led Bowen to a small windowed counter in the corner of the shop.

From out of a back room door came an alien. A Cinotarae, like Ramphry, Bowen recognised. Unlike Ramphry however, who reminded Bowen of a pig, this man mostly resembled a bull, horns and all but for his blue black skin tone and piercing grey eyes. He had a similar frame about him to Moryys, muscular and imposing, yet thick with fat and a small gut beneath his work clothes. He filled the service window almost completely he was so big. When he spoke his voice rumbled around the storehouse.

"Been a while."

"It has Nole." Quinn replied. "How have you been?"

"In here all the time now. At least I'm not down the pits any more. How's things off world? Keeping your head down?"

"I'm trying. It's the same as always out there. We're on our way to Obelisk and then on to Vibana."

"Off to see the money man? How is old Yoto Rex?"

"He's well last I spoke to him."

"Still as fat as he is rich?" Nole chuckled.

"What do you think?" Quinn replied. They laughed.

"So how can I help?" Nole asked.

"We've got our botanics ready to go again and we need some supplies."

"Just a moment." Nole said. He disappeared to the side and jingling keys could be heard. He soon emerged out of a side door and came out to meet them both. He and the Captain shook hands firmly. Quinn motioned to Bowen as he introduced him to Nole.

"Nole this is Bowen, he's our gardener in question. Bowen this is Nole, he's an old friend." Bowen shook Nole's huge hairy hand.

"Nice to meet you." Bowen said. Bowen noticed Quinn watching their interaction closely from the side.

"And you. So you're the one doing the supply run?"

"I suppose I am." Bowen confirmed. His eyes glanced over the shop and was struck by the sheer amount of choice before him.

"I'm paying." Quinn stated.

"That's okay then." Bowen smiled almost breathless.

"So what do you need?" Nole asked. Quinn motioned to Bowen to have a look around. The three of them began to walk around the storehouse. After an initial awkwardness, Bowen realised he was excited at the possibilities. Between them they formulated a list of what Bowen required. When they reached the seed bays Bowen felt like a child picking out sweets. Bowen chose only fruit and vegetables he was familiar with, everything from potatoes, carrots, tomatoes and peas to apples, oranges, strawberries and bananas. He had already marked out in his head where he was going to plant what in the garden. To ensure quick and healthy growth they arranged the correct dosage of growth hormones and nutrient compounds as well as ten tons of fresh soil. Bowen was relieved that he remembered all of the old information about how best to grow food quickly and correctly in space. Four giants tanks were ordered each containing a hundred thousand gallons of water that could be installed into the irrigation systems. They also requisitioned a brand new moisture collector and a humidity exchanger for the garden itself. Bowen was sized up for standard biped work gear and a fresh set of boots along with every tool he could want. Bowen imagined Mason and Nole would be fast friends if they were to ever meet. In a separate room Nole showed them the germination insects they needed. A whole colony of Laurentian Hoverflies, half a ton of frozen new appalachian ground worms and most importantly, a standard onboard apiary machine full of Saxon Pollinator Bees in a stasis configuration.

After some time, the three returned to the service counter where Nole began typing on his oversized keypad at a computer terminal. He finished inputting the data for their items and turned the box screen towards the window so Quinn and Bowen could see.

"All good?" he asked. Quinn turned to Bowen expectantly. Bowen had a quick run through of the list.

"Yeah that's all correct."

"Right then." Quinn said nodding. Nole tapped away at the keypad.

"You having them collected or dropped off at your landing bay?" he asked.

"Dropped off. Landing Pad B12." Quinn answered.

"No problem." Nole clacked away some more until a beep sounded. "Nine thousand eighty nine credits with drop off." Quinn reached into his pocket and retrieved a wallet made of old leather and pulled out a series of cards.

"You still accept free trade dona?" he asked.

"I do." Nole said. Quinn inserted his card into a reader. The payment went through and a paper transaction script was slowly printed out of the machine.

"Have you heard anything about Stormraven or the Titan? They were supposed to be here when we landed." Quinn asked. Nole leant forwards up to the service window.

"I heard Stormraven's been held up, they were hit by bad weather trying to leave Atlanticana. Apparently they had to make repairs in orbit." Quinn seemed to stiffen at the news.

"How far behind are they..?"

"About a week." There was a grim silence from the Captain. Bowen became somewhat wary overhearing such important talk so he pretended to be very interested in the shelving of sealant chemicals.

"What about the Titan?" Quinn asked.

"I keep hearing they've been picked up."

"Picked up..?"

"New regulations coming out from Metro into the quadrants. Eye Agents are stop searching Free Traders. Apparently Captain August had to dump something precious before they were stopped. Last I heard they'd been detained at Winter Star." Bowen heard Quinn sigh in frustration and he detected a sombre hint to his voice.

"How did regulations like that get passed..?"

"I don't know. But Stormraven is inbound, three days from now give or take. Captain Ishtar has it under control."

"I'm sure she does."

"Free Trading isn't what it used to be." Nole said. Quinn took a deep breath.

"No... it isn't."

"I still think about the Dragon sometimes." Nole said.

"It was a quite a ship." Quinn replied. "My offer's still on the table." he said. "I could use you out there." Nole exhaled as the printout finished from the machine.

"I might just consider it." Nole said as he tore it away. He folded it up in his hands and passed the order sheet through the hatch to Quinn. "My roots might be too deep."

"I understand." Quinn said. Nole disappeared to the side and emerged again through the door and stood before them both.

"Anything else I can get for you spacers?"

"I think that's everything for the garden." Bowen said. "Thanks a lot Nole."

"Not a problem. Anything else for you Captain?"

"No we're set."

"Right then I'll have the boys set to work and it'll be on the landing pad in the morning." Nole said outstretching his hand to Quinn. The two shook hands firmly and an unspoken history emanated from it. When Bowen shook Nole's hand it almost totally eclipsed his own. "Good to meet you Bowen."

"You too Nole." As they parted, Bowen was struck by a niggling sense of deja vu.

"Until next time Nole, thanks again." Quinn said opening the door for Bowen.

"Watch your self out there Zeke."

"I always do."

35.

Back out in the yard, the weather had picked up with an emerging sandstorm blowing in. The hot and heavy air was thick with pinkish red sand and it was hard to see too far ahead. Looking up, Bowen couldn't even see the top of the sky station that overlooked the city. Quinn donned his scarf over his face and pulled his goggles down over his eyes. He checked his shoulder slung weapon and patted Bowen on the shoulder.

"Come on let's go. Stick close Rhys before we look like an opportunity."

"An opportunity?" Bowen asked but Quinn didn't seem to hear him over the wind. Bowen walked with the Captain as they made their way back through the winding metal walkways of the city. The howling wind was billowing through the shade canopies testing their endurance. Where earlier there had been lots of people moving from place to place, now there was almost no one, the change in the weather had forced them inside. The sounds of the mining operations was mostly lost on the wind. After they turned a corner they had to stop. A huge metal gate had been closed off back to the market. Quinn tutted in frustration.

"We'll have to go another way." he said gently pulling Bowen back by the shoulder. They marched back to a previous turn and made their way through more alleys and through quiet strips of shuttered doorways. Bowen was glad he had worn his hat as he pulled the brim down to shield his eyes from the sand that blew through the streets that were like wind tunnels.

"You and Nole used to know each other, Captain?" Bowen asked as they rounded on a quieter spot.

"You could say that."

"Did he used to be a Free Trader?"

Quinn seemed to be distracted looking at weathered

signs and crooked direction posts as he answered.

"He was at Sovistan with us." the Captain replied absent mindedly.

"...us?" Bowen tried.

"I think we've taken a wrong turn." Quinn seemed to say to himself. He directed them to return the way they came and take another corner. Oasis City was proving to be a warren of alleys and walkways and it was poorly signposted. Without the reference point of the sky station above them, the city was a challenge to navigate. Bowen squinted through the blowing sand and his heart missed a beat. He put his hand on the Captain's arm.

"Captain." he said. Quinn stopped.

"What is it?"

"They're watching us." Bowen said as quiet as he could. Down an alleyway to their side were a couple of figures watching them from the shadows.

"Good spot." Quinn replied. "It's alright. Just keep walking, but slowly." he instructed Bowen. Bowen's heart had begun to beat faster. Quinn slowly took his weapon off his shoulder and held it upright in one hand, his other on Bowen's shoulder. As they moved, Bowen saw more dark shapes through gaps in walls and steel fences watching them as they passed. From lower levels, he saw others emerge silently from hatches and doorways. Some looked fairly squat and others appeared malformed at least from the way they moved, but they were all hooded and masked. Some, Bowen noticed were holding pipes, drills, wrenches and other tools like weapons. Bowen tried not to panic, but the fear was rising in his throat. Quinn's human hand on his shoulder reassured him a little, but the threat he felt was real. The only sound was the howling winds and their quick foot steps along with the creaking of metal hinges and clinking of the canopies above them.

"We should have stayed at Nole's." Quinn said to himself in frustration. They turned corner after corner as they looked for the market place and the exit back to the landing pads.

Every now and then Quinn stopped and considered their next move, but only for a moment. At one corner Bowen dared a look back behind them and saw that they were being followed.

"Captain who are they?" Bowen asked breathlessly as they briskly walked another route.

"Vermin dwellers. The bad weather's drawn them out. A lot of mining cities like this have them. They'll leave us alone when we reach the market." Bowen wanted to ask what they wanted or what they were going to do, but his questions caught in his throat as he imagined the answers. "Come on this is the only way we haven't been." Quinn said as he marched Bowen onward. The route opened up into a cluttered courtyard but it was not the marketplace Bowen noticed to his dismay. And their way was blocked.

Several vermin dwellers stood around the passageway ahead. Quinn's grip tightened on Bowen's shoulder, beckoning him to stop moving. Through the blowing sand, the vermin dwellers stood there silently. Some wore old welding masks, others wore goggles and visors. They hid their faces behind dirty rags and cloths and a couple wore broken mining helmets. Their patchwork attire was a mixture of tattered clothing and ragged uniforms. Bowen swallowed hard. Despite the rushing hot air Bowen felt a chill.

"Stay calm Rhys." The Captain whispered. "No sudden movements." Bowen wasn't sure he could move he was that afraid. The Captain let go of Bowen's shoulder. Bowen watched from the corner of his eye as the Captain began to slowly reach under his jacket to his belt. Through the wind, he heard a small clasp open. Bowen turned and saw that the dwellers who had followed them had silently blocked off the way they had entered the courtyard. Quinn quietly retrieved a handful of plasma rounds encased in reflective metal. Bowen kept his eyes on the vermin dwellers and tried to control his breathing. The Captain slowly and carefully entered the rounds into the feeder slot one after another, causing minimal noise as he did so. Bowen was breathing harder.

"Let us through!" Quinn shouted over the wind. They gave no response. It was impossible for Bowen to know if they had understood the Captain. Beneath the howling wind and the billowing sand, Bowen heard quick nattering, chirping and clicking. They were speaking to each other. "You know what this don't you!?" Quinn called as he cocked the lever of his rifle. A low hum emanated from the gun as the plasma cartridge flared within. The sounds made some of them back away slightly. Bowen was acutely aware however that there were only two of them and at least ten of the creatures. The Captain lowered his voice again. "Bowen when I tell you to move, you move fast you hear me? We'll only have a few seconds to get past them and it's a straight shot back to the market and the ship."

"Yes Captain."

"Alright. I'll be right behind you." One of the dwellers took a cautious step forward. In its hand was a rusted saw. Bowen couldn't tell if its red colouration was from the sandstorm or from blood. Quinn clicked the safety button off on his plasma rifle. The internal mechanisms whirred in anticipation and a red glow shone from the barrel. Bowen heard little and cautious footsteps behind him.

"Another step and I'll kill you!" Quinn warned the saw wielder. The creature either didn't understand or didn't care. It defiantly attempted a quick step towards Quinn. Bowen didn't have time to react. In an instant there was a flash and a bang that fizzed with red plasma. The vermin dweller's goggles shattered off his face as the back of his head exploded. Without a sound it fell to the floor like a rag doll. Bowen's ear rang. The noise of Quinn cocking the lever on the rifle cut through the muffled silence and the spent plasma casing flew across him steaming through the sandblasted air.

"Rhys go!" Quinn's voice sounded deeper and far away. A surge of adrenaline went through Bowen and his feet took charge. The death of the boldest vermin dweller had shaken the rest of them for a brief moment long enough for Bowen to sprint past them as they darted for cover. Bowen was on auto pilot as he ran along the metal walkways. He heard a further two shots from Quinn's plasma rifle as he ran. Before he knew it, he reached the sheltered marketplace. It was illuminated by harsh flood lights. The few people who were still around watched with minimal interest as Bowen sprinted past them with Quinn not far behind him. Bowen was sure he heard Quinn call out to him to slow down more than once, but the adrenaline wouldn't let him stop.

He finally stopped to look back when he reached the edge of the tarmac flats by a worker's shelter. The winds were still high, but the storm seemed to be easing off. Apathetic landing pad workers passed by and saw Bowen come to a stop breathless against a railing. Quinn caught up to him and was considerably less out of breath than Bowen was. Bowen was gasping for air as he removed his hat. Quinn unloaded his rifle before he slung it onto his shoulder again. He then removed his scarf from his face and rested the goggles on his forehead exposing his cybernetic eye.

"You're faster than you look." Quinn commented. Despite the compliment Bowen was more than ever aware of how out of shape he actually was. His breath was coming fast and hard.

"In through your nose, out through your mouth." Quinn advised.

"I... I forgot how hot it is." said Bowen.

"Here." Quinn thrust a canteen into Bowen's shaking hand who opened it and took a couple of swigs of the cool water within.

"I'm sorry Captain... I heard you shouting for me to stop." Bowen said. Quinn smiled with the corner of his mouth.

"I told you to run and you ran." he patted Bowen on the shoulder. Bowen looked off towards the hulking shadow of the Memento on the landing pad through the sand storm. His breathing had slowed.

"That man... that alien with the saw, he was gonna..."

Bowen tried.

"He was."

Bowen took another swig of water from the canteen. Quinn leant on the railing next to him. "You've never seen someone get shot before have you." It wasn't a question, the Captain correctly assumed as much. Bowen heard a tone in Quinn's voice that he hadn't heard before. For a moment, it reminded him of Mason.

"On the news a few times, but not for real..." Bowen said. Quinn took a deep breath.

"It might not feel like it, but you kept your head. I'm proud of you." the Captain said. Bowen looked at Quinn who beheld him with his yellow robotic eye. Bowen smiled bravely.

"Thanks." It was all he could say as he passed the canteen back to the Captain. He didn't quite agree that he had kept his cool, he had simply run for his life. Quinn patted him on the shoulder.

"Let's get back." he said.

They stepped out of the worker's shelter and began across the massive stretch of tarmac towards the Memento. The noise of the titanic fuel rig pumping away into the ship still sounded across the landscape and the distant sounds of the mine came from somewhere behind the city. The sandstorm was passing. The winds died down as they walked across the baking tarmac and the Memento greeted them from within the haze of the sweltering evening light. The cargo bay doors were slowly opening and the workers were resuming their duties. The loader mechs clomped their way in and out of the ship carrying crates and containers ready for the waiting trucks that were heaped in sand.

Bowen looked up at the clearing pink sky as they approached the ramp.

"That's just typical isn't it."

36.

Dear Bowen,
We're so pleased that you are settling in to your new job. We can't wait to see all the photographs of the places you've been to. Some bad news, we had to get a vet out to see Samhain because he wasn't eating much. The vet couldn't find anything wrong with him, we think he just misses you! We hope you are somewhere nice and that you are keeping warm and fed. Are you still on track for coming home after Obelisk station? We are so proud of you. Take care.
Mum and Dad
x

Bowen sat in the comm suite, illuminated by the green light of the screen. The nights after the encounter with the vermin dwellers, Bowen had a few restless sleeps, but he felt safe within the Memento. Safiya had been sympathetic to his story when he told her that night. If not for the fact that he had been with the Captain when it happened, Bowen suspected that she may have said I told you so. He was happy however to have received messages from his parents and one from Niamh.

Hello Bowen,
It's good to hear from you. Don't worry about not writing, I hardly have time to read messages these days, we're so swamped with work here. And where we are is quite patchy for communication as it is. It's great that your out there on a ship. It's not quite like we imagined is it? I hope you are enjoying space travel, I'm not sure I could ever permanently be planetside ever again. But I do plan on going back to Saxon in a year or two to see mum & dad, hopefully by then your

an established farmer like you said. The jungles here are dangerous but beautiful, some of the wildlife you wouldn't believe. Hope your adventure is going well. See you soon.

Niamh

xx

Bowen sat in his seat and re read both com-disks a couple of times. It was nice to feel connected to them all, even just like this. But at the same time they all felt so far away. It put a little knot in his stomach. They were staying on Davarak for a further two weeks, he still had time to think of his responses to his family. As he sat there alone in the comm suite, Jules found her way into his mind. He had still not replied to the message he had received the day he left home. Perhaps now was the time to say something back. There wouldn't be another stop until Obelisk station in another few months time, where he would be looking to get a flight home. If he was to reply to Jules, it would have to be soon.

From everything he had heard about Obelisk, it was massive. A station with its own warp gate, many times larger than either Pennine or Ganderonn, designed to propel the largest of star ships through space. He couldn't wait to see it, but it would herald the end of his journey, his adventure as Niamh put it. Just then Bowen noticed the time. He ejected the com-disk and stuffed the others into his bag. He didn't want to be late.

Bowen had spent the last few days in the garden. Nole had kept his word and was on the docking bay that next morning after they had seen him. Moryys and some other cargo workers helped haul the equipment up to the lower decks and Bowen had got to work. He installed the humidity exchanger and the moisture collector in one afternoon. He had become so wrapped up in his work that he almost forgot that he had agreed to see Safiya on the rec deck. Bowen apologised profusely and Safiya had said she understood, but he could tell she was angry.

That morning, before the post had arrived, he had been in the engine halls with Jothazar. The huge water tanks that had been bought could only be installed in a back corner of the engine halls and so Jothazar had grumpily agreed to coordinate their installation. The piping to the garden ran right through the series of shared walls. After a successful test, the water flowed freely into the garden. The last problem to be fixed was the wiring of the heat lamps. As Bowen ate breakfast that morning with Duggy and Ramphry after the post had been distributed, he pondered as to who he would turn to for help. It had been on his mind even as he was reading the com-disks.

Bowen left the comms suite and made his way to the crew decks. As he passed the stairwell atrium he saw a group of technicians opening wall panels. Vetura was with them. They noticed each other as she was setting up small floodlights. They exchanged smiles as he passed. Bowen began to climb the stairs. He smiled at those who he walked by. Finally he reached the hallway that connected to commercial seating. He was hit by the memory of the first morning he had boarded the ship. As he rounded the corner he found the others stood by the corridor to the departure tunnel. Moryys, Duggy, Ramphry, Zaren and Shillok greeted him as he approached.

"Here he is." Duggy proclaimed. Bowen received pats on the back and gentle punches to the shoulder.

"Our very own vermin dweller hunter." Shillok said.

"This human can't be stopped." Duggy said throwing his arm over Bowen's shoulder. "Don't get in his way or he'll kill you with a rake." Bowen smiled but he felt his face go red. Word had spread that the Captain and the gardener had walked off into Oasis City and that they had run into trouble with vermin dwellers. As was always the case, the story had morphed and twisted.

"This gardening business is just a front isn't it?" Zaren laughed. "The Captain's got you doing something top secret down there hasn't he?"

"Bio weapons." Shillok said suddenly. "He's developing micro cellular aggressors that kill from the inside out."

"Is he really?" Ramphry asked confused. The group laughed as one with Ramphry scratching his head. Kytos and the crocodilian Vargoth inspected their shore leave passes before they walked down the thin metal passage off the ship. As they walked across the landing pad in the late evening sun, Bowen hung back to speak to Moryys for a moment.

"The guys don't actually think I killed some vermin dwellers do they?"

"No." Moryys smiled. "I cant speak for other crew members though."

"Oh."

"I wouldn't worry about it. But if you notice people being extra nice to you or giving you a wide berth in the corridors that'll be why." Moryys said with a laugh.

As the group walked across the black in the late evening light, the sky was becoming a dark purple. Oasis City was beginning to light up preparing for the night with numerous huge flood lights flickering on across the rooftops. Bowen felt a pang of trepidation as they approached the metal walkways after what had happened recently. But he reminded himself that they were merely going for a drink in the local bar and not exploring the alleyways.

The city had become more crowded in the days since he and the Captain had visited Nole. More ships had arrived including Bowen heard, the Stormraven that Quinn and Nole had spoken of. When they reached the market, Bowen saw that it was fully set up and seemed to show no signs of stopping due to the influx of new arrivals. As the group made their way through the market, Bowen was almost sandwiched between Ramphry and Moryys, so he did not receive the same amount of harassment he had done the first time he was there. Up ahead, Bowen saw the front of the bar. The doorway had been propped open and there were patrons stood outside on a wide porch with drinks in hand. The working girls were out in full.

They had dolled themselves up with extra care for the evening and it seemed the most beautiful alien girls had taken the prime spots for themselves. Above the metal porch, the neon sign blared the words 'Miengu Waters'.

Bowen and the others wormed their way through the crowds in the market until they managed to enter the bar. Bowen was relieved to see that the place was not as crowded as it appeared outside but there was still a buzzing atmosphere. The bar itself was much larger on the inside than it first appeared. There was a low lit, smokey atmosphere, pierced with harsh neon lighting from the ceiling and from behind the bar. From the corner of the room the muffled sound of synthrash music came out of a large music player that stood as tall as the ceiling.

The group found their way to an empty table and they claimed some seats. Zaren had recently lost a bet with Shillok and so he got the first round. He returned with six tall glasses and a pitcher of iced Province Blue with some purple leaves from a Behemoth Baobab floating in it. Shillok stood up and shook his green tendrils behind his back as he lifted up his glass. He cleared his throat and got everyone's attention.

"Gentlemen. I'd just like to say cheers to Mr Bowen Rhys from Saxon for being our new gardener." Bowen felt his face go red as everyone raised their glasses to him.

"Thanks Shillok." he said smiling. As one they drank. Bowen winced as he emptied his glass. The hairs stood on the back of his hands and his tongue tingled.

"That'll put some scales on you." Duggy said to him. Zaren began to refill glasses with the pitcher as Ramphry let out a burp.

Before long, they were adding to the ambience with their raucous voices and they slowly made their way down to the bottom of the pitcher. Duggy spent some credits at the music player and exposed the bar to a synthrash band called Meteor Destroyer. At one point, Bowen was in conversation with Zaren concerning unlicensed weaponry and the next,

Ramphry was asking him about cows. After the Province Blue had emptied, Moryys took the next round and returned with pints of a dark drink called Deep Dark with a reddish foam. It was thick and bitter Bowen discovered but it had a warm quality. The conversations ebbed and flowed. Moryys told Bowen about some top priority containers each with their own power source that had been brought over from the Stormraven that had been placed in a secure zone in cargo. Bowen could feel the effects of the drinks begin to settle in. Despite the close encounter with the vermin dwellers, he was beginning to think this wasn't such a bad place after all.

A short while passed and they were surrounded by a flock of working girls who had spotted them. Ramphry was led away from the table by a couple of them who enticed him with a private dance. Shillok passed some dona over and a red skinned beauty with gold hair sat in his lap. Zaren and Moryys politely declined the attention. Moryys seemed ever so slightly bashful to Bowen's surprise. One girl with an abundance of curves approached the side of the table where Bowen and Duggy sat. Her jewellery jingled as she moved. Her sparkling orange eyes caught Bowen's attention and he noticed that much of her green skinned body was covered in tattoos.

"Hey, want a girlfriend for the evening?" As she asked him she ran her hand across his shoulder and down his chest. Bowen cleared his throat as his face flared red. Standing confidently in her knee high lace up boots, she was the same height as Bowen on his stool. When she threw her long white hair over her shoulder, she wafted her exotic perfume at him. Bowen recognised the smell from a long time ago. Bowen's head was a little fuzzy but he managed to answer.

"I uh. I'm sorry I'm sort of with Jules, I mean Safiya, Safiya I'm with Safiya." Bowen fumbled and winced at himself. He made eye contact with Duggy whose expression was half a grin, half a cringe. The working girl stroked the stubble on Bowen's face.

"Neither of them will find out. Promise." Despite the

increasing rush he felt in his lower half Bowen declined her affections.

"You're very pretty but no I'm sorry." The alien girl playfully pouted.

"Come find me if you change your mind." she said. Bowen smiled stiffly as she winked at him. "What about you handsome?" she said as she turned to Duggy.

"How much are we talking?" he asked.

"Fifteen for thirty minutes. Twenty five for an hour." As they agreed on price, terms and conditions, Bowen hiccuped as he nursed the bottom of his Deep Dark. The girl led Duggy away from the table towards one of the back rooms at the far end of the bar. As they left, she turned back to Bowen and blew him a kiss. Bowen grabbed a handful of spiced nuts from a bowl on the table as he found himself sat alone in the crowded room. The others were engaged in their own conversations. Ramphry returned from his private dance with a dim smile across his face. The girl on Shillok's lap was twiddling with the green tendrils on his head. Zaren and Moryys were arm wrestling. Despite the size of Moryys, Zaren was holding his own, his hidden muscles bulged from under the striped fur on his exposed arms. Bowen's mind had some breathing room. The lights above the bar were a little brighter than they were earlier and if he concentrated on it, the room was ever so slightly pulsing in his vision.

Try as he might, he couldn't stop thinking about Jules. He felt ashamed that despite his fairly happy romance with Safiya, Jules still occupied his unconscious thoughts. Things were quite different now than they were the morning he left home, and he had first read her com-disk. Maybe some time apart had been a good thing? Perhaps she genuinely did miss him and she was eagerly awaiting his reply? What if she was back home in New Mersey right now waiting for him? But then what of Safiya? Part of him knew that it was foolish to think that it would last.

Soon Bowen was shook from his thoughts by Moryys

taking the empty stool next to his. Moryys seemed untouched by the amount of alcohol he had consumed.

"Zaren's stronger than he looks." Moryys said massaging his forearm. "You okay?" he asked Bowen.

"Yeah I'm alright." he lied.

"What did you think of your Deep Dark?"

"It was okay, but I don't think I'll have another one."

"A bit strong isn't it? It's the local miner's drink."

"It's not for me I don't think." Bowen said as he pushed the empty pint glass away from him. Once again Bowen noticed five people approach his side of the table. They were not working girls, nor were they local miners. These aliens were spacers. Bowen didn't recognise them. They were not their fellow crew members. The man in the centre was a Feranahng like Steg. His canine face was as rugged as his uniform. He patted Moryys on the shoulder.

"Excuse me." he said. Moryys swivelled around on his stool and noticed the group. Before Moryys could say anything the man spoke again. "It is him, I told you!" A smile appeared at the corner of Moryys's big mouth. One of the other aliens, an ugly fish headed male grinned with sharp teeth.

"Mister Mega Fist!" he cried out. Moryys cleared his throat and greeted them.

"Fellas."

"Didn't expect to see you here." the first man said. One of the spacers, a short man with rough skin piped up.

"Say one of your lines! Strength is Power! or Choose your Defeat!" he shouted jumping up and down. Moryys rubbed the back of his neck and chuckled.

"I don't really do that sort of thing any more." he said. As they talked at Moryys, Bowen looked back at the table with a bemused smile on his face. His smile disappeared when he saw the others. Shillok and Zaren exchanged a look as the working girl on Shillok's lap kissed him on the cheek and left in a hurry. Ramphry was downing the last of his pint of Deep Dark and he stifled a burp. He wiped his hairy red hand across his snout.

Bowen didn't know Ramphry could look so serious. Duggy was still absent. Bowen suddenly felt a change in the atmosphere at the table as he turned back to look at the conversation. Moryys had turned his back to them and was looking into his drink.

"I thought he was still in MX-12?" said one of the strangers.

"Yeah I thought so too." replied another.

"I remember reading that his sentence was ten years?"

"Nah I heard fifteen?" Bowen's heart began to beat quicker in his chest as he noticed that nearby other people were beginning to look. He watched as the Fera-nahng popped a pill into his mouth and cracked it with his teeth. He then began to sniff and twitch slightly.

"He only was only in for six."

"He probably bought himself a shorter sentence behind the scenes." Bowen noticed that Moryys was biting his lip and his fist was clenching. Zaren appeared from Bowen's side and attempted to intervene.

"Come on guys, we're just here for a drink." Bowen took a deep breath and realised he was sweating.

"I reckon he's gone soft." said a spacer.

"I know he was a house villain but he took it a little too far wouldn't you say?"

"Oh yeah definitely." one jeered.

Shillok appeared to the other side of Moryys.

"I think everybody needs to back off a little."

"Was he arrested for the drug charges or for murdering his tag partner..?" said one of the men. At that, Moryys turned back around and stood up from his stool. Bowen was just intoxicated enough to not fully register what happened next. In an instant, Ramphry, who appeared from seemingly nowhere was stood in front of Moryys holding him back from the spacers. Shillok had his green hand against the chest of a spacer who was squaring up to him and Zaren was involved in a similar altercation. Bowen hadn't realised that he too was also on his feet. He was on auto pilot as a surge of adrenaline and testosterone commanded him to jump into action with his friends. It became a blur to Bowen who had gotten up too fast. He was aware that Moryys was bellowing. The spacers were goading him, some were laughing. He heard others around the bar, some voices from miners and other patrons were laughing and taunting the commotion. Working girls were scattering. Bowen found himself squaring up to the short alien who had his horrid little fists clenched into Bowen's vest with a mean grin on his face. Bowen was angry and a part of him wanted to fight. It was stronger than his urge to run.

Bowen didn't know who threw the first punch. The sounds of grunting and shouting filled the air as fists flew. The little alien had surprising strength. Bowen was shoved backwards where he felt the table wedge into his back. Glass shattered as drinks fell to the floor and the stools went flying. Without thinking he threw a wild fist into the face of the alien. That didn't make him let go, so he hit him again. The face of the alien contorted with angry pain. For a split second, Bowen had the urge to apologise. But as the moment passed a crack of pain went through Bowen's face as he was punched in retaliation. Bowen felt a warm splattering on his upper lip as his nose burst. Still at a disadvantage being held down against the table, Bowen attempted to kick the alien in his stomach, but his foot went wide into some loose clothing. The little man clobbered Bowen in his mid section, forcing the air from his lungs. Bowen held the strong wrist of the man as he was fast running out of options. To his horror, Bowen realised that the alien had his rough skinned hand around his throat. Bowen threw another punch but broadcasted it enough that the man simply moved his head back to avoid it, laughing as he did so. The synthrash blared out of the speakers that had been knocked into and was now playing the music at full volume. His ears rang as he felt another punch at the side of his head. His own blood now trickling into his mouth, Bowen desperately fumbled a free hand over the table. Without any forethought, he attempted to smash the pint glass he found in his hand into the alien's face, but he completely missed and ended up launching it over the chaos somewhere into the bar.

Just as real panic was about to set in, the table juddered from behind Bowen's head. His attacker had barely enough time to look up from Bowen as both of Duggy's feet collided into his face. Bowen gasped and began to pant as he was released from being choked. As he struggled to catch his breath back Bowen saw Duggy, who was naked from the waist down, pounding the face of the alien with both fists. Bowen's heart was on overdrive as another surge of adrenaline kicked in. Before he knew was he was doing, Bowen attempted to help Shillok who was grappling with a spacer. His feet took over and Bowen heard himself shouting as he ran forwards. Without a plan of action he tackled the man to the ground, who did not let go of Shillok. The three of them collided into a table that broke in half with their combined weight. Bowen's head was spinning. He felt himself be picked up off the floor by someone and was about to say thanks, but then was met by the curious sensation of flying as he was hurled across the room. He was numb to the crash as he fell into another table. He was wet with blood and various drinks and he felt the sting of glass in his skin. Bowen sat up dazed. He hadn't eaten enough that day. He carefully stood up, he needed to piss and he was hungry and he was horny. He wished he had paid to fuck that girl. He wanted to fight more.

The music was pulsing fast and hard. The windows shook and the lights bounced in their fittings. Bowen saw Moryys being ganged up on by a couple of the spacers. He fruitlessly yelled at them to stop. When they didn't it made him mad. His body took over again. In his hands suddenly was a stool. It was nowhere near as heavy as it should have been. Thunderous drums sounded and synthetic guitars screeched as Bowen swung the stool with strength he didn't actually possess into the back of one of the spacers fighting Moryys. The man howled in pain as he fell away to the side. Bowen watched in awe as Moryys grabbed the other man and lifted him into the air above his head. Bowen's jaw dropped as he saw Moryys throw the man across the room. In his distracted state Bowen was caught off guard. He felt something sharp smash against his face. His right eye was suddenly wet with blood. His body had had enough. He couldn't see out of his right eye and his left ear was swollen and ringing. Bowen felt the floor come up to catch him as another man was above him hitting him in the face over and over and over and over.

A boot saved him. It kicked the man in the face. Bowen felt a bloodied and broken tooth splatter onto him. The weight of the other man left him. He had seen that boot before. It was brown and knee high. The boots stood either side of his head. He could see someone's flight suit pants. They were red. From far away came a muffled gun shot. The music stopped and the speakers let out a whine of static. Another three gunshots fired in quick succession. Then everything stopped. Bowen again found himself being picked up a strong hand. His feet planted on the floor.

"On your feet Rhys." he heard. It was the voice of Garber. She stood with one hand on Bowen's shoulder and with the other she pointed her side arm into the air. The end of its barrel was smoking red. The bar was a mess. At least three tables were broken, stools were everywhere, broken glass littered the floor and there were puddles of drink with spots of blood here and there. The guys and the other spacers were the only people left in the bar but for a couple of bar staff peeking from cover. Another woman's voice called. She had been hidden in his peripheral and he had to fully turn his head to see her. She looked human. Scarred and stern with sharp features, she looked older than she was. Her silvery hair fell about her armoured shoulders and she wore a purple and black short cape. In her hands was an intimidating gas powered ballistic launcher with a snub nose. When she spoke, Bowen's ear rang and he winced.

"Causing trouble again!? After the shit we've been through!?" The other spacers suddenly looked like children being scolded. "All Stormraven crew members out and back to the ship, NOW! You five have forfeited your shore leave. You hear me!?"

"Yes Captain Ishtar." a few spoke together. The five spacers one by one marched out. Bowen watched as they passed them through the door. Garber squeezed Bowen's shoulder as they walked by. Captain Ishtar turned to face Garber and therefore Bowen. Bowen saw that she had purple eyes that seemed to glow slightly. She looked Bowen up and down before she spoke quietly to Garber.

"I'll have to see to this lot. I'll meet you at your landing pad in an hour?"

"Myself and Quinn will wait for you on our cargo ramp." Garber replied. Ishtar holstered her weapon.

"Roger that. Can you cover this? I'll owe you." she said motioning to the mess of the bar. Garber nodded.

"Sure, I'll hold you to that." she said.

"Solara."

"Magella." With that, Captain Ishtar left the bar. As the door closed, Bowen heard her muffled voice as she began to shout again. Garber said nothing. The only sound from the room was dripping from spilled drink and the occasional spark from the music station. From what Bowen could see, she was even more stern than usual. She took a deep breath through her nose.

"Can you stand on your own?" she asked Bowen.

"I, I think so." Bowen managed. At that, she let go of his shoulder and strode across the empty bar room, her trench coat billowing as she crunched over the broken glass. None of the others said anything as they watched her wrap her knuckles on the bar by the pay station. The bar staff came out of hiding looking shaken at the sight of their wrecked bar room. Garber placed her sidearm on the bar top and withdrew a small card from inside her coat.

"Apologies for the mess." Garber said stiffly. One of the bar staff, a small pink boggle eyed alien took her card and began a payment through the machine. From across the room Bowen heard the exasperation in Garber's voice as she sighed. She was tapping her blue fingertips on the wood as the alien processed her compensation. The guys all exchanged looks. Bowen didn't want to think about how much their night out had cost. After a painfully long time, the pay station pinged as the payment was complete. Bowen heard the barman thank Garber and she turned around to face them all again. Her frowning pink eyes fell on Duggy as she placed her gun back in her belted shoulder holster.

"I assume you didn't leave the ship dressed like that?"

"Left the rest of my clothes in the back room ma'am." Duggy said shamelessly. There was a quiet moment where the rest of them waited for Duggy to return with his pants and shoes back on. Garber stood with her hands on her hips tapping her foot. As Bowen stood swaying slightly, the pain caught up to him. His face and head were pounding as Duggy returned.

"Everyone out, back to the ship. And hand over your shore leave passes." Garber instructed them. One by one they shuffled over to the doorway. As they started to leave, the bar staff slowly began to sweep up and pick tables and stools off the floor. Garber waited for them all the leave and was the last one out. She marched them back through the market and towards the landing pads. The night had set in and the vast landing pads were illuminated by floodlights. The gigantic legs of the landing struts and the cargo ramp were illuminated as well as the boarding tunnel. As they crossed the tarmac, they were bathed in the orange light, Zaren and Shillok patted Bowen on the back as Zaren quietly joked about the fight. Duggy lit a purple cigarette next to Bowen whose head was becoming more blurry by the minute.

"You look like shit Saxon. You have a go at each of them did you?" Duggy asked.

"I'm not sure." Bowen said smiling weakly.

"If I'd known I would have pushed you to say yes to

that girl, or at least dragged you with us. She really liked you." Bowen smiled as much as he was able with his swollen face.

"How was it then?"

"Yeah, not bad for a soft-skin. I've had worse, I've had better. Nice girl, wants to be a teacher..." Bowen chuckled painfully.

"Hey man, thanks for jumping in with that little guy, he was about to really do me in."

"The little freak had it coming. Did you see him? Walking around looking like that." Duggy said as he exhaled a dark purple cloud that appeared black in the light of the landing pads. "How did it all kick off like that?" Bowen turned his head to make sure Moryys wasn't in ear shot. When Bowen saw him a ways back with Ramphry, he spoke quietly.

"The other spacers recognised Moryys from his fighting days and they started antagonising him."

"Ah right. Yeah that'd do it." Bowen cleared his throat and tried to keep his thoughts together in his throbbing mind.

"MX-12 is a prison then?" Bowen asked.

"Fortress facility on Harridan. Serious place." Duggy confirmed. Bowen remembered what the spacers had said. Drugs and murder. "I don't reckon it was like they said." Duggy said looking back at Moryys. "He's not the type."

"It hasn't come up."

"He'll probably tell you in his own time." Part of Bowen did want to know what happened. Moryys had been nothing but kind to Bowen since they'd met. And he had been a greater friend to him than Simon or anyone else had been for years.

Before long, the whole group followed closely by Officer Garber reached the opening of the boarding tunnel.

"Gentlemen." Garber said as he turned to face them all. "Would anyone be good enough to explain what happened back there?" Before anyone could react Moryys answered.

"It was my fault ma'am."

"I'm sorry ma'am that's not entirely correct." Shillok said.

"We were provoked." Zaren added. Bowen coughed and spoke up.

"Officer, it wasn't Moryys's fault they started fighting with us." Bowen turned to Moryys who gave him a smile and a gentle nudge with his giant elbow. Garber listened to them all and considered their input.

"You're lucky we didn't have to carry one of you back to the ship on a stretcher."

"Nah they weren't nothing." Duggy said.

"Zaren your security, you should be better than brawling in clubs." Garber said.

"Aye ma'am. I apologise."

"Well, I hope you all had a fun night. For the remainder of our stay on Davarak you can drink on the rec deck is that understood?" Everyone acknowledged her as she opened the door of the tunnel for them. Bowen was the last to enter. He held onto the door carefully as his head was throbbing.

"Bowen." Garber grabbed his attention quietly. Bowen stopped and turned to face her as the others walked up the tunnel chatting. Her blue skin looked almost brown in the orange light of the landing pad but her pink eyes still shone through. "Get yourself up to the doctor and have yourself checked out, you're by far the worst off out of all your friends." She said as she plucked a piece of glass from his sore and bloodied cheek.

"I think I'm okay." Bowen said as he began to lose his balance. The world began to twist and turn and a new darkness creeped its way in from the edges of his eyesight. Bowen felt himself stumble but Garber caught him with her arm. He felt her surprising strength heave his arm over her neck as she supported him.

"Right come on." he heard her say. "I'm taking you to the surgery."

"Okay." Bowen said. He felt his feet trying to walk, but only his tip toes were glancing the floor.

"Don't fall asleep that's an order."

"Yes ma'am."

37.

Bowen didn't remember being taken up to the doctor by Garber. Nor did he remember much of what happened when he was there. When he regained his awareness, he couldn't see. From what he could tell, he was wearing some form of oversized helmet. He could hear beeping and machinery quietly ticking over and he sensed a cool massaging feeling over his whole head. The pain in his head and face was more or less gone. The rest of his body was reasonably comfortable, he cautiously probed around with his hands and discovered he was on some sort of chair.

"Good evening Mr. Rhys." came the voice of Doctor Jinn-Quo.

"Where, what..?" Bowen tried. Jinn-Quo began to move unseen by Bowen in his clunky mechanical suit.

"Steady now, you're in the surgery. Officer Garber brought you here earlier this evening. She said you and your companions had been fighting in the local bar and that you appeared to get the worst of it." Bowen made a noise confirming the summary. "It appears you have a penchant for injuries to the head." Jinn-Quo said.

"It's not intentional." Bowen managed to say. "What is this?"

"It's a cranial assessment and triage dome. For the last couple of hours it has been easing your concussion. It should be done in a few minutes. The stitches in your face and hands will dissolve in a few days but some scarring may remain. I'm going to be sending you away with a course of painkillers."

Bowen felt too weak to say anything. He heard the doctor lumbering about and tinkering with this and that and he was content to sit and wait for the procedure to finish. He had no sense of time. He thought about asking the doctor but the words didn't come out. He assumed it was the middle of the night. There was no way to tell with the dome on his head. In the total black underneath the machine, his mind wandered. He remembered what he could of the events of the night with the guys. The drinks had dulled his memories to much of it.

His mind wandered further back and began a winding train of thought. He thought about how much time he realistically had left on the ship. He knew that his time was coming to an end onboard. And that meant a few things. The garden was only a temporary passion project. Would he have to pass on the responsibility to someone else? If so, who? To his knowledge, Bowen was the only person on the Memento with any interest in the place. Would it merely fall into disrepair after he was gone? Safiya had still not come to see it. Safiya was another issue. It felt like there was a conversation waiting to be had between them. And then there were the guys. It had been a few years since he had been part of a group. He had expected to get to know at least someone onboard through work, but what he hadn't anticipated was to fall in with a group of genuine friends. Perhaps they could stay in touch after he returned to Saxon? Would that be possible logistically? Would any of them even want to..?

His mum and dad emerged in the eye of his mind. He wondered what time it was on Saxon at that moment. He saw his parents in the kitchen. They were sat in their chairs by the fire with the radio on. The smell of tea and toast drifted at the edge of his mind and he heard Samhain purring. He had spent the last few years wishing that he could get away and attempt to make something of himself. But he realised then that he couldn't wait to go back.

Suddenly he heard a series of beeps and the sound of the doctor heaving about.

"That's it then." Jinn-Quo said. "I'm going to slowly remove the dome for you now, Bowen, I must ask you not to move." Bowen did as he was told. He heard clamps and switches being flicked and release valves hissing as they opened. The dome was slowly taken off his head and his vision was restored. The room was dimly lit but for small coloured blinking bulbs in the surrounding machinery as well as low strip lighting around the edge of the floor and ceiling. Bowen reached up and carefully touched his face. As the doctor had said, there was a line of stitches across his cheek that he traced delicately with his finger. His knuckles on both hands felt sore as he noticed the stitches there also from the poor punches he didn't quite remember throwing.

The doctor plodded around to face Bowen, illuminated inside his suit. In the dark of the surgery, the fluid within looked like vibrant blue water. The doctor's tentacled face was idly flicking at buttons and switches as he spoke to Bowen.

"How is your head?" he asked.

"Sore." Bowen replied. "But like the tail end of a really bad headache."

"Good that's what I wanted to hear." The doctor's artificial hand reached out to Bowen and he helped him stand with the use of his suit.

The doctor listed off precautions and advice for the coming hours regarding his head and he also gave Bowen his painkillers. When Bowen left the surgery it was confirmed to him that it was the middle of the night. The hallways and corridors of the Memento were mostly deserted. He didn't feel like going to bed, he felt rested enough from his period of unconsciousness in the surgery and so he wandered the ship. Eventually, he wandered into the atrium by the gym and the wet house. He found a row of vending machines across from the gym and bought himself a can of water and a bag of Gator flavour Jinkos. He lined his stomach with the Jinkos and took the first two pink and green painkillers with a can of water.

His feet took over and he wandered towards the rec deck. As he entered the double doors he didn't see anyone else. The digital window screen had been deactivated and beyond was the view of Davarak. He walked over to the wide strip of glass and was amazed by the view. A cloudless night sky above a seemingly endless dark desert. In the distance the dunes seemed to get bigger and bigger until they were the size of mountains.

"Bowen..?" came a voice from behind him. Bowen almost jumped in surprise. It was Safiya.

"Hey." Bowen said before they exchanged a kiss. "I didn't see you there. What are you doing here..?"

"I was about to ask you the same question." she replied. "And what happened to your face?" Safiya asked with some concern as she cupped the side of his head with her hand. As she did, he leant into her touch. The smell of her perfume was laced with alcohol. It made Bowen's head shimmer. "Look at your vest!" she exclaimed. It was stained with drink and spots of blood, some human, some not.

"I was out with the guys at a club and we got into a fight. I've been at the doctor's because I got a concussion."

"I told you didn't I? It's not a vacation spot."

"You did." Bowen admitted.

"Well I'm glad you're okay. Is your concussion better?" she asked after a moment.

"Yeah it is now, it's just sore. Anyway what are you doing here? At whatever time it is?" Bowen asked.

"I had to work late and I wasn't tired since I had a nap earlier today. It's been so hot in the kitchen you wouldn't believe. I can't wait to leave this awful planet."

"Honestly, my first visit to an alien world hasn't gone how I'd imagined." Bowen said. "And besides, me and the guys have had our shore leave passes taken off us for the remainder of the stay here."

"Serves you all right for fighting." Safiya teased.

"Hey we didn't start it."

"Oh I'm sure you didn't." Safiya was leaning into Bowen and she had her hands around the small of his back under his dirty vest. They just looked at each other for a moment. Safiya bit into her lip and kept glancing down at his mouth. His hands found a place for themselves at the dip of her waist. Bowen's mind began to swim as the painkillers took hold of him. He was horny again. He could feel her breasts push into him as she sighed and he felt his trousers become a little tighter. Out the window, the edge of the horizon was beginning to glow.

"It'll be morning soon." Bowen said.

"There's not much point in sleeping then is there?"

"Are you working tomorrow..?" he asked. She shook her head slowly. His hands began to explore her as she was tugging at his vest. Before he knew what was happening, they were hand in hand walking back through the atrium to the stairwells. Safiya got ahead of him as they climbed the steps and she exaggerated her hip movements for him.

When they reached the landing of the crew decks they came across a group of technicians at an open floor panel that were almost blocking the whole walkway. One of them in full overalls removed their welding mask and looked right at him. It was Vetura. Her white face almost glowed in his vision and with a gloved hand she dabbed at her sweaty forehead.

"V." Bowen said surprised.

"Hey." she said with a smile. He noticed she looked between him and Safiya.

"Safie this is Vetura. V, this is Safiya."

"Hello." Safiya said plainly.

"Hey." Vetura replied. "You're out late." she said to Bowen.

"Yeah, well you too." he smiled.

"We've been on the rec deck." Safiya stated matter-of-factly.

"Oh... cool." Vetura said. It was at that moment that one of Vetura's colleagues got her attention to return to work. "We've gotta try to finish before morning." she said to Bowen.

"Yeah no worries." Bowen said. "Maybe see you round?"

"I hope so." Vetura said to him. "Nice to meet you." she said to Safiya. Safiya grabbed Bowen's hand and began trying to pull him away.

"You too." Safiya replied with a slight wince in her

smile. Vetura gave Bowen one last smile before she donned her welding mask back on and turned away. Safiya virtually dragged Bowen down the corridor. While they were still in sight of the technicians, Safiya grabbed hold of Bowen and pushed him against one of the holographic ad boards and began kissing him.

Bowen's head was spinning as she said she wanted him. They both made their way down the curving corridor towards his cabin, stopping every now and then to kiss. Eventually they reached the door to his cabin. Safiya was virtually removing his belt from behind him as he was fumbling to get the door open with his card.

When finally they entered, Safiya closed the door behind them. The pre dawn glow of the planet outside peeked through the blinds. Still in the short corridor to his cabin, he pulled her by the waist and began kissing her until she took charge and moved him over towards his bed where she pushed him down onto the mattress. She ordered him to get undressed as she took a condom out of her bag and tossed it onto him. He didn't need telling twice. In a flash, he was naked on the bed.

Safiya moved towards the foot of the bed where she removed her own clothes. The light of the early morning shone on her in strips. A glint came off the ring of her nipple piercing. Her clothes had been quite restrictive he noticed as he saw extent of her thick curves. Lastly she removed her headscarf. Bowen's mouth fell open as she shook her black hair out and it fell over her breasts and down her back. Her amber eyes looked right into him as she made him wait just a moment longer. Bowen swallowed hard and his heart was racing. Safiya was upon him before he could think. She wasted no time making Bowen her plaything. He ran his hands through her thick hair as she took his cock in her mouth. She suppressed a gag more than once but didn't stop. She was good with her hands as well as her tongue. The smell of her perfume filled his head as he tried to think of something to distract himself.

In the gloom of the cabin he could see Safiya reach down

to her herself. She began to moan as she made herself ready for him. Her lips smacked off of him as she caught her breath. The mess of untameable black hair tickled him in the stomach. She took the condom with her free hand and with her teeth ripped it open. She placed it to her lips and placed it on him in one smooth motion. She mounted him and gasped as she took him inside her. Bowen's head was swimming as her large breasts rested on his chest. The bed began to complain as she fucked him. He was lost in the dark of her hair as his hands went exploring until she grabbed his wrists and restrained him. She had him at her mercy. She steadied herself as she brought her feet up until she was squatting above him. Even with the condom he could tell how wet she was. With one hand she began touching herself again. She began to shake and she squealed as she made herself orgasm. Bowen wasn't far off himself. She put her legs back down and he felt the sweat of her thighs against his sides. She allowed him the use of his hands again and she rocked him back and forth until he couldn't last any longer. Bowen's mind had melted. His heart began to ease down as he felt the sweat roll off of him.

Safiya relaxed herself and came down to kiss him. Bowen tried to speak but nothing happened. They breathed into each other for a moment before she dismounted him. With a swift motion she relieved him of the condom and left him on the bed. He watched her walk away from him towards the bathroom. When she switched the light on, he squinted and rubbed his eyes, his lack of sleep had caught up to him. He heard Safiya flush the toilet and run the tap before she threw him a roll of toilet paper to clean himself up.

"Do you mind if I shower?" she asked. Bowen fumbled to respond.

"No, go ahead." Bowen did his best to stay awake until she returned, but the running water of the shower had him asleep in seconds. He dreamed of Saxon rain.

38.

The heat of the cabin woke Bowen some time later. Still naked on the bed, he had barely moved in his sleep. Safiya was not with him, but a trace of her perfume lingered. It was unclear if she had slept with him or not. He half remembered a kiss goodbye from her, but whether it was from a few hours or a few minutes ago he couldn't know. Bowen's head complained at him as he sat up and his throat was extremely dry. Strips of bright daylight streamed into the cabin, Bowen suspected it was nearly midday. His stomach growled as it realised he had missed breakfast. Groaning with stiffness, Bowen sat at the edge of his bed.

It was then that he heard a familiar shuffling in the vents. He looked up and saw the reflective eyes of Toki. His mouth was puckering and widening into a cheeky smile. Bowen's voice was scratchy when he spoke.

"You been watching me you little weirdo?" he said. Toki chirped and hooted quietly from behind the grate. Bowen stood up and stretched his achy arms. He dressed himself with some clean clothes and opened the vent to let Toki into his room. The little creature jumped down onto Bowen's shoulders and immediately began grooming him with his tiny hands. Bowen flinched a little as his head was still sore. "Hello to you too." Bowen said. His stomach grumbled again and made Toki flinch. "Right I'm going to get something to eat and then I've got stuff to be getting on with." After scratching behind his fuzzy ears, Bowen coaxed Toki back into the vent who scampered off into the ship. He closed the vent grate back up and left his cabin.

By the time Bowen had reached the cafeteria it was lunch. The huge shield had been put across the windows to protect the room from the harsh daylight but here and there beams of light had found their way in. As he waited in line for food, Safiya occupied much of his thoughts. He had not had sex for almost a year, not since that last time with Jules. He was hit by a small amount of shame as he realised that once or twice during his encounter with Safiya, Jules had popped into his head for an instant. And then his brain opened up a whole line of questioning with itself. Since he and Jules never officially split up, was he now cheating on her with Safiya? Another part of his mind then spoke to him. He and Jules had indeed been an item, but had they ever specifically said that they were dating..? Bowen couldn't remember. It all seemed so long ago. Part of him wished that Safiya had been a little more intimate with him. He wished he had not been so tired, perhaps he might have remembered just lying with her in his bed, if she even stayed that was...

"What you having..?" the gruff voice of Jungga threw him out of his thoughts. Bowen had not even considered what to eat. The fresh food that the ship had acquired from Saxon was long gone. What was on offer now was still good food, but it was all tinned and frozen, courtesy of Oasis City storehouses. His responsibility with the garden prickled at the back of his head. In the end Bowen chose the second main of the day option, Vogodon sausage in a meaty red sauce with assorted frozen Midnight vegetables that were all shades of purple and black. He picked up two cans of water and a Detonator flavour Zordo bar.

He sat himself down at a table next to Duggy.

"Here he is, still alive." Duggy proclaimed.

"Just about." Bowen said smiling. Bowen was so hungry he devoured his food in moments before taking his painkillers.

"Got your first badges then?" Duggy commented motioning to his scarred face and knuckles.

"I think I fainted on Garber at the landing pad and she took me to the doctor."

"Oh yeah, she passed us all carrying you."

"That's embarrassing."

"Nah man you did good." Duggy said patting Bowen on

the shoulder. Bowen smiled.

"So." Bowen started. "Guess what me and Safiya did early hours this morning..?" Duggy who was lighting up a cigarette leaned in slightly with a grin.

"What's that?" he asked.

"Well, I ran into her when I left the surgery and we went back to my cabin..."

"You shagged her didn't you!?" Duggy shouted. He slapped the table as he did, turning some heads in the cafeteria. Bowen's face went red and he smiled as he tried to speak. "Yeah you did!" Duggy confirmed as he put his scaly arm around Bowen's shoulder and shook him firmly. "Go on then how was it, what did you do to her?" he asked. Bowen remembered the events of only a few hours ago.

"It was... great, yeah. She took the driver's seat really. I didn't have to do much." Duggy exhaled a stream of purple smoke.

"Nice." he said. "She enjoyed herself then?"

"I think so," Bowen joked, "I hope so anyway." Bowen's began to open his Zordo bar as someone approached their table.

"Hey, mind if I sit here..?"

"Hey V, no go ahead." Vetura sat down across from Bowen. She tucked into her modest lunch of cold meat and midnight salad with a tall can of Dizz.

"Thanks." she said. Vetura was dressed casually in what looked like a bed shirt with sleeves rolled up and she wore grey sweats. Her hair was scruffy and spoke of how recently she had gotten out of bed. She yawned as she opened her Dizz.

"V this is Duggy, Duggy this is Vetura." Bowen said.

"Hey." Vetura said with a tired smile.

"What's happening?" Duggy said nodding as he lit up another cigarette. "You're one of the techies aren't you?" he asked.

"That's right."

"Did you get your work done..? Bowen asked.

"Yeah we got it." she replied as she was salting the meat on her plate.

"What were you doing?"

"Some wiring got fried when we were on the highway and we've just been sorting it out." There was a moment of content quiet. Duggy smoked, Vetura ate and Bowen finished his Zordo bar and opened his second can of water. The painkillers were kicking in.

"Hey how's it going down in Botanics?" Vetura asked.

"It's okay thanks."

"Have you planted much?"

"Yeah plenty, fruit and veg. I still need some help with the tanks to set up the fruit trees."

"I can't wait for something fresh."

"I should see some growth in a couple of weeks." Bowen said.

"I'd like to come see it sometime if that's okay?" Vetura asked.

"Yeah sure, definitely." he replied beaming.

"It'll be nice to be around some greenery." she commented as she played with the sad looking salad on her plate. Bowen grinned. Another silence fell. The ambience of the cafeteria surrounded them. Duggy took it upon himself to fill the quiet. He leaned in and pointed towards Vetura, cigarette in hand.

"Hey, guess what?" he started.

"Hmm?" Vetura said as she looked up at Duggy with her black eyes.

"This guy joined the space corp last night." Bowen tried to interrupt but it didn't work. He knew where Duggy was going.

"What..?" Vetura asked in confusion.

"He got laid, didn't you?" Bowen went purple with embarrassment. He grimaced as Duggy nudged him in the shoulder.

"Did you?" Vetura asked as she looked to Bowen. Despite

the smile that played on her face, she looked down at the last of her food. Bowen fumbled an answer.

"Well, yes."

"That was your girlfriend I saw you with this morning then?" she asked. Bowen smiled stiffly and nodded.

"She's really pretty." Vetura commented as she looked down at her plate. There was another moment of silence, but this time Bowen was uncomfortable. Finally Duggy stubbed out his cigarette.

"Right well, I've gotta get to work. See you around private."

"Yeah see you." Bowen replied.

"And hey nice meetin' you V."

"Yeah you too." Vetura said smiling. They were left alone. Despite the air conditioning in the cafeteria, Bowen was sweating. He cleared his throat and broke the silence.

"Hey, you're a techie aren't you?"

"I am indeed." she replied. He cringed at himself.

"I might need your help with something if you have the time."

"Yeah, what's that?" Vetura said. She pushed her tray away from her and leaned onto the table towards him.

"A few of the heat lamps in the garden are a bit fucked and I think they'll need replacing. I was thinking you could help me install them?" Vetura let the question hang for a moment before she answered.

"Sure I can do that." She smiled at him. Bowen heard himself sigh in relief.

"Awesome thanks." Vetura looked expectant. Bowen looked confused.

"...what?"

"When?" she said.

"Oh," he laughed awkwardly. "Are you free later today? I'll be down there all afternoon."

"Sure, I've got some things to finish off but then I can come down there."

"Great, I've got someone from cargo helping me too so he'll be there."

"You're not great at this are you?" she said. Bowen almost choked on his water.

"What's that?"

"Well that'll be three you owe me." Vetura smiled as she got up to leave.

39.

Music echoed around the garden as Bowen worked. Moryys had brought his bulky tape deck when he had arrived to help and they were currently listening to some electronic dive. Bowen wiped his brow of sweat. The sprinklers were operating and the moisture exchangers had successfully been installed, but the garden was still steamy. Dressed in his overalls and new boots, Bowen stepped back from the potato patch and took a swig from his water. Moryys was clomping around in his loader mech setting up the glass cylindrical growth tanks for the fruit trees. With the help of Vetura when she arrived, the heat lamps would be installed and the trees could have a good start. Around him were the beginnings of the growth. Each patch was twenty feet square and he had worked himself ragged finishing off the seeding process. The ground worms had been defrosted and introduced into each patch. Moryys had helped Bowen install the nest of Laurentian hoverflies close to the centre of the room. It was a tall metallic installation with a series of glass pipes and windows exposing the internal environment. Bowen had programmed in a sonic wave attractor to ensure comings and goings of the insects. The pollinator bees would have a similar setup with their apiary machine but they were still in stasis waiting to be freed.

Bowen watched as Moryys carefully handled the delicate glass of the tree tanks as he set them up ready for use. Moryys made using the mech look easy. Ever since the eventful night in the club, part of Bowen wanted to ask Moryys about his time in prison and the hows and whys, but the right moment hadn't presented itself. Bowen watched him as Moryys bobbed his head to the music. Bowen was about to speak when the doors opened across the room and Vetura entered. Bowen brushed his top down of loose dirt as he made his way over to her.

"Hey, you came." he greeted her smiling.

"I said I would didn't I?" she replied. Vetura was dressed in her overalls boiler suit. On her back was a large backpack with various attachments and tools hanging from it and in her hand she carried another hefty toolbox.

"You look ready for anything." Bowen commented.

"No harm in being prepared." she replied as she set down her toolbox and undid the clasps on her pack. Bowen couldn't help but notice that Vetura had showered since last he saw her and she had styled her hair into a couple of neat buns at the back of her head. The shaved sides of her head were exposed and a deliberate single strand of black hair fell to the side of her face, which had also been made up.

Moryys clomped his way over to them and came to a stop. The hydraulics in the joints of the mech hissed and the internal mechanisms clicked and beeped.

"Vetura this is Moryys. Moryys, Vetura" Bowen said.

"Hey there." Moryys waved with the metal hand of the loader. "I've seen you coming and going in the machine shop downstairs." Moryys said.

"How's it going? Yeah I've seen you around too." Vetura replied as she buckled a tool belt around her waist.

"He's pretty hard to miss." Bowen joked.

"You know it." Vetura replied smiling. "So what have you got for me?"

"The main job is the heat lamps need new wiring. Moryys is setting up the tanks, but we have to fit the new lights before we assemble it all for the trees." As he spoke, Vetura was already unlocking her toolbox and rearranging what was outfitted on her tool belt. "Hope that's okay?" he asked.

"Sure, pretty straight forward. Let's get to it."

***

For the next few hours, the three worked. Moryys clomped around the garden fitting the glass tanks around the base of the trees ready for the lamps to be slotted inside. Vetura needed minimal instructions, in fact Bowen found himself being instructed by her more often than not. Before long, they found a rhythm as they worked. One by one the heat lamps were refitted and installed. Bowen found himself mostly holding a torch up for Vetura so she could see what she was doing inside the machines. He had to quickly learn the names of the various tools that she was asking him to pass her. He followed her up into the walkways above the garden as she worked. She opened up panels in the floor and the walls and carefully cut away into the ship. The garden periodically filled with a steamy atmosphere and the heat rose before the humidity exchangers circulated the air. Whilst Bowen was holding Vetura steady on a set of ladders by a circuit panel just too high to reach, she unzipped her overalls and tied the top half around her midsection. Underneath she wore a short vest top that exposed her midriff. As Bowen passed her more tools when she asked for them, she began to groan at a particularly awkward section of wiring. As she exerted herself his mind began to wander and he felt his face flush pink.

    Before long the siren blared to signal to the lower decks that it was time for dinner. Just as it happened, Bowen and Vetura were up on the walkways where they had installed all but two more lamps. Moryys brought the mech to a stop and powered it down by a charge point. Bowen watched from above as the whole front section of the machine opened up and exposed Moryys's body within. He reached up with his real hands and disconnected his headgear. When he stepped out of the machine, he winced as he began to do stretches and he cracked his neck with his hands.

    "We still eating down here?" he asked. "I could use the walk there and back." Bowen and Vetura confirmed to him from up high.

    "Make sure you take the stairs." Vetura advised. Moryys gave a thumbs up as he massaged his shoulders and neck with his other hand.

"So two cold meat selects and ice fruit pie?" Moryys asked as he made to leave.

"Please." Bowen said. "And plenty of water for everyone."

"Thanks." Vetura called. Moryys gave another thumbs up as he opened the double doors to the corridor. Vetura dropped a tool into the box at their feet and exhaled. Her white skin was glistening as she tossed him a clean cloth from a pouch on her toolbelt. Bowen wiped his brow and head with his as she wafted her vest top.

"I don't envy him using one of those things." she said as they moved their equipment over to the next tank.

"How come? I've always thought mechs were pretty kick ass."

"They are." She replied. "But if something goes wrong it could be seriously bad."

"Like what?" Bowen asked as he hefted the toolbox for Vetura.

"Everything from the neck down is in a form of stasis whilst he's driving it. That's why after prolonged use you get so stiff, especially in older models like that one. But if something gets damaged in an accident you could become paralysed. It's what happened to the head of engineering."

"Jothazar..?" Bowen said. Vetura was opening the main body of the heat lamp for the next tank as she continued.

"Yeah. That's why he's in that chair all the time. And he was lucky it only took the use of his legs from him." Bowen glanced down at the loader mech at the charging point. It looked different now.

"You ever seen those police mechs they have on Metro?" Bowen asked.

"Not for real. Could you pass me that driver cable please?" Vetura said as she began to work.

"I'd love to see Metro." Bowen said out loud.

"Yeah me too." Vetura replied. "The nice parts anyway." Bowen stopped talking as Vetura got stuck in with the machine. Bowen quietly admired her as he watched her confidently tinker with the complicated inner workings of the installation. "What the hell?" she muttered to herself.

"What's up?" Bowen asked, somewhat distracted. Vetura stood up in the hatch she had gotten into above the heat lamp. She brought the hem of her vest top up and wiped her face with it briefly exposing her bra to him.

"I don't know. This ship is weird." Vetura said with a sniff.

"How do you mean?"

"On the outside it just looks like most other old federation ships but under the skin it's a different story. It's like it can't decide if it's really old or state of the art." She attempted to show him two different examples of wiring configuration as she explained. It went right over Bowen's head but he tried not to let on.

One last stretch of steamy and sweaty work and they had finished. They both hastily made their way back down the walkways to the power station with the switches for the heat lamps.

"Moment of truth." Vetura said.

"No you go on, this was all your work." Bowen said as he motioned for her to flip the switch. She rubbed her dirty hand on her overalls and grasped the lever for the lights. She looked at Bowen and pulled. There was a humming sound from within the garden itself and a surge of power resonated from above them. One by one each light flickered on in a show of orange light.

Bowen was elated as he found himself jogging through the garden between the huge tree tanks. He turned around to face Vetura who had followed him.

"You did it." he said smiling.

"It wasn't just me though was it?"

"Thanks V." They exchanged a high five that became a hug. Vetura smelled like sweat, perfume, machine oil, burnt fuses and hair spray. Their sweaty clothes stuck to each other as they parted. Vetura played with her loose strand of hair as they smiled at each other. She had dirt and grease on her face and her make up had run a little in the heat of the garden.

Just then, Moryys returned with the food and Bowen's stomach let him know it was time to eat. The week previously Bowen had cleared and outfitted an old and forgotten break room within the garden with a wash station and old but comfy seats and low tables. Moryys had perked up a little since coming out of the mech. Bowen hadn't realised just how filthy he and Vetura had both become. They washed up and joined Moryys at the table where they ate. Bowen had installed an isolated air conditioning unit in the break room so it was much cooler inside than out in the garden to everyone's relief. The cold meat select was filling but disappointing, but the ice fruit pie was refreshing even though his was a little freezer burnt. They sat in content quiet for a while until Moryys spoke.

"Hey you two..." he started.

"Yeah?" Bowen replied.

"You wanna go snooping around cargo for a bit?"

"Why? Have you stacked up some crates to spell out your name or something?" Bowen asked.

"Not exactly." Moryys replied. "I don't know I just thought you guys might be interested to see the hidden door I found a few weeks ago..." Bowen noticed Vetura's sharp white ears perk up.

"What hidden door..?" she asked quietly. Moryys looked hesitant but excited.

"I was moving around stock before we landed and I noticed it. It's definitely a doorway, but there's no clear way to open it."

"Oh yeah I've gotta have a look at this." Vetura said.

"Have you finished what you were doing?" Moryys asked.

"The heat lamps are on aren't they?" she said sarcastically.

Moryys shifted in his seat.

"It's gotta stay between us three though right? The cargo crew don't know about it."

"Definitely." Vetura replied.

"I don't know about this." said Bowen. "Couldn't we get into trouble?"

"I've got clearance to be down there after hours." Moryys stated.

"And I'm a technician." Vetura added. "I can go all kinds of places around the ship." Bowen rubbed his chin where a beard was beginning to emerge. "Come on." Vetura nudged him. Bowen looked into her large black eyes, that glinted with a giddiness. Bowen sighed. He had a bad feeling, but he caved all the same.

"Okay."

"That's right." Moryys said standing up. "We won't be long. I'll get back in the loader and we'll take cargo elevator two."

Bowen and Vetura cleared away their trash from the area as Moryys clambered back into the loader mech. They followed him out through the doors into the empty hallway. Moryys clanked ahead in the mech, his steps echoing around the dimly lit corridors. Bowen was surprised to feel a rush of excitement as they were going off schedule, it felt like they were breaking rules together.   After a few turns they reached the wide doors of cargo elevator two. Moryys couldn't push the buttons with the large hands of the machine and had to direct Bowen and Vetura to call it from below. The wait for the lift felt long. The floor rumbled as the ship hauled up the platform to them. A green light shone above the door as the multi layered doorway opened for them. Moryys let Bowen and Vetura in first who stood by the buttons to the side. As Moryys joined them, the suspension of the lift shuddered under the enormous weight of the loader. Moryys again directed them what buttons to press to get down to the cargo bay. The elevator doors closed them in and they were plunged into darkness with only an amber light above the door. As the lift took them down into the ship, strips of bright light streamed inside in a steady pattern. Bowen felt a little anxious. He didn't notice Vetura looking at him.

The elevator shook as it slowed to a stop. The light above the door turned green and the doors opened. A rush of cool air came in from the dark cargo bay. The ramp was up and sealed. Moryys switched on a set of headlamps on the mech and lit the way.

"Why are all the lights off..?" Bowen asked.

"When there aren't any shifts they put the cargo bay in low power." Moryys responded. Bowen's eyes had trouble adjusting, but the mech showed them the way. Bowen and Vetura followed closely as Moryys walked ahead. The containers of many colours were tagged and stamped with all sorts of logos and lettering, some of which Bowen's implants did not translate. They had been stacked on top of each other almost to the ceiling high above in the dark. There was enough space for two mechs to walk side by side in the passages.

Towards a far corner of the cargo bay, they were met by a series of small metallic crates each evenly spaced and about the size of a double bed. Bowen counted ten that he could see. They blinked with blue and pink lights.

"What are these?" Vetura asked. She spoke quietly but even still, her voice echoed. She approached one of them and ran her hand across the top. There was a complicated control panel with a suite of buttons and a small screen.

"I don't know, it's what the Stormraven brought us from Atlanticana." Moryys replied. Bowen turned his head and saw that all the others not illuminated by the mech were glowing in the dark eerily.

"So what's inside?" Bowen asked. Moryys surveyed the crates with the light.

"Usually a set up like this, each with its own power source is organic material." he said. "We were told it's priority one cargo." Vetura was fascinated. Bowen shuffled on the spot, he couldn't shake the feeling they were being watched.

"Can we carry on? This isn't even what we're down here for." he said. Vetura looked up and was silhouetted against the headlamps of the mech.

"You getting freaked out?" she jested.

"Yes." he admitted. He couldn't see the smile that played out on her face.

"Right come on it's not far." Morrys said as he turned to leave, the loader's feet clomping across the floor. Vetura walked close by to Bowen.

"I want to know what's in those boxes." she said quietly. Secretly, Bowen did too.

They emerged out from the maze of crates in a cavernous far corner of the cargo bay. The head lamps of the mech shone out ahead, but hit nothing. Bowen swallowed. It was like they had walked out into space, or were at the bottom of an ocean. Bowen turned around and saw the blackness of the cargo bay behind them. He could still feel eyes on them.

"Straight on." Moryys said. The mech lumbered forwards into the black. Bowen felt Vetura's smooth hand on his forearm.

"Hey, you good?" she said. Even in the gloom of the cargo bay he saw a glint in her large, black eyes.

"Yeah, thanks." he replied. They walked on further than Bowen thought they would have to until they found a single empty container against a wall. With the loader mech, Moryys grabbed a hold of the huge metal box and effortlessly lifted it and placed it to the side. When the head lamps turned back to the spot it was revealed. A wide metal doorway. Bowen thought it looked similar to the doors he glimpsed up to the bridge.

"There it is." Moryys said. Vetura approached the door and ran her hand on it.

"It's the same style as the upper decks." she said. "Reinforced and blast proof."

"There's no keypad or card slot." Bowen noticed. "Why would there be a set of doors like this down here?" No one had an answer for him.

"Moryys can you shine the light over here?" Vetura said as she moved to the side of the door. Moryys angled the mech and switched to a wide angle lense and most of the wall was illuminated before them. Bowen watched as Vetura unclipped a couple of tools from her belt and began to tinker with a wall panel.

"What are you doing?" he asked her.

"Just seeing something. Give me a hand here please?" Bowen reacted without question. He helped her undo the bolts and fittings from the wall panel and they lifted it off and rested it on the floor. She retrieved a small handheld device and plugged it into an opening. The device began to beep and flash in her hands. "See that?" she said pointing into the wall. Bowen just saw complicated wiring and circuitry with flashing lights.

"Yeah..." he said.

"Something behind this set of doors has its own power supply. And it's stronger than anywhere I've seen on the ship besides engineering."

"Is it dangerous?" Bowen said.

"Doesn't look like it. No sign of radiation."

"The Memento's schematic's don't show anything behind here." Moryys said. Bowen swallowed. He felt a nervous excitement. Vetura bit her black lip as she looked at the door.

"Do you think you can get us in..?" He asked. She smiled at him and he smiled back.

"Maybe. I'll need an emergency override console to make it open up. And I'll need to get my hands on a power diversion kit to mask the power surge from engineering."

"Can you get all that?"

"It'll take a little while but yes, I can. I'll have to file some bullshit paperwork to get the stuff out of the machine shop." she said. She shook her head and tutted putting her hands on her hips. "Only thing is, even then it might need authorization from a member of crew command. Bowen and Moryys exchanged a look.

"We could try your card…" Moryys said.

"What..?" Vetura asked.

"There's nothing to suggest that would work." Bowen replied.

"Wait what are we talking about here?" Vetura asked. Bowen took a deep sigh.

"Months ago when I first joined the crew, my card accidentally opened up a restricted door I shouldn't have been allowed into."

"Where?"

"The Navigation Suite."

"Why did you try to get into Navigation?" she asked with an intrigued smile.

"It's a long story." he sighed.

"But did you ever get into trouble for it..?" Vetura asked.

"No but… if we open this door," Bowen started. "And we're not allowed to, wouldn't someone be alerted, like a break in?"

"It would depend on how the ship registers authorised entry to restricted areas." Bowen rubbed the back of his neck and shuffled on the spot.

"What do you say man?" Moryys asked.

"I don't know."

"Come on, just a peep…" Vetura tempted.

"You guys won't leave me high and dry if we get caught..?" he asked them both.

"Nah man, no way." Moryys said.

"Course not. I swear." Vetura said. Bowen took a deep breath.

"Okay." Bowen said finally. "How long will it take you to get the things you need?"

"A couple of weeks to not cause suspicion, so we'll be back on the highways. I might need to call in one of those favours you owe me."

"What for?" he asked.

"You sign my paperwork for some of the kit, we'll say it's

for the garden."

Bowen swallowed.

"I do owe you a bunch."

"You do."

"We'll have to find a night where all of us are free." Moryys said.

"Easy done," Vetura said. "We can coordinate all that in the cafeteria when we see each other, keep it all low key." Bowen was nervously excited. Vetura's enthusiasm for rule breaking was infectious.

"This seems like it's becoming your plan." he said.

"It does doesn't it?" she said with a grin.

"Okay then." Bowen smiled.

"I'm almost on low power, I'll have to put this back in garage at the other end of cargo." Moryys said.

"No problem." Bowen replied. Bowen helped Vetura replace the wall panel and Moryys replaced the empty container before they left the hidden doorway. They walked all the way back through the dark maze of containers and past the mysterious cargo. Moryys parked the mech with the others in a maintenance garage. Without the light from the mech, they were plunged into near total darkness. The only light came from security lights lining the walls and high up on the ceiling. As they walked through the gloom, Moryys lead the way to the elevator. His shape disappeared from Bowen after a few feet. Bowen's eyes had difficulty adjusting as he took cautious steps forwards like a baby. He felt Vetura's hand on his arm.

""Come on," she said. "Just walk forwards."

"See in the dark can you?"

"Not properly, but better than humans can." They both laughed as they walked to the elevator. Ahead he could see Moryys enter the lift as he stood under the green light inside. Vetura chuckled to herself as she walked Bowen to the elevator.

"What?" he asked.

"I told you this ship was weird didn't I?"

40.

Bowen sweated through his shirt standing in the garden a few days later. The patches were already showing some significant growth. The pollinator bees had been released from stasis and were happily buzzing around. It was nice to be around animals even these space faring creatures. Even the trees had emerged from their huge soil bases, but they still had some weeks left to go. To Bowen's calculations there might be time for one harvest before they reached Obelisk station.

The doors opened and Vetura entered dressed in her overalls equipped with her tool belt and a work satchel.

"It's coming on in here already isn't it?" she commented.

"Yep, it's looking good so far." he replied as she came to join him by a patch.

"What's this going to be?" She pointed down into the patch next to them.

"Watermelon." he said.

"Any good?"

"I think so."

"You sign the paperwork?" she asked.

"I did." Bowen said as he pulled a neatly folded piece of blue paper out of his pocket. He handed it to Vetura and she opened it up and scanned it over.

"Sweet, come on then." They both left the garden and made for the nearest elevator.

As the elevator moved about the ship towards the engineering deck, Bowen was still sweating. He had made their rule breaking official by signing the falsified paperwork. But still, Vetura's confident and calm presence helped.

The doors opened up on engineering, showing a wide hexagonal corridor with metal grate flooring and bright strip lighting. The engines of the Memento were pulsing like a sleeping monster. On Vetura's directions, they walked side by side following the corridors until they came to a huge atrium. Around the sides were a small number of crew members at consoles and terminals all working away. Jothazar was trundling about looking grumpy who acknowledged them with a nod. They passed the huge water tanks that fed into the garden and Bowen saw one wall that was dominated by a gigantic doorway similar to the one for the incinerator room but much larger. Massive stencilled red lettering read

ENGINE ROOM RESTRICTED

Vetura ripped Bowen away from looking at the door. They walked through another heavy metal doorway to the machine shop causing a claxon to sound off. Inside, the shop was one large room separated into sections where machines had been stripped. The walls were a mess of hanging tools and parts in both hectic displays and separated into neat shelving. Whole areas of the floor were painted with hazard stripes. Mobile work stations cluttered the room and across the floor as well as thick wiring hooked up to compact computer terminals. Bowen and Vetura carefully tip toed their way across the room to a corner where a loader mech arm was hanging on a set of chain hooks from a sturdy frame. The arm was stripped down to its wiring and circuitry as it was being worked on. Bowen saw a woman dressed in grubby orange overalls with her back to them. Sounds of work echoed around the room.

"Hey Yuki!" Vetura called out. Yuki turned around and lifted a pair of welding goggles off her face and rested them on her forehead.

"Whose this?" Yuki asked looking at Bowen.

"Bowen, he's the gardener."

"Hey." Bowen said. Yuki looked Bowen up and down.

"You better not be traipsing dirt into the shop." Bowen recognised Yuki as another Fujugante native like Bao Bao, but unlike Bao Bao she was tall and slim. Her electric blue hair was a mess of buns at the back of her head that matched her striking crystal eyes. Her stern but pretty face was pierced in numerous places and Bowen caught a glimpse of colourful tattoos around her neck that disappeared beneath her work clothes. Bowen had seen her in the cafeteria a few times looking sullen.

"Oh yeah, wouldn't want to ruin the furnishings." Vetura remarked sarcastically. Yuki forced a smile at Vetura.

"What do you want?" she asked. Vetura retrieved the paperwork from an inner pocket of her overalls and handed it to Yuki who opened it and started reading it over. Yuki sighed as she held the paperwork to a nearby torch light. Bowen shifted nervously. "I'll be back in a minute." Yuki said as she turned to fetch the equipment they needed. "Don't touch anything." she snapped as she disappeared through a series of rubber strip curtains.

"So the paperwork was okay..?" he asked Vetura quietly.

"Just relax, we've got this." Vetura replied. "Stop sweating so much."

"I can't help it."

"It'll be fine."

Yuki soon returned with a large green box on a cargo trolley that she wheeled over to Bowen and Vetura. "One emergency override console for the happy couple." Vetura began looking over the machine on the trolley.

"Alright that'll do it."

"Good, I'm glad." Yuki replied. "Now get lost the pair of you." Vetura unlocked the brakes on the trolley and began wheeling it away with Bowen in tow.

"Bye bitch." she called to Yuki.

"See you at dinner slut." Yuki replied as she donned her goggles back on and resumed work on the loader arm. Bowen helped Vetura haul the trolley back out into the atrium of engineering.

"Is she always like that?" Bowen asked as they reached the hallway to the elevator.

"Yuki?"

"Yeah, or was she just having a bad day?"

"Don't take it personally. She's good at what she does." Vetura smiled. "She's just a snarky cunt. She hasn't had a good fuck in a while though too which doesn't help her mood." They entered the elevator with the trolley and pressed the buttons to go to cargo.

As they moved through the ship on the elevator Bowen came back to the matter at hand and felt a little anxious again.

"So there shouldn't be anyone in the cargo bay now..?"

"Shouldn't be no." Vetura reassured him.

They emerged out of the elevator into the dark cargo bay and heaved the trolley into the room as the doors closed. Vetura handed Bowen a head mounted torch from her satchel and she fitted herself with one. Now with the ability to see clearly, they both wheeled the trolley through the maze of containers. Moryys on his shift had left small secret markings for them to follow through the containers.

"Nice one man." Bowen said quietly as they followed the subtle directions. They would have had serious difficulty trying to make their way through the cargo bay without them. They came out of the containers quicker than Bowen anticipated and began heaving the trolley across the stretch of darkness. Vetura cleared her throat.

"So how's things with your girlfriend, I'm sorry I don't remember her name."

"Safiya..?" Bowen asked.

"Yeah that's it."

"Yeah it's going okay." Bowen said after a moment.

"You sure..? You had to think about it."

"I just..."

"What..?"

"...I don't know." He wasn't sure what that thought was, but he could feel it somewhere inside himself.

"You'll figure it out." Vetura said after a moment of silence as they reached the hidden doorway. They found the spot that Moryys had marked out on the floor. There was a splodge of white paint on a particular floor tile. Vetura instructed Bowen to move the trolley bed next to the marked spot as she crouched down with a drill tool to open the floor tile. As Vetura worked, Bowen looked about them into the darkness with his torch. Again, he felt eyes on them from somewhere. He swallowed and took a deep breath. Vetura finished opening the floor tile and began to unfold the sturdy handles on either side of the huge green box. They both took a handle each and carefully lowered the console into the floor. There was just enough space. Bowen helped Vetura lower the floor panel back in and she secured it back in place with her drill. It was totally hidden. Bowen took one last look at the empty container blocking the hidden doorway before they made to leave.

"Not bad." Vetura said as she looked back. "You'd never know it was there."

"Yeah we did okay." Bowen said.

The trolley, now much lighter was easier to manoeuvrer as they made their way back to the elevator. As they turned the last corner, they had a view of the elevator out on front of them. It wasn't there.

"Where's the elevator?" Bowen asked.

"Someone's called it." Vetura said as they both exchanged a look. Then Bowen heard it, the sound of the elevator coming down from the floors above. Bowen's heart missed a beat. Someone was coming down to the cargo bay. The metallic sound of the elevator was getting louder and louder.

"Shit we have to hide." Vetura said. They abandoned the trolley where it was and ran back a way down the path of the containers. Behind them Bowen heard the elevator's creaking mechanisms and the thud of the machine coming to a stop at the bottom. They were about to be right in view of whoever it was. Bowen frantically looked left and right for any nook and cranny available. Without thinking, he grabbed Vetura by the hand and pulled her to the side as he shoved her by the shoulders into a tight gap between a couple of containers just as he heard the elevator doors opening.

Bowen and Vetura both quickly fumbled to turn off their head lamps and they were plunged into total darkness. They were squashed in tight. Bowen felt Vetura's hard breath on his sweaty neck and their chests were pressed together. If they spoke they would be heard. They had a view of the pathway between the containers, but it was only a sliver. Bowen heard footsteps. At first it sounded like one person, but soon it was two or three pairs. Blaring torch lights came down the way and illuminated where Bowen and Vetura just were moments ago. Whoever it was who had entered was talking. Bowen couldn't make out what they were saying, but their voices were getting closer. Bowen looked down towards Vetura. In the darkness, he could see the glint in her black eyes looking back at him. Her breath was a lot steadier than his was. He felt a tightness on his shirt as he realised she had a hold of him.

"I've managed to convince the Captain to leave in the morning. None of this bullshit waiting around for other Free Traders." It was Officer Lennox. It took Bowen a moment to realise who the other voices were.

"I discovered the Stormraven is headed for Oryx in a few days time." Bowen recognised the voice but couldn't pin it.

"Where is that..?" came a third voice. Bowen focused hard until he realised it was Comms Officer Horner.

"The other side of the arm." came the unknown voice.

"Ishtar's prone to her fancies, she could end up anywhere." Lennox said. Bowen swallowed. He looked back to Vetura. She was still looking at him in the dark. Lennox, Horner and the other two walked further until they passed the gap in the containers, torches in hand. Bowen's heart stopped. He found himself gripping Vetura as they moved by. Bowen recognised the third person as Officer Denton. Bowen swallowed as he also recognised Murrow, the dark, bird-like navigation crewman who was friends with Simon.

"Talk to me about Kaldr." Lennox asked.

"I received comms this morning sir." Horner replied. "They haven't made it yet." Lennox sounded flustered.

"What do you mean?" he demanded.

"They had to take a detour through the Velta region since the pirate raids on the Echo Reach recently."

"Hayashi." Lennox spat. "They are all as bad as each other."

"Sir." Denton began. "Obelisk Enforcement Division are still prepared for our arrival."

"Are your men in Navigation briefed?" Lennox asked.

"Yes sir." Denton confirmed as Murrow clicked his beak. Bowen's breath caught in his throat as he was sure for a moment that Murrow's beady eyes glanced over at where he and Vetura were hiding as they passed.

"Make sure they are." Lennox said. "Security know what to do."

"What about Garber?" Horner asked.

"She's oblivious as usual. Too busy running around after the Captain." There was sheer bitterness in Lennox's voice.

"Sir is it true?" Denton asked.

"Is what true?" There was a moment of silence.

"That it's really him? *The* Ezekiel Quinn?"

"Yes. It is. According to Captain August." Lennox confirmed grimly.

"So that means this is..?" There was another silence. "How is that possible..?"

"Stay focused Denton."

Bowen's heart was racing as he strained to listen. Vetura dared to shuffle slightly on the spot and her leg grazed the inside of his thigh. The voices were getting fainter. Bowen wasn't listening all of a sudden. He felt a bead of sweat drip off his nose. It was getting stifling in the small gap he had stuffed himself and Vetura into. She was very close to him. The voices were just echoes now. He looked down at her face. Her white skin was almost glowing in the dark. Her large, black eyes were still fixed on his own and her hands were still gripping his shirt tight. Bowen swallowed. Suddenly there was a thunderous mechanical sound as from the far end of the hold, the cargo bay doors opened up and orange light washed inside from the floodlights on the landing pads. The cargo bay was now full of noise. Vetura used the moment to speak to Bowen, the echo of her voice was muted by the sound of the doors. She stretched up and spoke into his ear.

"We should make a break for the access stairwell."

"Now..?" Bowen mouthed. She nodded. They both shuffled out of the gap. Bowen cautioned a look. Lennox, Horner, Denton and Murrow were obscured by the mass of containers. The doors were still opening and the noise was bouncing off the walls, masking their frantic footsteps as Bowen and Vetura ran for the stairwell that ran parallel to the elevator. They reached the upper walkways and Bowen dared a look back down before they left the cargo bay. The huge doorway was still opening, but the four men were silhouetted leaving down the ramp into the night.

41.

The view from the observation deck was clear and the sun shone down on the Memento. Bowen looked through his binoculars at the red dunes and marvelled at the great rock pillars that reached up into the pink sky. He spied winged creatures that were just too far away to see clearly even with the binoculars. His first look at alien wildlife. They were circling the tops of the rock pillars where they were roosting. Bowen counted twenty of them before he lost count as they dove in and out of the sky. He wondered if there were hidden rock pools between the huge pillars and perhaps secret tunnels and caves that led deep underground. He would have loved to have gone exploring, but now he might never know. Bowen swapped out the binoculars for his camera and captured the Davarak landscape. Safiya sighed behind him.

"You alright..?" he asked without turning away from the view.

"Hmm?" she replied. Bowen turned around and lowered his camera. Sitting on a front row seat, she was reading a magazine and cooling herself with a colourful hand fan depicting a Phoenician landscape.

"What's up?" he asked. She stretched out and yawned.

"I'm just a bit over this place." she said. Bowen sat back in his own seat next to her.

"Not long now." he replied. Captain Quinn and the command crew had interrupted breakfast to announce their departure that afternoon. Not an hour later Garber had commanded via the intercom system that all passengers were to find a place in commercial seating. Bowen was sad to be leaving.

The Memento's engines had been firing up since before sunrise and the occasional rumble was felt through the floor even in the observation deck. It was an eight hour flight through open space until they reached Mordarak Gate and then another four months on the highways until Obelisk station. Bowen rubbed his head and sighed.

"Are you okay?" Safiya asked him.

"I'm fine. I ran out of time to send my messages and now it's too late."

"Who were you writing to?"

"My parents." he said. "And a friend or two." The second part was a lie.

"You'll have the chance when we get to Obelisk to let them know where you are." There was a quiet moment. The ship awakening filled the silence. Bowen just looked out into the pink and red landscape of Davarak. He thought of green hills and muddy fields.

"So where are you going after we get to Obelisk?" he asked finally.

"I'm not sure. I might see what other ships are docked and whether any will be going past Phoenicia."

"You going home?"

"I think so. I've had my fun out here now."

"Hmm." Her words sank on top of Bowen. He just looked out of the giant windows. The winged creatures were still circling in the distance. Safiya would be going home and so would he. He felt a little stupid for being naïve. Their relationship was always going to be temporary and there would be no point in despairing.

They sat there a while. The sun beat down on the red sands and the horizon shimmered. Garber's announcements for take off came and went. Bowen took some photographs, some with Safiya, some without. He did care about her and he felt that she cared for him too, but that was all it would be. Jules still swam into his mind from time to time, but the guilt that had followed with those thoughts was easing. By the time he made it back to Saxon he would speak to her about everything and ask all the burning questions he had been storing in his mind.

Before long, the Memento's final preparations for launch were initiated. Bowen and Safiya sat in their seats as the ship began to rumble. Bowen felt a pressure in his ears as the air conditioning was shut off and the Memento was locked and pressurized. A series of beeps and fragments of transmissions came through the overhead speakers as the flight crew started take off procedures. Bowen took one last look at the view of Davarak. The winged creatures in the distance dipped and dove over the sweltering red sands. The engines roared and the Memento fired upwards. The seats in the observation deck wobbled and compensated the turbulence of the launch. Unlike the take off from Saxon through the storm, the cloudless pink sky of Davarak was open to them. The expanse of red dunes was thrown out before them as they rose higher and higher. In the ever growing distance, Bowen saw dark rocky mountains rise up over the sands but they were getting smaller by the second. It was incredible. He felt a pang of sadness mixed with his excitement and fascination as he realised that realistically, this would be the last launch he would experience.

The colours of Davarak grew fainter and fainter. As they soared into the upper atmosphere, the horizon began to curve and the black of space emerged. The turbulence eased and the engines relaxed having won the fight against the gravity of the world. The roar of the ship disappeared completely as they began the flight to Mordarak Gate.

***

Bowen and Safiya enjoyed each others company in the observation deck. They talked and kissed and enjoyed the view. As they went to lunch together hand in hand, Bowen felt a melancholic twinge. Neither spoke, but their hands intertwined tightly. They found a quiet corner of the cafeteria to eat. Bowen remembered how awkward he had been when they first met and he realised as he watched her across the table that that part of him was gone. His mind thought of home and his parents. Samhain and Virgil. His bike, his room and Jules. Part of him considered talking with Safiya about it all, but the words wouldn't come. After eating they left the cafeteria and made for Gricky's. They bought drinks from the freshly stocked vending machines and a magazine each and made their way back to the observation deck in a content quiet.

***

A few hours went by and the Memento was passing an immense purple gas giant with far reaching rings that stretched out before them like a huge floor. Bowen was stood by the window taking pictures of the planet and the rings through the windows as it passed them by. More than once he enthused about the view, but Safiya didn't reciprocate. As he looked through the view finder and zoomed in and out from the rings, he noticed something odd. A shape was growing larger. It looked as if a piece of the ring had been thrown towards the ship. It glinted in the light from the far away sun as it approached them.

"What's that?" Bowen asked out loud. Safiya looked up from her magazine.

"What?" she said. Bowen lowered his camera and pointed through the glass down towards the rings.

"Look there, can you see? It's coming towards us."

"It looks like a big chunk of ice from the ring." Safiya said.

"But it's coming at us isn't it..? I'm not imagining that..?" Bowen asked bewildered.

"I think you might be right." she replied.

"About which?"

"That it's coming at us... But it'll miss us surely." Bowen hadn't heard Safiya ever sound nervous before. Bowen saw a flash from the object.

"It's definitely metallic, did you see-" They were both thrown to the ground as the ship was struck by something. Bowen looked up at the glass ceiling of the observation deck as he lay flat on his back.

"What was that..?" he said as a surge of pain went through his back. Safiya groaned in pain nearby. A harsh metallic clattering sounded from above them. Huge metal shutters were deployed from the top of the observation deck windows. They covered the glass piece by piece until they thudded into place, throwing the room into total darkness. Bowen's heart began to thump faster as he tried to sit up.

"What's happening?" Safiya asked.

"I don't know. Are you okay?"

"I think so." she sounded shaky and her breath was coming fast and short. A series of red lights flickered on illuminating the large room. He could see Safiya in the red gloom, she looked worried. Bowen hoped he didn't appear as terrified as he felt. Before he could open his mouth, the overhead speakers chimed and the voice of Garber came through.

"Attention all crew and passengers. We have an emergency. Pirates off the starboard side approaching fast, repeat pirates off the starboard side approaching fast. All passengers are to immediately make their way to their cabins. This is for your safety. A lockdown timer had been started, you have three minutes before cabin doors are sealed. Security teams gear up. Situation Zeta. All crew members remain at your posts. Off duty personnel-"

Garber's voice was suddenly cut off. The hairs on Bowen's body stood on end as a jolt of static electricity passed through the ship. The emergency lights flickered.

"What happened?" Safiya cried.

"They did something to the power." Bowen assumed. A cold fear came over him and he felt himself sweating. "What should we do?" he asked.

"Maybe we should stay where we are..?" Safiya

suggested. "There's no reason why pirates would come in here, is there?" Bowen swallowed and tried to remain calm. The ship began to groan as a pulsing sound emanated from deep within it. His mind raced. Garber said three minutes until the cabins were locked. But the pirates had shut the power off. They needed to be somewhere away from most people or anything too valuable. Somewhere quiet and where no one would think to look.

"Botanics, we can hide in the garden! We'll be safe there!" Bowen said as he hastily packed his camera into his rucksack. He grasped Safiya by the hand and they ran for the door. The door was loose and the atrium was illuminated red like the observation deck. There was no one around as usual, but now it made Bowen feel exposed. He thought of the high walkways of the garden, the equipment closets in the break room and the blind corners of the tree tanks. They ran through the atrium as a series of shudders went through the ship that made them both stumble.

"What was that?" Safiya asked.

"I don't want to think about it." he reacted. They reached the elevator doors and mashed the call button.

"It's out!" Bowen cried.

"Of course it's out.!" Safiya shouted. Bowen's heart was thumping in his chest.

"The stairwell, come on!" Bowen realised. They ran though the doors and descended the stairs, their steps echoing up and down the dark shaft. The overhead speaker system buzzed and flickered. The red light pulsed and the ship shuddered. Further and further down they descended. The sound of frightened people made the situation that much more real. Bowen and Safiya reached the atrium by the cafeteria and the rec deck. Bowen tightened his grip on Safiya's hand as they ran past crew and passengers scrambling to find their own places to hide.

"The stairwell from the rec deck leads down to botanics and cargo!" Bowen shouted. Out in the atrium, a handful of security were attempting to calm and herd a crowd of people. The security were fully armed and armoured, their weapons were drawn and their mounted torches shone through the red emergency light of the atrium. There was another shudder and a crash as everyone was knocked off their feet. Cries of fear echoed around them. A series of metallic thudding sounds were proceeded by a screeching noise that sounded like a drill or a saw. The security were losing control of the situation. One was attempting to contact command crew on a short range radio, but was failing. Bowen helped Safiya get to her feet again.

"Come on, we have to get to the stairs!"

"We should stay here!" Safiya protested as he led her through the crowd towards the doorway.

"It's not safe!" Bowen shouted as he tried to muscle his way past people. The metallic screeching made everyone cover their ears as they reached the doorway. Then came an odd electronic sound. A descending fractal tone emanated from all around as Bowen felt his feet lift off the floor. Screams came from the crowd as the artificial gravity began to fail. Bowen held Safiya's hand tight as she to began to scream as she lifted off the floor. With his other hand, he gripped the door handle to the stairwell with all his strength. Bowen's heart was in his throat and his head was trying to make sense of what he was seeing. All around them, members of the crowd in the atrium were slowly floating away from each other. The few security scrambled and magnetised their boots to the floor. They did their best to help who they could around them but it was an increasingly uphill battle.

"Bowen don't let me go!" Safiya cried.

"I won't!" Bowen replied. The high atrium was filled with the panicked screams of others and fruitless calls from the security. Some people had already drifted upwards into the centre of the space. Another fractal tone sounded as the artificial gravity shifted again. Bowen's breath caught in his throat as he felt his hand rip away from the door handle as they fell towards to far wall. Screams echoed in the atrium as the crowd of crew and passengers fell, some of them at great distance. Bowen and Safiya crashed against the wall panels. They had missed the vending machines by a fraction. A shattering of glass and plastic came with a burst of sparks as someone else was not so lucky. The breath was driven from Bowen's lungs as they impacted together. Safiya squealed in pain as people fell on top of them. With a surge of adrenaline, Bowen shrugged off whoever had landed on them. He struggled to his feet and his stomach turned as his brain attempted to make sense of the situation. People lay around them in heaps, some were crying out for help, others sobbing in fear. He looked up and saw the door to the stairwell now on the ceiling. Bowen's head throbbed and there was a serious pain in his side. He saw the security crew, still magnetised to the floor, but now they appeared to be standing on the wall. They rushed down and took odd looking steps onto the new floor and tried to aid injured people.

"Safie are you alright?" he shouted over the din of the crowd. Bowen didn't hear her response as he lifted her to her feet. A metallic thud shuddered the ship and gravity shifted back. Bowen pulled Safiya close and wrapped his arms around her. Bowen closed his eyes and braced for the fall back to the true floor. Screams filled his head and caused his ears to ring. Safiya held onto Bowen tight as they fell with everyone else. A sharp pain went through Bowen from his back as they crashed to the metal floor panels. Around them was the sickening thuds of people landing painfully, some fell still and quiet.

Bowen's head was spinning and he felt nauseous. He felt Safiya's head on his chest. He kept his eyes shut. For a moment he willed them to be in his bed. Everything sounded distant. Amongst the cries of pain and fear he heard someone vomiting and another person begin hyperventilating. A hot crackling sound came from the main double doors into the atrium. The torch beams of the security crew wheeled around like search lights. Bowen felt a pair of soft hands on either side of his face and he faintly heard someone shouting for him. A flickering bright light came from across the atrium and Safiya's face was illuminated in his vision.

His body took over and he stood up with her help. A shot of adrenaline fired within him and his hearing cleared. The main doors to the atrium were suddenly breached. A cloud of smoke erupted out of the doorway as the shooting started. Pirates armoured in full electroplate armour stormed the atrium. Their faces were hidden behind intimidating monstrous helmets with glowing eyes. The guns they wielded emitted confusing strobe lighting that burned at the back of Bowen's mind.

There was no where to hide for either side in the open atrium or for the bystanders caught in the middle. The red emergency lighting, the cloud of smoke, the strobe lighting, the plasma fire and muzzle blasts of the firefight, it took everything Bowen had to not fall to the ground and cover his head in fear. He grabbed Safiya by the hand and made a break for the stairwell doors across the room. The floor became uneven and soft in places. He didn't dare look down. Bowen risked a look back as they reached the doors and to his horror they were being followed. Two pirates were muscling their way through the crowd specifically for them. He threw his weight into the door and they crashed through.

As they descended the stairs, a low whirring sound resonated through the ship and the lights came back on along with a piercing sound from the overhead speakers. The power had been rebooted. A harsh alarm began to fire, that echoed through the cold shaft. Above them, Bowen heard heavy footsteps and muffled shouting. Bowen's heartbeat was in overdrive as they burst through the doors on the botanics level.

A crack of white light and Bowen felt his shoulder hit the floor.

"Pick him up!" he heard through ringing ears. Bowen felt a pair of hands on his shoulder wrench him upwards.

Bowen's head was spinning as he felt the metal ring of a gun barrel at the side of his head. He heard Safiya struggling to his side and the slap of a hand across her face. An armoured forearm grasped Bowen around the neck.

"Hold them!" shouted one of the pirates. Bowen's vision stopped tumbling. They had been caught by at least six pirates. The one barking the orders was stood in front of Bowen. He wore red painted armour with a helmet that sported the appearance of an alien skull. Bowen couldn't move his head to look at Safiya. The leader of their captors held a wired device up to Bowen's face. Bowen's mind raced as his heart stopped. He winced in anticipation of excruciating pain, or even death. A beam of green light fired out and traced Bowen's face.

"It's him! Let's go! They'll be on us any minute! Bring the female!" Still in a headlock, Bowen was forced forwards. For a moment, he was able to see Safiya to his side. He tried to speak but it was impossible. She was in a similar position. Her clothes had been torn at and her face was red and puffy. Her expression stuck in his mind. He felt a rush of regret and anger at himself. If only they had stayed in the observation deck. They were hurried right past the garden and towards the access stairs to the cargo bay.

As they moved through the bowels of the ship, Bowen thought of all the possible things that might be in store for them. A screech of transmission came through the speaker system.

"Attention this is the Captain! Crew decks secure! Security teams Green and Orange hold position! Red and Blue teams regroup on my coordinates!"

"Hurry, they know where we are!" one of the pirates yelled as they ran through the ship. They turned the corner and were faced with a reinforced sealed doorway to the cargo bay. A red emergency light glowed above. Bowen was released and shoved forwards. He turned and faced the pirates who all pointed their guns at him. Safiya was quietly sobbing. He swallowed hard and he was drenched in sweat. The leader stepped forwards.

"You! Open the door!" he yelled. Bowen looked at the sealed entrance. A huge metal barrier had been extended and the hinges had been bolted.

"I, I can't it's been locked down..." Bowen attempted. The pirate leader cracked Bowen across the face with an armoured red fist. He fell against the door and a bloodied broken tooth fell out of his mouth. With a shaking hand, Bowen reached into his pocket and retrieved his id card.

"Please, it won't work, I don't have authorisation..." The pirate leader turned to the others. He motioned to the one who held Safiya to bring her forwards. She was brought in front of Bowen. Her head scarf was gone. The pirate with the skull helmet pointed a heavy barrelled side arm at Safiya.

"Open the door." he commanded. Bowen looked at Safiya. She was terrified. She knew that he didn't have authorization to access a sealed door just as he did. The metal id card shook in his hand.

"Please don't..." Bowen tried. A white flash and a crack. Safiya screamed. Bowen's heart missed a beat. Safiya sank to her knees and held her arm as blood ran down her skin and onto the floor. Bowen cried out for them to stop but the pirate held his gun at Safiya's head. He threw up his hands.

"No, no! Okay! Look please I'll show you!" Bowen turned to the keypad and swallowed. On the screen it read in red lettering,

EMERGENCY LOCKDOWN
AUTHORIZED ENTRY ONLY

His brain showed him everything he loved all at once as his breath slowed. When the door didn't open he would be shot in the head or worse and Safiya too. Bowen took a breath and entered his card into the key pad slot. There was a moment where nothing happened. But then, a shift in the door was heard and the red light turned green. His mouth fell open as he looked at the key pad screen. In green lettering the screen read,

>   EMERGENCY LOCKDOWN LIFTED
>   LIEUTENANT RHYS
>   OVERRIDE ACCEPTED

Bowen's mind stopped as he read the words. He felt a strong hand on his shoulder and he was forced to enter the cargo bay. He heard Safiya moan in pain as she was picked up. They entered onto the upper walkways. One of the pirates withdrew a small scanner device and pointed them in a direction as they descended the metal stairs. The cargo bay looked relatively the same despite the gravity failures, but for odd tools and cargo trolleys on their side. Luckily all the cargo containers were fitted into position.

When they reached the bottom, one of the pirates ran off towards the loader garage and began jacking into one of the mechs. A couple of the others ran off and began frantically ripping container doors open looking for loot. Bowen once or twice tried to look around to see Safiya but every time he did, he was forced onwards by the pirate who had a hold of him.

The pirate with the scanner was directing them.

"A strong power signal this way!" he informed his leader. Soon they emerged at the far edge of the containers where the mysterious small crates where. They hummed with their own power supplies and glowed in the dimly lit cargo bay. Bowen was thrown to his knees before one of the crates.

"What's inside?" the leader demanded. Again Bowen felt a gun at his head.

"I don't know." Bowen replied. The pirate growled behind his helmet and cracked Bowen in the side of his head with his firearm. He distantly heard Safiya sobbing. The pirate leader commanded one be opened. Two of the pirates with immense effort and great difficulty pried open the first crate. A cold fog erupted from within. Bowen couldn't see what was inside. He turned and saw that Safiya was close by on her knees. She had gone very pale and her arm was covered in blood. The pirate with the scanner ripped a panel off the side of the open crate and attached his device with some wiring. There was a moment of quiet. All that could be heard was the echoing alarm through the ship.

"What do we have here?" the leader asked as he peered inside. The other scanned the contents with his device.

"Stasis frozen. Ninety percent intact. Brain dead."

"Take them."

The words bounced around Bowen's sore head. The leader called for the stray looters to return. Two of the pirates quickly reattached the lid of the crate as the others emerged with arms full of technical packs and loose gear. The one who had stolen the loader mech clomped over and began wrenching the crates off their secured spots on the floor. Another two pirates ran off towards the closed cargo bay ramp door. They were equipped with blow torches and industrial saws. Bowen's stomach dropped. He looked to Safiya. A pirate held her by the hair and pointed a gun at the back of her head. She didn't seem far off from passing out. Their plan was becoming clear. The pirate in the mech was ripping the crates off one by one and sliding them across the floor of the cargo bay towards the ramp doors. If no one was coming for them, they were going to die. Bowen couldn't think of a worse way than to be sucked out of the ship into the void of space. Perhaps their bodies would fall to the big purple gas giant and be lost forever. Every time the mech ripped a crate off the floor it sparked. A blinding white light came from the cargo ramp doors as the pirates breached it with their saws and torches. It would only take them a couple of minutes to rip a hole in the ship and then they would suffocate instantly whilst being sucked out of the hole. The pirates would escape with their prizes and that would be that. The end of his adventure. And it would be all his fault. If he hadn't tried to be heroic and whisk Safiya to safety they might have lived. He thought about Moryys, Duggy and the guys. What had happened to them during the attack? He would never know. He thought about Vetura. And he thought of home.

The mech was ripping up the last of the crates when there was a bang from behind them. The pirate in the mech let out a cry as a small explosion burst from the back of the machine. Another bang and a zip as a plasma shot cut through the air. There was a metal clang from over to the side. Bowen turned his head. One of the pirates cutting through the door had dropped to the floor dead. His armoured space suit was hissing from where he had been shot and dark blood seeped away from him. The other pirate tried to run but another bang and he was on the ground motionless.

Bowen felt the pirate leaders hand grab him by the throat and rip him around onto his feet. He felt the gun barrel at his temple. He was being used as a shield. The other pirate did the same with Safiya. The other two pirates drew their guns and looked at each other. Captain Quinn, Garber and nine geared up security crew ran down the steps and approached them. The mech driver was still groaning, trapped in the machine.

"Let them go." Garber commanded. The pirate didn't answer. Bowen's heart was in his throat. The pirate leader had a vice like grip around his neck and Bowen's legs felt weak. The other pirate who held Safiya broke. He kicked her in the small of the back and she fell to the floor before he started firing wildly. As he and the others were brought down in a hail of gunfire, Bowen was released as a hot strike cut through the air right by his head from high above them. He fell to the ground as the pirate leader's skull face plate exploded.

"Stand down!" Quinn commanded everyone as the chaos ended. Bowen turned his head and saw up on the walkway was Lennox with a high powered plasma rifle. The barrel was smoking red.

Quinn's cyborg hand rested on Bowen's chest.

"...Safiya." Bowen tried to say. He was crashing from the adrenaline and his head was beginning to spin. He heard

Garber shouting commands to the security crew. Quinn spoke to Bowen, but he couldn't hear him. The last thing Bowen saw was Quinn's robotic yellow eye before he passed out.

42.

Bowen stirred. He knew he was awake but he didn't want to open his eyes. The Memento hummed and rocked gently, it felt alive again. Bowen's memories were hazy, his whole body ached, willing him to get up. Finally he conceded and opened his eyes. Bowen blinked and stared at the ceiling of his cabin, he couldn't remember getting there. All of a sudden his body convulsed and he felt a rush of panic. Bowen sat bolt upright in his bed and threw the covers off himself before he leapt off the mattress and darted to his bathroom. His heart rate had tripled. He sank to his knees in front of the open toilet and waited to vomit, but it didn't happen. Bowen's breath was coming hard and uneven. After a moment, he reached up and ran the cold tap in the sink. The noise of running water helped him slow his breathing down as he slumped back and sat against the wall.

What memories he had came back to him. The observation deck, the attack, the chaos in the atrium. The pirates, Safiya, the gunfire, the blood. He cupped his hands over his face and winced in pain. His tongue acquainted itself with a new false tooth that was in his mouth, it was noticeably different to all the others. With wobbly knees, Bowen got to his feet and saw himself in the mirror. There were stitches across his cheek where the pirate had punched him. He hadn't felt it at the time, but his armoured fist had ripped open the skin on Bowen's face. He bared his teeth in the mirror. His lower right canine was metallic. The light scarring from the fight in Miengu Waters was barely noticeable in contrast to his new injuries.

Gently Bowen ran water over his face before returning to his cabin. He sat on the edge of his bed and saw a plastic tube of strong painkillers. Another memory returned of being carried into a surgery bay. There had been an air of commotion and the nurses had been rushing about. There was another blank spot but Bowen remembered some metal instruments about his face and in his mouth, then nothing. He picked up the tube of pills and read that he should take two three times a day. He checked the time and saw that it would be dinner soon, but he didn't really feel like eating.

He sat on the edge of his bed and took a deep breath. The blinds in his cabin were closed but a blue light streamed inside, they were on the highways again. He had missed the passing of Mordarak Gate which meant he had been out of action for at least a day. He opened his blinds and leant on the window frame a while, watching the roiling blue energy. Things that Mason had said were ringing true. Space travel was dangerous.

Bowen dressed himself and sat on his bed. He picked up his rucksack that was resting by the side and idly inspected it. There were a few dark patches on the back. His fingers recoiled from touching them as he realised it probably wasn't his blood. He reached inside and brought out the belongings he had with him when the pirates attacked the ship. The magazine he had bought, some trash from the snacks and his camera. When he pulled it out, his heart sank a little. He remembered the spike of pain he felt in his back when the ship's gravity had malfunctioned. He had landed on the camera more than once during the chaos. He pressed the activator button, but nothing happened. He turned it over in his hands and it rattled as he saw the cracked lens. It was broken. He set it on his bedside table and sniffled, it seemed a silly thing to get upset about, he could have died after all. Safiya could have died, but he was getting teary eyed over his camera.

A few minutes went by and there was a knock at his cabin door. Bowen jumped at the sound. He took a deep breath and went to answer. He sighed in relief when he opened it.

"Hey V."

"Hey, can I come in?" Vetura asked.

"Yeah sure."

Vetura walked inside the cabin and Bowen closed the

door behind her. As he turned to her she threw her arms around him. He didn't question it. Bowen felt a little dizzy from the smell of her hair spray and her perfume. He wrapped his arms around her carefully.

"I heard what happened." she said. "How are you doing?" They didn't let go of each other.

"I'm... alright. I think. I don't remember much. How long have we been on the highway?"

"About ten hours."

"Are you alright?"

"Yeah. I'm good." she whispered. He felt her caress his back before they pulled away from each other.

"You wanna sit?" he asked. She perched on the edge of Bowen's bed and he joined her with his back against the metal headboard. "What happened?" he asked as he motioned to her face. She had a plaster on her forehead and the beginnings of a bruise on her white skin.

"I was getting out of the shower when we got hit. Smacked my head on the floor." He leaned forwards and turned her head to the light gently.

"It looks pretty gnarly."

"It's not so bad, not the best time to be stark naked though. When the gravity failed I broke my mirror." She lowered her vest top and showed him a series of small cuts on her shoulder and collar bone. "You were in the atrium by the cafeteria weren't you?" she asked.

"I was." Bowen said remembering it all too well.

"It must have been awful. Some people died."

"Yeah? No one we know I hope?" he asked cautiously. His mind rifled through Moryys, Duggy, Wotll and others.

"A couple of security crew. And a few passengers. Someone died of a heart attack. Most people were in their cabins or got sealed inside priority areas."

"Security..? Anyone called Zaren or Shillok..?"

"No, I don't think so." Vetura replied. Bowen took a deep breath as Vetura idly traced his stitches with her finger. There was a moment of quiet but for the humming of the ship. "Your face has been through it lately." she said.

"Just a bit. Look at this." he showed her his new metal tooth.

"Honestly that's a good look for you." Vetura said.

"Right."

"For real." They both laughed. For a moment Bowen forgot his stress. "Has Safiya come to see you..?" Vetura asked.

"No, at least I don't think so. Is she alright?"

"She's fine. You two were rushed up to the med bay pretty quickly."

"They shot her in the arm..."

"I heard. Apparently she's quit her job in the galley."

"I should probably go and see her when I can." Bowen said.

"Are things okay between you two?"

"Sort of. It's kind of my fault what happened."

"How do you mean?"

"She wanted to stay in observation where we were, but I thought we'd be safer in the garden. We ended up running right into trouble." His hand started shaking. Vetura placed her hand on his.

"You were just trying to look after her..." For a moment, Bowen just looked into Vetura's large, black eyes. He swallowed.

"My camera broke." he said.

"Can I see?" she asked. Bowen reached across the bed and took the camera off the bedside table. He handed it to Vetura and she turned it over in her hands inspecting it.

"Doesn't seem too bad. I might be able to save it."

"That'd be great." he said with a smile. Vetura beamed. Bowen's stomach growled so loud Vetura raised her eyebrows.

"Was that you?" she asked.

"It was." Bowen smiled. Vetura hung the camera around her neck. She stood up outstretched her hand to Bowen.

"Take me to dinner?"

43.

On the way to dinner there was a quieter vibe to the ship. Bowen and Vetura passed crew and passengers taking meals to their cabins. There were closed off corridors and sections where repairs where being worked on. Despite this, they chatted as they walked. Bowen discovered that they shared a love of similar music and that Vetura was something of a cinephile too. She even challenged him on a piece of behind the scenes trivia that he had misremembered. By the time they entered the canteen, Bowen had almost completely forgotten the pirate attack.

The food the Memento had picked up on Davarak was substantial but its quality was more of the same frozen ready meals. Apparently it was the best that could be hoped for from a mining city. The cafeteria was busy, but the atmosphere was subdued. One by one, they were joined by others, each with their own minor injuries from the attack. Duggy arrived first with some food from the vending machines and a lit cigarette in his mouth. Bowen hugged him and laughed.

"What I say? This man can't be stopped." Duggy said as he admired Bowen's false tooth. Moryys arrived with a tray of food and lifted Bowen off his feet when they embraced.

"I'm glad you're okay man." he said.

"Vermin Dwellers, Free Traders, Pirates, he's fights them all." Duggy said. "He could take on a Federation Riot Squad on his own." Soon the table was full. Bao Bao, Gricky, Ramphry, Zaren and Shillok joined them one by one. Vetura swapped a few cigarettes from Duggy in exchange for the leftovers of her dinner. Bao Bao and Shillok congratulated Bowen on his new scars and the table even began to talk lightly of the pirate attack. Bowen felt himself becoming relaxed again.

Vetura leant in to Bowen as the rest of the guys were joking around.

"Hey by the way..." she said quietly. "Are we gonna talk about what happened in cargo..?" Bowen swallowed hard. He had almost completely forgotten that last night on Davarak. Bowen remembered stuffing himself and Vetura between cargo containers. He remembered her gripping his shirt tight and her warm breath on his neck. Her black eyes glinting in the dark as she looked up at him and how she had shifted her thigh between his legs.

"What do you mean..?" he coughed. She seemed to wait for a moment and she glanced down at his mouth.

"A pretty shifty conversation to overhear wouldn't you say?"

"Oh yeah, yeah it was." Bowen shuffled in his seat as he went red in the face.

"I knew there was a bit of drama behind the scenes between Lennox and Garber, but it seemed a little more serious than that," she said. "And what exactly would the navigation crew need to be prepared for..?" Bowen thought of Simon.

"I thought they were just talking business." He said.

"Quietly down in the dark of cargo? I'm not so sure. Do you remember how Denton was talking? I've never heard him that nervous."

"He was talking about the Memento and the Captain." Bowen said as he tried to remember.

"It seems we aren't the only ones onboard on the tail of secrets." she said. Their conversation was cut short as the table talk absorbed them again.

One by one, the table emptied until the only ones left were Bowen, Vetura and Moryys. In a moment of quiet, Bowen spied Simon across the cafeteria sitting alone. His initial reaction was to call out for him, but Bowen stopped himself. Simon's hair had grown out a bit and he looked very tired. Bowen watched him finish a cigarette and leave the cafeteria in a hurry.

Before Bowen could react Moryys spoke.

"So, I don't know about you two, but I'm free to check

out cargo." Vetura shuffled in her seat.

"It depends whether Bowen still wants to. He might not want to go back down there after what happened."

"Yeah, sorry, I didn't think." Moryys said.

"No. I do want to." Bowen confirmed.

"Okay then." Moryys smiled. Bowen reached into his pocket, withdrew his id card and showed it to them.

"When the pirates got a hold of me and Safiya, they took us down to the cargo bay doors that were sealed off with an emergency lockdown. It said authorised personnel only. They forced me at gunpoint to open the door. If it hadn't have worked they would have murdered us both."

"I'm glad that didn't happen." Vetura said.

"Me too."

"I've heard the odd bit of talk." said Moryys.

"How's that?" Bowen asked.

"Well we've got their ship down there, a little cruiser thing. it's gonna be stripped down. The Cpatain's confiscated their flight computer but I heard from the guys that uninstalled it that the pirates were on Davarak for weeks. They left the same day that you went out with the Captain and must have spotted you both and flagged you." Bowen swallowed. He remembered walking through the dusty backstreets and how they were watched.

"Can I see your card please?" Vetura asked. Bowen handed it to her and she looked it over. "Nobodies come to say anything to you about how you got into the cargo bay during the attack?"

"No."

"I think this is our ticket in there." she said.

"How are we gonna do it then?" Bowen asked.

"We'll have to leave it a few hours until the night shift." Moryys said.

"Okay so we waste some time and then meet up down there tonight?" Vetura asked.

"Sounds good," Moryys said, "What do you say Bowen?"

"I'm in."

44.

Bowen checked his watch as he walked the quiet crew decks. The low lighting illuminated the way and the shifting ad screens glowed in the dark as he made it to Safiya's door. He knocked and for a moment there was no response. Part of him considered leaving until he heard the locks shifting. Safiya's face appeared.

"Yes?" she asked.

"Hey," Bowen said, "I thought I'd come to see you." She looked away into the cabin before she returned.

"I'm not really in the mood for company." she said.

"Are you alright..? How's your arm..?" he asked carefully. She opened the door a little more and he saw her in full. She looked tired and dishevelled, he had never seen her without her jewellery or make up and her hair looked uncared for. She rolled up the arm of her plain sweater and showed him her arm. There was a fresh bandage. She didn't say anything. Bowen's heart dropped a little. "It's all my fault. I'm sorry."

"How is it your fault?" she asked.

"We should have stayed in observation."

"Maybe. I don't blame you for this though." she said. Bowen swallowed. There was a difference in the air between them. He waited for her to comment on the stitches on his face, or anything, but she just stood there looking down at her feet.

"Are you going to be alright..?" he asked.

"I will. I'm just counting the days until Obelisk and then I'm going home."

"Fair enough. I think I'll be doing the same." There was another silence that was more than a little awkward.

"I'm glad you're okay too... Thanks for coming to check on me." she said finally.

"No problem. I'll leave you to it. See you around

maybe..?"

"Yeah, maybe." she said with a half smile. Bowen smiled stiffly. "Goodbye Bowen." She closed the door on him and he left.

**

Later that night, Bowen made his way down through the ship with a heavy heart. Ever since leaving Davarak, the ship felt much cooler. He walked slowly as he entered the atrium where he and Safiya were when the gravity had failed. He noticed the doors had been replaced. The vending machine was out of order after the unfortunate passenger had crashed into it. It had been cordoned off along with a few wall panels that needed repairing. A few sections of the floor had been cleaned and buffered, Bowen could only think of one reason why. He reached the elevator and pressed the button to go down to the lower decks. As the machine carried him, he realised that his face was a little wet with tears. He balled up the sleeve of his jumper and wiped at his face.

Before long he reached the garden where Vetura and Moryys were waiting for him. Vetura was wearing her overalls and equipped with her tool belt.

"You good?" Moryys asked.

"Yeah. One sec." Bowen answered. He peeked his head inside the garden and flicked the lights on. Luckily the heat lamps had kicked back in when the power had rebooted. There was a mess but nothing too serious. Bowen had worried that it would be a bomb site after the gravity failure. Some of the plants needed a prune, but overall the growth was coming on nicely. Vetura poked her head in next to his.

"Is it still there?" she asked. Bowen smiled.

"Yeah just checking." he replied. She looked down at his lips as she smiled back.

"Come on then." she said.

The three of them walked off down the wide hallways

towards the cargo bay. They rounded the corner and found the doorway to cargo that Bowen had been forced to open. Moryys opened the door and walked through. Bowen stopped in his tracks. He noticed a small dark patch on the floor where Safiya had been brought to her knees. His heart beat a little faster. Vetura's hand found his arm.

"Hey." she said quietly. "...we can forget this if you want?" Bowen swallowed.

"No, I'm alright." he said.

"Okay then." Vetura smiled at him.

They followed Moryys into the cargo bay and emerged onto the dimly lit metal walkways. Moryys was already down by the mech garage starting up a loader. As they met him in amongst the containers he illuminated the way with the head lamps on the mech.

"Fucking pirates man." Moryys exclaimed.

"What's up?" asked Vetura.

"They only went and jacked one of the best rigs. It'll be in repairs for weeks."

"Lennox sniped the driver from the walkways." Bowen said remembering the events.

"Yeah Yuki wasn't pleased when it was brought up to her." said Vetura.

They reached edge of the containers where the pirates had taken Bowen and Safiya. Looming in the dark of the cargo bay was the shape of the pirate ship. It was covered in scaffolding and various cranes were dotted about as well as floodlights that had been switched off.

"Those powered crates have been moved." Vetura noticed.

"Yeah we got orders to move them." Moryys replied. Bowen cleared his throat.

"The pirates tried to steal them when they found them. They brought me and Safiya down here and opened one." Moryys and Vetura stopped walking.

"What was inside?" Moryys asked.

"I didn't get a look, but it was refrigerated in stasis. They scanned whatever was inside and they said it was brain dead."

"Shit." Vetura said. "You think there was a person in it?" There was a silence between them.

"They ripped them all up real good." Moryys said. "It took the guys most of yesterday to clean up what they'd done to the floors around here."

"Once they ripped them up they were going to tear open the cargo bay doors and let them be sucked out into space with me and Safiya along with them." Bowen said. He looked over to the dark edge of the room where the pirates tried to cut open the doors into space.

"I'm glad that didn't happen." Vetura said.

"Yeah me too." replied Bowen.

"So where are those boxes now?" Vetura asked.

"We got orders to move them up to priority storage on deck one. Handed them over directly to Officer Garber and the Captain. We'll probably never see them again."

"It'll bother me to no end." Vetura said.

"What?" Bowen asked.

"Never knowing what was inside. And why. What the hell is Ishtar doing delivering Captain Quinn bodies?"

"If that is what they are…" Moryys said. "Could have been iced Kovostoyan Great Ox. Apparently it's great. Very rare."

"Right, so the Captain's got his own supply of special cow meat." Bowen joked. The three of them joked their way to the hidden door behind the empty container.

Moryys hauled it away with the loader mech whilst Vetura and Bowen lifted up the floor panel where they had hidden the emergency override console. They both heaved it out carefully and set it over by the wall. Vetura set about opening the access panels closest to the doorway and she began to fiddle with the internal components as Bowen opened up the emergency override console. It unfolded into a large computer terminal with a complicated keypad and numerous attachment outlets. Moryys left the head lamps shining on the doorway, but he exited the mech and came to stand with them. Vetura switched on the override console and it began to boot up as she unravelled wiring that she brought to the wall and hooked it up. From her tool belt she took a loose keypad like the ones all over the ship and she connected it to both the console and the inner workings behind the wall panel. She returned to the emergency override console and it flickered on. Bowen stole a glance at the machine as green text appeared on the black screen.

EMERGENCY OVERRIDE
MANUAL DIAGNOSTIC RELAY
GAMMA PATTERN
PROGRAM ECHO/9/THETA/X

PLEASE WAIT...

Vetura crouched down and sat cross legged on the floor and began typing code into the machine. She brought out her own id card and inserted it. She worked quickly and quietly. Moryys and Bowen could only watch as she was illuminated by the headlamps and the green screen of the console. Bowen peeked over her shoulder and saw a confusing string of console commands and data packets. After a minute she stepped up.

"Okay it's reading the doorway and trying to patch in, might take a few minutes." she said.

"So are we going to be able to cover our tracks with this thing..? Will we be able to lock the door again after we're done?"

"We will indeed. Just a reversal of the program."

"Oh, sweet." Bowen replied.

"I'm the whole package."

Moryys began to pace and after a while Bowen's hands were becoming twitchy. There was a beeping sound from the console and Vetura took hold of the portable keypad.

"Okay Bowen, your id card..?" she asked with her hand outstretched. Bowen took a deep breath and handed it over. Moryys had come to watch as she inserted his metal id card into the keypad. The three of them faced the doorway. They all huddled around the pad in Vetura's hands. On the screen a wall of orange text appeared with a flurry of code and data. Then a loading bar appeared and they watched with baited breath as it filled up. The orange text became green.

AUTHORISATION
RECOGNISED
LEIUTENANT RHYS
OVERRIDE ACCEPTED

There was a clunking sound from the wall as internal locks loosened. They watched as a whole section of the wall shifted. As it did so, a thick layer of dust was shook off. Old mechanisms whined and strained as the panels shifted and moved to the side. There was only blackness beyond as everything stopped. No one spoke. Vetura lowered the keypad onto the floor and retrieved a torch from her belt. The head lamps from the mech offered some light, but not enough.

All three of them walked forwards as one towards the darkness beyond. Vetura flicked her torch on and shone it into the doorway, but the light hit nothing. As they stood on the threshold of the blackness, Bowen's heart was beating faster. He had not considered what was actually in there. Perhaps it was hidden for a reason? What if there was something dangerous inside?

Vetura was the first to step inside. The step of her boot echoed into the darkness. Bowen and Moryys followed close. Vetura turned to the side and shone her torch onto the inner wall.

"What are you doing?" Bowen whispered.

"There must be a light or something." Bowen and Moryys exchanged a look. Bowen felt very exposed. Vetura equipped a tool and was grunting with an access panel before she flicked a switch. A deep whirring sound came from a hidden power source. Dust fell on them as the room began to shake and power was distributed into the darkness. The sound of generators firing began to rise as lights flickered on one by one all throughout the room. Bowen's mouth fell open.

"Would you have guessed it?" Moryys said.

"No way." replied Vetura.

Hung like bats in a cave were two rows of star fighters. Walkways ran between them and up above them. Bowen counted ten as they began to move down the central walkway. The floor beneath the fighters looked like closed jaws for a drop deployment. Each of the ships was heavily built, yet sleek in their design. They were a matte black, but some of the paint had chipped off and revealed the metal beneath. Behind each star fighter were small, one man elevators that came down from somewhere else in the ship. The doors were locked and unused. Moryys turned his head to read the stencil words on the hull of the fighters.

"Gun Dog." he said out loud.

"No way. Bowen said.

"What?" asked Vetura.

"My great grandfather flew a Gun Dog." He smiled as he remembered the photograph on the table in the lounge at home.

"They only made a certain amount of these." Moryys said impressed.

"I'm getting a weird feeling here." said Bowen.

"What's up?" Vetura asked. "Are you okay?"

"Yeah I'm fine. I just… I don't know."

"These things were experimental." Moryys said. "Some of the fastest star fighters ever made. They flew at hypersonic speeds."

"This looks like a proper hanger bay." said Vetura. "Like

on a naval ship or an army station. But there's only ten ships."

"What are you saying?" asked Bowen.

"Well, why the hell are they here? It's a hidden hanger bay on a Free Trader vessel. Doesn't that strike you as odd?" Vetura said. Bowen's head was spinning.

"Who do you think knows how to fly them?" Moryys asked

"They look like they've been here for years." Bowen commented.

"The Captain and Lennox for definite." Moryys wondered.

"Garber too probably." Vetura added as she explored a corner of the hangar. Bowen absent-mindedly began to climb a metal ladder by the side of one of the Gun Dogs. He reached the upper platform and got a peek inside the cockpit that faced downwards.

"I don't know what to make of all this." Bowen said as he came back and leant on a railing.

"Pretty badass." Moryys commented.

"I guess." Bowen replied.

"Hey look over here." Vetura called. Moryys and Bowen looked over and saw that she was stood by the doorway of another room. They both joined her and they all exchanged a look. They were standing in front of a secure heavy duty doorway.

"It's unlocked." Vetura said. They all exchanged a look before she opened the doorway. Bowen and Moryys followed her closely as she entered. Again she found a light that struggled to activate. Once the room was illuminated they saw what was inside. In the centre of the room was a series of complicated computer terminals that surrounded a chair similar to the one in the surgery. In the head rest and down the back of the chair was a mess of cables and wiring that connected to the terminals. There were no surgical tools or operating equipment, in fact no signs of medical use at all. Surrounding the room were work benches and metal cabinets all cluttered with mess from the gravity failure and perhaps long before. No one had been there in a very long time.

"What is all this?" Moryys asked.

"It looks like and old launch control room," Vetura replied. "but it's been converted to some kind of workshop." Bowen found himself looking at the largest computer terminal set into the back wall. It was much bigger than the other ones. He idly ran his hands across the keyboards and was struck by the strangest feeling.

Vetura sat herself down at another terminal in another corner of the room. Bowen and Moryys both at the same time looked around and saw that she was activating the console. They exchanged a look and joined her. Bowen watched as she entered lines of code in a backdoor program.

"Now then." she said quietly as the screen changed. The blur of static and code slowly disappeared as she hacked her way inside. Bowen wanted to express his concerns but the words wouldn't come. He just watched as she opened files and began searching.

"What are you looking for?" he asked quietly.

"I'm not sure, but I'll know it when I see it." she replied. Moryys and Bowen exchanged a look.

"What the hell?" Vetura said finally.

"What is it?" Bowen asked. All he could see was a wall of small text. Vetura leaned in to the screen.

"The system's fighting me at every turn."

"Maybe we shouldn't be doing this?" Bowen said finally looking over their shoulder at the door.

"Just a couple of minutes. There has to be something." she said. Bowen watched as her white hands dashed across the keyboard blindingly fast. "This has to be incorrect." Vetura said finally.

"What's up?" Moryys asked. Vetura traced her black nail across the screen as she read out loud.

"The Federation recognises the exemplary bravery of those who fought and died at Mausoleum..." her finger traced more as she skim read. "These dates can't be right..." Bowen swallowed as she continued. "The battle was turned with the daring actions of Flight Commander Ezekiel Quinn and the noble effort of Security Chief Zoltan Hayashi." The three exchanged a look before Vetura continued. "Their dedication and bravery ensured the end of conflict with the fringe world Mausoleum brought into the Federation." Vetura clicked some keys carefully and a picture appeared on screen. It was slightly distorted but there he was in black and white, Captain Quinn in full ceremonial dress with medals on his chest. He was younger by some years and he sported no cybernetics. Next to him was the infamous pirate leader Zoltan Hayashi. He too looked younger, but his distinctive white hair was unmistakable. Dressed in the same formal military dress, next to Quinn displaying medals on his overcoat.

"What the hell?" Moryys said. "Zoltan Hayashi's never been in Federation Command. He's been in and out of prison since he was a teenager."

Vetura sat back in her chair. "More to the point, Mausoleum isn't a federation world. We were defeated weren't we?" she sounded unsure.

"We were..." Bowen said sweating.

"Do you know that for sure?" she asked. Bowen swallowed.

"My... grandad died in the fighting. My great grandad..." he said.

"What the fuck?" Moryys said. There was a silence between them all. The screen shifted and blurred. Vetura started frantically typing.

"Dammit." she exclaimed. "It's shutting me out. Whoever set this up didn't want us to see it." Bowen looked over his shoulder. "Fuck I've lost it!" she cried as the terminal shut itself down. "I won't be able to get any of that back. And there was a lot more that we didn't see, a lot more..."

"Maybe we should get going before someone finds us."

"Yeah I think you're right." Vetura agreed.

45.

That night, Bowen, Vetura and Moryys had covered their tracks in the secret hangar bay and they had returned the emergency override console to the machine shop. Bowen stressed that someone would ask them questions, but no one did. Vetura was sure she had stumbled onto something big and secret, but Moryys believed that the data they had found was scrambled from out dated files after Vetura had hacked her way in. When he was alone, Bowen considered the impossibility of it. Quinn and Hayashi were younger than his great grandfather Arnold Rhys by almost fifty years, and the conflict at Mausoleum that had claimed Arnold's life ended decades ago. Moryys was right, the data was scrambled as the ship detected Vetura's activity. But the image of Quinn and Hayashi stayed in Bowen's mind.

The galactic highway carried the Memento across space and the days began to blur again, and the mystery of the secret hangar bay faded from Bowen's mind. The stitches on Bowen's face began to dull somewhat and he stopped noticing his metal tooth as much. Around the ship as the repairs were carried out and finished, the air of caution and hesitancy eventually cleared. Like everyone on the ship, Bowen found himself consumed with his work as he spent a lot of his time in the garden. He monitored the sub routines and tweaked the power distribution when needed and fed the plants with growth hormones. Before long, the garden was bustling with greenery and the humidity exchanger was working around the clock. On more than one occasion, Bowen enlisted the help of Vetura and Moryys for a pair of extra hands. Every time they did so, they wound up hanging out in the break area after the work was done. Once or twice, Vetura came to the garden whilst Bowen was working, just to sit and read.

The days became weeks and soon enough, Bowen was

asking for help to harvest. For a whole day, Bowen, Vetura, Moryys, Duggy and Gricky scoured the garden of all fruit and vegetables. The word had gotten out that some fresh food was on its way and Captain Quinn came down to observe the results. They were just about finished when he arrived and had filled up special crates and containers onto cargo trolleys. Bowen was pleased with the outcome of the grow as much of the produce was significantly larger than he had anticipated to the point where they had to requisition extra boxes from cargo. Bowen received a firm handshake from Quinn as well as pats on the back from everyone. Duggy was particularly interested in the potatoes. Vetura had to stop herself from drooling as Bowen helped her pack the oranges and strawberries. With some help from Gricky, Bowen reset the pollinator bees and the hover flies back into stasis before as one, they all hauled the harvest through the access corridors and made for the lifts up to the back end of the galley.

When they came through with crate after crate of fresh food, Wotll almost did a backflip from joy. Bowen received a huge hug from her after she inspected the contents of the packages. What galley staff were present at the time were excitedly vying for a spot to look at the new food. There was an instant change in the kitchen as the staff were suddenly giddy and positively ecstatic at the prospect of cooking with fresh ingredients. Bowen went bright red but he couldn't contain his own pride.

"This'll more than see us through until Obelisk!" Wotll exclaimed as Bowen received pats on the back from people he didn't know the names of.

Later that evening, the cafeteria was buzzing with activity. By then everyone had heard about the fresh food and the queue for the serving lines snaked around the edge of the room. Bowen had not seen the place that full since he first joined the crew. Crew from every deck and department were present, even the command crew had come down from their executive suite on the deck above. Bowen sat at the busy table between Duggy and Vetura. The tables seemed to be full of colour as everyone ate the fruit and veg. There was still the frozen cuts and canned meat, but it was made suddenly tolerable by the addition of the fresh food. There was an almost child like rumour that was spreading like a fire that the kitchen staff were preparing a huge fruit salad for the following day. The sweet smells seemed to fill the air. For the first time in a while, the cafeteria echoed with a happy ambience. Next to him, Duggy had discovered a passion for roasted turnip soaked in red butter whilst at Bowen's other side Vetura was tearing apart an oversized orange. Bowen smiled as he ate his lemon battered fish with fresh cut salted chips and buttery peas. He wondered what his parents would think of him if they knew. He thought of them both as he put a spoonful of sweetcorn into his mouth. Across from their table, Bowen spied Erin and her parents tucking into their own meals. Erin noticed him and she waved her small hand at him. Orla and Colum noticed and they exchanged smiles and nods.

As the majority of crew and passengers were seated, suddenly a harsh ringing sounded from over by the serving line as Wotll got the attention of the room. The quiet spread throughout the cafeteria. Wotll was stood on the end of the serving line with a view of the whole room.

"Ladies and gentlemen, I'm sure you'll all join me in thanking the provider of this evening's food, Mr Bowen Rhys the ship's farmer!" she pointed over towards him and the room erupted in applause, cheers, whistles and banging cutlery on the tables as all eyes were on him. Bowen felt his face flare red as he failed to hide his smile. His hand was thrust into the air as Duggy grabbed his wrist and raised it upwards. Bowen dared a look around. Cargo crew, technicians, engineers, medical staff, janitors, security, even the command crew were congratulating and thanking him. His gaze fell right next to him and his eyes met Vetura's. She was beaming at him. His embarrassment died away and he just smiled back at her. Wotll continued as the noise lowered a touch.

"There's plenty to go around so enjoy!" He looked over to Wotll who blew him a kiss from her frog mouth before she was helped off the serving line.

Over the course of the dinner rush, Bowen was met by pats on the shoulder and calls of appreciation from complete strangers as crew and passengers walked by. Bowen turned to Vetura who was lighting up a thin pink cigarette.

"So you like oranges then?" he asked. She simply nodded at him slowly as she took a long drag of her cigarette. "Good, I'm glad." he smiled. Bowen had gotten for himself a bowl of mango and melon as desert. He had almost finished as he felt another pat on the shoulder. Bowen turned and was surprised to see Simon.

"...Simon. Hey man." Bowen said. Simon looked just as dishevelled as the last time he had seen him. His red hair had grown out significantly and he was brushing it out of his tired eyes. He was not in uniform and his clothes looked unwashed.

"Good job with dinner." Simon said. Bowen was struck by the comment and fumbled for a response.

"Yeah, no problem." he replied. "You okay Si..?"

"I'm fine." Simon replied rather curtly. "Listen you fancy a drink upstairs?" Bowen was caught off guard by the question. He looked around for Simon's crew mates from navigation, but they were nowhere to be seen. He carefully swallowed his mouthful of melon.

"Okay yeah. You wanna go now?" Bowen asked.

"Sure, sounds good."

"Well give me a minute I'll be with you." Bowen said. Simon turned around and walked over towards the vending machines where he stood looking rather vacant.

"That your friend from home?" Vetura asked him.

"Yeah, yeah it is."

"Well let me know how it goes?" she asked.

"Yeah will do." he replied. "I don't mean to bail like this..." She shook her head.

"Don't sweat it, I'm gonna go to bed and rub one out

thinking about oranges." Bowen's mouth fell open and a single gasp of laughter left him. "I'm just kidding." she said as she stood up to leave with her tray. She exhaled a pink cloud of smoke as she turned back to him. "Or am I..?" she added with a wink.

46.

The rec deck was quiet. The walk down from the cafeteria had been somewhat awkward, as Simon had barely spoken. Bowen tried to initiate small talk but Simon seemed to only half hear him. Part of Bowen expected Simon to suddenly call it off and leave but that didn't happen. They were the only two sat at the bar as Techno walked up and down wiping surfaces and constantly neatening the place up. The music player was on low and played old earth electro jazz. The holographic window display that hid the galactic highway from view showed off a sunset on a tropical coastline.

"What are you having?" Bowen asked Simon as he considered the menu.

"Just, whatever you have." replied Simon.

"Hey." Bowen got the attention of Techno. It turned and looked at him blankly with its blocky head. "Two Sun Fossils." he asked as he placed his id card on the bar. The machine took Bowen's card and moved away to get the beverages.

"Still don't like robots?" Simon asked. His voice was flat. Bowen was pleased that Simon was perhaps snapping out of his emotional funk with the question but he barely looked his way when he spoke.

"They have their uses, but no I'm still not fond of them." Bowen said. The robot returned with the two tall glasses of Sun Fossil and Bowen took his card back. He took a sip of his drink and watched Simon take a swig of his. He watched as Simon pulled out his old cigarette tin from his pocket and began to roll himself one. "So…" Bowen started. "How are you doing?" he asked. Simon licked the edge of the paper and began to roll the cigarette in his hands.

"I'm alright." he replied finally.

"You been up to much lately..?" Bowen asked. Simon twisted the cigarette into a point, retrieved his lighter and ignited it. He leant on the bar with his elbows as he answered.

"I've been digging through the ship's data archives."

"Oh right."

"Just busy work. Navigation runs out of things to do pretty quickly once you set off."

"You found anything interesting?" Bowen asked. His mind replayed the events of the night in the hidden hangar bay. For a moment, he was afraid that Simon would somehow know that they had trespassed. Simon took a long drag of his cigarette and the smoke poured out of his nostrils like a waterfall as the question hung in the air. Bowen took it as a no. "So where were you when we got boarded by the pirates?" Bowen asked as a change of subject.

"I was in the server room. I'm in there a lot recently."

"That was... scary." Bowen remarked as the events of the attack replayed in his head.

"I heard you were in the thick of it?" Simon asked.

"Yeah, that's why I've got all these stitches. One of them clocked me."

"I'm... glad you're okay." Simon replied. Bowen swallowed his mouthful of drink and shuffled in his seat. He couldn't remember the last time Simon had said anything remotely similar.

"Thanks. I'm glad you were away from it all when it happened." Bowen said.

A quiet broke out between them. Simon smoked his cigarette and nursed his drink. Bowen watched Techno move around behind the bar endlessly cleaning and the electro jazz played on quietly. Bowen swirled the last of his drink in the glass and broke the silence.

"We must be coming up on Obelisk station soon?" he asked. Simon nodded as he took a swig of his Sun Fossil.

"Yeah, a few weeks now. Are you going home when we get there..?" he asked. Bowen sighed and pushed his empty glass away from himself.

"I am. I'll have a see what ships are going back that way

when we get there."

"There'll be something. The big cargo haulers will get you back in about a month or two on the express lanes." Simon said. "I hear there are plenty of hotels on Obelisk if you have to wait around." Bowen's heart sank a little at the notion.

"I take it you're staying on?" Bowen asked. Simon downed the last of his Sun Fossil. He nodded and smiled stiffly.

"I won't be going home for a while yet." Simon said. Another quiet fell. Bowen began tapping his finger on the counter before he dared to voice his next thought.

"It'll be nice to see Jules again." he said. Simon shuffled in his seat.

"So she's home again..?" he asked.

"She should be by now." Bowen said. "She's said she wants to see me."

"I've not heard from her for a while..." Simon commented.

"Really." Bowen replied flatly. "I've been in touch with her since before I left home." Simon's discomfort was poorly hidden. There were still unanswered questions burning in Bowen's mind. Bowen tried to force the words but they would not form. Part of him wondered if there was a point. He would be headed back in a matter of days. And hopefully he would be home in a couple of months. He would speak to Jules himself.

Bowen took a deep breath as he began to let it drop. Simon got the attention of Techno.

"Another two." he ordered as he placed his crew card on the bar. The machine began to work again. Simon reached into his pocket and pulled out a plastic tube of pills as two more Sun Fossils were placed in front of them. Bowen just watched as Simon popped a couple of the pills into his mouth and swallowed them with a gulp of the orange drink. After a moment, Simon cleared his throat before he spoke. His demeanour was a little different all of a sudden. "Look at us eh? A couple of spacers. Who would have thought?"

"Yeah..." Bowen replied.

"Do you know roughly how far away from home we are right now?" Simon asked.

"No... no I don't." Bowen answered. Simon sniffed as he began rolling another cigarette.

"It gets hard to wrap your head around after a point. But you can't imagine how far. It'd take you a long time to write out the number in miles."

"Yeah?"

"I mean if we didn't have the gates and the highways it would have taken us three or four years just to get to Davarak."

"I know it's mad isn't it?" Bowen replied. Simon seemed to be on the verge of becoming erratic. Bowen had a suspicion those pills were not painkillers.

"You know over the last century there have been six attempts by the federation to miniaturize warp gate technology?" Bowen took a long swig of his drink and Simon didn't allow him to respond before he carried on. "They've all failed. Every time for one reason or another."

"Wow." Bowen managed. He sighed as Simon waffled on next to him.

"Imagine if a warp engine could be installed into a ship this size or even smaller."

"Yeah..."

"A Tyrannus Core. No need for Crystalak fuel. We could jump across the galaxy and fuck up anyone who started anything.

"Imagine." Bowen replied. Bowen rubbed his face and took a deep breath as he rested on the bar. Simon had slumped and he looked tired again.

"What's going on with you man? You're a mess." Bowen snapped. Simon didn't seem to hear him. Simon took a deep breath and sat up. He leaned over the bar and prodded Techno in the arm.

"Hey give me a shot of something." he said lazily. The machine turned and fetched a couple of shot glasses and began pouring out a dark green liquid that sparkled silver. The bottle was inscribed Hiraeth.

"I don't want one." Bowen said to Techno as it poured out two shots anyway. "Whatever." he said as he picked it up and knocked it back. Bowen felt the warm drink pour down his insides. He watched Simon shakily pick up his own and look at it.

"Hey Bowen..?" Simon began.

"What?" Bowen responded with a sigh.

"What did we do for your twenty first birthday?" Bowen was surprised by the question, but he cast his mind back all the same.

"We... got the hyper track over to New Mersey and had a night out. We met up with James and Mosh at Allchester central and met the others at Lennon's platform."

"Yeah, I remember..." Simon said with a weak smile. "Phillip tried it on with that girl didn't he?"

"Yeah he got shut down immediately." Bowen remembered.

"What about my birthday that year, my twenty second?" Simon asked. He was still holding the shot in his hand and looking at it. Bowen had to strain his memory but he did remember.

"We went to watch Vorpal Snake at Maker's Park didn't we?"

"You were there weren't you?" Simon asked.

"Of course I was." Bowen remarked. "I've got a guitar pick in my bedroom that I caught out of the air at the end."

"Right... yeah..." Simon said. He drank his shot slowly. Bowen frowned.

"What's got you so nostalgic? That's not like you..." he asked. Simon pushed away the shot glass and casually tossed his crew card at Techno that fumbled to catch it. He took a deep breath and turned to Bowen. His wild red hair was slick with sweat and his piercing blue eyes were sunken.

"I just wanted to remember."

47.

Dear Mum and Dad

I hope you are both well.
I'm sorry I haven't written in a while,
I'll be coming home soon.
I'll be getting a flight home from Obelisk station,
I might be on my way already when you get this,
but I'll write to let you know when I'll be getting back to Saxon.
I miss you both.
I can't wait to come home and tell you about everything.
Love Bowen
x

Juliette,

I know it's been ages since you wrote to me,
I've been away for a while.
I'll be coming back to Saxon in a couple of months.
We should talk when I get home.
Bowen

Bowen sat in the dark comms suite. He re-read both of his messages a couple of times before he finalised the com-disks. As the computer terminal worked, he looked over the the far end of the room. The door to the server room was shut. Bowen wondered if Simon was inside. The conversation they had in the rec deck a couple of weeks ago had devolved into Simon rambling about this and that to the point where Bowen had just left him to it. By the end, Simon was barely responding to what Bowen did have to say. Simon had popped another couple of whatever his pills were and began the cycle again just before Bowen threw the towel in and left for his cabin.

The terminal beeped and the second com-disk was presented to him. He took it and put them in his bag and he stood to leave for the Comms Office. There was a buzz about the place as they were nearing the Obelisk system. Davarak had not been a substantial enough rest stop, but from what Bowen had been told about Obelisk it would more than make up for it.

He reached the Comms Office and joined a small queue as others were also writing their messages to be sent off as soon as they landed. When Bowen finally reached the front, he saw officer Horner sat behind the glass screen. His dark skin was glistening with sweat and he looked overworked. Bowen tried to make idle conversation with him, but Horner didn't seem interested. Horner's uniform was unkempt and he was unshaven. When Bowen handed over his com-disks he saw that Horner's hands were shaking a little.

"Nearly there now." Bowen said with a smile through the glass. Horner looked up at him with his brown eyes and forced a smile of his own. Bowen noticed around him on his desk was the evidence of excessive coffee drinking.

"That's right." Horner managed in response. "I'll get these sent off when we dock at Kaldr. Obelisk sorry." he corrected himself and laughed it off.

"Okay thanks…" Bowen said as he turned to leave. As he walked away, he felt as though a weight were lifted off him. He had finally responded to Jules. He walked around the ship at a leisurely pace until he came to the rec deck atrium. The ambience had returned to the area. There was noise from the gym further down and beyond that the wet room laundry was busy with people coming and going with their sacks of clothes. His mind replayed the first time he used the laundry and the first time he met Vetura. He sat on a bench across from the vending machines that were now fully repaired. He considered the fact that he would be leaving soon and the people he would not see any more. Vetura, Moryys, Duggy. Everyone swam through his head one by one. He would try to exchange details with them so that he could stay in touch, but that seemed like a faint hope. The sheer distance and the time between messages would interfere. And the fact that everyone was so busy. His old friends had disappeared into space and he had not heard from them again. The friends he had made on the Memento were different. It was enough to try all the same.

***

That evening at dinner, Bowen was sat with everyone at a table. The crew had been treated to a special fruit cake that the galley had prepared. The staff had proudly served it around the room. Kabé came and brought the servings for their table, perfectly balancing bowls up his arms and on his masked head. The food had lifted everyone's spirits and the cafeteria again had an atmosphere. Afterwards, Bao Bao and Ramphry started arm wrestling that Moryys and Zaren got in on. Gricky, Shillok and Duggy began planning a last guys night for when they got to Obelisk. Vetura, who was sat next to Bowen, retrieved a small bag from under the table. She pulled out Bowen's camera with a new lens and a newly installed battery pack.

"You fixed it?" Bowen asked amazed.

"I said I would didn't I?" she replied.

"Thanks V." Bowen leant over and they hugged. From over Vetura's shoulder, Duggy appeared in Bowen's eyeline from over Shillok's side and raised his scaly black brows giving a suggestive smile. Bowen went red as he realised he and Vetura were holding each other for a moment longer than he might have expected. They let go of one another and Bowen cleared his throat. She just looked back at him as he rested his camera on the table.

"Hey uh..." he started.

"Hmm..?" Vetura replied as she leaned in slightly.

"So, you know how I'll be going home to Saxon?"

"Yeah..?"

"Can we stay in touch?" he asked. Vetura smiled.

"I'd like that." she replied. They exchanged federation identification numbers there and then. When they were done, Vetura picked up Bowen's camera off the table. She removed the new lens cap as she leaned into him. She raised the camera up into the air in front of them and took a few photographs. She messed up his hair in one and she stuck her black tongue out for another. Bowen caught himself beaming as they got increasingly silly. As Wottl passed by, Vetura asked for her to take some for them. Wotll obliged as Vetura whistled for the table to assemble. All the guys crowded around them both and each posed in their own way. Duggy rolled up his sleeves and flexed his lizard muscles which made Moryys do the same and Zaren and Shillok threw up military hand signals. Gricky stood up on the table and waved his spindly arms as Bao Bao raised a whole huge watermelon above his head. They all packed in together at Wotll's command so much that Vetura hopped into Bowen's lap for the big picture. The flash blinded Bowen and before his eyes readjusted he felt a kiss on his cheek. He felt Vetura hop off him as he rubbed his eyes. The camera was thrust back into his hands as he smiled stupidly.

Before Bowen could react, the doors to the cafeteria opened. The chatter died down as the command crew entered. Captain Quinn and officers Garber and Lennox stood by the windows and made their announcements. They would be exiting the highway in a mater of hours during the night shift. By the time breakfast would be served they would have docked. Garber stated that the ship would be pulling into a repair bay to fix the remaining damage from the pirate attack. Quinn reminded the crew of the correct disembarking procedures and that they would be stopped at Obelisk for a few days at least. Bowen did his best to pay attention but he was growing more and more tired by the minute. As the command crew exited, the ambience resurged around the room, but Bowen saw Quinn move through the cafeteria over to their table. The guys each addressed the Captain appropriately and nodded in respect as he reached Bowen.

"Gentlemen. Madam. A moment of your time Mr Rhys?" he said to Bowen.

"Of course." Bowen replied. He stood up, camera in hand as the Captain patted Bowen on the shoulder. He looked back at Vetura who waved at him. He and Quinn walked through the strip of tables towards the main doors. As they walked, Bowen saw on each table happy messes of food and passengers and crew enjoying it all in the various forms the kitchen had prepared. As they left the cafeteria Quinn spoke.

"You did excellently with the garden. The fresh food came just in time."

"Really?" Bowen replied.

"Really. What we picked up from Davarak was not substantial in the slightest." They walked through the atrium beyond the doors and down a few corridors and stopped by a long window where they were bathed in the blue light from the highway.

"Well I'm glad I helped." Bowen said.

"You did more than help, I think you saved the crew from rioting."

"Yeah?"

"Have you seen them in there these last few weeks? It's like the last days of school. People need good food and you provided them with it." Bowen felt himself go red but he smiled.

"Thank you Captain."

"You've done so well that I've given you a bonus on your pay."

"Really?" Bowen asked stunned.

"An extra three thousand kardonna." Bowen stifled a laugh.

"I don't know what to say. Thank you Captain."

"You deserve it Bowen." Quinn said. Bowen looked out into the blue and smiled. "On top of that I have a proposition for you." Quinn added. Bowen looked back at the Captain who observed him with his yellow cyborg eye.

"Yes?"

"How would you like to become a permanent member of my crew? I'll have a new rank drawn up for you. Botanical Science Officer." Bowen's mouth fell open. "It would come with a higher pay bracket along with some measure of responsibilities like sourcing the materials and equipment you need wherever we stop." Bowen cleared his throat and closed his mouth. His mind raced as he imagined himself in such an official position on the Memento. He saw himself in a proper uniform, rubbing shoulders with the likes of Lennox, Doctor Jinn-Quo and Garber, but his mind crashed back to reality and he thought of home. He thought of his parents. He thought of the rain soaked walls of Allchester and the bells and ribbons hanging from the Old Woman in the great square. The fields and the hills. With the money he had already earned and with the bonus that Quinn had paid him, he could start his own farm on Saxon immediately. Bowen rubbed his mouth and found the words.

"That's an amazing offer Captain really." he started. He was about to continue when he laughed.

"What?" Quinn asked with a smirk.

"It's funny." Bowen said. "I spent so much time wanting to get away from Saxon, but now all I can think about is going home."

"I understand." Quinn replied. He patted Bowen on the shoulder.

"I've never been away from my family for this long."

"Yes… me neither." the Captain said looking out into the blue. As he did so he squeezed Bowen's shoulder before he let go.

"With the money I've earned I can really think about starting a farm of my own."

"You should. If the food you produced here is anything to go off, you'll make a fortune for yourself." Bowen beamed.

"Thank you Captain."

"How's this?" Quinn started. "I'll give you another thousand. To help your farm get started." Quinn reached into his pocket and handed him his encoded free trader comms details. "Send me a message when you have things up and running. We'll be coming back around the galactic arm in a couple of years. Keep your eyes on the interstellar shipping forecasts for us and I'll come and do business." Bowen didn't know what to say. He was almost overwhelmed. He felt a tear try to escape the corner of his eye. He looked down at the free trader id card.

"Thank you Captain. You'll have to stop by for a drink and something to eat."

"Some of that famous Saxon hospitality." Quinn replied with a smile. "I can't wait."

48.

Bowen woke early. When he opened the blinds in his cabin he saw billions of stars. The engines were off completely and the Memento was silent. During the night they had left the highways and made the trip across the system to Obelisk station. From Bowen's window he could not see any of the station, but he strained his neck to look down and he could see massive servo cranes hovering into position on the hull of the ship. Bowen took a deep breath. He showered and dressed himself and made to leave.

On his way down through the ship, he stepped off the stairs down from the crew decks. Ahead of him was a queue of passengers waiting to leave the ship. Bowen noticed a colourful headscarf and a flash of black hair. He stopped his instinct to call out to Safiya, just as she left through the departure tunnel onto the station. With a heavy heart, he watched her until she was lost to the crowds.

Bowen was one of the earliest to the cafeteria. The kitchen staff could be heard clattering away behind the doors preparing breakfast. But Bowen's attention was fully on the windows. His mouth fell open as he approached the glass. Out before him was the biggest structure he had ever seen. The warp gate of Obelisk station dominated the view. A colossal blue portal full of roiling energy that sparked constantly like a storm. The thick ringed structure of the station was massive, many more times larger than Pennine gate above Allchester. He saw queues of glinting specks lined up before the gate and his heart skipped a beat. The sheer size of Obelisk gate was enough to send a shiver through him. They were currently docked in a repair bay and the station itself sprawled out towards them. It was much like what he remembered from Pennine but much more, an endless cluster of metallic structures covered in gigantic signposts and billboards. Sticking out of the station were titanic radio towers and signal dishes. They also covered the gate itself. Alongside the Memento were other ships in dock. Bowen looked up and saw many more. The same if he looked down too, there were hundreds of ships. Bowen managed to tear himself away from the view to have a hurried breakfast.

  Bowen wasted no time and was the first in line. He was so distracted he barely noticed what Jungga served him. He ate alone in the canteen watching the window. Afterwards Bowen walked briskly through the ship he felt an anxious hurry within himself. He doubled back to his cabin, threw on his leather jacket and pocketed his wallet and id card. He made his way down through the crew decks and flashed his crew card to Vargoth and Zaziik at the departure tunnel. They waved him through and he walked the sloped tunnel off the ship.

  Bowen took his first step onto the station. He was immediately struck by the smells of the maintenance bay. A mixture of fuel, exhaust fumes and hot metallic smells. He began to follow large electronic signs for the main body of the station through a caged tunnel with the noises of the busy repair bay echoing all around. He heard men shouting, engines revving, saw blades, drills, laser cutters and massive bolt guns firing as the bays were buzzing with activity. Bowen walked for a long while before he looked back at the ship through the steel wire cage. The Memento looked small now, nestled in amongst others bigger than it. The station workers had assembled scaffolding over parts of the hull with the hovering cranes. He saw them coming and going from out into space behind the ship from out of an energy field. They were stripping off damaged portions of the ship's hull. Bowen watched them disappear into huge dark tunnels that were marked as interior scrap yard levels lower down. The ship was tethered to the station in numerous points with huge mechanical arms that had tightly packed wires inside like veins. Bowen made himself look away and carried onward.

  He eventually came to a wide open space that was

covered with an astronomically big glass dome. Through the glass was the view of the massive gate. It looked faraway and incredibly close at the same time. Many paths led away from the area towards the main body of the station. Bowen walked to the flight terminal buildings where massive digital screens were ever changing with details of ships coming and going and their destinations. He spied the Memento that was bound next for Vibana. Bowen was a little sad that he would never see it. He scoured the destination screen and had to wait for it to revolve around twice before he saw the name Saxon. A towing ship called the Benign Summer was heading directly for Saxon on hyper lane fourty seven b twelve.

 Bowen recited the name of the ship to himself in his head as he approached the terminal ticket office. He queued for some time until he reached the front where he enquired about a passenger ticket and paid for an ensuite cabin. Papers were printed for him and stamped. The Benign Summer was docked across the station from the Memento and was due to leave in eight days time on the morning rotation which would be after the Memento would be gone. For a moment he was distracted by the thought of having to watch the Memento leave. He asked about hotels and was directed to a multitude of options all over the station from the most cost effective to the more luxurious. When asked, the ticket officer told him that the trip to Saxon would take roughly six weeks non stop. They were scheduled to exit at Himmelwald Gate and land in the industrial city of Engelreich. Engelreich was just over seven hundred miles from Allchester, about a three hour ride on the hyper track.

 He thanked the ticket officer and walked away, papers in hand. He carefully folded them and put them in his pocket before he explored the station for a hotel to book for a few nights. It was official, he was going home.

 Bowen wandered into the heart of the station. It was a bustling and busy metroplex made of brick, stone and wood as much as steel and iron. A local hyper tram suspension circuit driven by robots zoomed in and out of all districts and armed and armoured station security patrolled in twos and threes. Wide open food courts gave way to entertainment blocks. Arcades and movie theatres, department stores and wildlife biodomes were overlooked by clusters of high rise structures. He past digital sign posts for sports arenas and race tracks as well as the station's red and blue light districts. Everywhere was decorated with hanging vines, potted trees, marble water fountains and carved stone statues. Bowen did his best to not become distracted.

He found a modest hotel with an attached alien bird sanctuary and paid for room and board for as many nights until the Benign Summer departed. He walked away with a room key in hand and made his way back to the Memento.

***

Having decided to remain on the Memento for as long as possible, Bowen took every opportunity to spend time around the ship. He was no longer a crew member and was just a passenger. He spent his remaining days with the others, but their work schedules had kicked back in since they were docked and he ended up spending more time alone than he might have liked. Moryys was on shift in the cargo bay and Vetura was on call for minor repair jobs. There had been an influx of new passengers and the kitchen staff and clean up crew were back on their routines in force. Despite being a passenger, Bowen took to walking around the ship with his camera taking candid shots. With Bao Bao and Gricky he engaged in a small scale game of Usurper one evening on the rec deck. Another evening he watched a couple of action flicks with Moryys in his cabin, but Moryys was so tired from working that he fell asleep before the end of the second film. He didn't catch much of Vetura, other than passing her at work in the corridors once or twice. Every so often when he used his camera he would think of her.

On the penultimate day of his stay on the ship, he got all his laundry done and he spent some time in the garden. He made sure that the hover flies and the bees were back in stasis and he switched on the deep freeze protocol over the dirt patches that would preserve the soil and the worms inside for whoever may take up the task of growing food in the future. Bowen tidied up the place and organised all the tools and equipment back into their rightful places. He took to the upper walkways and remembered Vetura helping him with the heat lamps. He snapped pictures of the garden to show his parents and hoped they would be proud. That night, he stayed up late and left the blinds open to see the stars from his bed. If he listened for it he could faintly hear the sound of the repair crews working on the hull through the night shift. It didn't bother him, he wanted to take in every last moment. Bowen played idly with his camera. Before he fell asleep, he decided he would look for a film development lab on the station to take his memories home.

49.

The last day went by too fast for Bowen's liking. He overslept and nearly missed breakfast. On the serving line, Wotll commented on how shaggy his hair had become as she served him muesli with fresh bananas and strawberries. Bowen ate alone in the emptying cafeteria looking at the impossibly big warp gate. In a way he was sad he would not be crossing it with the rest of the crew, but he enjoyed the view whilst it lasted.

The overhead speakers chimed around the room and the voice of Garber came through.

"Ladies and gentlemen this is Officer Sol Garber speaking. All crew members will be required to attend the Captain's briefing this evening immediately following dinner service. This message will repeat throughout the day, Officer Sol Garber signing off."

Bowen heard the sound of rolling metal wheels as Duggy came by with the collection trolley coming to a stop. He retrieved a pack of cigarettes from under his apron and took an unofficial break.

"Morning." Duggy said as he lit a purple cigarette.

"Hey man what's up?" Bowen replied finishing up his breakfast.

"Last day today?"

"Yeah it is." Bowen said with a stiff smile.

"So our boy Zaren tells me we're leaving tomorrow around midday." Duggy stated.

"Yeah?" Bowen asked. Duggy nodded as he exhaled a breath of purple.

"Know what that means don't you?" Duggy asked.

"What?"

"Big night out that's what it means." Duggy said. Bowen smiled.

"Awesome. Who else?"

"Everyone. You, me, Ram, Bao Bao, Gricky, Moryys, Zaren, Shillok, the full house."

"Sweet that sounds great. Where are we gonna go?"

"There's a cage fight in the Hot Box we're watching, ultra heavyweight four v four match. Then we're hitting Madame Valentha's, the best strip joint on the station."

Bowen smiled.

"Sounds good."

"Don't worry it's a classy establishment, fire dancers, zero g sex shows, everything. They serve everything man I mean everything, great food too. You might wanna eat light at dinner and wait til we get there."

"I can't wait."

"You're getting at least a dance this time, there's no escape." Bowen's cheeks flared pink.

"If you insist."

"I do. Everyone's shuffled their shifts around to make it work. Well most everyone."

"What do you mean?"

"I'm just fucking off work tonight to go out."

"Really? Will you not get in trouble?"

"I don't give a fuck, Steg can give me an earful tomorrow. It's your last night with us you know?"

"Thanks man." Bowen smiled. From behind the collection trolley came Wotll.

"Come on you get back to it." she said to Duggy shooing him along. Duggy put the last of his cigarette in between his sharp teeth and took Bowen's tray away from him.

"Would sir care to see the desert menu this morning?" he said putting his black hands together sarcastically. Wotll's throat inflated and her eyes bulged as she slapped him in the side with a dish rag. Bowen laughed as he stood up to leave.

On his way back to his cabin he crossed paths with Vetura in the stairwell. She was dressed in her work overalls and she was listening to music through her chunky headphones. When they saw each other she lifted them off her head and sat them round her neck. She flattened her hair and threw her long black braid over her shoulder as she came to a stop on the step above him.

"Hey." She said with a smile.

"Hey V." Bowen beamed.

"I didn't know if you'd left already."

"No, I'm gonna leave in the morning, just on my way to go pack now. I've got plans for this evening actually."

"Yeah? What are you doing?"

"The guys have planned a night out on the station after the briefing."

"Ah okay. You going anywhere nice?"

"Apparently we're going to watch a fight and then go to a strip joint." Vetura shook her head smiling.

"Don't have too much fun." she said.

"I'll be okay, I think." Bowen replied a little red faced.

"It's cute that they're taking you out like that."

"You doing anything tonight?" he asked. "Maybe you could come with..?"

"On a guys night out to watch a fight and go to see strippers?"

"Yeah sorry that was stupid." he said.

"No it wasn't." she said with a smile. "I actually would, but I have to work late."

"Oh right, no problem."

"I'm working with Yuki in the machine shop. We'll probably just have dinner, hear the briefing and go back downstairs. We're gonna have a late night drink on the rec deck afterwards though." Vetura played with her braid in her white fingertips. She looked down and for the first time since he had known her, Bowen detected a timidness about her. "You know... if you don't get back too late you should swing by and say hey..? If we're still there that is..." Bowen smiled.

"Yeah okay, ...I'll come see you."

For a moment they just looked at each other as crew and

passengers passed them on the stairwell.

"So you got a ride home..?" Vetura asked him finally. The question brought Bowen's head back to reality.

"Yeah. I've bought a ticket on a big cargo hauler. It leaves in few days."

"How long of a trip have you got?"

"Just a few weeks."

"That's awesome. Listen I've got to get back to work, but hey you know," Vetura started as she took a step down closer to him. "If I don't see you later tonight, write to me so I know you got home safe?"

"Will do." he replied. She brought her arms around his neck and they hugged each other. Her perfume filled his head as his hands found the small of her back. "I still owe you a bunch of favours."

"I know." she said as she stroked his scruffy hair. "I'll call them in some day."

50.

Sitting at the edge of his bed, Bowen tied up the laces of his boots. His hair was a little frizzy after he had showered and he felt fresh for the night on the station. His stomach grumbled. He stood and turned into the cabin. All of his clothes were packed into his trunk that was now stood at the foot of the bed and his satchel was resting next to it. Everything was set.

He left his cabin and locked it behind himself. Bowen walked down the crew cabin hallway that was illuminated by the digital wall ads and the ceiling lights that had just switched to evening mode. He joined the throng of crew and passengers walking down to dinner. As he reached the atrium he ran into Orla with Erin on her hip stood by the vending machines outside the bathrooms.

"Hi Bowen!" Erin called out to him. She was wearing her bunny hat with the floppy ears.

"I know you." he said as he stopped. Erin beamed a little smile at him.

"Someone looks nice." Orla said as she noticed him over her glasses.

"I'm going out with some friends later." Bowen replied.

"You're not working in the kitchen any more?" Orla asked him.

"No I'm actually going home in a few days." he said.

"Back to Allchester was it?"

"Yeah that's right, Meath village."

"That's lovely. You have somewhere to stay on the station until your flight?"

"Yeah I've booked into a hotel next to a bird sanctuary."

"We went there the other day didn't we Erin?" Orla said.

"Yes I liked the birds." Erin said as she peeked at Bowen from behind Orla's mess of red hair.

"We fed the Wallamingos didn't we?" Orla said.

"You did?" Bowen said in a child like way to Erin. "I might go and see them tomorrow." Bowen said. Erin nodded with a cheeky grin at him. At his side Colum appeared from out of the bathrooms.

"Hello again Bowen." he said fixing his watch nervously.

"Evening. Still a long way until Bolgotha." Bowen commented as they all began to walk across the atrium to the cafeteria.

"Oh yes," Colum said. "It'll be worth it though."

"I hope so." Bowen replied.

"Hey man!" Moryys called from the stairwell. He was with Duggy and Gricky. Bowen waved to them over the crowd before he turned to Erin and her family.

"Hey listen have a good trip you lot." To his surprise Orla came and hugged him whilst still carrying Erin. A bemused smile spread across his face.

"You get home safe Bowen." she said to him. For a moment he was reminded of his own mother.

"I will." he said as she gave him a peck on the cheek. She pulled away and Colum shook his hand warmly.

"Good luck son." he said to him.

"You too Colum." Bowen replied. "Bye bye Erin." he said. Erin waved at him as the three of them disappeared through the crowd into the doors of the canteen.

He was met by Moryys, Duggy and Gricky. Gricky gave Bowen a high five with his spindly insectoid hands.

"My dude."

"Grick." Bowen replied with a smirk.

"I'm starving." Moryys said as he stretched out his big arms.

"Let's get in there it looks packed already." Duggy said. As they turned, Simon emerged into view coming out of the cafeteria. He walked past Bowen and the others completely. Bowen stopped and tried to turn back. Moryys, Duggy and Gricky carried on oblivious as Bowen did a double take to watch Simon. He was walking over to the elevators. Bowen made a snap decision and followed Simon. He caught him just as he was calling the elevators.

"Si." Bowen said. Simon looked at him as he pressed the button to summon the elevator.

"Bowen..?" he said. Simon's hair had been trimmed and his clothes were much more tidy that the last time Bowen had seen him, but his eyes were still darkened. When he looked at Bowen there was a moment of shock. "I thought you were going home when we got to Obelisk?"

"Well… I am." Bowen said. "My flights in a few days, I wanted to stay on the Memento as long as I could." Simon began pressing the button impatiently for the elevator. He didn't respond to what Bowen had said. "What are you doing? Aren't you having dinner?"

"I have to be in the server room." he said without looking at Bowen as the doors to the elevator opened.

"Hey Saxon!" Duggy cried from over the atrium. Bowen looked back and saw them waiting for him at the side of the cafeteria entrance.

"Simon wait." he tried, but Simon had already pressed the buttons to close the doors. He got a last look at Simon's gaunt face and a flash of his ice blue eyes before the doors closed.

Bowen turned and walked back to the guys.

"What happened?" Duggy asked.

"Nothing. Sorry." he said.

As they stood in the long queue for food, Bowen replayed what had just happened in his head. It had hardly been a goodbye. But that might have been it unless he happened to catch Simon in the morning. Bowen's thoughts were dashed aside as they got food. Kabé served him a side of tinned Zuko bird meat in a tangy green sauce with some of the potatoes and carrots he had grown himself in the garden. The cafeteria was indeed packed out. The influx of new passengers had swelled the ranks, but Bowen noticed that practically every crew member of the ship was present. Jothazar trundled around in his chair with Toki on his shoulder nibbling at his ear. Some of the clean up crew were already out and about getting a head start on their shift. Bowen saw Steg, Qirus, Jist and Roo working with two separate collection trolleys. Bowen smiled when he saw Roo looking grumpier than ever.

Bowen and the guys found the rest of their party at a table fairly close to the serving line and the talk quickly turned to the night out. Bao Bao was keen to get a double dance at Madame Valentha's whilst Zaren and Shillok debated over who was going to come out on top at the big cage fight. Duggy was itching to get going. Moryys and Gricky prepared Bowen for how excitable Duggy was likely to get watching the fight. Ramphry had gotten a head start on the night by piling his tray high with food and stuffing his red pig face with as much as possible. Bowen was keen for the briefing to be swift so they could leave. From over the bustling canteen he saw Vetura and Yuki in their work overalls finding somewhere to sit. She was too far away to hear him if he called out for her. Part of him hoped they wouldn't be out too late. Duggy was tapping his fingers on the table by the time they had all finished eating. Ramphry let out a belch.

"Come on let's get on with it." Duggy said impatiently. He had smoked almost constantly in a jittery energy throughout dinner.

"It'll be okay man, command crew will be here in any second." Bowen said.

"Briefing's gonna take what, two minutes?" Moryys said.

"Come on why don't we go now?" Duggy said to the table in a hushed voice. "We know what he's gonna say, yadda yadda pass through the gate tomorrow, blah blah we'll be on the highway for however many months until we get to Vibana. Big deal we can miss that." Bowen secretly thought it was a good point. Zaren leaned across the table and chimed in.

"You know what command crew are like they're sticklers for protocol." he said.

"Yeah dude, we could get our shore leave taken away for good." Gricky said. Duggy threw his hands up in defeat.

"Yeah yeah, bunch of space rangers the lot of you." Bowen took a swig of his can of water and looked around. He would miss the ambience of the Memento. He watched Jothazar snoozing in his chair nearby whilst Toki inspected his head with his little hands. He saw Kabé balancing a meat cleaver on his open palm at the enjoyment of Jungga. Over the other side of the room he saw Yuki and the back of Vetura's head. Bowen remembered what Niamh had said in her com-disk.

"I'm not sure I could be permanently planetside ever again." Bowen wondered if he would end up thinking the same. He felt like a changed person in some ways.

Duggy nudged him in the side gently and threw him out of his thoughts. He leaned into Bowen and spoke out the side of his mouth.

"You and me Saxon let's blow this off what do you say? We'll get some kick ass seats at the cage."

Bowen was about to say yes when the main doors to the cafeteria were flung open. Duggy tutted and Bowen smiled at him as Quinn entered followed by Garber and Lennox.

"Captain on deck!" Garber called. The usual hush fell over the room. The three of them walked over towards the window and faced the room one by one. All eyes fell on the command crew. Duggy shuffled in his seat impatiently beside Bowen. Bowen tried his best to concentrate on the briefing, but the irrelevance of it to him played on the edge of his mind. He continued to glance around the room. At each of the main doors there were security crew members. He didn't remember them taking up those positions when they left Pennine or Davarak. Perhaps he had just never noticed, he thought. Or maybe it was some special protocol because they were on Obelisk station. Bowen made himself pay attention as Quinn continued to speak.

"...We will be on the super highway for one month until

we reach the Vibana system..." Quinn said.

Bowen's eye caught some more people quietly filtering in from the side entrance doors. More security. He noticed Vargoth and Ziziik. They were in full dress like the others in their armoured flight suits and they were armed with their weapons like normal. He also noticed the members of the navigation crew among them, Qizic, Liio, Murrow and Denton. Simon wasn't with them. Bowen's attention fell on Toki of all things. Jothazar was still softly snoozing in his chair. Toki's furry back was up and his little eyes were darting about the room. Bowen quietly moved to turn around. He saw that the security team members who had entered were quietly closing the doors behind themselves.

"...Any problems you encounter that your supervisor cannot help with, you are free to reach out to Officer Sol Garber and to First Officer Harper Lennox." Quinn continued. Bowen's heart rate upped a gear.

"What's up..?" Moryys whispered to Bowen from his other side.

"I don't know." Bowen whispered back.

"What is this all about..?" Duggy quietly said to himself. Bowen noticed what he was looking at. Slowly and surely, security and navigation were walking through the tables throughout the cafeteria. Bowen looked about discreetly. Garber seemed to have also noticed the odd behaviour and she seemed to be slowly moving her hand under her trench coat. He noticed that Kabé had emerged silently from behind the service line. He held the meat cleaver down at his side.

"Anything you would like to add..?" Quinn said to both Lennox and Garber. Lennox took a step forwards. Toki shrieked and leapt up into the air. He grabbed hold of a ceiling fan and scampered up into the air vents.

"Doors!" Lennox called out. Bowen snapped his head around and saw that every doorway was being shut off by security. Some people began screaming. Lennox drew his side arm and pointed his gun into the face of Captain Quinn. There was a wave of sound as everyone who possessed a weapon seemed to draw it at the same time. The security members at the doors and even the navigation team withdrew guns. Garber took a side step and withdrew her weapon pointing it directly at Lennox.

"What the fuck is this Harper!?" she demanded. Captain Quinn seemed unfazed as he held Lennox in his gaze. The armoured security team began weaving in between the tables. A few reached Bowen's table as they all as one tried to stand.

"Nobody move!" one of them shouted from behind their mask. They were accompanied by Qizic who also pointed a gun at them, clicking his mantis mandibles in a show of intimidation. Bowen's heart was in his mouth. He glanced around the room wildly. There was a chaos developing barely being contained by the security.

"What the hell is this!?" Zaren shouted at one of the security. Despite being security himself he was met with a crack to the face with an armoured fist. He fell back into the arms of Gricky who only just caught him. Nearby Lennox was still pointing his gun at the Captain. Officer Denton had joined Lennox and was pointing a gun at Garber. Quinn merely stood there with Lennox's gun in his face.

"Ezekiel Quinn, you are under arrest for charges of desertion and theft of top secret federation technology. The ship is surrounded!"

"What the fuck!?" Garber cried in shock.

"Enough out of you!" Lennox barked at her.

"The whole time..?" Quinn simply asked. Denton retrieved a small communicator from his belt and spoke into the receiver.

"Gamma team, Echo team move into position!"

"Obelisk Law Enforcers are boarding the ship through cargo." Lennox said. "Federation cruisers are circling the station. There's no way out of this. You've got some explaining to do." Bowen's heart was pounding against his chest. The security crew herded them away from their table at gunpoint.

Bowen saw that it was happening all around the room. From the side of the cafeteria towards the serving line, Bowen saw Kabé slink underneath a table with the knife in his hand. He silently crawled on all fours until he found a spot on the open floor. No one but Bowen had seen him. Bowen was breathing fast and hard. Around the room, people were protesting, crying out and wailing in fear and despair. For a moment, Bowen tried to look for Vetura in amongst the chaos. He was sandwiched uncomfortably between Moryys and Duggy against a side wall.

"You're making a mistake Harper..." Quinn said to Lennox. Lennox wasn't having it.

"You'll be on trial by the end of the week for what you've done." he said.

"This is mutiny you bastard." Garber spat at Lennox.

"Take her." Lennox commanded. From behind, a couple of security cracked Garber across the head and snatched her gun from her hand. In an instant Bowen saw the situation change.

Kabé leapt onto a table and flipped the meat cleaver in his small frog like hand until he was holding the tip of the blade. There was a flash of metal as Kabé launched the knife through the air. Lennox screamed as his gun hand fell away from him. A gush of blood poured from his open wrist. A gunshot fired and the cafeteria fell into chaos. Screams bounced off the walls and shots fired. At his side Moryys rushed a security guard who turned his back on them for a moment and he tackled him to the floor. The room was in chaos as members of the crew began raging against the mutineers. Qizic began to panic and waved his gun around until his aim fell on Bowen. Bowen's breath caught in his chest. The crowd surged behind him.

"Hey come and have a go at me fly boy!" Duggy challenged him. Bowen felt Duggy's clawed hand grasp him at the chest and he was shoved to the side. Bowen fell into the crowd as he heard two gunshots. Bowen lost his footing and he felt the cold floor hit him in the face. A sharp pain went through his back as someone stood on him. A flash of white went through his head as someone kicked him in the face. Fear shot through Bowen until the fat, tattooed hands of Bao Bao grabbed him under the arms and lifted him onto his feet. Bowen didn't get the chance to thank him as the panicked crowd moved him along. There was a crush of people at the main doors of the cafeteria that had been locked. Adrenaline surged through him and he had a moment of clarity. He turned his head and looked to the side. One of the side entrances was unguarded. He planted his feet and forced his way to the side. On his way he was hit in the side of the face by frightened people as the mass of the crowd pulsed. Bowen clambered over a table and scattered plates and cutlery. Gunshots were still ringing around the room. Bowen chanced a look back. For a moment he saw the flash of a metallic arm as Quinn swung his cyborg fist in a chaotic melee. He carried on for the lone doorway. In a sheer panic all Bowen thought about was getting out of the room. He would shout for the guys and they would follow him. They hadn't done anything wrong, they would be okay. Absurdly he thought that if he was quick enough perhaps he could dart up to his cabin and get his luggage.

Bowen's thoughts carried him across the stretch of the floor towards the exit. He didn't register having to run over people who were lying on the ground. He breathed a momentary sigh of relief as he reached the doorway and turned the handle.

"It's locked…" he said quietly. In an adrenaline haze, he turned his head perhaps to tell someone it wouldn't open. His heart stopped as a panicked crowd came rushing towards him. In an instant Bowen was trapped. All around him the cries of others tore at his ear drums. His face was shoved against the door and he felt a crack in his upper torso that he was sure was a rib. A true terror flooded through Bowen as he realised his feet were no longer touching the floor and it was hard to breath. He was being crushed. People he had worked with, people he had fed with food from the garden, those same people who had all congratulated him days earlier were now slowly killing him in a panic to get through a locked doorway. More gunshots fired. Sparks came from the ceiling as stray bullets hit wiring and a light fitting exploded.

Suddenly all the lights flickered and the room was cast in darkness. A red emergency light replaced it. A jolt of movement came from the door as the sheer weight of the crowd crushed against it. Bowen's right arm became loose. He tried to cry out to go back, but it was useless. In a blind panic he began punching and elbowing whoever was near him. Suddenly he felt the sensation of falling as the doors gave way.

Now out in a hallway that led back to the atrium, his back was on the broken door. Scared people stood on his chest and drove the breath from his body. Someone next to him lay silent and still. Bowen looked into their dead face before he felt himself being picked up. He didn't see who was responsible for saving him. All of a sudden he was being forced backwards on his feet as more and more people flooded out of the cafeteria.

Bowen's feet took over as another wave of adrenaline hit him. He fought through the crowd as much as he was able and he made for the stairwell. As he rounded the corner, through the red glow of the emergency lighting he saw streams of green laser sights and from out of the gloom strode Obelisk law enforcement in heavy armour. They began threatening the crowd with arrests, but the fear was too widespread and they began opening fire, some with electric shocker rounds and some not. Bowen shoulder charged his way through the crowd and reached the stairs. Despite the savage pain he was in, he began to run up the stairs two steps at a time. As he ran, the power surged back and the lights flickered on the brightest setting of daylight. With every step, blood gushed from his broken nose. He looked down as he ran and saw blood on his boots that he couldn't be sure was his. He was on auto pilot as he darted around the corridors looking the comms suite. Bowen's mind raced in a blind panic. He would grab Simon and they would find a way off the ship. He would meet the guys out in the station, and Vetura would be there, and they would all be okay.

He burst through the doors into the dark comms suite. He ran blindly for the server room and crashed his way inside.

"Simon!" he called out. Inside the server room were huge standing towers that blinked with all colours of lights. Wires were fixed onto the floor and they hung from the ceiling. It was a small maze as Bowen ran about looking for Simon. Eventually he rounded a corner and found Simon hunched over before a terminal with a screen that was as big as the wall. Simon glanced up at Bowen with his wild blue eyes. He was illuminated by the screen that was just a torrent of data and code. Bowen ran over to him.

"Simon we have to go something crazy is happening!"

"You weren't supposed to be here..." Simon said quietly as he lowered his head.

"Come on man let's go, there's a mutiny, there are station police downstairs and Lennox tried to kill Captain Quinn..." Simon hunched over the computer and took a deep but ragged breath. Bowen reached out and grabbed Simon by the shoulder. "Simon!" he cried. Simon grabbed Bowen's hand and ripped it off of him.

"You weren't supposed to be here!" Simon yelled.

Bowen recoiled in shock. Simon stood up and confronted Bowen. His eyes were wild. Bowen glanced down and saw a bottle of pills spilled out on the floor. "You were supposed to go home!"

"What are you talking about?" Bowen asked.

"I should never have told you about this ship."

"What..?"

"You had to tag along didn't you? You weren't content with your perfect little life on Saxon were you?" Bowen's blood was starting to boil.

"Simon, this isn't the time for this..." Bowen said through a stiff jaw.

"And to think I tried to stop Murrow and Qizic from fucking with your implants."

Bowen's thoughts tumbled. Shock and anger fused together in his mind.

"I could have gone blind or deaf... I could have had brain damage..." Bowen seethed as Simon had lied to him. Bowen's words went unheard. Simon turned back to the computer and began frantically typing on the keyboard. Bowen watched him work on the terminal and he glanced at the screen. He was scrambling all the Memento's data. "What are you doing..?" Bowen said but his mind was filling in the blanks. "You're part of the mutiny." he concluded.

"You're best friends with the Captain aren't you?" Simon said as he continued typing. Bowen was lost for words. After a moment of confusion Bowen found his courage again.

"Simon what the fuck are you into? We need to leave!" Simon didn't respond. Part of Bowen told him to run, but he didn't. "Is this why you've been so secretive lately? On top of you being off with me for a fucking long time before we even left home..!?" Bowen felt it all about to come out. "What's the story with you and Jules!? SIMON!" Bowen's heart was on fire and his fists were balled tight. His pain was secondary now.

"Don't talk to me about being secretive..." Simon said quietly as he typed frantically.

"What!?" Bowen demanded.

"Look what I found in the ship's archives..." Bowen's attention was drawn to the wall sized screen. Simon summoned a federation log.

"This is from the Federation archive vaults in Fortress High Command on Metro." Simon said as he pointed at the screen.

- - - - - - - - - -

FEDERATION ARCHIVES
ALPHA / CENTURY / DC99X
TOP SECRET

OPERATION SKYFIRE
SOVISTAN HIGH ORBIT

SHIP DESIGNATION: Victory Undivided

TEST CAPTAIN: Flight Commander Ezekiel Quinn

TEST FLIGHT RULING: TOTAL FAILURE

LOSS OF LIFE: COMPLETE

Bowen opened his hands in disbelief.

"What? According to the Federation Captain Quinn is dead..? From a test flight of some other ship. It must be wrong..? It is wrong. And what does any of this have to do with me being secretive..?" Simon didn't take Bowen on. He merely turned back to the screen. Bowen tried one last time to reach out to Simon.

"Simon come on please. Let's go home."

"Look..." Simon said. Bowen saw as on screen the data shifted to a different program as Simon opened up the Memento's deep archives. The screen shifted numerous times and the programming seemed to struggle to open up. Whatever Simon was about to show Bowen it had been hidden well.

MEMENTO
INTEL - ARCHIVE
ENCRYPTION BYPASS: I09-43F9J

OPERATION SKYFIRE
SOVISTAN HIGH ORBIT

SHIP DESIGNATION: Victory Undivided

TEST CAPTAIN: Flight Commander Ezekiel Quinn

TEST FLIGHT RULING: SUCCESS

CREW LOG: Victory Undivided

FLIGHT COMMANDER:

EZEKIEL QUINN – Missing in Action

Bowen observed a monochrome image of Captain Quinn. He seemed younger and he had no cybernetics. The list continued and Bowen read on.

CHIEF SURGEON OFFICER:

Jinn-Quo Gayama – Missing in Action

GUNNERY STAFF MAJOR:

Nole Russik – Killed in Action

FIRST OFFICER:

Magella Ishtar – Missing in Action

CHIEF SENIOR CARTOGRAPHER:

Syrus August – Killed in Action

ENGINE MASTER:

Jothazar Zaditch – Killed in Action

WARDEN ACADEMIC PROFESSOR:

Wilhelm Volkov – Missing in Action

- - - - - - - - - - -

SECURITY SERGEANT FIRST CLASS:

Zoltan Hayashi – Killed in Action

- - - - - - - - - - -

As Bowen read down the list his head was spinning. Each entry was accompanied by a monochrome photograph. Each seemed to be taken from years ago, with each person looking noticeably younger. As Bowen read each entry his mind turned over. Doctor Jinn-Quo was not missing and Nole was very much alive on Davarak. So was Ishtar as Captain of the Stormraven. Nole had mentioned Captain August of the Bastard Titan was being held at a place called Winter Star, Lennox had also mentioned his name. Vetura had said that Jothazar had been injured years ago driving a mech, but he was definitely not dead. At present he couldn't know if Zolton Hayashi was still alive, but he assumed as much. Wilhelm Volkov was Niamh's science team leader and Captain of the Glass Library on Saurophos. Bowen thought she would have mentioned it if he was dead. It made no sense. And what was this ship called the Victory Undivided? Bowen scanned to the bottom of the page where there was one final entry in the crew listing. His heart stopped and his mouth fell open.

- - - - - - - - - - -

JUNIOR LIEUTENANT GRADE I:
Bowen Rhys – Killed in Action

- - - - - - - - - - -

Accompanied with the entry was a photograph. It was him in the picture, he looked much as he did when he was in his late teens, there was no mistaking it. Whatever this was, according to the Memento, he was dead and had died years ago.

"It... it can't..." Bowen tried. Simon turned to him and he looked back at Simon. "Simon... I..." A flash of white cracked across Bowen's head as Simon punched him. Bowen fell against a server tower and he felt stabbing pains through his back.

"Tell me it's wrong..." Simon ordered with a manic look on his face. "Explain this to me!" Simon yelled. Bowen shook his head and managed to stand up.

"Of... of course it's wrong I'm here aren't I!?" Bowen shouted. His blood was boiling and his head was spinning. "Simon I don't know what it means."

"It's no wonder the Captain took a shine to you, you already knew him didn't you somehow?" Simon was walking over to Bowen. He was silhouetted against the bright screen and Bowen could no longer see his face.

"Simon are you hearing yourself this is crazy!"

"I'm sorry Bowen."

"What for..?" Bowen asked.

"I've transmitted the Memento's archive logs to the Obelisk data board. You'll be just as wanted as Quinn soon."

"You..." Bowen started. He glanced over Simon's shoulder and saw the screen. There was a large red flashing icon that indicated a transmission. "Why? Why would you do that!?" Bowen cried out in sheer confusion. "You've known me your whole life! That can't be me on there it just can't!" In the gloom of the server room, Bowen saw a glint in Simon's eyes.

"You should have ran back home as soon as we got to Obelisk. Maybe you could have had a few months of your perfect life back before they came for you." Bowen clenched his fists.

"You've always had a chip on your shoulder. You've always been jealous of me, of my parents. You were jealous of me and Jules ...weren't you? Why don't you just tell me already..?" Bowen was shaking. His nose was dripping blood and his head was pounding. Simon snickered under his breath as he stood right in front of Bowen.

"Tell you what..? That I was fucking her for mon..." Bowen saw red. He had a hold of Simon by the throat in one hand and with the other he was pounding him in his face. Bowen's eyes were suddenly streaming with tears. They both fell backwards and crashed into the computer terminal. Simon's tech box fell to the side and all manner of tools and instruments scattered across the floor. A shudder went through the ship as they rolled around on eachother. A powerful pulsing rippled through the walls and through the ceiling. Bowen barely noticed as he was on top of Simon pummelling him. He tried to speak but he just roared in anger and confusion. Simon was smiling under Bowen's assault. Another tremble went through the ship and Bowen's breath caught in his throat.

The ship shuddered again and a powerful hum emanated through the Memento. It rippled right through him. It was in his brain. Bowen raised a hand to his head. Simon's heel found Bowen's gut. He felt something rip as he cried in pain. Suddenly he was on his back and Simon was now cracking him in the head. He felt technical equipment in his back as he was lying in the mess on the floor. With every hit from Simon, Bowen felt his skull rattle. A snap went through Bowen's eye as he felt Simon break his eye socket and his vision blurred. He barely had the strength to fight back. All he could do was raise his hands. Bowen felt Simon's jaw and his cheek, then his teeth, then his brow. Bowen felt a furious white heat in his chest as he felt the resistance on his nail from Simon's eyeball. Simon shrieked as he let go of Bowen for an instant. Bowen's hands flailed about him for anything to grab hold of. He felt something solid and heavy find its way into his hand.

The ship began to judder violently. Something new was awakening from somewhere deep within the Memento. The lights flickered on and off. The server room screen began to flash a harsh pink colour in error. Bowen tried to sit up but an excruciating pain tore through him as Simon thrust a tech screwdriver into Bowen's upper chest. Bowen felt it scratch on his rib. He cried out in pain. His body reacted and with the last push of strength he had, he swung whatever was in his hand at Simon's head. There as a dull metallic smack and Simon fell away from Bowen. The Memento fell still again, but the pulsing from below continued like a colossal drum. Bowen managed to get to his feet.

Simon was slumped on the floor leaning against the server room screen. The impact of his body had smashed it and it was flashing static. Bowen looked down at his hand and saw the steel terminal wrench in his hand. There was a smattering of Simon's blood on a rough cut edge. Bowen took a few deep breaths. The screwdriver was sticking out of his chest. There was blood all over him and on the floor and blood dripped from his face. His mouth was slick with it. Bowen tried to speak but blood spurted out of his mouth onto the floor.

"Simon..? I'm sorry..." Bowen said quietly. Simon lifted his head slowly and looked at Bowen. His face was covered in blood from where Bowen had hit him. "We could have left... We could have..." he tried, but Simon just looked at him. "I can't go home." Bowen realised. A quake ran through the ship. The humming came back and was now more powerful than ever. Simon made an odd noise. Bowen took a step forward.

"Sh..." Simon tried to speak. Bowen took another step. "She..."

"What..?" Bowen asked. Simon vomited onto himself. There was blood. Bowen felt his stomach turn with a mixture of anger, sadness and guilt.

"She... loves... me..." The server room darkened as another surge of unreal power ran through the ship. Simon began laughing to himself. Bowen didn't think. He swung hard with the wrench. There was a wet crack and a dull snap of metal on bone. Bowen let go of the wrench as it stuck in Simon's head. Bowen watched as he began to convulse. The wrench fell and clanked on the floor as a spurt of blood came from Simon's head. One of his eyes filled with blood and a black stream ran from his nostrils. Bowen took a step back.

He watched in horror as Simon juddered violently until he fell limp and a froth formed at the edge of his bloody mouth.

51.

Bowen stood rooted to the spot for what felt like an hour, his eyes fixed on the dead body before him. The Memento pulsed like an giant anxious heart and the vibrations resonated through Bowen's legs. His feet began to move him out of the darkened room leaving the corpse on the bloodied floor. Drenched in sweat and blood and with the screwdriver still protruding from his chest, he began walking the corridors. Bowen's vision began to shake and blur. Distantly he heard shouting and gunfire. At the top of the stairwell Bowen gripped the banister with a weak hand and looked down the shaft. Cool air was blowing up from below that eased his stinging face. Down there was a way off the ship, he could find a spare door that wasn't being watched and he could leave. He could walk to his hotel and sleep until he departed on the Benign Summer back to Saxon. Tears ran down his face as he thought of his mum and dad. What would he say to them? How could he explain? How could they understand? Bowen looked down the stairwell and wished he had never left home. He could have waited for Jules to come back and maybe everything would have been alright, but it didn't matter. Everything was different.

Bowen walked back from the railing and moved through a haze of pain, his thoughts becoming muffled by the second. At another stairwell he began to climb, following the noises of the shouting and the guns. The Memento shook violently and the humming increased, it was a power Bowen had never felt before. Every step felt like it would be his last. At the top of the stairs on the main deck his legs gave out, but someone caught him.

"Bowen? Bowen!?" A distant voice was calling him. He recognised it, but he couldn't remember where from. A face white as frost came into his vision. The features were sharp and there were large, black, alien eyes. They were beautiful. He reached out to touch the face.

"V..." he tried. He heard gunshots distantly and more yelling. He felt his arm wrap over her neck as Vetura shouldered him down a corridor. They passed under a bright light as they ascended the ramp to the bridge and his vision came back to him for a moment. Vetura was calling out to someone, but he didn't hear what she said. Bowen felt his other arm become supported as they entered the bridge. It was Kabé, he was drenched in blood. He heard the voice of the Captain and Garber, she was shouting as she fired her weapon through the open doorway. Bowen felt a carpeted floor against his back as he was lay down. He felt soft hands on either side of his face as Vetura cradled his head in her lap. Through the blood and the tears, Bowen saw a huge window as the Memento was pointed out into space. Captain Quinn was sat in a master seat and surrounded by a suite of buttons and keypads, his hands ran across them blindingly fast. The door to the bridge was sealed shut. Distantly Bowen heard Garber.

"We're still tethered to the station!" she cried. Her hair was loose and she had lost her trench coat. Quinn didn't answer as he operated the command consoles. Vetura stroked Bowen's face. He wanted to sleep, more than anything he wanted to sleep. A horrid whining sounded as the Captain forcefully ripped the ship free of the constraints of the docking bay. Bowen's head was wracked with pain as the Memento lurched violently to the side.

"Quinn, they've shut off the warp gate!" Garber yelled.

"We don't need it!" Quinn shouted back. Bowen heard the voices but like they were underwater. His pain was fading.

"Bowen stay with me..." Vetura said to him. Simon's face went past his mind's eye, then Jules, his parents and his sister, Duggy, Moryys and the others. The ship juddered and the bridge rocked as the stars wheeled across the view screen. The Memento was alive like never before. Bowen saw his bedroom and he heard Saxon rain. He felt the wet grass under his feet and the cold wind on his face. He felt Samhain purring on his chest. Vetura whispered in his ear as she held him tight. "I've got you..." He felt her tears run onto his skin. The ship fell silent as it looked out into infinity. Bowen's eyes failed him and everything became dark. Then came a final tremor and a blinding white light as the Memento blasted into the depths of space.

ACKNOWLEDGEMENTS

Thank you to Jack, Mat, Izzie, Lauren and Elizabeth for being my first readers, your honest feedback was vital.

Thank you to Ian for the tech wizardry.

Thank you to Uncle Mark and Aunt Chrissie for their support and insight.

Thank you to Jodie for believing in me and your tireless efforts to make this book possible.

The biggest thank you to Mum and Dad for everything you have done for me.

Printed in Great Britain
by Amazon